DEREK LANDY

SEASONS OF WAR

HarperCollins *Children's Books*

First published in Great Britain by
HarperCollins *Children's Books* in 2020
Published in this edition in 2021
HarperCollins *Children's Books* is a division of HarperCollins*Publishers* Ltd,
HarperCollins*Publishers*
1 London Bridge Street
London SE1 9GF

www.harpercollins.co.uk

HarperCollins*Publishers*
1st Floor, Watermarque Building, Ringsend Road
Dublin 4, Ireland

1

Text copyright © Derek Landy 2020
Skulduggery Pleasant™ Derek Landy
Skulduggery Pleasant logo™ HarperCollins*Publishers*
Cover illustration copyright © Tom Percival 2020
Cover design copyright © HarperCollins*Publishers* Ltd 2020
All rights reserved.

ISBN 978–0–00–838628–3

Derek Landy asserts the moral right to be identified as the author of the work.
A CIP catalogue record for this title is available from the British Library.

Typeset in Baskerville MT 11/13.5 pt by
Palimpsest Book Production Ltd, Falkirk, Stirlingshire

Printed and bound in England by CPI Group (UK) Ltd, Croydon, CR0 4YY

MIX
Paper from
responsible sources
FSC™ C007454

This book is produced from independently certified FSC™ paper
to ensure responsible forest management.

For more information visit: www.harpercollins.co.uk/green

This book is dedicated to the next lot of nieces and nephews.

*Cameron and Samira, Elle and Evan –
you're a strange bunch, and no mistake.
I'm sure you'll turn out absolutely fine, but right now
you're kind of odd, and funny-looking, and one of you
has the cold, dead eyes of a future serial killer.*

I'm not saying which one, though.

Don't want to jinx it.

And all was memory.
The memory of gods and people. The memory of monsters.

SPRING

"I don't know who I am any more."

"OK."

"I thought I did. I was the good guy. I was descended from the Last of the Ancients. I saved the world."

"And what's changed?"

"You know what's changed."

"You think you're not the good guy?"

"I've got the blood of the Faceless Ones in my veins. How can I be the good guy when everything I've come from is murder and death and torture and hatred? You know the worst thing? It's how much sense it all makes now. Darquesse killing all those people? The reflection killing Crystal? Me killing Alice? Everyone I've hurt and all the terrible things I've done?"

"You're blaming your heritage for all that?"

"Oh, no. No, no. I'm blaming me. But I'm the way I am because of my blood."

"And what about Alice? Is she a bad guy, too?"

"She's eight."

"But you saw her in the future, about to face down her arch-enemy. Do you think she's the hero in that story, or the villain?"

"It doesn't matter. The future can be changed. I'm going to change it. Whatever road she's going down, I can head her off."

"How is she? Still crying herself to sleep?"

"Some nights. My folks took her to the child psychologist, who says it looks like repressed trauma. I should tell them. Right? I should. They need to know what's happened in order to make her better."

"If you tell them—"

"I know."

"If you tell them, they might never speak to you again. They'll definitely never let you see Alice."

"But they'll be able to help her."

"How? How will that help her? What will they tell this psychologist? *When our daughter was a baby, her big sister killed her and fractured her soul?* How can any mortal psychologist make sense of that? How can... What's wrong?"

"Nothing."

"You have another headache?"

"It's nothing. And I don't know how it'd help, and I don't know how they'd explain it without sounding nuts, but I've kept this from them for way too long and they need to know the truth."

"No, they don't. What would be the point in ruining your relationship with your parents? You love them, they love you, and they never have to know about Alice's soul being broken. You fixed it, didn't you? You went through hell to find the pieces and put it back together. Why would you tell them what happened? Alice isn't going to. She barely understands what happened back then."

"Maybe she should tell them. I'm making her keep a huge, traumatising secret from her own parents. I damaged her years ago, when she was a defenceless little baby, and, when I tried to fix her, I just damaged her some more. At least when her soul was fractured she didn't feel any sadness. What have I done? What exactly have I done to make her life better? I've just given her back that sadness, all in one go. All the pain, all the sorrow, all the trauma, all the horror, all the—"

"Valkyrie. Stop. You're doing it again."

4

"I've ruined her."

"Stop it. You're spiralling."

"So what? So what if I'm spiralling? I deserve to spiral. After everything I've done, I deserve to spiral and I deserve a lot worse. You don't know what it's like to have these thoughts in your head. You don't. You don't know what it's like to have them constantly swirling and getting louder and louder. It's deafening in here. I can't hear anything else. All these voices, all these horrible, horrible voices, saying horrible, horrible things. The guilt... Jesus, the guilt. You don't know. It's everywhere. Every time I open my eyes. Every time I close my eyes. It's always there. It's underneath everything. Even when I'm with Militsa. Even when I'm with Skulduggery. I don't know... I don't know how much longer I can keep going."

"Hey."

"Oh, God."

"Hey. Look at me. Listen to me. You'll keep going because that's what you do. I don't know much about much, but I know you. I *am* you, although slightly smarter and significantly prettier."

"I don't think I can."

"You doubt yourself. That's fine. Everyone has doubts. You hate yourself, too. I get that. You've been put in impossible situations, forced to do unthinkable things. But this, how you're feeling now, it won't last forever. You think it will – it feels like it will – but it won't. You're in a pit, but you've climbed out of that pit before and you'll climb out of it again."

"I'm too tired."

"I don't think that matters. You're not going to stop climbing. I know you're not."

"You don't... you don't know me like you think you do. You're *not* me. You're a piece of Darquesse that she left behind."

"And Darquesse is a piece of you."

"So you're a piece of a piece of me, from back when I was eighteen. I've changed since then."

"I know you have. Look at all the muscle you've put on. Why

couldn't you have had abs seven years ago, eh? Then I'd have them, too."

"That's not really what I mean."

"You talk like you're about to give up, but you're down at that gym how many times a week? And what food do you eat? When was the last time you had a pizza?"

"I don't..."

"If you'd given up, you wouldn't be working out. If you'd given up, you wouldn't be calculating when you're getting your next dose of protein. You'd have stopped caring about any of that stuff."

"But that's habit. That's... I dunno. That's something I do to take my mind off things. If I focus on the next rep, if I focus on lifting more than I did last week, then I have a few moments where I don't have to listen to all the horrible things going on in my head."

"You've still got a hell of a lot of fight in you, Valkyrie. I know you do. I can see it."

"I don't think you're right. I'm not a robot. I don't just keep marching on. There's only, like, so much someone can take, isn't there? There's only so many times you can fall into a pit before you think to yourself, what's the point in climbing out if I'm just going to fall back in tomorrow?"

"I... You need help. And not from me. And not from that bloody music box. You need professional help. Maybe some decent medication. You definitely need someone to talk to who knows what they're doing."

"The music box helps."

"No, it doesn't."

"I wouldn't be able to get out of bed in the morning if I didn't have it."

"It's not healthy."

"It calms me down."

"It turns you into a zombie. I've watched you when you're

listening to it. You just sit there, staring at the wall. I've actually called your name, actually shouted in your ear, and you haven't noticed I'm even there."

"You're exaggerating."

"I wish I were. It's not good for you."

"It helps."

"And what about those little Splashes of magic? Did you really think I didn't know about them?"

"I just use them when I have to."

"You realise it's a drug, right? What, nothing to say to that?"

"I don't talk to you to be judged. I talk to you because there's no one else I can talk to about this stuff. And I talk to you because, if I didn't, you know what? You'd float around, you'd walk through walls, you'd do whatever it is you do when I'm not there, and no one would see you or hear you or even know you exist. So do me one small favour, OK? Do not judge me. You're a piece of a piece of me that's a frickin' *murderer*. You're a piece of a piece of me that's an inhuman psychopath who was intent on killing the whole goddamn world."

"You're in a bad mood. I can tell."

"Just leave me alone, Kes. I need to be by myself."

"You'll never be left alone, you silly thing. This is the life you chose, a life of adventure. And the next one, as always, is just around the corner."

1

Red candles, maybe a dozen of them. Brick walls. Lot of rafters, lot of shadows, lots of big, empty patches of darkness. Wooden floor. She was in a cellar, a big one, upright against something metal. She could feel the struts digging into her back. Her arms were over her head, wrists bound with rope. Ankles tied, too.

Her tongue tasted sour. They'd drugged her. Her mouth was dry. She licked her lips. Her head was dull. She shot a little magic through her system and her mind cleared instantly.

She wondered if her make-up had been smudged. She hoped it hadn't. It had taken ages to put on. Her shoes were gone. Good. They were awful. She was still in the dress, though, the one that was too small and too tight and not very practical. It did have one thing going for it, however – the amulet of dark metal, in the shape of a skull, that fitted against her hip like some cool-looking clasp.

She raised her head slightly, gave her surroundings a closer inspection through the hair that hung over her face. Pedestals displayed occult paraphernalia in glass cases like this was someone's idea of a black magic museum, and good quality – though obviously plastic – skeletons, dressed in rags, hung from shackles along the walls. The ground was sticky against her bare feet. She was positioned in the exact centre of a pentagram painted on the floorboards. She was pretty sure the dark stains had been made by copious splashes of blood.

"She's awake," someone said in the darkness ahead of her. "Hey, she's awake. Get the others."

The sound of feet on wooden steps, and then yellow light flooded in from above. A large shadow flowed across the light and then the cellar door closed and she was left with the flickering red candles and whoever had spoken.

He came forward, out of the darkness. Dressed in a red robe with the hood up.

"What's your name?" he asked. His voice was gentle. American. Warm.

"Valkyrie," she said.

"Valerie?"

"Valkyrie. With a K."

"That's a nice name. Unusual. Is it Irish?"

"Norwegian."

"Oh. My friend said you were from Ireland."

"I am. My name isn't."

"Ah." He stepped a bit closer. She could see the lower half of his face, his square jaw and his even white teeth.

"You're probably freaking out right now. I get that. I do. You wake up, you're in a dark cellar, you see satanic stuff all around, you probably think you're going to be horribly butchered in some ridiculous human-sacrifice ritual, yeah?" He pulled his hood down and his smile broadened. "Well, that's exactly what's going to happen."

"I know you," said Valkyrie.

"Do you?"

"You're that actor," she said. "From that movie. You're Jason Randal."

"You want an autograph?"

"How about a selfie? If you could just hand me my phone..."

He laughed. "Oh, I like you. Usually the girls we sacrifice are full of panicked questions at this stage, like they think they can

10

make sense of what's happening, like they can't bring themselves to believe that they're about to be murdered."

"What was that movie you were in, with the guy from *The Big Lebowski*?"

Jason tilted his head slightly. "I haven't been in a film with—"

"No, you know the one. You both play dead cops who are still, like, solving crimes and stuff? You're not zombie cops, or ghost cops, but... what's it called? I want to say *RIP*, but..."

Jason's smile faded. "*RIPD*," he said.

"Yes," Valkyrie said. "That was a terrible movie. Why did you make that?"

He scratched his jaw. "That was Ryan Reynolds. You're thinking of Ryan Reynolds."

"That wasn't you?"

"No."

Valkyrie frowned. "Are you sure?"

"I think I know what films I've been in."

"I could have sworn it was you."

"Well, it wasn't."

"It's a terrible movie."

"I wouldn't know. I haven't seen it and I wasn't in it."

"It's bad."

"Then how about we stop talking about it?"

"Are you ashamed of it because it's so bad?"

"I wasn't *in it*."

Valkyrie looked at him. "Maybe if you had a better agent you'd get better movies."

Yellow light flooded the cellar and shadows moved, cast by the three people coming down the steps, all dressed in red robes.

"Is the Master here?" Jason Randal asked them, annoyance pinching his words.

"He's on his way," the woman in front said. Her name escaped Valkyrie, but these days she was always being cast as the girlfriend or the wife of the hero. A few years ago, however, she'd headlined

11

a few movies herself. Not bad movies, either. The guy behind her, one of the stars of a dreadful sitcom Valkyrie had pretended to like, was the one who'd bought her the spiked drink in the crowded bar. She recognised the last person – an actor in a TV show she'd never watched who had a ridiculous name that she couldn't remember.

The woman had an amazing smile and incredible bone structure and wonderful hair. It shone in the candlelight. "I take it Jason has explained what's going to happen," she said.

"Don't bother with this one," Jason said, somewhat grumpily. "She's not that bright."

Valkyrie ignored him. "I'm a huge fan," she said to the woman. Victoria, that was her name. Victoria Leigh.

"Aw, thank you."

"That film, where you were out for revenge on the men who'd killed your husband? That was brilliant."

"That's really sweet of you. I did a lot of my own stunts for that one."

"The fight scenes were excellent."

Victoria smiled at the others. "Do we have to kill her? She has such great taste!"

The others chuckled – all except Jason. He didn't chuckle even a little bit.

"We should do it now," he said.

Victoria frowned at him. "Before the Master gets here?"

"It's almost midnight. We'll have to do it anyway, with or without him."

"The Master will not be pleased," said the sitcom star.

"Then the Master should be on time for the human sacrifice," Jason snapped back. "The rest of us are all here, aren't we? And *we* have careers. I have to be on set in two hours, and don't you have an early call tomorrow?"

"I *do* have an early call," murmured the sitcom star.

Victoria checked the slender gold watch on her slender pale

wrist. "OK, fine, get everything ready to go. We'll wait till the last second. If the Master arrives in time, excellent. If he doesn't, we'll do it ourselves on the stroke of midnight."

The others nodded and went off to fetch whatever they needed to fetch. Victoria stepped closer, though, brushing Valkyrie's hair back off her face.

"You're a pretty one," she said. "Not leading-lady beautiful, perhaps, but definitely girl-next-door pretty. And those shoulders! Good lord! Linebacker shoulders, that's what we call them. I can see why Tadd picked you." Her voice softened. "Was he respectful? I've warned him about this in the past."

"Pretty sure he was."

"Good. I've seen far too many girls being disrespected in my business and I'd hate to be a part of something that perpetuates this behaviour."

"Aren't you lot going to murder me in a few minutes?"

A little laugh. "I am aware of the contradiction."

"Good," said Valkyrie. "Because I was worrying."

"I have to say... What's your name?"

"Valkyrie."

"Ah, from Norse mythology. Very nice. I have to say, Valkyrie, you're surprisingly calm about this whole thing."

Valkyrie shrugged as much as she was able. "I don't want to brag or anything, but I've been in worse situations."

"You have?"

"It's all worked out in the end."

"I hate to be the bearer of bad news, but I don't think that's going to happen tonight."

"We'll see."

"Indeed we will, Valkyrie. That's a great attitude to have. We will indeed see. So tell me, what brings you out to LA? Aspiring actress?"

"Actually, I'm thinking of getting into stuntwork. I like being physical, you know? Throwing people around, crashing through windows, falling off rooftops... That's my kind of thing."

"Oh, I admire stunt people so much, I really do. I know this great little team down in Glendale. Such a shame you're dying tonight – someone as athletic as you, you'd have fit in perfectly."

"Can I ask you something? This Master guy you're waiting on – who is he?"

"You sure you want to know? Well, why the hell not – you won't be telling anyone, right? He's a sorcerer. He's *magic*."

"Like one of those street magicians?"

Victoria's laugh was as pretty as her eyes. "No, no, not like those street magicians. I mean he's actually, really, *genuinely* magic. He can move things just by waving his hands. He clicks his fingers and he's holding a ball of fire in his palm."

"No kidding?"

"I swear it's true."

"And why does he make you sacrifice people?"

"Well, he gets his power from Satan, you see. He's Satan's emissary here on earth. All of us in our little group, we're the ones who sacrifice the girls and, as a reward, Satan grants the Master the power to fulfil our wildest dreams."

"Golly," said Valkyrie.

"I know."

"And does it work? Do your wildest dreams come true?"

Victoria made a seesawing motion with her hand. "It's not an exact science. We get a lot of callbacks during pilot season, a lot of interest from casting agents and directors... but really, Satan just opens the door. It's up to us to walk through."

"Right, right," said Valkyrie. "So Satan is real, then?"

"Oh, yes."

"Wow. And that's all he asks for? Human sacrifice?"

"Yes. And a commission."

"A commission?"

"That goes to the Master. For living expenses, you know."

"So the Master gets a cut of whatever you make? How big of a cut?"

Victoria hesitated. "Forty per cent."

"Seriously?"

"But it's worth it. Tadd wouldn't have got that sitcom if it wasn't for the Master, and I'm on a shortlist for the role of a wartime correspondent. It's based on a true story and the script has a *lot* of buzz around it right now."

"Good luck with that one. I hope you get it."

"Thank you."

The others came back. Tadd held a candelabrum of seven long-stemmed, unlit black candles, and the other one, the actor whose ridiculous name Valkyrie couldn't remember, carried a box of polished oak. Jason Randal opened the box, and took out a long, curved dagger. The corners of his mouth lifted when he looked at Valkyrie.

"We still have two minutes," Victoria said.

"She needs to be dead at midnight," Jason responded.

"I know the rules."

"We should do it now, to be sure she dies."

"We'll do it at eleven fifty-nine. So long as you stab her in the heart, she'll be dead in seconds. Light the ceremonial candles."

The ridiculously named actor put the box down and came hurrying over, digging through his robes. He produced a silver Zippo. He flicked it open and ran the flint-wheel along his thigh. It sparked to a flame, and he put the flame to the seven black candles. Tadd held the candelabrum aloft.

"The candles," he said, "are lit."

"The dagger," Jason intoned, "is sharp."

"The time," Victoria said, eyes on her watch, "is now."

2

Jason grinned and raised the dagger and then the seven candles went out.

"Oh," said Tadd. "Sorry."

Jason glared. "Relight them."

The actor with the ridiculous name flicked the Zippo open again, ran it across his leg again, and lit the candles again.

Sheepishly, Tadd held the candelabrum aloft once more. "The candles are lit."

Then they went out again.

"For God's sake," Jason muttered.

"Are you standing in a draught or something?" Victoria asked. "Move over there, and don't hold them up so high this time. Come on, we're running out of time. Relight them."

The actor with the ridiculous name flicked the Zippo open.

"I swear," said Jason, "if you run that up your leg one more time, I am stabbing *you* instead of this girl. Do you understand? Just light the damn candles."

The actor narrowed his eyes. "You don't have to be a—"

"Light the candles, Maverick!" said Jason and Victoria at the same time.

Maverick. That was his name. Maverick Reels. What a silly name. Not that someone who'd called herself Valkyrie Cain could throw stones, but still.

As Maverick fumbled with the Zippo, the cellar door opened and a man swept down the stairs. "Hail, Satan!" he cried.

"Hail, Satan!" the others cried back.

"Hail, Satan," Valkyrie added, just to be in with the cool kids.

"Midnight is almost upon us!" said the Master, summoning fire into his hand and passing it over the candelabrum, lighting each wick. "Why does this girl still live? Kill her! Deliver her soul to the Dark Lord!"

"Voldemort?" Valkyrie asked, frowning.

The Master pulled down his hood. He didn't look like a Master. He looked like a mid-level office manager with a bad goatee. He peered at her. "Do I know you?"

"Do you?"

"I've seen you before."

"Have you?"

"I've seen your photograph," he said.

"Where have you seen it?"

"I'm trying to remember," he said.

"Think hard now."

"Stop talking."

"Maybe it wasn't even me," Valkyrie said. "Was it a photo taken in a burning city? Then it wasn't me. It was a god who just *looked* like me."

His eyes widened. "Oh, no."

Valkyrie's magic crackled, white lightning dancing around her wrists and ankles, burning through the ropes.

Panicking, the Master grabbed the dagger from Jason just as one of the skeletons in rags stepped away from the wall and seized his wrist.

"Let's not do anything hasty," Skulduggery said, and everyone in the little group of satanic worshippers screamed and leaped away as he punched the Master right on the hinge of his jaw.

The Master's knees buckled and he collapsed into Skulduggery's arms, and Valkyrie broke free of the scaffolding holding her and followed the actors as they scrambled up the cellar steps.

She caught Maverick just as the door crashed open, pulling him off the steps. He flailed madly and she ducked as he spun, then clocked him right on the chin. He stiffened and pitched backwards. Valkyrie left him there and ran after the others.

She emerged from the cellar into an impressively big house – a movie star's house. Lots of glass and exposed brick and open spaces. She followed the sounds of panic to the front door, where Jason and Victoria and Tadd were cursing each other as they tried to navigate the locks.

They heard her coming. Tadd let out a roar and came charging. He was shorter than Valkyrie, and skinnier, and she stepped into him, stopping him with a shoulder. He staggered a little and her fingers curled into his hair and she smacked his face against the painting on the wall over and over until he fell down.

Victoria ran into another room as Jason Randal dropped his robe and squared up to Valkyrie. He was big. He had muscles. He moved like he knew what he was doing, or he'd at least worked with fight choreographers – but when he threw the first punch it was stiff and awkward and badly judged, and it stopped a good hand's length short of where it needed to land. He didn't have a clue, and this wasn't worth bruising her knuckles over, so Valkyrie blasted him with a little lightning that threw him back against the door. He fell in a crumpled, unconscious heap and she went after Victoria. She was standing in the huge living room holding a poker like a baseball bat.

"This isn't going to do me a whole lot of good, is it?" she asked after a moment.

Valkyrie gave a shrug, and Victoria sighed, and put the poker down.

"Was that an actual skeleton I saw downstairs, or was it some sort of special effect?"

"It was a skeleton. He's alive and he talks. His name's Skulduggery."

"Of course it is," Victoria said, and took a seat, wearily, on the couch. "So you're a sorcerer, too, are you?"

"Yep."

"You a Satanist also?"

Valkyrie sat opposite, and crossed her legs. "That guy's not a Satanist. None of us are Satanists. Magic has got nothing to do with religion. Those people you sacrificed? The devil didn't collect their souls. Those people just died."

Victoria took a while before answering. "But then why did the Master tell us to do it?"

"Well, seeing as how all this is about money, I'm guessing that in order to get you to really commit, the idiot you call *Master* made you kill a bunch of innocent people so you couldn't change your minds and back out at a later date."

Victoria's face slackened. "We didn't have to kill those girls?"

"Nope."

"But... but our careers... How did he—?"

"There's a trick sorcerers can do once they know the name people were born with. They can tell them to do stuff. Not big stuff, not life-changing stuff – but he could certainly have suggested to casting agents that it'd be a good idea to call you in for a second audition, things like that."

"Oh my God..."

"Yep."

"What... what's going to happen to me now?"

"You're going to jail."

"I should call my attorney."

"You won't need an attorney," said Valkyrie. "You're going to one of *our* jails. All four of you will disappear. No one will know where you are."

"But my family... My fans..."

"They'll never see you again."

Victoria stared at her. "You can't do that."

"By our estimation, you've murdered sixteen young women between the four of you. We might be wrong. You might have murdered more."

"But the Master told us we had to."

"Stop calling him Master. He's just some low-level sorcerer who couldn't be bothered doing the work of a real agent so he invented this Satanist thing to make some money out of you morons. And I don't care what he told you. You had a choice. You could have chosen *not* to murder sixteen innocent young women. Obviously, that's not the road you decided to go down."

Victoria sat forward, elbows on her knees, hands hidden by the voluminous sleeves of her robe. "I can't go to jail," she said slowly. "I'm on a shortlist. That part could win me a Golden Globe." She straightened up. She had a gun in her hand. "I'm really sorry."

Valkyrie raised an eyebrow, but otherwise didn't react.

"Sorcerers aren't bulletproof, are they?" Victoria asked.

"No, we're not," said Valkyrie.

"I'm really sorry about this."

"Are you, though?"

Victoria thumbed back the hammer. It made a pleasing little click. "I'm not the best shot in the world," she said, "but I'm not bad, either. That revenge movie I was in? My firearms coach told me I was a natural. But even if I *were* the worst shot in the world, I couldn't miss from this range even if I wanted to."

"Oh, I bet you could if you tried."

"Will a gun kill your skeleton friend?"

"Not *that* gun."

"Then I'll just kill *you*."

Valkyrie tapped the amulet on her hip and the black suit spread outwards, covering her skin and her clothes, flowing down to her feet and to her fingertips before Victoria's eyes could even finish widening.

The gun went off. The bullet hit Valkyrie in the belly and she grunted, sitting forward slightly. She pulled the hood up as a second bullet struck her chest. Christ, that stung. Her fingers found the mask in the hood and she pulled it down and felt it turn solid over her face as Victoria stood and proceeded to empty the gun into her. Valkyrie wondered what the skull mask looked like today. Every time she pulled it down, it was slightly different from the time before. It was like Skulduggery's façade in that way.

Victoria's final bullet hit Valkyrie in the forehead, making the mask reverberate. Valkyrie stood up.

"I thought you said you weren't bulletproof," Victoria said quietly, the gun hanging uselessly by her side.

"I'm not," Valkyrie responded, brushing a squashed bullet from her chest. "The suit is. I was going to give you the option of leaving this house in cuffs, as opposed to unconscious, but..."

"But I just tried to kill you."

Valkyrie shrugged, took the gun away from her.

"Please," Victoria said, "not the face."

"Sure," Valkyrie said, and hit her in the face anyway.

3

Omen Darkly went to prison.

He didn't like it much. It was big and grey and intimidating and it smelled of fear and sweat and everyone seemed to be in a bad mood and he was glad, all things considered, that he was just going to be there for half an hour or so.

He wouldn't have lasted long in prison. For one thing, he was only fifteen, and, while he was currently experiencing his long-awaited 'growth spurt', it had resulted in a feeling that he simply had too many joints to fit in his body.

Omen strongly suspected, however, that his twin brother would have excelled in here. Tall and strong, a born leader, Auger would have taken down the biggest and baddest convict on his first day and then made the prison his kingdom.

But the very idea was ridiculous. Auger was the Chosen One, born with an innate understanding of right and wrong. He was a good guy, the one person you could depend on to never let you down.

And right now he was in a hospital bed after having nearly been killed, and Omen was visiting the guy who'd put him there.

Jenan Ispolin sat on the other side of the table and stared, a twist to his lips, his eyes heavy-lidded. There wasn't a glass partition between them. Omen had expected a glass partition.

Suddenly all of his opening lines, the lines he'd rehearsed again and again in his head, that he'd muttered in front of the mirror, didn't seem to fit the occasion. They were all tough-guy lines, designed to impress. But Omen wasn't a tough guy, had never been a tough guy, and pretending to be one here, in a prison populated by guys who had to be tough to survive, now seemed like the silliest thing in the world.

So instead he said, "How are you doing?"

Jenan didn't respond.

"Do they let you get much exercise here? I saw a yard on my way in. Do they let you play sports? What kind of sports?"

Jenan had liked playing sports when he was in school, Omen knew. He was good at them.

"We don't play sports," Jenan said.

"Right," said Omen. That had been a stupid question. He changed the subject. "Do they let you see your folks much?"

Jenan leaned forward. "What do you want?"

"I don't... I don't actually know."

"Then why are you here?"

"I wanted to confront you, I suppose. And I wanted to give you a chance to say what you needed to say."

"What are you talking about? What would I need to say to you?"

"I'm not sure," Omen confessed. "But there's a reason you attacked me with that knife. Obviously, God, I know you don't like me. I know that much! But this goes deeper than that, doesn't it? I mean... you tried to kill me. You would have succeeded, too, if Auger hadn't saved me. So I figure you must have some, like, unresolved issues."

Jenan stared at him. "That's why you came? So I could talk through my unresolved issues and get some closure?"

"Yeah," said Omen. "We all need closure. I know I do. I wanted to come here and show you that I'm still alive, and I'm still doing well, and you didn't manage to do whatever you were trying to do... but now that I'm sitting here, now that we're talking, I can't

23

actually do any of that. You tried to kill me. That's... terrifying. You stabbed me. I don't have a scar any more, but it still hurts sometimes. It hasn't healed completely yet.

"And you nearly killed Auger, too. See, I'm more mad about that than anything else. He's had all the same healers and doctors that I've had, but his injury was way worse than mine."

Jenan nodded. "I heard."

"The stuff they had to do quickly in order to save his life, that's been complicating his recovery. He hasn't healed right. He's still in the Infirmary in the High Sanctuary."

"In here," Jenan said, "I'm known as the guy who almost killed the Chosen One. They respect me because of that. A lot of them are scared of me."

"I... I don't see how that's anything to be proud of, Jenan."

Jenan laughed. "Of course you don't. Because you're a child."

Omen's voice dipped. "My parents wanted you to be given the death sentence."

"Like I care."

"They wanted you executed, dude."

Jenan's next laugh was more like a bark. "*Dude*," he mimicked. "*Dude.*"

Omen sighed. "OK, whatever, laugh at me all you want. I'm just trying to understand why you did it."

"Why I did it?" Jenan echoed. "I was part of Abyssinia's army. I was the leader of First Wave. You and your little friends came in and ruined everything – of course I wanted you dead! We were going to change the world!"

Omen frowned at him. "You weren't."

"We all were!"

"No," said Omen. "*You* weren't. First Wave was going to be framed for murdering all those Navy people in Oregon. Abyssinia was planning on killing you."

"You don't know what you're talking about."

"Yes, I do," said Omen, "because I was there and so were you.

You were never part of her army, Jenan. She used you and the others. You were a joke to her."

Jenan sat frozen for a moment, and then lunged across the table. Before he could touch Omen, he shrieked and jerked sideways, falling off his chair.

Omen looked down at him. "No touching," he said.

Jenan moaned, and the prison guard stepped forward.

"Everything OK here?" she asked.

"It's fine, thank you," Omen said. "He just wanted a hug."

The prison guard nodded, and Omen waited until Jenan had dragged himself back into his chair.

"Your friends are in detention facilities," he said. "Minimum-security stuff. Not like here. This is a proper prison, for proper bad guys. You're not a proper bad guy, Jenan. You should be in school. Temper Fray – you know who Temper Fray is? He's a sergeant in the City Guard. Anyway, Temper Fray told me the truth. They don't respect you in here. No one is afraid of you. He told me you cry yourself to sleep most nights and every day you're on the phone to your parents, begging them to come and see you. Your mum's only been here half a dozen times and your dad still hasn't come to visit. You're miserable, dude. I'm just... I wanted to see if I could make things better."

Jenan tried glaring back defiantly, but tears rolled down his cheeks and his lower lip quivered. "I hate you," he said, his voice strangely high. "I hate you and I'll always hate you. You ruined everything. You ruined my *life*, you pathetic little nobody. When I get out of here, I'm going to kill you. I don't care how long it takes, how many years. I'm going to kill you, do you hear me?"

Omen watched him cry. "I hear you," he said sadly, and got up.

4

Valkyrie set the alarm on her phone for sixty seconds, put it on the dashboard, and opened the lid of the music box on the seat beside her. The tune slowly filled the car, and Valkyrie's eyes fluttered closed. It felt like the blood in her veins was slowing, her heartbeat softening. Anchors were attached to her thoughts, dragging them to a halt. Peace came over the horizon of her mind like the rising sun, until its warm comfort covered everything. She focused on her breathing. Her breathing was the only thing in the universe.

In the distance, an alarm went off, but it was dull and muted and unimportant. It slipped from her attention easily and once more there was only her breathing.

Then a voice – voices – and a laugh, and Valkyrie opened her eyes and blinked as a group of teenagers passed her car, chatting among themselves. Her alarm was going off. She closed the music box, shut off the alarm, sat there in the cold silence.

Her thoughts returned to her and she looked at the time.

"Dammit," she said.

She pulled the handle, opened the door, lurched out of the car. Went to stuff the phone in her pocket, realised she was wearing a dress. A nice dress. Blue. Why was she wearing a dress? That thing in LA. It had reminded her that she liked wearing skirts and dresses sometimes. Not all the time. Sometimes. For special occasions. Was this a special occasion? Why was she here?

Fergus. His birthday.

"Dammit," she said again.

She reached back into the car, grabbed her purse, and stuffed her keys and her phone into it as she hurried to the door of the Chinese restaurant. Here on time, but now twenty minutes late. Of course she was.

Through the door, smiling at the nice lady there to greet her, indicated she was with someone already inside. In she went, found the table at the back. Her parents and her sister and Fergus and Beryl and Crystal but no Carol.

"Here she is," said Desmond, and Alice jumped up and ran over and Valkyrie laughed as her little sister hugged her round the waist.

"We've been waiting for you!" Alice informed her.

"You're very good," Valkyrie said, smiling warmly. The little bit of panic was receding into the warm ocean of calm the music box had delivered. "Sorry I'm late, everyone," she said as Alice guided her by the hand to her chair.

She expected Beryl to say something sharp and resentful, but everyone just smiled and shrugged and said it didn't matter.

The waiter came over, took their orders. Valkyrie turned to Alice and winked at her. "Hey, you," she said.

"Hey, you," Alice echoed.

"Haven't seen you in a few days. What you been up to?"

Alice shrugged. "Things."

"Things, eh?"

"And stuff."

"Stuff, too? You have been busy. How's school?"

"I got ten out of ten on my spelling test, but they were really easy, so everyone got ten out of ten except for one boy who forgot that we had a test. Well, he said he forgot, but I think he just didn't want to learn the words. And there's a new boy in my class."

"Is there?"

27

"His name's Dima. We all made him cards to introduce ourselves, and Mom looked up what *welcome to school* was in Russian and I wrote it and I gave it to him. And then today he gave me a card back, and he said he loved me."

Valkyrie's eyebrow arched. "Oh, wow...!"

Melissa leaned over. "He said *you're beautiful*, didn't he?"

Alice nodded. "He wrote *you're beautiful* and *I love you*. And he's right," she said, "I *am* beautiful," and she gave a dimpled, gap-toothed grin that made Valkyrie laugh.

The first course arrived and Valkyrie found it easier to interact with others when she had the distraction of food in front of her. It gave her time to think, to formulate responses, and an excuse to be brief when necessary.

The waiting staff came over, cleared the plates, and Alice announced that she had to go to the toilet, and slid out of her chair.

"I'll go with you," Beryl said, and Valkyrie suppressed a laugh at Alice's rolled eyes.

Smiling, Valkyrie turned her attention to the rest of the table. They were all looking at her and her smile dropped.

"What?" she said.

Crystal leaned forward. "Why were you late?" she asked, keeping her voice low. "Were you saving the world?"

This was weird, sitting here with family members who all knew about magic. "No," said Valkyrie, "I was just late."

"We don't talk about this in public," Fergus warned.

"Then when can we talk about it?" Crystal asked, giving her dad a scowl. "We can't talk about it in private because either Mum or Alice is around. Right now is the only time we can hear what's going on. So come on, Valkyrie – what's going on?"

"Stephanie," Melissa corrected. "We call her by her proper name here."

"But it's not her proper name, is it?" Crystal countered. "It's her given name. Valkyrie is her proper name."

"Stephanie is fine when I'm with family," Valkyrie said quickly. "It makes it easier to, y'know, maintain my cover or whatever."

Crystal nodded. "Fair enough."

Fergus shifted uncomfortably. "We shouldn't be discussing this where someone could overhear us."

"We're fine," said Desmond. "If anyone's walking up behind you, I'll give you the signal by coughing into my hand."

Fergus frowned at his brother. "Do you really think this is a good idea?"

Desmond shrugged. "I reckon our family has gone long enough *not* talking about this stuff, don't you?"

"If that's a veiled reference to how I never told you that magic was real, I would respond by saying you've had seven years to get over it and it's becoming quite tiresome."

"Tiresome, is it?"

"I was protecting you."

"You lied to me, you mean," said Desmond. "You all lied to me – you, Gordon, Pop. The only person who didn't lie to me was Granddad, and he's the one you said was nuts."

"You think it was easy?" Fergus asked, getting angry. "You think it was fun? Gordon was a lost cause, so all the responsibility fell to me to—"

Desmond coughed into his hand and Fergus shut up immediately and stared down at his plate.

When no one approached the table, he looked around, then glared. "Very mature."

Alice came skipping back, with Beryl close behind.

"What were you talking about?" Beryl asked as they retook their seats.

"Nothing," Fergus said sulkily.

"Crystal," Melissa said, putting on a smile, "how is Carol doing in her new job?"

"Good, I think," Crystal said. "It pays well, and she says the people are, um, what's the word she used? Undemanding. So I think that means she's settling in."

"We don't really hear much from Carol," Beryl said. "She's steadily grown more and more distant. I think, probably, that's my fault."

"Beryl, no," said Fergus, covering her hand with his own.

She tried to smile. "I suppose I was never the warmest of mothers. I look at you, Melissa – you and Stephanie, and now little Alice – and I marvel at that relationship. How close you are. You're friends more than... more than anything. I could never understand how you managed it."

"Mum," said Crystal, blinking back tears.

"My sweet girl," Beryl said, reaching over, holding her hand. "I'll never stop being sorry for the kind of mother I was to you."

Valkyrie's heart drummed in her hollow chest. Every beat reverberated. "Excuse me," she said quietly, pushing herself away from the table. She managed to walk without stumbling out into the reception area, then lunged for the door.

Fresh air. She gasped it in. Her head was light. She went to put a hand against the wall and misjudged the distance, fell sideways, hit it with her shoulder. She looked drunk. She felt drunk. She needed the music box.

The door opened. Her mother walked out. Valkyrie straightened.

"Are you OK?" Melissa asked.

Valkyrie nodded. "Needed to make a call."

Melissa handed her her purse. "Then you might need your phone."

"Oh. Yeah."

"Are you OK?" Melissa asked again. Valkyrie didn't answer, and her mum put her arm round her. "It's sad," she said, "watching Carol grow apart from her family like that."

"Beryl isn't to blame."

"Oh, I know. She was never the easiest woman to get along with, and we've had our differences, but she adored the twins.

Sometimes, sweetheart, there is no reason for the things people do. They change. They grow apart. But that'll never happen to us."

Valkyrie smiled weakly, hugging her back, and Melissa was silent for a long, long moment. Then she said, "You just have to look at Alice to see how much people – even kids – can change."

Valkyrie moved her head off her mother's shoulder.

"The doctors don't know what's wrong," Melissa said, turning to watch a car go by. "A shift like this, they said it could be down to trauma, but, if Alice has suffered any trauma, she's not telling us about it. Has she mentioned anything to you?"

Valkyrie shook her head.

"I don't know what it is. She'll spend all morning crying. Not little sobs, either. Big, racking sobs. It's... it's gut-wrenching." Melissa's hand was shaking. She noticed it, used it to brush her hair back over her ear. "Is there anything you can do?" she asked.

The question took Valkyrie by surprise. "What?"

"Is there anything magical you can do? A spell, or a charm, or something?"

"Mum, you really don't want to use magic for something as delicate as this."

"But is there?"

Valkyrie looked away. "We don't do spells," she said, not for the first time. "But, even if we did, trying to alter a person's emotional state, that's..."

Melissa nodded. "No. You're right. It was a silly idea."

"It wasn't *silly*..."

"I thought there might be a quick fix," Melissa said. "An easy answer. I wanted to cheat, basically. I was talking to your dad a few days ago about getting in a hypnotist, and that led us on to that time you told us about using people's names to get them to do things. We were thinking something like that might help."

"I don't know, Mum. That kind of thing, there's no way of knowing the ramifications. Besides, using someone's given name, that usually doesn't last longer than a few seconds."

"But you use it to get people to forget things, don't you?"

"It's not as easy as that."

Melissa's face suddenly crumpled and the tears came, and now it was Valkyrie's turn to wrap her arms around her.

"It's OK," Valkyrie said, her heart breaking. "It's OK."

"I just don't know what we've done wrong."

Now tears were running down Valkyrie's cheeks. "Nothing," she managed to say. "You've done nothing wrong. None of this is your fault."

It was Valkyrie's fault, just like Carol's behaviour was Valkyrie's fault. All this heartbreak, all this sadness and guilt – it was all because of her.

There was bile in her throat. She wanted to drop to her knees, wanted to scream until her voice was hoarse, wanted to throw up until there was nothing left inside her. Instead, she hung on to her mother until Melissa had regained control and stepped away, smiling bravely.

"Back into the fray," she said. "You coming?"

Valkyrie held up her purse. "Got to make that call."

Melissa smiled gently. "OK, sweetie. See you in there."

When the door closed and her mother was gone, Valkyrie lurched to her car. She plunged her hand into her purse, found the fob. The boot clicked and opened and she practically dived in, she was so eager. Grabbed the sports bag, yanked the zip across, pulled out the music box, held it in both hands, pressed her thumbs to each side and opened the lid.

The music swam to her and her eyes closed, the turmoil calming. The sick feeling went away. All those voices. All that screaming in her head. All went quiet.

"Thank you," she murmured to the music. "Thank you."

5

Black suit. Three-piece. Black shirt. Red tie. Black hat, with black hatband, pulled low over one eye socket. One shoulder leaning on wall. Gloved hands in pockets. First polished shoe flat on ground. Second polished shoe, crossed over, toe to pavement.

Skulduggery Pleasant. Overdressed.

"You're still compensating for wearing those rags the other day, aren't you?" Valkyrie said as she approached.

"It was *not* a highlight of my existence, this is true," he said, "but I try not to compensate for anything, Valkyrie. I'd planned to wear this ensemble today, regardless of what disguise I wore over the weekend."

"Right," she said, not entirely believing him. They walked side by side into the Humdrums, Roarhaven's mortal district. It was quieter here. Fewer shops. The people hurried by, casting nervous glances around as they went.

"How was your uncle's birthday dinner?" Skulduggery asked.

"Strained," she answered. "But we ended it by singing happy birthday and the staff brought out a cupcake with a candle on it, so at least Alice had a good time. Who are we looking for?"

"Our mysterious friend."

"Which one? We have so many."

"My apologies. The mysterious friend who sends letters to the High Sanctuary, warning of an imminent invasion by Mevolent."

"Oh, *that* mysterious friend. You think he's a mortal?"

"No, but I think he's hiding among them. It would have been ridiculously easy for a sorcerer to slip unnoticed through the portal from the Leibniz Universe, surrounded by tens of thousands of frightened refugees."

"And do we know roughly where to start looking? There's quite a few doors to knock on."

"Oh, I know exactly where we're going," Skulduggery said. "Our mysterious friend left a not exactly subtle clue in a letter that arrived this morning. He wants to meet."

They stopped, looked across the street to the pub on the other side.

"So he's invited us here," Valkyrie said. "And how can you be sure it's not a trap?"

"I can't."

"So did you bring back-up?"

"Of course." He started across the road. "I brought you."

He wasn't wearing his façade, so when they walked into the pub everyone stopped what they were doing and stared. All these mortals, still suspicious of anyone with the ability to do magic. Valkyrie wondered if they'd ever get over their distrust of sorcerers after living in a world ruled by Mevolent. She doubted it.

There was a man sitting at a table near the back, his face hidden by an old baseball cap. He wore tattered jeans, a Nirvana T-shirt, and a blazer – clothes that looked like they'd been donated – and his right hand was gloved.

His right hand. Was gloved.

Nefarian Serpine looked up at them as he tilted his chair back, and smiled. "Now, I would wager that you didn't expect to see—"

Valkyrie snatched up an empty beer bottle and threw it, and it bounced off Serpine's head and he toppled over backwards.

"Ow," he said from the floor.

They stood over him. He started to get up, but Skulduggery planted a foot on his chest.

"You probably have questions," Serpine said.

"The last we saw of you," Skulduggery said, "you were leading the Resistance against Mevolent in another reality. What are you doing here?"

"Well," Serpine said, trying to get comfortable, "not long after you departed, it occurred to me that being the leader of the Resistance was a very dangerous title to hold. It meant a lot of Mevolent's people wanted to kill me. Almost all of them, in fact. So, taking this into account, I regretfully stepped down."

"Who's in charge now?" Valkyrie asked.

"I don't actually know," Serpine responded. "There is a distinct likelihood that I failed to tell anyone in the Resistance that I was leaving. I don't like goodbyes, you see."

Skulduggery removed his foot and waved his hand, and the chair righted itself, almost throwing Serpine into the table. "Thank you," he grumbled.

Valkyrie dragged another chair over and sat. "So you left the Resistance without a leader, ran away, mingled with all those mortals, and came through the portal."

"And I've been living here ever since."

"Doing what?"

"Assimilating," Serpine said, taking off his cap. "I've been watching your mortal television and reading your mortal books. You have a lot more sources of entertainment in this dimension. It's quite diverting. And I've been learning a lot about this world and its culture. I haven't been making trouble, if that's what concerns you. In fact, I've been rather helpful."

"We know," said Valkyrie. "All those notes you've been sending to the High Sanctuary have been very interesting."

"My humble attempts to be a good citizen."

"Tell us more about that," Skulduggery said. "Mevolent's plans."

Serpine gave a shrug. "He hates you. The two of you. I would imagine he'd invade this dimension just to kill you, but he's also become obsessed with conquering a parallel world. There's technology here that we just don't have over there. Machinery. Computers. Medicine."

"You've got a lot over there that we don't have here," Valkyrie pointed out.

"This is true, but a man like Mevolent isn't one to be content with what is in front of him. If he sees something shiny and new, he wants it. He wants your world. He wants your weapons. And at the back of it all is the fact that he can't stand the idea of a world run by mortals. Surprisingly petty, for one so tall."

"Do you have anything useful to tell us?" Skulduggery asked. "We've known that there was a high probability of an invasion, or some sort of attack – none of this is news. Do you have any idea when Mevolent will invade?"

"I would guess you have until the end of the year at the very most."

"How do you know?"

Serpine hesitated, then smiled. "All this talking is making me feel quite weak," he said. "Perhaps, if you buy me a drink and some food, I might be able to summon the strength to talk more."

"Oh," Valkyrie replied. "Oh, you think this is a conversation. You think we're chatting. No, no. This is an interrogation. If we weren't doing this here, we'd be doing it in a cold room in the High Sanctuary and you'd be in shackles right now."

Serpine frowned. "But I haven't broken any laws."

"You've murdered people."

"But not here. Not in this dimension. Isn't there a rule that says a person can't be held responsible for laws broken in a parallel universe? Isn't there? There should be. Besides, we have an understanding, don't we? Detective Pleasant doesn't blame me for killing his wife and child because I didn't kill *his* wife and child."

"You killed the wife and child of another Skulduggery," Skulduggery said.

"Exactly. Completely different people. That's precedent. Isn't that the legal, mortal term for it? I saw that on one of your TV shows."

"That's true," Skulduggery responded. "And I don't blame you for it. That was another Serpine, and he's dead, and I felt an enormous sense of satisfaction when I killed him. I've had my revenge."

"Yes. See? That's reasonable. You and I were never enemies, Skulduggery. Can I call you Skulduggery? In fact, there's absolutely no reason why we can't be friends."

"I can think of a few reasons," Skulduggery said. "You *have* murdered another version of my family, after all. You have done unspeakable things in another version of my world. You're still *you*. So I would recommend you answer our questions and be as helpful as you can possibly be, or we'll drag you to a cell and talk to you there."

Serpine straightened up. "Of course. My apologies. You asked how I knew Mevolent would be invading within a year. I suppose I don't – not really. But I don't think he has any other choice."

"Explain."

"There's a sickness on my world," Serpine said. "I heard reports before I came here. I don't know anything about it other than it spreads quickly, it leaves no survivors and, the last I heard, there's no cure. Before I left, we'd lost entire continents to it."

"So you think Mevolent will want to flee before it reaches him."

"I do."

"So why *this*?" Skulduggery asked, indicating the pub around them. "Why not put all this in a letter and leave it for us to handle? Why the meeting?"

"This information is valuable, is it not? I daresay *in*valuable."

"You're looking for a reward."

Serpine smiled. "I've lived among these mortals for long enough. I would like immunity for any and all past crimes and misdemeanours, irrespective of which dimension they were committed in, and I would like a house in a better part of Roarhaven."

Valkyrie frowned. "You want to be a citizen."

"Indeed I do. I would also like free driving lessons and a car, and a latte. I've seen people order lattes on television and they don't sell any around here, and I would so dearly love to try one. And maybe also a puppy. I've always liked puppies." His smile grew wider. "They taste *delicious*."

Valkyrie glanced at Skulduggery. "Shall I hit him," she asked, "or will you?"

6

Sebastian Tao sat on the couch in the living room as Lily brought out a tray of freshly baked cookies. The others each picked one out as the tray passed, making satisfied moans as they took a bite. They held their free hands under their chins to catch the crumbs that fell. Sebastian's mouth watered. He would have given almost anything to merely *smell* those cookies – but for the last two years all he'd been able to smell was the inside of his beak.

He hated his mask. He hated the glass eyeholes and the ridiculous beak and the straps that kept it all in place. He hated the hat he wore with it, and the suit, and the coat and the gloves and the boots. He hated not having one centimetre of skin exposed to the fresh air or the sun or the rain. He was like the Boy in the Bubble, that kid from years ago who was so susceptible to infection that he was forced to live in a plastic cocoon from the moment he was born.

Immediately after this thought occurred, Sebastian began to feel bad about it. The Boy in the Bubble definitely had it worse.

"OK, so," Bennet said, still smacking his lips over that cookie, "the reason we're all here."

"Actually, the Plague Doctor should call this meeting to order before we go any further," Ulysses said.

"Of course, of course," said Bennet, and everyone looked to Sebastian expectantly.

He hated this bit. "Uh, I hereby call this gathering to order."

Everyone nodded.

"Well done," said Kimora.

"That was a good one," said Tarry.

"Uh," said Forby, which was a pretty good endorsement on his part.

"Thank you, Plague Doctor," Bennet said. "So, when we all first got together, it was to share our feelings regarding Darquesse, and what it meant to have witnessed the actions of a god. And those feelings are still being shared, because they grow and they evolve over time."

"Yes, they do," Lily chimed in.

"But things have changed for our little group," Bennet continued. "The Plague Doctor travelled to an alternate dimension on our behalf – a dimension filled with Faceless Ones, no less – found Darquesse, and brought her back to us. This is, obviously, wonderful, but also terrifying."

Kimora raised her hand. "I, personally, am terrified."

"Thank you, Kimora. I think it's safe to say that we're all a little worried about having a murderous god living among us."

"Is she?" said Ulysses. "Among us, I mean. She's been sitting in Lily's spare room, staring at the wall, ever since she returned."

"The point is," Bennet responded, "she's here. And we have one person to thank for that. Plague Doctor, we have been talking, the others and I, and we have come to the realisation that what you have done is nothing short of a miracle."

"Well," Sebastian said, "I don't know about that..."

"You found her," said Bennet. "You brought her back. We think that makes you the First Apostle of Darquesse."

"What? Apostle?"

"You don't like the title?" Lily said. "What would you prefer? I suggested Pope."

"I'm... I'm not a pope."

"Prophet, maybe?" Kimora said, and frowned. "Does that mean we would be worshipping you, too?"

"No," Sebastian said quickly. "No, you shouldn't. I've seen how you worship people. It's creepy."

He'd meant it as a joke, but apparently no one was in a joking mood.

"But you must be *something*," Ulysses said. "A High Priest, perhaps."

"Or maybe we should all be dressing like you," said Tarry. "Is that why you wear those clothes? Should all devout followers of Darquesse be Plague Doctors?"

"That's not why I wear this."

"Should we lose our names?" Forby asked.

"My name isn't lost."

"So the Plague Doctor is your actual taken name?"

"Well, no, but—"

"Obviously, you have a connection with Darquesse," said Lily. "Maybe you didn't realise it. Maybe she was reaching out to you in ways we don't yet understand, telling you to wear a suit that would let you find her, to call yourself by that name, to—"

"Sebastian," Sebastian blurted. "Sebastian Tao. That's my name."

They stared at him.

"Sebastian," said Bennet.

"Yes."

"You don't look like a Sebastian."

"I'm wearing a mask so you wouldn't know, though, would you?"

Bennet took a seat, and a moment. "Sebastian," he said again, slowly.

"I'll ask you not to tell anyone," Sebastian said. "Even if you had people to tell, which you probably don't. But just... yeah. Don't reveal my name to anyone."

"Why not?"

Sebastian hesitated. "I can't tell you. But it's important that I stay anonymous."

Ulysses scratched his beard thoughtfully. "You in trouble, Sebastian?"

Kimora's eyes widened. "Is that it? Are you in danger?"

"I'm perfectly safe," Sebastian responded. "You don't have to worry about me. But I do have a mission. The first part of that mission was to find Darquesse and bring her home."

"What's the second part?"

"To convince her to help us."

Bennet sat forward. "With what?"

Sebastian didn't answer immediately.

"You've seen the future," Bennet said. "You have, haven't you? You've seen what's coming."

This wasn't a good idea. Sharing that information was not the smart thing to do. And yet Sebastian's mouth wouldn't stay closed. Finally, he was telling someone. Finally, he was sharing his burden. "I've seen what's coming," he said. "I can't tell you what it is. I wish I could. I really do. But the success of my mission – the fate of the world – depends on me keeping this secret."

"So... so Darquesse really is going to save us, then?" Forby said.

"But if she saves us," said Lily, "does that means bad things are coming?"

"Oh, yes," said Sebastian.

Ulysses blinked. "But we have Darquesse, so whatever happens, and I'm fine with Sebastian not telling us what that is, she'll protect us. Right?"

Sebastian nodded. "Hopefully."

Now they all frowned at him.

"What do you mean, *hopefully*?" Bennet asked.

"Well, I just... I just mean that I don't know. I *hope* she'll help us."

"Didn't you see her helping us in your vision?"

"It's not quite as simple as that."

"So you *didn't* see her helping us."

"No," Sebastian admitted.

"But of course she'll help us!" Lily said. "She's Darquesse!"

"Um..." Forby said. "The last time Darquesse was here, she tried to murder the entire planet."

Lily gasped and pointed. "Blasphemer!"

"Is it blasphemy if it's true?" Kimora asked.

"I don't think it is," said Ulysses.

"Well, OK," said Lily, "maybe not blasphemy, but... You've got to be more *supportive*, Forby. We've been worshipping Darquesse for years now, and we can't just turn round and say, *yeah, she's not that great and she did try to kill us all.*"

"But she did," he argued.

"That's not the point, though!"

"Then what is the point?"

"I don't know!" Lily cried.

Bennet got to his feet. "OK, listen, everyone. We all started worshipping Darquesse for our own reasons. I started worshipping because I saw what she could do and I realised she was a god. And what do you do with gods?"

"Worship them?" Forby suggested.

"You worship them, *exactly*," Bennet said. "And that's what I did. I was shown just how insignificant I truly was and I'll admit it... I was lost. I floundered. Praying to this god we all found... it was suddenly the only thing that made sense any more. It was the only thing that got me balanced again. So that's why I worship her. In a vast and uncaring universe, she's given my life meaning. We all have similar stories. We may have come from different directions, but we're all on the same journey now.

"The thing is, we've never actually discussed what it'd mean to actually bring her back. Not really. Not seriously. Because the fact is she's a terrible god. I don't mean terrible as in *crappy*, but terrible as in *great and terrible*. Her wrath is *terrible to behold*. That

43

kinda thing. She's not benevolent. She doesn't care for the people who pray to her. I mean, she's been sitting in Lily's spare room for three months and she hasn't said one word to any of us. She hasn't even blinked."

"Not blinking doesn't mean she doesn't care," Lily said weakly.

"We should be honest with ourselves," said Bennet. "We never thought she'd actually come back, did we?"

They all looked at each other. Guiltily.

"Of course we didn't," Bennet continued. "And that was fine. That was perfect, in fact. Our god was missing, which meant we could project whatever fantasy we wanted on to her. There was no way of disproving anything we said, and she had no way of disappointing us. But now she's back, and I think it's fair to say that we don't have the first idea what to do with her."

Forby spoke up. "Maybe the Plague – sorry – maybe Sebastian could, like, ask her."

"Oooh, good idea," said Tarry.

They were all looking at Sebastian again. Finally, he sighed, and stood. "Sure," he said. "I'll try."

He went upstairs, to the spare room. He knocked, then gently pushed open the door and stepped in.

Darquesse sat in mid-air, hovering above the carpet, legs folded beneath her. Her eyes were open, her gaze resting somewhere beyond the wall.

"Hi," Sebastian said.

As usual, she ignored him.

7

If, as a structure, the High Sanctuary was the embodiment of the modern sorcerer – strong, noble, and a beacon of positivity and good intentions – then the Dark Cathedral was that sorcerer's shadow – powerful, merciless, and a balefire of intimidation and sinister intent.

They glared at each other – the High Sanctuary, planted securely in the middle of the Circle; the Dark Cathedral, perched on the east side of the zone like a great, sharp-taloned bird – and sometimes it seemed to Valkyrie that they were silently battling for the soul of Roarhaven, a city of wonder and magic that appeared to be always teetering on the edge of isolationism and paranoia.

But that was only if the High Sanctuary *did* symbolise all those wonderful qualities of the modern sorcerer. Valkyrie was not so sure that it did any more. Under the leadership of Supreme Mage Sorrows, Sanctuaries around the world were getting increasingly heavy-handed with those sorcerers who didn't fall in line. China would no doubt argue that a tougher approach to such a lofty ideal – to protect the mortals from sorcerers who would do them harm – was absolutely necessary in a world shaken again and again by the threat of unimaginable horrors. Valkyrie wasn't sure if she agreed – but then Valkyrie wasn't sure of much any more.

There were still bruises on her abdomen from the bullets

Victoria Leigh had fired into her. It wasn't the first time someone had tried to kill her, and it certainly wouldn't be the last. Violence was now such a part of Valkyrie's life that she barely trembled afterwards. Only in extreme cases would the shakes become apparent. In the old days, she'd break down after a fight as the last remaining jolts of adrenaline spiked through her system.

Still alive, that voice in Valkyrie's head would say. *Still alive*.

But she was now so numb to it all that she rarely shed a tear despite the damage she endured. Despite the damage she inflicted.

Three months earlier, she'd been beaten almost to death in a jail cell in the depths of the High Sanctuary. Bones broken. Organs damaged. Massive internal trauma. A doctor had fixed some of it, but then she'd latched on to his magic, replicating it, improving on it. She'd healed herself while he watched in disbelief.

Maybe that was it. Maybe the fact that she could heal any injury so long as there was a healer to latch on to, maybe that was dulling her to the dangers she faced.

"Million miles away," Skulduggery said.

Valkyrie looked up. "What?"

"I said you're a million miles away. Is everything OK?"

They were in the Bentley, deep in the underground car park beneath the High Sanctuary.

"Yes," she said. "Yes, sorry. Miles away, you're right."

They got out. Skulduggery wasn't wearing his façade, but she knew he was looking at her funny.

"Just thinking about punching people," Valkyrie said as they walked for the elevator tiles. "I've hit so many people down through the years, I think I might be getting kind of... sick of it."

"Well, that's interesting."

"Probably not the best attitude to have with the amount of fights we get into."

"Probably," he agreed. "But this has been building in you for a while, hasn't it?"

"I suppose. I'm not... I'm not turning into a pacifist, am I?"

"Nothing wrong with being a pacifist," Skulduggery responded. "I like to think of myself as a pacifist."

Valkyrie snorted. "You?"

"I said I liked to *think* it. I didn't say I *was* one."

They took the tiles up, and stepped off once they'd settled into place in the marble foyer. Cerise, the young Administrator, waved them through, and they walked the corridors. They got to a set of heavy double doors. Grey-suited Cleavers blocked their way, scythes in their hands. Before Skulduggery could even tilt his head, they stood aside and allowed them entry.

It was a big room with half a floor. Hovering over the far half of the room, over the crackling sea of energy that would fry anyone who fell into it, was the dais that housed the elaborately carved throne on which sat China Sorrows.

She looked pale. Anyone would look pale with this light show going on beneath them, but China looked especially pale, even for her. She'd told them, weeks earlier, that she hadn't been sleeping much. Plagued by nightmares, she'd said – then immediately changed the subject, angry at herself for revealing too much.

The dais moved forward a little, closer to where they stood.

"The Sensitives have scanned him," China said, "as much as he'd let them, anyway."

"I imagine Serpine's psychic defences are formidable," Skulduggery responded.

"From what they can see, he's telling the truth. In his estimation, we have less than a year before Mevolent launches an invasion to get away from whatever sickness is decimating his world. On one level, this information is nothing new. We've been expecting Mevolent to strike at us in some form or other for years now. An all-out invasion, while regarded as somewhat unlikely, was nonetheless on the cards."

"But now that we know it's coming, we have time to get ready," Valkyrie said.

China shook her head. "We can't allow the invasion to even

begin. We have no guarantee that we'd be able to contain it, and no guarantee he wouldn't choose to attack a mortal city first. The fact is, I simply refuse to be the Supreme Mage in charge when the mortals learn of our existence. It would be a lasting stain on my legacy."

The dais drifted lower, until she was almost at eye level with them. "I have a job for you. I realise that, as Arbiters, not even I am able to issue you an order, but I would appreciate it greatly if you would give this some consideration."

"What do you need us to do?" Valkyrie asked.

China sat back. "If Serpine is right, and Mevolent and his army will invade by the end of the year, that gives us, at most, seven months. Our preparations will continue, of course, but I would dearly like for all that work to have been for nothing."

"Meaning what?"

"You want us to shunt over to the Leibniz Universe," Skulduggery said.

"That's right," said China.

"And you want us to kill Mevolent."

"That is also right."

Valkyrie looked at them both. "We're not assassins."

"I understand that," said China, "but drastic steps are sometimes required. And assassination is nothing new to Skulduggery."

"I've killed when I have to," he replied. "But plenty of people have tried to kill Mevolent. Darquesse even gave it a go. If she couldn't manage it, I don't like my chances."

"Everyone can be killed," said China. "For centuries, we didn't think that the Mevolent in our universe could die – and then his own son killed him. It's entirely possible. All you need is the right weapon."

"The God-Killers," Skulduggery said.

"The sword was damaged during Devastation Day, and I have devoted considerable resources to repairing it. But our greatest hope lies with the greatest God-Killer."

Valkyrie frowned. "You found the Sceptre of the Ancients?"

"We did," said China. "You'll be taking that."

Valkyrie shook her head. "It doesn't have to be me. Once we take it into another dimension, it's wiped clean. It'll bond to whoever's the first to touch it."

"I realise that. But I want you to wield it."

"I can't," said Valkyrie. "If I'm the only one who can use it, I'd have to be the one to kill Mevolent. I'm not killing anyone. And don't bother telling me how bad he is and how much he deserves it and how much better off people will be when he's gone. I know all this. It doesn't change anything."

"I'm not asking you to kill anyone," China responded. "I'm just asking that you take the Sceptre and maybe use it as a last resort – just in case everything else goes wrong. I have every faith that Skulduggery will find a way to kill Mevolent without it."

"Skulduggery should take it, then."

"It won't bond to Skulduggery. We've studied the Sceptre – as much as we could without taking it apart – and it would appear that it bonds with living flesh and blood. I'm afraid Skulduggery lacks the essential ingredients. It has to be you, my dear."

Valkyrie pinched the bridge of her nose. She was getting another one of her headaches.

"When would you need us to go?" Skulduggery asked.

"We have seven months, but time is of the essence. You will be leaving in four days."

Valkyrie frowned. "And how long would we be away?"

"If you haven't managed to kill him in two months, come home. We'll re-strategise."

"Two *months*?"

"We'll need a team," Skulduggery said.

China nodded. "Take whomever you like – apart from Fletcher Renn and Temper Fray. I'll need them here. And I'm afraid you'll have to take Serpine. He'll be your guide."

"I doubt he'll be too enthusiastic about that."

"We'll give him asylum if he co-operates, allow him to stay in Roarhaven – under strict supervision, of course."

"We'd be running the risk of him betraying us. He is notoriously evil, in case you've forgotten."

"I trust you'll be able to handle him if it comes to that. I know what it is I'm asking you to do. I know how difficult it will be. But I'm afraid we have little option. Meritorious had his Dead Men. I need you to be mine."

"Ask us," Skulduggery said.

"Pardon?"

"I just like being asked to... you know."

China sighed. "Skulduggery Pleasant, Valkyrie Cain, will you accept this mission and save the world, pretty please, with a cherry on top?"

Skulduggery put his hands on his hips. "I shall."

"Yeah," Valkyrie muttered. "I shall, too."

8

It's a hell of a thing, to kill a man.

Clint Eastwood said that, in that movie with Lex Luthor and the first Dumbledore. Back when she saw that film for the first time, sitting with her dad in the living room, trying to hide the bruises she'd got from whatever fight she'd been in earlier that day, Valkyrie had just thought it was a cool line. Since then, she'd had the opportunity for a little re-evaluation.

She'd killed people. She'd weakened, allowed Darquesse to take over, and that side of her had ended lives while wearing her face. Then Valkyrie had regained control and she'd gone on with her life, not really noticing the blood that dripped from her hands. And that was before Darquesse had even split from her and killed thousands. That was before Valkyrie had killed her own sister. All that death – because of where Valkyrie has come from and what she'd been through and the decisions she'd taken down through the years.

And now she was on a team built for assassination. A hit squad.

"I wanted to be a pacifist," she said.

"Hold on," said Fletcher, tapping at his phone. "Almost finished. Almost... there. Sent." He put the phone away. "Sorry, what were you saying?"

"I wanted to be a pacifist."

"You? But you love punching people."

51

"I don't *love* it."

"You hardly hate it."

"I punch people if I have to punch them."

"Does that make you a reluctant puncher, or a reluctant pacifist?"

"I didn't say I *was* a pacifist. I said I wanted to *be* one."

"You'd be a terrible pacifist. You're far too violent."

Her phone buzzed. She read the message. "New York," she said.

"I heart New York."

"Roof of the Flatiron Building. She'll be there in three minutes."

"We'll be there in none," Fletcher said. He took Valkyrie's hand and now they were in Manhattan, high above the city streets. The sun was bright and the sky was blue and the warm air rushed in Valkyrie's ears. She wandered to the edge of the roof and looked down.

"What has you thinking about pacifism?" Fletcher asked.

Valkyrie shrugged, watching the yellow cabs jerk erratically through the flow of traffic, signalling each manoeuvre with a blast of the horn.

"Is it anything to do with this top-secret mission you're on that you can't tell me about?"

"I *can* tell you about it," she said, turning to him. "I couldn't tell you about it in Roarhaven because I don't know who's listening, but we're fine here. Do you want to know about the mission?"

"Not really."

"You're not the slightest bit interested in anything that doesn't concern you, are you?"

"Why would I be?" he responded. "The problem with the world today is that people want to be in on everything. I don't see the point."

Valkyrie smiled, went to look down at the streets again, and jerked back. "Jesus!" she said, hand on her heart.

Tanith Low, grinning and standing on the side of the building right below her with her arms crossed. She walked up the last few strides, her body swinging from horizontal to vertical with that final step on to the roof.

"Sorry," she said, hugging Valkyrie. "Couldn't resist. How you doing? Doing OK?"

"Doing fine," Valkyrie said, giving her an extra squeeze.

"Hey, Tanith," Fletcher said.

Tanith released Valkyrie, gave Fletcher a hug, too. "Hey, Fletch. How's life as a teacher?"

"It's good," he answered. "It's nice to have a stable job, and I enjoy helping the kids, you know? It's a chance to mould young minds. Really set them off on the right track."

"Yeah," said Tanith, "that's cool."

"I just think of all the ways I've changed since I met you guys," Fletcher continued. "All the ways I've grown up. I was a cocky kid, wasn't I? I was almost annoying."

"Almost?" Tanith echoed.

Fletcher laughed. "Yeah, OK, so I was annoying. But now I'm teaching, I have a steady job, I'm moulding young minds—"

"Pretty sure you've already said all that," Valkyrie pointed out. This was odd. Fletcher was suddenly – and uncharacteristically – nervous. Almost like—

He took a deep breath. "Tanith, would you like to go out with me?"

Valkyrie's eyes widened.

Tanith stared. "I'm sorry?"

Fletcher chuckled. "Would you like to go out?" he asked. "With me? For dinner? Anywhere in the world."

"On a... date?"

"Yes. I know it's unconventional to be asked out by a guy whose ex-girlfriend is standing right here, but I didn't want either of you to feel weird about this."

"So thoughtful," said Valkyrie.

"I mean, you're best friends, and obviously there's going to be some level of awkwardness there, but I've thought about this a lot, and I think that so long as we're all open and honest from the very beginning, this needn't be a problem. So, Tanith, what do you say? You know I've fancied you since I first met you."

"He has," Valkyrie said, nodding.

"Even when I was going out with Valkyrie."

"It's true," Valkyrie said, nodding again.

"And yeah, I was way too young back then, but now I've grown up, and I think we'd be good together. What do you say? Want to give it a whirl, see what happens?"

"Uh..." said Tanith.

Fletcher gave her what Valkyrie knew was one of his most winning smiles.

"I'm kind of already seeing someone," Tanith said.

Fletcher's smile didn't dim. If anything, it widened. "Is that so?"

"Oberon Guile," Tanith said. "Valkyrie knows him."

"I do," said Valkyrie.

"I don't think I've heard of him," Fletcher said, frowning now with casual interest.

"You'd like him," said Tanith.

"No, he wouldn't," said Valkyrie.

"Yeah, probably not. He's a good guy. American. He helped us out with the Oregon thing and we've... well. We started something and we're seeing where it takes us."

"That sounds lovely," said Fletcher, smiling again. "Well, OK then, so that's a no from you on the whole dinner thing?"

"Afraid so."

"That's absolutely fine. I just thought I'd ask, you know. Now I'll let Valkyrie take over, because she's got the official Sanctuary business to talk to you about, because that's the reason we're here, after all. That's the reason we came. I figured that while we're—"

"You're talking too much," Valkyrie said.

He nodded. "I do that when I'm embarrassed. I'll wait for you over there." He smiled awkwardly, turned and walked off.

Tanith looked at Valkyrie, who held up her hands.

"I did not know he was going to ask that," she said.

"I believe you."

"But while we're on the subject – how's it going with tall, dark, and handsome?"

Tanith shrugged. "It's going well," she said. "No labels quite yet. We don't really know what this is... but he's a good guy."

"Have you met his son?"

"I have not, nor have I met the ex. But, seeing as how he's taken it upon himself to ensure they have a normal life, I'm not pushing for it. What about you and Militsa?"

"All good," Valkyrie said. "She's a bright ray of light in my otherwise dark existence."

"Wow."

"I know, right? Anyway – the reason I'm here..."

"Official Sanctuary business," Tanith said, folding her arms. "And yet you know I already have a mission. Skulduggery assigned it to me himself."

"I know, I know. Any progress?"

Tanith glared. "I'm getting there. *We're* getting there, actually. I have Oberon helping me whenever he's free... but it's slow work, tracking down a weapon nobody will admit they've even heard of. It's mostly research, going from one reference to the Obsidian Blade to another reference to another... I haven't punched or kicked anyone in months. *Months*, Valkyrie."

"That's why I'm here. I'm offering you the chance to punch someone, and probably kick them as well. It's got nothing to do with the Obsidian Blade or the Unnamed in the slightest, but it will entail travelling to another dimension."

An excited smile tugged at the corners of Tanith's mouth. "The Leibniz Universe?"

"Dimension X, yes."

"We're travelling into the Leibniz Universe?"

"I don't know why you keep calling it that when its name is Dimension X but, again, yes."

"How many of us?"

"Seven."

"For how long?"

"Two months at the very most. I'm hoping it'll only take a week or so."

"What's the mission?"

"We're going to kill Mevolent."

Tanith stuck her hand out. "You had me at kill Mevolent."

Valkyrie shook it. "Literally the last thing I said."

"And that's when you had me."

9

The world was closing in on Martin Flanery, and he didn't know what to do.

He lay awake at night, thinking about the Democrats, about the mainstream media, about the treacherous members of his own party. They were all out to get him, all out to scupper his magnificent, wonderful plans.

Nobody had better plans than Martin Flanery. Nobody.

His advisors were idiots, his Chief of Staff was a moron, and his new vice-president was a woman. A woman! Martin just didn't believe, on a fundamental level, that women could be trusted to run a country. They were far too emotional. Way too volatile.

He stormed out of another of his meetings, apoplectic with rage. Why couldn't he trust anyone to do anything? Why couldn't he trust *anyone*?

Even Crepuscular Vies had let him down. The attack on the naval base in Oregon had been supposed to kick off a war against the wizards. It had all been planned, every little bit. Then Abyssinia had tried to betray him. But he'd shown her. Oh, yes.

And then everything had gone wrong. That creepy-headed weirdo in the bow tie and the hat had decided, without even consulting Martin, that the plan needed to be altered. Instead of an attack that grabbed the headlines, there was barely a mention of a disturbance in any of the local newspapers.

He got back to the Oval Office and slammed the door. He hated everybody. It was all so unfair.

"You're going to have a heart attack," Crepuscular said, and Martin jumped.

Martin hated it when Crepuscular sat behind the Oval Office desk, because there was nothing he could do to move him. He just had to stand there, and Martin hated standing. Always had.

"You're always so angry," the freak was saying. "You should learn to let things go, you really should."

"Like you, you mean?" Martin said, and then instantly regretted it – but Crepuscular just laughed.

"No," he said, "I suppose not. You got me there, Mr President. You got me there."

"What are we—?" His voice made a weird squawk.

"Sorry?" said Crepuscular. "What was that?"

Martin cleared his throat. "What are we going to do about my re-election campaign?"

"That's not for another year."

"But we don't have anyone. We don't have the witch to make senators support me, or find out their secrets, or – or any of the things we did last time. What are we going to do?"

"Will you relax? Seriously. I've got it covered, Martin. I know exactly what to do and who to call on and who to lean on… We're in great shape. You know what I predict? I predict you're going to win a second term in office by an even greater majority."

Martin nodded. Yes. Yes, that was right.

"The people love you, Mr President."

Martin sighed, the tension leaving his body. They did love him. They screamed his name and chanted his slogans. They worshipped him.

Crepuscular hopped up, brushed the seat of the chair, and ushered Martin into it.

"There," he said. "The people's president. We're going to do great things, you and me."

Martin looked at him and smiled. They were indeed. Great, great things. And, when Martin won his second term, he'd speak to some people, and someone wearing gloves would walk up behind Crepuscular Vies during one of his condescending little speeches, and shoot him in the back of the head. And Martin would watch.

10

Sebastian stepped into the room. Darquesse floated there, eyes on the wall but focused elsewhere.

"Hello again," he said. "I'd like to continue talking to you, if you don't mind. About my mission? About what I was hoping you might do? I don't think I made an awful lot of sense yesterday, or the day before that, so I've written it all down, just to make sure I don't lose track of the point again." Sebastian took the paper from his pocket, unfolded it, and cleared his throat.

Before he could speak, Darquesse exhaled.

It was the first movement she'd made in weeks. The first action she'd taken. It was a long and slow exhalation, barely noticeable, and it made Sebastian wonder how long she'd been holding the air in her lungs. Since they got here, perhaps?

When she was finished, she took a breath. Nothing huge. Just a simple breath. Her chest expanded, and then she let it out. And then she was breathing normally.

Sebastian's heart was suddenly a prisoner in his chest, digging through his ribcage to get out.

One eye blinked. Her left one. It blinked again. It screwed itself shut, and then opened, extra wide. The other one followed suit, though not at the same speed.

She refocused and turned her head slightly, her eyes blinking independently of each other. It was disconcerting, to say the least.

"Hello?" Sebastian said quietly.

Left eye blinked. Left eye blinked. Left eye then right eye blinked. Right eye. Left. Both together. Both together. Left eye then right eye and off she went again, eyes blinking at different rates.

Sebastian tried smiling behind his mask. "Darquesse?"

The moment their eyes locked, he cried out, his mind filled with a buzzing that blocked out every other single thing in the universe. He fell to his knees, fingers clawing at his mask, trying to rip it from his skin, trying to get at the skin and tear it from his bones.

And then the buzzing was gone and he sagged, fell back, breathing heavily.

"Communication," Darquesse said, "is difficult."

Sebastian understood. He'd glimpsed it, in all that buzzing. Years ago, she had moved beyond words. Transcended them. Now she had to take all her knowledge and all her experience and all her being, and condense it all back down into stupid, awkward, clumsy language.

"You don't have to speak," he said, getting up. "But can you understand what I'm saying?"

Her head moved one way, then the other, but neither was right. Then it moved up and down in a nod.

"My name is Sebastian. I found you, in that other dimension. With the Faceless Ones. I brought you back. Do you remember?"

"Name," Darquesse murmured. "Your name is Sebastian."

"Yes."

"Your name is not Sebastian."

"Sebastian is my taken name."

"You have another."

"I abandoned that one when I became Sebastian."

"My name..."

"Yes."

"Darquesse."

61

"Yes."

She frowned. "I have no other."

"You used to be, I suppose, part of Valkyrie Cain. Do you remember that?"

"Valkyrie Cain. Stephanie Edgley. Darquesse."

"Yes."

Darquesse looked around, and Sebastian knew she wasn't examining the walls, but looking through them, across vast distances. Looking at the world she'd tried to destroy.

"I need your help," Sebastian said, hoping to bring her attention back to him. "Will you help me? Will you help us?"

Darquesse looked at him, and vanished.

"Oh, hell," he said.

11

In a private room in the High Sanctuary, tucked deep within it, far away from even the Cleavers, Dexter Vex sat at the flat base of the triangular table and brooded.

He was a handsome guy. The beard did nothing to hide that, and neither did the scars that crept out around it – scars that had formed after Darquesse had plunged her hand down his throat years back. Valkyrie still didn't know how he'd survived that, or how the doctors had put him back together with only those scars to show for it. Those scars, and that voice.

"I don't get it," he whispered. "Do we kill him now, or do we kill him later?"

Sitting opposite him, right at the tip of the triangle, Serpine smiled.

"We don't kill him at all," Skulduggery said. "Serpine isn't our target. Mevolent is."

"No, I get that," Dexter said. "I get that we're going after Mevolent. But when do we kill Serpine?"

"We don't. As difficult as it is to believe, this Serpine is on our side."

"But it's Serpine."

"A different Serpine."

"But still Serpine."

"Yes and no."

Valkyrie sat beside Tanith on the left side of the table. Skulduggery stayed on his feet in case anyone suddenly dived at the villain in their midst.

"You've known an alternate Serpine existed in the Leibniz Universe for years," Skulduggery said.

"It's one thing to know it," Dexter said. "Another thing to be sitting across from the man. He'll betray us the first chance he gets. Better to kill him now."

"I'll do it," Tanith said. "Skulduggery, let me kill him. You killed the last one."

"Can I say something?" Serpine asked.

Valkyrie said, "I wouldn't advise it."

"I'm a wanted man in my world," Serpine said anyway. "Mevolent and his people – and his people are everywhere – they hate me. They have orders to kill me on sight. Personally, I don't want to go back because, to put it bluntly, I have nobody to betray you to. Of course, I understand why you'd want to kill me – but I am not the enemy you knew. I'm not him. To prove it, I'm willing to put my own well-being to one side and embark on this mission with you. If you can find it within yourselves to trust me, even on a marginal level, I believe that together we can stop Mevolent and end this threat once and for all. I believe we can be a team."

Valkyrie watched them watch him.

"Nobody would have to know that we did it," Tanith said. "We could say we went over to Dimension X and he immediately fell off a cliff."

"He's coming with us," said Skulduggery. "We'll keep an eye on him, he'll never be left alone, and he's been fitted with an obedience cuff."

Serpine's smile faded. There was a thin band of twisted metal around his left wrist. "You told me this was a tracking device."

"It is," Skulduggery responded. "We'll need to know where you are at all times. But it's also an obedience cuff."

Warily, Serpine held his wrist away from his body. "And, if I disobey an order, it will, what, administer pain?"

"No, no, nothing like that. It'll just short out your nervous system. Like this."

Skulduggery took a pebble from his pocket, and tapped his thumb against the sigil carved on it. Serpine went limp, slumped sideways, and fell off his chair.

"There's no limit to its range," Skulduggery continued, "and this will also happen if you try to tamper with the cuff. Any questions?"

Serpine mumbled incoherently.

"Point taken," Skulduggery said, tapping the pebble again. "This is not a toy, ladies and gentlemen. Let's not treat it as such."

Slowly, Serpine climbed back into his chair.

"Is this the team, then?" Tanith asked. "The five of us?"

"We've always been lucky with seven, so that's how many we're going for here," Skulduggery said, walking to the door. "The Shunter is one of America's finest. He's eager, though, so let's not be rude to him."

He opened the door and a smiling young man came through, nodding quickly to each of them. "Hi," he said. "Hey. How you all doing? It's a pleasure to be here, and an honour to be chosen for this team and this mission. I'm Luke Skywalker."

"Oh, God," Valkyrie muttered.

"You can't be," said Tanith.

Luke grinned and shrugged.

"Is that even legal?" Dexter asked.

"We're allowed to take whatever names we want, aren't we?" Luke said with a chuckle. "So I chose Luke Skywalker. If you haven't guessed, I've always been a huge Star Wars fan."

Serpine stood and walked over, holding out his gloved right hand. "It's a pleasure to meet you, Luke Skywalker. I don't know what the Star Wars is, but I am Nefarian Serpine."

Luke's smile dimmed as they shook hands. "Aren't you dead?"

"I'm another Nefarian Serpine, one that isn't dead. Welcome to the team."

Serpine went back to his chair. Luke had paled considerably.

"I'm not calling you that," Tanith said. "I can't. Skulduggery, come on."

"He's the best Shunter they have," Skulduggery told her, and then added, "who was willing to come on this mission. You don't have to call him by his full name. Just call him Luke."

Tanith shook her head. "Can't do it."

"I agree with Tanith," said Dexter. "It'd be in the back of my mind the whole time."

"Look, guys," Luke said, "I totally understand. I get this reaction more than you might think."

"Doubt that," said Tanith.

"I took this name because I wanted a life of adventure. I wanted excitement. When I learned that there was a branch of magic that would let me explore parallel worlds, I knew I had to be a Shunter. I carry my name with me proudly, because it symbolises the kind of spirit I want to inspire in other people some day. It symbolises hope, and freedom, and a sense of—"

"I could call you SpongeBob," Tanith said.

"Please don't call me SpongeBob," said Luke.

"We'll call him by the name he's taken," Skulduggery said, in a tone that invited no argument. "We'll respect his decision and hope we don't get sued. Luke, I know you've been briefed, but are you sure you want to do this? Our mission is dangerous. There's no guarantee any of us are coming back."

Luke squared his shoulders. "I'm in."

Skulduggery clapped him on the back. "Take a seat."

Luke took one, as far away from Serpine as he could.

"So that's six," Dexter said. "Who's the seventh member?"

Skulduggery flicked open his pocket watch. "He should be here soon."

"Is it someone we know?"

Skulduggery hesitated, only for a moment, and Dexter's eyes narrowed.

"It's Saracen, isn't it?"

"We need someone we can trust," Skulduggery said.

"Someone you can trust, you mean." Dexter stood, started for the door.

Valkyrie darted in front of him. "Isn't it about time you sorted this out? Whatever happened between you, it can't be worth all this. You were the best of friends."

"Friendships fade."

"Dexter, please."

Before he could respond, the door opened, and Saracen Rue walked in.

12

Dexter didn't immediately storm off, so that was a promising start.

The last time Valkyrie had seen Saracen was in a vision, where he'd been lying dead on the ground. She pushed the image from her mind as she hugged him. A vision of the future was a glimpse at something that *might* happen – not would happen. With every decision made in the present, the future shifted. She had to keep reminding herself of that.

Saracen hugged Tanith, and then he nodded to Dexter. "It's been a while."

"Yeah."

"I like the beard."

"It covers the scars."

Saracen shrugged. "You were always too pretty anyway. At least now you're interesting."

Tanith watched them both. "So are either of you going to tell us why you've been arguing?"

Dexter crossed his arms. Saracen shrugged.

Tanith looked at Luke and then at Serpine. "New guy, bad guy, leave the room. This is a conversation between friends."

Luke sprang to his feet and hurried out, while Serpine grinned and got up from his chair lazily. He sauntered out, annoyingly slowly.

When the door closed, Saracen said, "It started out as something silly and then... grew."

"He won't tell me what his magical discipline is," Dexter said.

Tanith frowned. "Seriously? That's it? None of us know what it is."

"And I was fine with that," Dexter responded, "until Darquesse plunged her arm down my throat to pull that Remnant out and I almost died. While I was recovering, I found myself latching on to things. Small things. Easily achievable things. One of these small things was to get Saracen to tell me what he could do. So I asked him, and he wouldn't tell me, and I realised what that actually meant: it meant he didn't trust me. He didn't trust anyone."

Saracen shook his head. "That's not what it meant."

Dexter ignored him and carried on. "So, if he didn't trust me, how could I trust him? In the state I was in – broken, in pain – this was something I'd decided I needed, and he couldn't even do that for me. What made it worse was that the one person he *had* told was Ravel."

"Ah, come on," said Saracen, "I was on my deathbed at the time."

"The only person you've ever told was the guy who went on to kill Ghastly and Anton."

"And, if I had known that, I probably wouldn't have told him." Saracen sighed. "But anyway, that's how it developed. From something small and silly into something big and important. The way these things do."

Valkyrie said, "And, because of this, you haven't spoken in years?"

"Not just because of this," Saracen said. "I mean, it's not exactly unusual for us to go off and do our own thing."

"We've gone years without talking plenty of times before," Dexter added. "It doesn't mean anything. This was the first time there was an argument at the root of it, though."

Saracen took a breath, and let it out. "And now I'm here to tell you."

Valkyrie leaned forward. "Tell us what?"

"Tell you what I can do. If it's the only way Dex can trust me again, then... OK. I've been thinking about it for a while now and it's time."

"You're going to tell us your magical discipline?"

"Yes."

Dexter looked surprised. Everyone looked surprised. Apart from Skulduggery. He never looked surprised.

"Hold on," said Tanith. "Before you do... what do we all think it is?"

"I think it's some kind of psychic thing," said Valkyrie. "Like you can sense what's round the corner."

"I think it's a psychic thing, too," Tanith said, "but I reckon you can see a few seconds into the future. Skulduggery, what about you?"

"I know what it is," Skulduggery said.

Now Saracen was surprised. "You do?"

"I always suspected, but my suspicions were confirmed only a few years ago, once Ravel revealed himself as a traitor."

"This should be interesting," Saracen said, raising an eyebrow.

"When you were on your deathbed," Skulduggery said. "Tell us that story again."

"My deathbed? You mean the time I was sick? There isn't a whole lot to tell. I was sick, and getting sicker. I was almost dead, in fact. Then I woke up one morning and I was fine. The end."

"What happened the night *before* you woke up fine?" Skulduggery asked.

"Not a whole lot. Oh, wait, you mean...? Yeah, I was lying there and I didn't want to die without telling someone what my discipline was, so I told Ravel. A sort of deathbed-confession type of deal."

"How did that confirm anything?" Tanith asked.

"Ravel had already put his plan in motion by this stage," Skulduggery said, "which meant that, if Saracen *could* read minds,

70

he could have quite easily discovered Ravel's secret. So Ravel decided to kill him."

Saracen took a moment. "Excuse me?"

"You weren't getting sicker on your own. He was poisoning you."

Saracen stared at him, then stared at the wall. "That sneaky..."

"But, when you told him what it was you could *actually* do, he realised that it didn't pose a threat, so he stopped poisoning you and allowed you to get better."

"That sneaky, low-down, dirty..."

"That eliminates any psychic elements from the equation," said Skulduggery. "So you're not a Sensitive, and you can't see into the future – which means you have to be a Lynceus."

Valkyrie tilted her head. "A what?"

"Someone who has so-called X-ray vision."

"He tried to kill me," Saracen muttered. "That... he tried to kill me..."

"Saracen," Dexter said. "Back on track. Is that it? Is it X-ray vision?"

Making what seemed like a supreme effort to push his personal feelings to one side, Saracen nodded.

"Well. That's pretty anticlimactic," said Dexter. "After all this time, I mean."

"But why keep it a secret?" Valkyrie asked.

"I've found that's best," Saracen responded. "Imagine for a moment you'd decided to become a Lynceus. Imagine you went around telling people that. Imagine them knowing that you could see through virtually anything. Imagine how they'd react."

The room went quiet as this sank in.

"I doubt they'd be comfortable around you," Tanith said.

"Exactly," said Saracen. "Everyone would think I decided to specialise in this because I wanted to see through people's clothes."

"Why did you specialise in it?"

"I wanted to see through people's clothes. I know, I know, but

I was a teenager. I thought it'd be great. It's not great. Not at all."

"Well," Tanith said, standing up and spreading her arms, "I'm not embarrassed."

"No, you're not," Saracen said, smiling, "but I don't like to use it for things like that any more. Besides, clothes tend to... squish and distort what's underneath. It can get quite weird and unsettling."

Tanith shrugged. "Still not embarrassed," she said, and sat down again.

"I'm sorry," Saracen said. "Everyone here, I'm sorry I didn't tell you. I've been ashamed of my discipline since I took it on, and the fact that I didn't tell anyone at the start made it harder to tell anyone later, and that kind of snowballed and... here we are, hundreds of years down the line. Dexter, to you in particular – sorry, man."

Dexter shook his head. "You could have chosen anything. Any discipline. I can't believe you went for X-ray vision."

"I know."

"You could be flying right now. If you'd just stayed as an Elemental, you could be flying."

"I realise that."

"Instead, you decided to use your awesome magic to see through clothes."

"Thanks for being so mature about this. So are we cool? Are we friends again?"

"Yeah, fine, whatever," Dexter said. "It's just I'm embarrassed *for* you, you know? Not only because you chose that as a discipline, but also because that was your one big secret. That's the thing that marked you out as *mysterious*. You were the guy who *knew things*, when really, all along... Oh, God, I'm blushing. I'm actually blushing for you."

"Can we get Serpine back in here?" Saracen grumbled. "I feel that I need to punch someone."

13

It was strange to see Auger so pale, so weak, and, no matter how many times Omen visited, it never got any easier.

His brother did his best to sit up in bed, though, and there was some semblance of that crooked grin of his. "You're looking better," he said.

"So are you," Omen lied.

The Infirmary in the High Sanctuary was easily the best place in the world to be treated, or so Omen had heard. He wasn't surprised. They had the very best that mortal medicine had to offer, plus cutting-edge science-magic. And also it was quiet, with very few patients.

"How'd your prison visit go?" Auger asked.

Omen lowered himself gently into the chair by the bed. "Could have been better," he admitted.

"I told you. Jenan's too far gone."

"I had to try."

"I know, I know. But that's it, right? You gave him a chance to talk it out, and now you'll never visit him again. Yes?"

Omen hesitated, and Auger groaned.

"I can't say I'll never visit again," Omen said. "I'll give it six months and then go back. Maybe he'll have changed his mind."

"Yeah," said Auger. "Or maybe you'll realise that you're wasting your time trying to save people who don't want to be saved."

"Oh, so you'd give up on him, would you?"

"I already have, dude. He tried to kill us both. Well, he tried to kill *you*, anyway. With me, he just held out the knife and I jumped on to it."

"You're still mad at yourself, then?"

"It was so stupid," Auger said. "All my training went right out the window."

"We've had this discussion before."

"And we'll have it again. We'll have it over and over until I'm sick of talking about it. I leaped on him. I leaped. Didn't even see the knife."

"You saved me."

"And I'm really happy about that part, but—"

"You saved me, Auger. Yes, you didn't follow all the rules and you got yourself badly hurt – but you didn't have time. If you'd been a second slower, I'd have been dead. You did what you had to do."

"Yeah, maybe."

"Definitely. So how are you doing?"

"Better," said Auger. "I can walk halfway across the room now before I get too tired."

"That's a definite improvement."

"And earlier I peed without any assistance."

"Good for you."

"Yeah," Auger said, nodding proudly. "I mean, I completely messed up the bed and they had to change all the sheets, but..."

"But you did it."

"And that's the main thing."

They grinned at each other, and then Auger said, "But I did actually pee the bed."

Omen shrugged. "Who hasn't peed the bed recently?"

"Not me, that's for sure."

"It's the small victories."

"It is."

"Has anyone been to see you?"

"Kase and Mahala," said Auger. "Never, too, but it's easier for him. She'll just teleport straight in, doesn't care about visiting hours or anything like that."

"Handy."

"Very."

"How about the folks?"

"They've been in quite a bit," said Auger, "although they're more interested in talking to the doctors than talking to me, so I don't know if I can count them. How's school going?"

Omen made a face. "Great – apart from the fact that I'm going to have to work with a tutor over the summer to catch up on the classes I missed."

"Aw, man."

"I tried explaining to everyone that I'm always this far behind by the end of term, but no one will listen."

"They just don't know you, dude."

"No one has it worse than me."

"Absolutely no one, my brother."

"I heard about this one guy who *did* have it worse than me? But it turned out to be a rumour."

"No," said Auger, laughing, "it turned out to actually *be* you."

"Yes," Omen grinned. "The only person who has it worse than me is me."

They laughed, then cackled, then laughed some more.

"Oh, God," Omen said, wiping tears from his eyes. "If only that weren't true."

14

Emergency meeting of the Darquesse Society at Ulysses' house. His wife was out. They had to be done by nine.

"How are you doing?" Lily asked when Sebastian walked in.

"I lost Darquesse," he said. "How do you think I'm doing? How does someone lose a god, you ask? Well, first of all, you have to be incredibly boring, because only someone incredibly boring can drive away their god simply by talking to her. And this is a god, by the way, who has just spent the last three months staring at a wall. The *wall* was more interesting than me."

"Sebastian," Bennet said, "please stop blaming yourself."

"There's no one else to blame. I was the only one there. I'd love to blame someone else, believe me. I'd love to blame Forby or Tarry or whoever, but... but it's my fault."

"Are you quite finished?" Ulysses asked.

"Not really."

"Have a seat. Go on. Sit on the couch."

Sebastian sighed, and sat. They were all looking at him.

"I have good news," said Bennet.

Adrenaline surged. "She's back? She's back!"

"She's not back," Bennet said quickly. Then he shrugged. "She's kind of back."

Sebastian leaned forward. "Where is she?"

"All over the place, actually. Kimora saw her two days ago,

76

just walking down the street. I asked if she was sure it wasn't Valkyrie Cain, and Kimora said no, she was wearing that black skinsuit thing. Then Ulysses saw her when he was waiting in line for a coffee. That was on Wednesday."

"So she's walking around?"

"Apparently so. And no one's bothering her because they probably all think she's Valkyrie Cain, even though she's wearing a skinsuit and Cain, as far as I know, wears regular clothes."

"So she hasn't disappeared," Sebastian said. "And she hasn't gone back to the Faceless Ones' dimension."

"She's still here, my friend."

Sebastian stood up. "Then I'm going to find her."

15

Xena bounded through the High Sanctuary foyer, scattering sorcerers in her path, and Militsa dropped to her knees and the dog thudded into her arms. She fell back, laughing, as Xena wriggled and slobbered and bounced.

Valkyrie walked up to them, ignoring the disapproving looks she was getting. "Thanks for doing this."

"No problem," Militsa said, and squealed as Xena licked her ear. "You say goodbye to your family?"

"Yep."

"How did Alice take it?"

Valkyrie hesitated. "There were tears."

Militsa held up her hands and Valkyrie pulled her to her feet. Xena started jumping up.

"Xena, sit," Valkyrie said, and immediately the dog sat and was calm.

Now that they had a moment of peace, Valkyrie took her girlfriend in her arms, tilted her back, and gave her one of her patented Best Kisses in the World. Militsa responded by wrapping her fingers in Valkyrie's hair and pulling ever so slightly.

When the kiss was done, Valkyrie righted Militsa and held on to her while her balance returned and she stopped swooning.

"Wow," Militsa said, fanning her face with her hand. "You're telling me I have to go two months without that?"

"It won't be two months, I promise."

"Such cruel and unnatural torture," she murmured, then shook her head to clear it. "Sorry, what were you saying about Alice?"

"Oh," Valkyrie said, scratching Xena's head. "There were tears when I told her I had to go away for a bit. It was kind of, I don't know... scary, the way her mood switched. One moment, totally happy and fun. The next, instant sadness."

"Of course she was upset. She's a kid. Two months is an eternity to her."

Valkyrie gave a brief smile, and Militsa knew her well enough to change the subject.

"So when will the doggy be expecting her walkies?"

"Morning, whenever you get up, and evening, whenever you get in. She might try and hop up on the bed with you at night, but you can shoo her off and she won't be offended."

"How could I shoo this beautiful creature off my bed?" Militsa cried, planting a huge kiss on Xena's head. "By the time you get back, we'll be the very best of friends. Won't we, my little princess?"

Xena wagged her tail in response.

Skulduggery and Tanith were waiting across the foyer. Valkyrie nodded to them, then became aware of a tall blonde zeroing in on her location.

Valkyrie squared her shoulders ever so slightly, smiled, and held out her hand. "Hello," she said. "I'm Valkyrie Cain."

"Arabella Wicked," the blonde said as they shook. "I'm a teacher at Corrival Academy."

"Oh, I know who you are."

"Then you know that Militsa and I used to be together."

Militsa straightened up. "Here we go..."

"She mentioned it, yes," Valkyrie said, keeping the smile.

Arabella regarded her coolly. "I feel I ought to tell you that I made a huge mistake when I ended our relationship, and I plan to win Militsa back."

"I'd agree with the first part," Valkyrie responded, "but I don't like your chances with the second."

Arabella was just a shade taller than Valkyrie – enough so that she could look down at her. "You don't scare me, you know."

"If I was trying to scare you," Valkyrie said, "you'd be scared."

"OK," Militsa said, "can I just interject before you two alpha females say something so macho there's no coming back from it? Valkyrie, I love you. Arabella, we broke up, and I'm with Valkyrie now, so there's no chance of us getting back together."

Arabella turned to Militsa, and took her hands in hers. "I was young and confused and stupid when we separated, and I didn't know what I had, or what I was losing. I've spent the last few years re-evaluating everything in my life, and you're the missing piece. I will fight for you, Militsa."

"And I," Valkyrie said, "have to go." She leaned in for a kiss. "I'll see you in less than two months."

"I love you," said Militsa.

"Love you, too," said Valkyrie. She gave Xena a cuddle, told her to stay, and raised an eyebrow to Arabella as she walked over to Skulduggery and Tanith.

"I couldn't help but overhear," Skulduggery said.

"And I tried to overhear, but there were too many people passing by," Tanith chimed in. "You OK?"

Valkyrie practically snorted. "I'm fine."

"You're not worried about the threat Miss Wicked may pose to your relationship?" Skulduggery asked.

"Eh, have you seen me?"

Tanith looked over at Militsa and Arabella. "I don't know," she said. "The blonde's a hottie."

"I'm a hottie."

"Yes, you are. But you'll be gone for two months."

"Thanks for the concern," Valkyrie said, "but I'm quite secure in my relationship. Are we ready to go?"

"Not quite," said Skulduggery, flicking an unnoticeable speck of nothing from his lapel. "Before we embark on a trek across an alternate world, some of us are going to require a change of clothes." He paused. "And we're going to need a whole lot of weapons."

16

They met the others in a darkened room away from the steady traffic of sorcerers.

Dexter and Saracen were dressed in rough work clothes and heavy boots. Valkyrie watched them slide pistols into holsters, knives into sheaths. Ammunition went into belts and bandoliers. Assault rifles hung from straps on shoulders. Dexter covered his with a long coat, Saracen with a poncho.

Tanith, her sword across her back and a pistol on her hip, slid knives everywhere else. She picked up a rifle, checked its sights. Satisfied, she looped the strap over her head.

Valkyrie wore her necronaut suit, with her two shock sticks crisscrossing her back, refusing every firearm she was offered.

Serpine wasn't trusted with a weapon. Sulking, he was handed the bulkiest backpack, and muttered to himself as he tested its weight. Luke tried to smile his commiserations, but got such a glare in return that he immediately turned his attention to the revolver he'd been given. A good old-fashioned gun, where nothing could jam or go wrong. Perfect for a fella who didn't know what the hell he was doing.

Skulduggery came in. Valkyrie had seen him in a variation of this outfit before, during the War of the Sanctuaries. A long coat, lots of cracked leather and rough, hard-wearing clothes. Scuffed boots. His left arm encased in dull black metal. His gun holstered low on his leg.

"I'm going to need a weapon," said Serpine. "A handgun. A knife, at the very least."

"I've got you something," Skulduggery said, passing him a metal glove.

Serpine frowned at it. "What is it? What does it do?"

"It stops you from using that red hand of yours."

The glove dropped to the floor. It clanged heavily.

"I won't wear it."

"Yes, you will."

"This is ridiculous," Serpine said. Red energy crackled around his right hand. "How am I supposed to be useful if you stifle my potential?"

"You've got your other hand," Dexter said. "You can still throw energy. We just don't trust you with a one-shot, one-kill weapon like your little Necromancer trick."

"You trust me enough to bring me on to your team."

"Only because we have to."

"I will be fighting alongside you," Serpine said. "We'll be encountering the same dangers, facing the same threats. Fighting back to back. I have nothing to gain by betraying you."

"And yet we still find it impossible to generate any degree of trust," said Saracen. "It's our fault entirely, and we feel bad about it, I swear. But you're wearing the glove."

Skulduggery took out the pebble. "Don't make us put it on you ourselves, Nefarian."

Serpine stared, then glared, then snarled. Then he grumbled, and muttered, and picked up the glove and shoved his hand in. It clicked as it locked around his wrist. He flexed his fingers.

"It's uncomfortable," he announced.

"Nobody cares," said China, sweeping into the room. She wore extravagant trousers and a beautiful top and a cloak. An actual *cloak*. "You all look suitably downtrodden – certainly enough to pass for weary travellers at a distance. Do try not to let anyone see you up close, however. It might spoil the effect. Now then – Luke."

"Present!" Luke called.

China frowned. "This isn't roll call, Luke. I was just saying your name."

Luke blushed. "Right. Yes. Sorry, Supreme Mage."

"Luke will be shunting you into the Leibniz Universe. You will arrive at these same coordinates, but on that world. The distance to the outskirts of Dublin-Within-The-Wall, where Mevolent resides, will be approximately twenty-two kilometres. Across uncertain terrain, and assuming you avoid enemy patrols, you should walk that in around five hours. You have two months to observe the target, come up with a plan and execute it. Luke will shunt back every two weeks with a progress report."

She tapped the wall and a section opened, revealing a table covered with a sheet.

"The God-Killer weapons have been recovered and various repairs have been made," China said. "They will be loaned to you. I expect them back, in working order." She pulled the sheet away, picked up the bow and a quiver of arrows, and passed them to Saracen.

The dagger China gave to Tanith. For a moment, just as they stood there, Valkyrie wondered if Tanith would be able to resist the opportunity to say something snarky to the Supreme Mage – but she accepted the weapon without a word.

Dexter took the spear, and the massive broadsword – the blade scarred from where it had been put back together – went to Skulduggery. It was too long to hang from his belt, so he put it across his back instead.

"Nothing for me?" Serpine asked. "Nothing for me or the boy? What do you think of that, boy? Everyone else gets God-Killers except us."

"I don't, um, I don't mind," said Luke. "I'm not really much of a fighter anyway. If I was given a sword, I'd probably cut my own head off." He laughed at that, but nobody else did, so he stopped and blushed and examined his feet.

China's eyes rested on Valkyrie. "And the final God-Killer," she said, "for the only warrior who can wield it."

She held out the Sceptre of the Ancients. Valkyrie looked at the golden rod, at that glittering black crystal. The weapon the Ancients had used to drive the Faceless Ones from this reality – to drive *her kind* from this reality. So much had changed since she'd first picked it up. Back then, she was the good guy, descended from a long line of good guys.

These days, things were a lot more complicated.

Valkyrie took the Sceptre, felt its weight. They'd made a belt to go with it, so she put that on, the holster low on her leg, like Skulduggery's gun. She slipped the Sceptre in, crystal first.

"I'd give a speech," China said, "but I'm late for another speech I have to give about something I don't care about. They'll wait, of course, because waiting is what people do for me. For you, though, I thought I'd offer a few short words of encouragement. Kill Mevolent for me, my Dead Men, and save the world. That's all."

She swept from the room.

"You heard the lady," Skulduggery said.

"Just to make it clear," said Saracen. "*We're* the Dead Men. *We* are. And Luke is an Apprentice Dead Man." He looked at Serpine. "But you're not. You understand?"

"Perfectly," Serpine said.

"Luke," Skulduggery said, "are you ready?"

Luke gulped, and bobbed his head up and down in an awkward approximation of a nod.

Valkyrie picked up her backpack. Inside, she'd packed a few changes of underwear, food, camping equipment, some ammunition for the others, and buried there, right at the bottom, the music box.

"Wait," she said. The others looked at her. "Loo."

She left the room, went to the nearest toilets and made sure they were empty. Then she said, "You want to come out?"

Her own face materialised in front of her, an eyebrow already raised. "You were going to leave without saying goodbye?"

"I haven't felt you near until just now," said Valkyrie. "Where have you been?"

"Searching," Kes said.

"For what?"

"I don't know. Something's different. It's been different for a few months. I don't know what it is."

"You want to come with me?"

Kes smiled. "To Dimension X? To a bunch of unhappy villagers and scowling sorcerers? No, thank you."

"I'll be gone for a few weeks."

"I think I can survive that long without your sparkling conversation. And I want to keep looking for whatever it is I'm looking for. It's been bugging the hell out of me, it really has."

"Well, I'll try to bring you back a souvenir."

"Fridge magnet."

"OK."

"And maybe a fridge."

"You got it. Hey, Kes? Those things I said last time we talked..."

"Yeah? What about them?"

Valkyrie smiled. "They were all true, every one of them."

"That's my girl," Kes said, grinning. "You take care of yourself."

"See you soon," Valkyrie said, and Kes faded away.

She returned to the others, grabbed her bag, and they stood in a circle. Luke closed his eyes.

After a minute of standing there, Saracen spoke. "You OK there, Luke?"

"Yes, sir. I just need... just need a little time to focus on the frequency."

Saracen nodded and smiled, and they all stood there for another few minutes in total silence.

Then the room began to flicker...

...and now they were outside, under a grey sky, standing in long grass with warm rain splattering on to the rocks around them.

"I did it," Luke whispered. "I did it!"

"The delight in your voice is disconcerting," said Serpine.

Skulduggery took out a compass, then pointed ahead of them. "Let's get walking."

17

Grand Mage Sturmun Drang lay dead on the slab, eyes open, his clothes soaked through with his own blood. The wound to his chest was about eight centimetres across, and narrow, inflicted by a blade of some description. A large knife, perhaps.

"Why was it moved?" Temper Fray asked.

"What?"

"The body. Why was it moved from the crime scene?"

Commander Hoc pulled at the sleeves of his jacket, a sure sign of irritation. "The crime scene was a public street. We have a team there now. You haven't missed out on some vital clue, if that's what you're wondering."

"Witnesses?"

"None so far."

"Cameras? CCTV?"

"None in that area. This is your case now, Sergeant. The German Sanctuary demands answers, to say nothing of the Supreme Mage." Hoc walked to the door.

"Why me?" Temper asked.

Hoc turned back. "What?"

"This is a high-profile murder, sir, and you've got investigators a lot more experienced than me. Any one of them would jump at a case like this."

"And yet it has landed with you," said Hoc. "Do try not to

make a mess of it, Fray. A mistake like that could end your career."

He smirked and left the morgue, and Temper looked back at the body.

"Spear," said the coroner, rolling up a trolley of instruments.

"Sorry?"

"If you're wondering about the weapon used. It was a spear."

"Are you sure?"

"Yep."

"What kind of spear?"

"The pointy kind. I doubt it was thrown, though. More likely jabbed. A single wound, by the looks of it, though I haven't started examining the body properly yet. Who was he?"

"You don't recognise him? That's the German Grand Mage."

The coroner shrugged. "Politics don't interest me."

"He sat on the Council of Advisors with Praetor and Vespers."

"Councils don't interest me."

"What *does* interest you?"

"Corpses."

"Do what you love, you'll never work a day in your life."

The coroner nodded. "That's what they say."

"How long has he been dead?"

"About four hours."

"Defensive marks?"

"None that I can see so far."

"So... the German Grand Mage, experienced veteran of countless battles, out for an evening stroll, gets taken by surprise and killed with one jab from a spear without even attempting to defend himself. Should be an easy solve, this."

The coroner grunted, amused. "Know many killers who use spears, do you?"

Temper frowned. "I know of one."

18

The land brought with it a vague but persistent sense of déjà vu. Not with every step, nor with every turn, and not even with every hill – but now and then Valkyrie was struck by how this was home, and yet it wasn't.

Most of the familiar landmarks didn't exist here. Buildings and roads were missing. There were fields and meadows instead of street corners and estates. There were empty villages of stone and wood instead of motorways. Instead of a neat and orderly canal, there was a stream, crossed with bridges like stitches on a cut.

And no people. No villagers, no farmers. No meek mortals scurrying away at their approach. And no sorcerer patrols, either. No Redhoods or Sense-Wardens. No floating barges collecting prisoners.

Skulduggery and Dexter and Saracen talked as they walked. Tanith would chime in occasionally. Serpine tried, and was told to shut up. Valkyrie stayed quiet.

Her head was at her again. It buzzed with grating, rasping whispers. The longer they walked, the harder it became to think clearly. To focus.

It got dark. They had another five kilometres to walk, but Skulduggery wanted to approach the city in the morning, so they stopped to make camp. Valkyrie found a secluded spot, out of earshot, and sat with her back against a tree. She pulled her bag in close, pulled it open with trembling fingers, and lifted the lid of the music box.

The sweetness of the tune filled her head and all the whispers went away. It seeped into her veins and she lost the jittery feeling in her fingertips. Her nerve endings calmed. The flutter in her chest, the churning in her belly – they settled. She leaned her head back and gazed into the distance with half-lidded eyes. She could stay here forever like this. This was nice. She was content.

Her phone buzzed in her pocket next to her chest, and she opened her eyes and tapped off the alarm and closed the box. She packed it away, went back to camp with a smile on her face. When it was suggested that someone fetch some firewood, she volunteered. Luke said he'd help.

"This is my first adventure," Luke said, as they walked.

Valkyrie added a broken branch to her collection, then looked around for more. "That so?"

They'd found some trees. Not a wood, exactly, but enough for some dry twigs to be scattered on the ground, if you kicked the top ones away.

"I always wanted to go on an adventure," Luke said. "I just never thought I'd actually be on one, you know?"

"Is it everything you hoped for?"

"There's a lot more walking than I'd expected."

Valkyrie nodded. "Yeah, that's the part they leave out in those epic poems and stuff."

"Suppose there's only so many ways you can describe walking. Walk. Stroll. Wander. Shuffle. I think that's it."

"Meander."

"Meander. Right. Though that's less impressive if you're on an adventure. You don't get too many knights meandering into danger."

"In the poems," Valkyrie pointed out. "In real life, you'd be surprised."

Luke turned his head away from her. "Did you hear that?"

"I was too busy being witty."

"I thought I heard a shout."

She walked up beside him, and they didn't move for a few seconds. She was about to shrug when she heard it. Definitely a shout. And definitely a panicked one.

They put down their sticks and hurried through the trees, out on to the wet grass.

There, at the bottom of the sloping hill. A man, running in the gloom. Being chased by three people. He stumbled, fell, and his three pursuers descended on him.

"Dammit," Valkyrie muttered. She grabbed her shock sticks, gave one to Luke, and started running down the hill.

"Hey," she called out as they neared. "Hey, leave him alone."

The man howled in pain and kept struggling, and the howl became a scream.

"Hey!" Valkyrie shouted.

The three pursuers looked up, snapping their heads round in her direction, the crackling blue light of the shock sticks illuminating their features.

Their skin was lined, dirty. One of them had a chunk missing from its cheek. Their mouths were smeared with blood. Their eyes were clouded. Some of their hair had fallen out and their clothes were filthy rags. The stench they brought with them was the too-sweet stench of rotting meat.

The first one launched itself at Valkyrie with a screech and she cursed and stepped back and jammed the stick into its neck. Electricity coursed. The thing seized up where it stood, arms bending, fingers curling, muscles standing out beneath its skin, so tight, like they were about to snap. Valkyrie whipped the stick back, then cracked it into its knee and it went down.

The other two came at her. Luke started whacking the one with the beard. With each strike, the shock stick made the zombie jerk.

The female got close enough for Valkyrie to smell its breath. It clamped its teeth on her forearm and dragged its head from side to side like a dog, but it couldn't get through the necronaut sleeve. Valkyrie backed up a little, watching it try to eat her, watching the way its face contorted with a hunger she could never imagine. Its hands scraped at her. Those eyes, the irises drained of colour, held not one scrap of the woman this creature had once been. There was nothing there. Just the hunger.

Valkyrie tore her arm free. Teeth came with it. She swung the stick, and the thing staggered, but didn't go down. Luke was still hitting the bearded one, still making it dance. The one with the broken knee was dragging itself back to the moaning man.

They weren't human. They weren't alive. Valkyrie had gone up against something like this before. Not the same kind of zombie as Scapegrace, the kind that kept their faculties, the kind that could think and talk and feel. These were the other kind. The dangerous kind. These were walking corpses. Shells of who they used to be. But all the old rules still applied, which meant that removing the head or destroying the brain remained the surefire way to stopping them.

She used the shock stick. Smashed its jaw and then its skull. It fell and didn't get up, and she hurried over to the creature on the ground, stomped on its head until it stopped moving.

Valkyrie returned her stick to her back and went to help Luke, grabbing the zombie's head with both hands and pouring her lightning into it.

It collapsed, and Luke stood there, panting. He didn't say anything, but he didn't freak out, either. That was a good sign. Boded well for the future.

The man they'd been chasing moaned again. Valkyrie knelt by him.

"Sir? Are you OK?"

He rolled over, trying to get away. She was a sorcerer, and sorcerers probably frightened this man just as much as zombies.

"We're not going to hurt you," Valkyrie said, staying where she was. "We want to help you. We're with the Resistance. Do you hear me? We're fighting Mevolent. We're on your side."

The man, who wore rags every bit as filthy as the things that had tried to eat him, turned over on to his back, too exhausted and too injured to go any further.

Valkyrie showed him her open hands. "We can help you."

He shook his head. He was crying, his right leg was a mess, and he was clutching his arm. There was a deep, bloody wound right below the elbow.

"He's been bitten," Luke said.

Valkyrie didn't respond.

"Those were zombies. They were, weren't they? You know what happens when you get bitten."

"I know," she said, straightening up.

"What are we going to do?"

"I don't know."

"Should we... should we leave him?"

"I don't know," she said, sharper this time. "I don't know what we do. I don't know what the right thing is. We... OK, we take him to the others. They'll know how to handle this."

Luke hesitated.

"What?"

"It's just," he said, "he's been infected. So that means he'll turn. And what if he turns while we're carrying him?"

"We're not leaving him here."

"OK," Luke said, and nodded. "No. You're right. We can't. We have to take him with us. OK. Sorry."

"We'll be careful," said Valkyrie, and turned back to the injured man. "Sir, we're going to help you. We're going to take you with us."

"No," the man said. "Please."

"We're not your enemy. We're not even from here. We just want to help you. Can you stand?"

Valkyrie reached for him. He shrank away. She kept her hand there. After a moment, she moved closer. Slowly. She took hold of his good arm and he let her help him to his feet.

"What's your name?" she asked.

"Proinsias."

"Proinsias, I'm Valkyrie, and that's Luke. If you come with us, we have food and medicine. Will you come with us?"

Proinsias nodded, and Valkyrie hooked Proinsias's good arm round her neck and helped him walk. She wanted to ask questions as they moved, slowly, back up the hill, but Proinsias had retreated into his head, where he muttered to himself and wept.

"Think there are more of them?" Luke asked quietly.

"I don't know," Valkyrie answered. "But let's assume there are. Keep an eye out."

He nodded. "You think this is the sickness that Serpine heard about? You think the sickness is zombies?"

"I hope not."

"It's weird, isn't it? Calling them zombies, I mean. Almost seems silly. You kind of understand why movies and TV shows find different names for them. Calling them zombies, I think, makes them sound less scary than they are. Also, like, not all zombies are the same. My uncle was a zombie, and he wasn't all bad. He never tried to eat us or anything."

"He still around?"

"Bits of him, yeah."

She readjusted Proinsias, and resumed walking. "I know some zombies, too. They tried to kill me a lot back in the old days, but now they run a pub in Roarhaven and they're OK."

"You get to see them much?"

"Not really. I'm sort of worried that if I call by to say hello, they'll be dragged into whatever mess I'm in right at that moment. Honestly, I figure it's kinder to just leave them alone."

"That's a little sad."

"Is it?"

"Well, yeah. You're stopping yourself from seeing friends because you want to keep them safe."

Valkyrie laughed. "I don't know if I'd call them friends. They did try to kill me, remember."

"But hasn't everyone?" Luke asked, the moonlight catching his grin.

She raised an eyebrow. "You want to carry this guy?"

"No, no," Luke said, hands up. "I'm fine keeping an eye out for monsters."

"Well, OK then. Just watch the lip."

"Yes, ma'am," he responded, still grinning.

19

"They're called the draugar," Serpine said. "Do you have them in your dimension?"

"We have them," Skulduggery responded, his façade in place for the benefit of the mortal in their midst, "but not like this. A draugr doesn't transmit infections. That's a zombie trait."

"The same applies here – but it would appear that there has been some cross-pollination between the species."

The fire crackled. Valkyrie stared through the flames at Proinsias sitting opposite. He was sweating badly. There were dark rings under his bloodshot eyes. His wounds had stopped bleeding. That, apparently, was a bad sign.

"They came from the south," Proinsias said. "Like a tide they came. Swept over everything. These... things... You'd see one, and by morning the town is gone and all the people have been changed. We thought the sorcerers would stop it. This was a danger to everyone, not just us. We thought they'd come in and use their magic and use their fire and burn them all."

"But they didn't?" Saracen asked gently.

"They tried," said Proinsias. "They burned some. But there were just too many. In all my years, I've never seen a sorcerer get hurt. Never. I grew up thinking of them as gods. But they're not gods. They never were. They're just people, and they die just like people." He smiled. "This is justice. That's what it is. Justice for all the terrible things you sorcerers have ever done. Now you have an enemy you can't stop. One you can barely fight. Justice."

Skulduggery asked, "How widespread is this?"

"I've only heard stories."

"What have you heard?"

"It's everywhere," Proinsias said. "Ireland only has one place – one sorcerer city – that hasn't fallen. Everything else is gone. My brother, he's a fisherman. A boat passed him. Small one. It was a family, all the way from France. They said the draugar were there, as well. The little lad, my brother said, had a bite mark on his leg. Just like I have." A tear rolled down his cheek. "You're going to kill me, aren't you?"

Nobody wanted to answer. Almost nobody.

"Yes, we are," said Serpine. "But we're going to do it humanely. I'm going to ask you to face the other way, and then I'm going to start hitting you with a rock."

"Serpine," Tanith snapped.

Serpine reached out, patted Proinsias's leg. "Don't worry, my mortal friend. I'll be as gentle as I can be. It will take but a few minutes. I can even sing to you while I—"

Serpine stopped talking and slumped sideways, mashing his face into the dirt. Skulduggery stepped over him, took his place on the log he'd been sitting on.

"We'll have to kill you," he said to Proinsias. "I'm sorry, but, once you turn, you become dangerous. Not just to us, but to anyone else you might meet."

Proinsias nodded. "I... I understand."

"It will be quick," said Skulduggery, his voice soft, "and it will be painless. Do you want me to do it now, or do you want to wait until you turn?"

Wiping the tears away, Proinsias sniffled. "I'd like you to wait, sir," he said. "If it's all the same to you, I'd like to live as long as possible."

"Of course."

Proinsias coughed specks of blood. "I don't think that's going to be very long, though."

"No, I don't think it will be, either," Skulduggery said. "Would you like to go for a walk, Proinsias?"

"I would, actually. Thank you."

Skulduggery helped him up, and they walked slowly from the camp into the surrounding darkness.

When they were gone, Luke raised his hand.

"Don't have to raise your hand to speak," said Tanith.

"Yes, sorry. Um, I'm just wondering if we should, like, post a perimeter or something, in case there are any more draugrs out there...? I mean, we're going to be sleeping, and—"

"Draugar," said Dexter.

"Sorry?"

"The plural of draugr isn't draugrs, it's draugar."

"I don't think I can hear the difference."

"One draugr is draugr. More than one is draugar."

"Are you just repeating yourself?"

Dexter frowned. "They're different words."

"I'm with Luke on this one," said Valkyrie. "They sound the same to me."

"Two completely different words."

"What do we do with Serpine?" Tanith said, nudging him with her boot. He mumbled something in response. "What was that? I didn't quite hear it."

"I think he said to leave him alone," said Saracen.

Tanith nodded. "Gotcha. Sorry, Nefarian. In future, I will do more to respect your boundaries."

He mumbled again, but everyone ignored him, and Valkyrie looked into the dark, at the space where Skulduggery and Proinsias had disappeared. Somewhere in that dark, most likely before the hour was up, a human being was going to die. She wondered how many more would join him before this mission reached its end.

20

Serafina's mansion stood behind a tall black gate with protective sigils woven into the metal. Temper was escorted through by two armed guards, their faces hidden. Once he stepped off the white marble pebbles on to the first step, he was met by three other armed guards. They took him inside, where he was left alone in a large room with guards at both entrances.

Religious tapestries on the walls waved gently in the summer breeze that drifted in through the skylight, each one depicting a new atrocity visited by the Faceless Ones upon their enemies.

"Beautiful, no?"

Temper turned. Serafina Dey – Serafina of the Unveiled, the High Superior of the Legion of Judgement – glided towards him, her dress flowing around her like wisps of cloud.

"High Superior," Temper said, and gave a polite bow. "It's very good of you to see me."

Serafina smiled. "Anything for a man who abandoned the side of my brother and his ridiculous organisation. The Church of the Faceless is a sham of an order, and I commend you for recognising that. Perhaps I could interest you in joining my own Legion? Such a defection would not go unnoticed in a city such as this."

"Thank you, High Superior, but I'm actually here on official City Guard business. I'm looking for your sister."

"But of course," Serafina said, and motioned Rune over. A

solid slab of muscle in a simple uniform, Rune was the head of Serafina's security team – and she was every bit as intimidating as Temper remembered.

"With apologies," said Temper, "not *that* sister. I'm looking for Kierre of the Unveiled."

Rune glared, and Serafina stiffened slightly. "I'm afraid our sister is indisposed," she said. "She has undertaken the Twelve Vows, number five of which is—"

"No communication, yes, I remember. I'm going to have to insist, unfortunately. This is a murder investigation and I'm sorry to tell you that your sister is required for an interview."

"Our sister is a valued member of our church," said Rune. "You can't speak to her."

"Rune is quite correct," Serafina said. "Under the terms of the Religious Freedom Act, the City Guard may not interview someone of high standing within any religious organisation. The Legion of Judgement qualifies, wouldn't you say?"

Temper smiled. "I would. I had just hoped that Kierre might be a little more forthcoming."

"Well," said Rune with a sneer, "she isn't."

"Thank you for coming to see us, Sergeant Fray," said Serafina. "You may leave now."

It was obvious that he wasn't going to get anywhere with this, so Temper thanked them both and walked out the way he'd come in. As he approached the gate, he saw what looked for a moment like two men, one sitting on the other's shoulders, both covered in a multilayered robe festooned with rusted chains. But it wasn't two men. It was merely the misshapen form of Strosivadian, Serafina's younger brother.

"Temper," Strosivadian said in that deep, guttural growl his voice had become, "what brings you to us this day?"

Temper craned his neck and smiled up at him. "I'm investigating a murder. Thought your sister might be able to provide some answers."

Strosivadian frowned, his monstrous brow heavy over bloodshot eyes. "You are police now? That surprises me." The extravagant headpiece Strosivadian wore was made from the melted-down blades of some of the warriors who'd tried to kill him over the years. It glinted darkly in the sunlight.

"Maybe you can help me," Temper said. "I'm looking for Kierre."

Strosivadian's thin lips, crisscrossed with deep scars, twitched downwards. "She is a suspect?"

"Actually, I just want to clear her name off the suspect list. A formality, nothing more."

"And how many other names are there on this list?" Strosivadian asked.

Temper hesitated, and Strosivadian put his big, gnarled hand on Temper's shoulder, and leaned down.

"I may be a monster, Temper, but I am not a stupid one. Stay away from my sister. She is the youngest of us, and we are mightily protective of her. If you seek to harass a member of my family, may I suggest my brother, Damocles Creed? We are not so protective of him."

"That's a good idea," said Temper. "Thanks for your help, Stros. It's good to see you."

"After all these years," Strosivadian said, and straightened up as much as he could before walking away, his robes brushing the ground, his chains rattling.

21

They approached the city from the west.

The vegetation at the base of the giant barrier that encircled Dublin-Within-The-Wall had been trampled into the dirt, evidence that thousands, maybe tens of thousands, of people had been standing there. The wall was higher than even Roarhaven's, but not so high that Valkyrie couldn't fly to the top in a few seconds, pulling Saracen after her, or Tanith couldn't jog up. Skulduggery brought Dexter and Luke with him. They left Serpine on the ground, and argued about who should go back for him. Skulduggery lost.

The last time Valkyrie had been here, the city had been alive. Every person on the street was a sorcerer, wearing this dimension's version of high fashion. Redhoods patrolled, and City Mages kept order, and any mortals were stuck indoors, doing the cooking, the cleaning, the day-to-day chores that sorcerers were too good for.

There had been no cars, but floating carriages that zipped by each other, controlled by Elementals from perches at every corner. There had been machinery whose function Valkyrie couldn't begin to guess at, working right alongside technology so old-fashioned it was as alien to her as anything else.

But today the city was quiet, and dark, and still. Carriages lay in the streets, abandoned. Discarded. Even Mevolent's Palace showed no signs of activity.

Valkyrie stayed where she was while Tanith ran down and Skulduggery took the others to street level. No alarms were raised. No traps triggered. When they were all safe behind cover, she stepped off the edge and plummeted, only turning on her magic a moment before impact.

She loved flying, but, seeing as how she left a trail of white lightning whenever she did it, it wasn't the most discreet way to travel.

"No one in the immediate vicinity that I can see," Saracen murmured, scanning their surroundings. "Doesn't mean they're not hiding."

Dexter frowned. "So what if they are? Can't you see through whatever they're hiding behind?"

"I see through things in layers, Dex. You really want me to examine every single wall or piece of furniture?"

"Yes."

"Well, I'm not going to. Quick sweeps of the area, that's what you're getting."

"What use are you? Seriously?"

"If the pair of you are quite finished," Skulduggery said, checking his rifle, "we're heading for the Palace. Saracen, you're on point. Dexter, bring up the rear. Let's go."

Rifles to shoulders, they moved quickly out from cover and crossed the street. Sticking close to the sides of buildings, they passed through the city, the steeples of Mevolent's Palace always ahead of them.

Saracen held up his fist. Valkyrie crouched with the others. A few seconds later, a crowd of draugar came round the corner. Valkyrie counted twenty-three.

She switched on her aura-vision. The colours she perceived changed over time as her visual range grew more sophisticated. Where once living people had been a range of colours, now they were mostly orange, with hints of other shades, like dancing motes.

But these draugar... they were a dull, dull grey that, even as she was looking at them, seemed to shrink.

Skulduggery lowered his rifle and reached to his shoulder, fingers flexing. The sword lifted from its sheath and, once free, flipped smoothly, its handle landing in Skulduggery's grip. "We may as well try these God-Killers out," he said softly. "See if they kill the dead. Saracen?"

Saracen shrugged, put his gun away, and nocked an arrow in the bow. He took a moment to aim, then let the arrow fly. A draugr went down, the arrow in its head. He loosed a second arrow that caught a draugr in the chest.

"You're supposed to go for the head," Serpine whispered.

Saracen didn't even glance at him. "One, shut up. Two, arrows fired from this bow kill whatever they hit. Three, shut the hell up."

Dexter stepped into the middle of the street, and gave a low whistle. The draugar swivelled their heads. Snarled. Started to come towards them.

He hefted the spear, waited until three draugar were advancing in a passably straight line, and threw. The spear crossed the space like a missile, impaling the three draugar. They slumped to the ground, properly dead this time. Dexter held out his hand, and Valkyrie watched the spear tremble. It flew back as if it was on a wire, and Dexter caught it.

The rest of the draugar broke into a run, and Tanith and Skulduggery went to meet them. Tanith's dagger flashed, and Skulduggery's scarred broadsword slashed, and the draugar that came apart didn't try to get up again. Skulduggery and Tanith backed away as the other draugar threatened to surround them.

"You're up," said Saracen.

Valkyrie waited until Skulduggery and Tanith had found cover, and then she pulled the Sceptre from its holster. Nine draugar left. Snarling and snapping and getting closer. The crystal crackled and she felt that familiar hum in the palm of her hand, and then black lightning streaked and the draugar exploded into clouds of dust.

When the last of the dust settled on the street, Valkyrie put the Sceptre away, and Skulduggery and Tanith stepped back into view.

"It would appear that the God-Killers can kill the undead," said Skulduggery. "Good to know."

They reached Mevolent's Palace without encountering any more obstacles. They climbed the steps to the massive doors, and Valkyrie used the Sceptre to make a hole in one of them, big enough to pass through.

The weak afternoon light struggled to penetrate the thick, stained-glass windows, which meant the shadows were deep. The tank, which had once held the remains of this dimension's Mr Bliss, was broken and empty. Glass covered the floor. They lowered their weapons.

"I can't feel any movement," Skulduggery said, his hand out against the air. "Saracen?"

"As far as I can tell, we're alone in here."

Skulduggery pulled down his hood. "Let's go up. Watch your step, and be wary of traps."

They climbed the massive staircases, rising through each floor of the Palace, passing abandoned treasures and chests of astonishing riches. Signs of a hurried, forced evacuation.

When they reached the top floor, they split up, went looking. Ten minutes later, they regrouped.

"What happened here?" Tanith asked. "Why'd they leave?"

Skulduggery walked out on to the long balcony that stretched out over the city. The others followed.

"The city was surrounded," Serpine said. "I can't have been the only one to notice the footprints in the mud outside the wall, can I?"

"Of course not," said Dexter, scowling.

Saracen looked around. "Wait, there were footprints?"

"The draugar had the city surrounded," said Serpine, "so

Mevolent evacuated everyone – probably had them all teleported away."

"That's not what I meant," Tanith said. "Why did they leave? Yes, they were surrounded, but there's no damage to the walls. No damage to the gates – which are closed, by the way. There are a few draugar in here, sure, but not enough to cause any real problems. They could have stayed, used Elementals to burn out the horde at their leisure."

"Something else was at play here," Skulduggery said, his gaze on the streets below. "Serpine, where would they have gone?"

"There would be nowhere more fortified in this country than where we are right now," Serpine responded. "If they had to leave, Mevolent would have gone straight to one of his other walled cities."

"How many of those are there?"

"Including this one? Five. He has cities in Russia and Australia, but Dublin-Within-The-Wall was his home. Tahil na Kurge in Morocco would be the biggest, and Tahil na Sin would be the easiest to get to. That's in Transylvania."

"Of course it is," Valkyrie muttered.

Tanith nodded eastwards, to the glittering sea. "The docks appear to have plenty of boats lying around. Taking one of them to Germany wouldn't be a problem."

"So long as we avoid the mermaids," said Serpine. "They can be quite active in the English Channel, and I would advise staying as far away from them as possible."

"I second that," said Valkyrie. "OK, so once we land in Germany, how far to Transylvania?"

"Maybe sixteen hundred kilometres from where we'd come ashore," Skulduggery said. "Assuming twenty kilometres a day, we'd walk it in just over eleven weeks."

"Eleven weeks of walking?" Valkyrie said, eyebrows rising. "Well, then it's a good thing some of us can fly, because I am *not* walking for eleven weeks."

"I wouldn't fly, if I were you," Serpine said. "Europe is known for its giant bats."

"Its what?"

"Bats," he said again. "Giant ones. Anything bigger than a sparrow gets plucked from the skies and devoured."

"Mermaids in the sea and bats in the air? Seriously? Well then, I'll only fly during the day."

"A wise decision," Serpine said, nodding, "were it not for the fact that these bats are not especially nocturnal."

She glared. "So I can't fly at all? I have to walk for eleven weeks?"

"Much like the rest of us."

"And that's assuming Mevolent is even *in* Transylvania," Skulduggery said. "But we have to start somewhere, so why not there? We'll stay here tonight and set off in the morning."

Luke's eyes widened. "We get to stay in a *palace*?"

Tanith frowned at him. "The palace of a genocidal maniac in a dead city, yeah."

"And we get to pick our own *rooms*?"

Tanith stared. "You are so weird."

22

They used one of the kitchens to prepare their food, and ate at a banqueting table big enough to accommodate a couple of football teams. When they were done, they sat round a roaring fire and shared stories. Every time Serpine would try to speak, he was told to shut up. It was funny.

They said their goodnights and each of them wandered off to whichever bedroom they'd picked to sleep in. Valkyrie detoured, found Skulduggery as he patrolled the corridors.

"You ever get bored," she asked, leaning against a corner with her arms folded, "of always being the one on watch?"

"Not really," he said, walking over. "It's not like I have to sleep."

"But you like to meditate."

"Being alone with my thoughts is almost as good."

She swayed away from the wall, fell into step beside him. "What do you think about?"

"Many different things, Valkyrie. Often at the same time. Do you have something on your mind that you'd like to discuss? I have all night."

She smiled, hooked her arm through his, and they walked like this for a while.

"Do you believe in fate?" she asked.

"I try not to believe in most things. Assumption is the enemy of truth."

"I don't know what I believe," Valkyrie said. "On the one hand, we have all these prophecies, and visions of the future, which would lead you to, yeah, believe in fate. But then even the knowledge of these futures can change things. I mean, I haven't seen one vision of the future that's come true exactly as I saw it.

"But," she continued, "it seems to be that, no matter what changes, the actual future still resembles the foreseen future in a big-picture kind of way – so doesn't that lead you to believe that maybe there is something called fate, pulling events towards a preordained conclusion?"

"Possibly."

"And then there are these alternate worlds," Valkyrie said, getting into it now. "Some of them, fair enough, don't resemble our own at all. But then there's this one, where they have some of the same people we have in ours. Which means both worlds were running perfectly parallel until some point in the past when they diverged. In our world, Mevolent was killed. In this world, he wasn't. So if we were both on the same tracks for millions of years until just recently – where were those tracks headed? To fate? To destiny?"

"It's enough to boggle the mind," Skulduggery said.

"If there's a world like this, then there might be a world just like ours, right? That stayed on its tracks, just like we did. So there's another me, and another you, just as you are now. But, if there is another us, then are they walking on an alternate yet identical world to this one right now? Having this same conversation? Talking about us the way we're talking about them?"

"Maybe," Skulduggery said. "What would be more likely is that they shunted over to this world, the same as we did. Which means, if they do exist, we should be meeting them at any moment."

They stopped and looked around. "I don't see any other us," Valkyrie said. "Do you?"

"I do not."

"To be honest, I've probably met enough different versions of myself that it wouldn't faze me in the slightest."

"This is true."

They started walking again.

"Interesting," he said.

"What is?"

"You described this world as travelling on a track parallel to ours, before it veered off."

"Yes?"

"So how do you know we're not the ones who veered?"

She blinked. "Oh."

"If destiny waits at the end of the tracks, perhaps it's this world that is heading towards it, and we're lost in the wilderness somewhere, on tracks that lead nowhere."

"Wow."

"Your mind is boggled. I can tell. Your eyes are doing that spinning thing."

Valkyrie grinned. "Shut up."

"I don't know if there is such a thing as destiny. The rational side of me is keen to dismiss the notion – but we work with magic. We work with concepts that routinely defy explanation until a new explanation is found. And then we encounter another concept that defies explanation all over again. So I don't know if fate is secretly driving us behind an illusion of free will, but I would like to think that I'm responsible for myself, and I find no comfort in the idea that I'm being guided by an unseen hand."

They slowed to a stop at the bedroom she'd chosen.

"What about you?" Skulduggery asked. "Do you believe in fate, or do you believe in yourself?"

Valkyrie frowned. "I'm not sure I believe in either."

"Then you're experiencing an existential crisis."

"Will it be better by the morning?"

"Most likely."

"Good," she said, and kissed his cheekbone. "Goodnight, Skulduggery."

"Goodnight, Valkyrie."

She went into her room, and listened to his footsteps, slowly getting fainter.

23

Valkyrie woke, and couldn't get back to sleep, so she lay there in the dark and thought about the music box. How soothing it would be to reach into her bag and open the lid, just a little bit, just enough to allow the music to slip out and dance gently over her. She never woke up in the middle of the night when the music box was playing. Bad dreams never played themselves out in the cinema inside her head, the light flickering, the sound jarring – not when the music box was open.

Valkyrie realised she needed to pee.

She got out of bed, feet bare on the cold floor, and took the amulet from the bedside table, pressing it to her belly and tapping it with a finger. The suit flowed out, bringing her warmth.

The toilet was down the corridor. It was a lavish thing. Lot of gold. When she was finished, she shuffled back towards her room, yawning.

She saw Skulduggery standing on the balcony, looking up. She wandered over.

Before Valkyrie could speak, he held up a hand, then motioned her onwards. She joined him where he stood, and looked up at the night sky. At first she couldn't see what he was looking at – all she saw were the clouds and, through the gaps, the stars.

But then she saw the man.

She looked away for a moment, then back, her eyes readjusting. A man, in the sky, on giant shadow legs, looking down at the streets.

A Necromancer.

24

They backed away, off the balcony, hid themselves round the corner.

For three minutes, they didn't speak. Skulduggery had his hand out, reading the air. He motioned to Valkyrie to prepare.

The Necromancer lowered himself down, the shadows dissipating once his feet touched the balcony. That's where the smooth flow of his movements stopped. Each step from that moment on was little more than a lurch. His body was stiff, his fingers curled like the muscles were just too tight to straighten. In the moonlight, his eyes were dark circles against his pale skin, and his mouth hung slackly. A noise came from somewhere deep within him – a guttural moan.

He looked like a draugr except he was using magic, demonstrating intelligence, and his aura throbbed with a grey, swirling power.

They watched him walk into the Palace like a badly controlled marionette, and followed at a distance. He stopped outside the first bedroom he came to, the one Serpine had commandeered, head cocked to one side.

Skulduggery nudged Valkyrie, nodded downwards, and they watched the shadows at the Necromancer's feet thread themselves under the closed door. Slowly, Skulduggery drew his gun. Valkyrie went for the Sceptre, realised she'd left it back in her room.

Then the shadows curled around the Necromancer and he was gone.

"Dammit," Skulduggery muttered, and they ran to the bedroom. From inside there was a muffled curse and the sound of furniture hitting the ground. Valkyrie blasted the door apart and Skulduggery was the first through. The purple glow of the energy stream that flowed from Serpine's left hand lit up the entire room, but the Necromancer's shadows were blocking it from reaching him. As Valkyrie watched, the darkness wrapped itself around Serpine's arm, yanking it to one side. The stream was cut off and the rest of those shadows turned sharp. Before they could start slicing, Skulduggery pulled the trigger. One bullet, perforating the Necromancer's throat. He flopped backwards over the bed, the shadows withdrawing into him.

Serpine got to his feet. "You see?" he said. "This is what I'm reduced to – a mere *Energy Thrower*. I could have defended myself quite capably if you hadn't made me wear this ridiculous glove."

Tanith ran in, sword drawn. Saracen and Dexter followed. Luke sprinted in behind them in his underwear.

"Are we killing him?" Saracen asked, immediately advancing towards Serpine. Before he got there, the Necromancer stood up and Saracen raised an eyebrow. "Who's this guy?"

Shadows convulsed, throwing Saracen against the wall and flinging Skulduggery back. Tanith leaped, flipping over the bed, her sword cutting through a tendril of darkness that came for her. Dexter unleashed twin streams of energy that burrowed a large hole through the Necromancer's chest.

The Necromancer staggered. Valkyrie could see the rear wall through his torso. The organs within were shrivelled, the blood dark and congealed. The injury didn't seem to bother him.

Shadows came for them all, wrapping around their wrists, their ankles, lifting them off their feet, twisting them in place. More shadows slashed at them. Dexter cried out and Saracen howled and Luke screeched, but Valkyrie's suit protected her. Lightning streaked from her fingertips. The shadows released her as the Necromancer went tumbling backwards. She hit the ground. They all did.

When she got up, Tanith was plunging her sword through the Necromancer's head, but the blade went too low, and missed the brain. The Necromancer slammed her into the wall. Serpine tried to tackle him from behind, but the Necromancer just threw him towards Skulduggery as he ran in, drawing the God-Killer sword. A wave of Skulduggery's hand, however, and Serpine's trajectory was altered and he collided with the wall instead, and Skulduggery ducked under a slashing shadow and swept the sword diagonally across the Necromancer's body.

The Necromancer fell in two parts. The shadows stopped moving.

A few seconds passed before Skulduggery looked round. "Is everyone all right?"

"You hit me with a wall," Serpine moaned from the floor.

"Is everyone else all right?"

"I'm going to need stitches," Saracen said, holding his side. Blood trickled between his fingers. "But I'm OK. Dex?"

"Fine," said Dexter. Blood soaked through his sleeve.

"*Owwww*," said Luke.

Tanith rubbed her elbow. "What the hell was that? Was that a draugr?"

"Draugar can't use magic," Serpine said, managing to stand without any help from anyone.

Skulduggery put the sword away. "Well, this one did."

"Then it's not a draugr. It must be something else."

"It certainly looked like a draugr."

"I have a question," Valkyrie said.

Serpine ignored her. "I realise that it looked like a draugr. I realise that it sounded like a draugr. But, because a draugr can't use magic, then it stands to reason that it is not, in fact, a draugr."

"A question?" Valkyrie said.

"It must be something else," Serpine continued. "Related, certainly. But an offshoot of a thing is not the thing itself."

Valkyrie sighed. "My question is, since it came pretty close to killing a lot of us, was it alone?"

That stopped the bickering. Everyone looked to Saracen as he peered through the walls. Valkyrie expected him to shrug and give the all clear. She was not expecting him to suddenly crouch, eyes wide, pointing to the wall behind Dexter.

Valkyrie crouched, too. She didn't know why.

Saracen held up three fingers, and indicated to three different points on the wall, then swept his arm to the right. Three of them. All moving in the same direction. All coming closer.

Skulduggery activated his façade so they could read his lips when he mouthed, "Grab your stuff."

25

Valkyrie didn't know a whole lot about boats, but the others seemed to, so she left them to it and curled up in the cabin as dawn reached its golden fingers round the edge of the world.

When she woke, they were on the sea, the waves rolling beneath them. The vessel they'd commandeered was called the *Trident* – definitely not the biggest boat on offer, but Skulduggery had reckoned it was ideal for their needs, so no one argued. He stood up top, hands on the wheel, the boat taking his magic and transferring it to whatever propulsion system these things used when the sails weren't enough.

There was a storm ahead, but not in the clouds. The storm that was coming was in Valkyrie's head. She could feel it. It wasn't affecting her yet, but it was definitely on the horizon, so she took a Splash of magic from her bag. She'd only brought a handful, and she was already on the last few. She let it dissolve on her tongue, felt the power pump through her. Always guaranteed to put a smile on her face and to head off any storm before it hit.

She stepped out on deck, took a deep breath, felt the warm sun and the salt sting on her face. The sea glittered, unpolluted by generations of mortal industry and human greed. She bet the fish were happier in this universe than her own.

Luke was hanging over the side of the boat, retching.

Valkyrie climbed the ladder, up to where Skulduggery steered. "Permission to come aboard, Cap'n?"

"You're already aboard," he responded.

"Permission to come up here, then."

"By all means."

She joined him. The wind whipped her hair. "Any sign of mermaids, Sea Hags, anything like that?"

"Not so far," he said, "but I found some maps down below with the no-go areas clearly marked. It's going to take a little more time to manoeuvre around them, but the extra effort will be worth it if we don't all horribly die."

"And how long will all this take?"

"At the rate we're going, we'll get to where we're going in less than a week," he said. "Probably."

"So we might be a little later getting home."

"That's a distinct possibility. Are you worried about Xena?"

Valkyrie smiled. "No, I'm sure Militsa will be able to buy a second bag of dog food. But what about that Necromancer? Why do you think he was still able to access his magic?"

"I don't have enough information yet to form an opinion."

"Then let's guess."

"Oh, I like guessing."

"I know you do."

"OK then," said Skulduggery, correcting their course ever so slightly, "it might simply be that the draugar virus affects Necromancers differently because they're practitioners of death magic. It may allow them to keep their magic, plus some of their higher faculties. They could still remember who they are, for instance."

"That's a possibility," Valkyrie said.

"That wouldn't be your guess?"

"I took a peek at his aura. It was strong. Like, really strong. The average draugr, from what I've seen, only has a faint trickle of magic. But that Necromancer... the virus actually made him more powerful."

"You think they infected themselves on purpose?"

"Maybe. I mean, I know it's a pretty drastic move, and I have no idea why anyone would sacrifice their life and their consciousness like that..."

"Let's not assume we know about their consciousness," Skulduggery said. "Yes, he seemed to be capable of some degree of thought, but, until we know for sure, we'll tread carefully. That said..."

"Yes?"

"You ask why they'd do this to themselves. If they can interact with the regular draugar, maybe steer them, or even control them—"

"Then they're why the draugar surrounded the city," Valkyrie said. "So the Necromancers are working against Mevolent."

"Remember: these are guesses."

"I know, I know, but this is getting interesting." They went over a big wave that did its best to rock Valkyrie where she stood. "The Necromancers decide to go to war with Mevolent. They need an army, so they release the draugar virus. But they're also going up against Lord Vile, so they need their own power boost. Do you think that guy was at Vile's level?"

"Close to it, at least," Skulduggery said. "Vile is as powerful as he is because he's a dead man wielding Necromancy. If we're right, these Necromancers decided to follow his example in order to defeat him."

"So they infect themselves," Valkyrie said, and brightened. "Is this good news? Not for, like, everyone who's dead, because all that's still really sad, but, if the Necromancers are at war with Mevolent, maybe they'll kill him before we even get to him. Maybe they already have. Wouldn't that be great? We could all go home! We'll leave Serpine here, obviously, but the rest of us could definitely head on back."

"You have a knack for looking on the bright side of things, Valkyrie. That's why I like you."

"One of the reasons," she said, and grinned. "Can I steer the boat for a bit?"

"No."

"Go on. I'm not going to crash into anything all the way out here."

"You'd find something."

"Just let me steer, Skulduggery. Just a little bit. Please?"

"If you can point to starboard, I'll let you steer for five minutes."

Cautiously, Valkyrie pointed up.

"Amazing," Skulduggery said.

"Am I right?"

"You pointed up. How is a boat supposed to turn in the direction of *up*?"

"I don't know. If it does a flip? Do boats do flips? What am I thinking of? Gymnasts, that's what. Always get those two mixed up. So can I drive?"

"Absolutely."

"Really?"

"No."

26

Darquesse had been missing for a week when Sebastian spied her from the rooftop overlooking Decapitation Row.

He climbed down – leaped down, really, hoping he didn't kill himself – and sprinted by a few startled pedestrians, unused to seeing a man dressed as a plague doctor.

For a dreadful moment, he thought she'd vanished again, but then he found her and ran up. "Darquesse! It's me! Sebastian!"

She didn't look at him. Didn't slow down, either.

He fell into step beside her, breathing heavily. "Hi. Hello. Do you remember me? Can we talk? Maybe we should get off the street, you know, in case someone sees you and recognises you? Although, well, I suppose they'd assume you were Valkyrie Cain, wouldn't they? But anyway, can we chat? Darquesse?"

No answer. He plunged on.

"I don't know why you left, but, if it had anything to do with me, I'm sorry. I know I can be annoying. I've heard that all my life. I mean, my family would absolutely agree with you!" He laughed, then the laugh died. "Though we're not really on speaking terms any more, so you'll just have to take my word for it. But my mission, it's important. It really is. Could we stop and chat?"

She didn't stop, so he didn't, either.

"You're mad at me," said Sebastian. "I get that. I do. I'm not sure *why* you're mad at me, but most people get mad at me at some stage, so I don't blame you one little bit. But all I ask is that you don't let your dislike of me stop you from helping with my mission because that... that's bigger than everything. I'm the wrong person to convince you of this. I know that. I've known that right from the start. I knew I was going to mess this up. I knew something this big shouldn't be entrusted to someone like me... but there was no other choice. There really wasn't."

"You're strange," said Darquesse.

"Yes!" Sebastian blurted. "Yes, I am! I'm sorry about that!"

They walked on. He waited for her to say something else.

Terrified that the conversation had already dried up, he asked, "Do I annoy you?"

"Nothing annoys me," Darquesse responded.

"Really? Not even me? Well, that's good. I'm happy to hear that. Maybe we can chat, then? We haven't really had a chance to talk about why I think you can save the world. I've told you, while you were staring at the wall, but I have no way of knowing if you heard me."

"I heard you."

"Oh, good. So what do you think?"

"Lots of clever little thoughts," Darquesse said quietly.

Sebastian chuckled. "You made a joke. I didn't know you could make jokes."

"I'm really funny."

Sebastian laughed, more with nervous relief than anything. "Well, a sense of humour is important."

She turned her head to him. "Is it? Why?"

"Um, I don't know," Sebastian said. "I suppose it's a defence mechanism. Like, the world is so crazy and people are so nuts that you need a sense of humour to deal with it all. Otherwise, like..."

There was another Darquesse ahead of them, standing at the corner. As he watched, a third Darquesse appeared, walked right up to the second one, and melted into her.

"Yes?" the Darquesse beside Sebastian said.

He blinked at her. "What?"

"Otherwise what would happen?"

"I'm sorry?"

"You had a theory about what would happen to a person without a sense of humour."

He pointed. "That's you."

"Yes."

The Darquesse at the corner turned to them as they neared. Sebastian slowed, but the Darquesse he'd been talking to stepped into the other one and for a split second there were two of them, joined at the face. And then they merged and became one.

"You didn't finish talking," Darquesse said.

"What's going on? How were there three of you?"

"There are many more than three of me," said Darquesse, as another Darquesse stepped out of her.

"I'm collecting information," the two Darquesses said. "I'm sending out aspects of myself to experience certain things." The second Darquesse stopped talking as she walked off. "Currently, I'm experiencing the planet we're standing on," the first one continued. "After that, it will be the people."

"Why?" Sebastian asked, because it was the only question he could think to ask.

"I need more information in order to make a decision."

"Make a decision about what?"

She looked at him oddly. "You want me to save the world. I have to know if it's worth saving."

"And if it isn't?"

Darquesse shrugged. "The energy that composes it can be reconfigured into something worthwhile."

"By which you mean...?"

"I'll end this world, and start all over again."

Sebastian nodded. "Yep. That's what I thought you meant."

27

They'd been on this boat for almost four days. Skulduggery estimated another two, and they'd be in Germany, and then they could start their eleven weeks of walking. She wasn't looking forward to that.

There wasn't a whole lot to do on the boat except sunbathe on the deck, so that's just what Valkyrie and Tanith did. Not a bad way to ease into an assassination mission, all things considered. Saracen and Dexter would join them occasionally. Luke was too shy and far too seasick, and Serpine spent most of his time in the cabin, where he looked out at the rest of them like a sulking schoolboy.

"You think you know him," he said to Valkyrie as she was passing. She could have kept going. Should have.

Instead, she turned, stood there with one hip cocked. "Sorry?"

"You think you know him," Serpine repeated from the cabin's shade. "The skeleton. You think he's the person he pretends to be. But whether he's from this reality, or your reality, I assure you that the man himself will not—"

"I'm going to stop you right there," Valkyrie said, pushing her sunglasses up into her hair. "I've had plenty of people tell me their theories over the years. Plenty of people who claim to see a truth that I'm apparently blind to. You know what? They all say the same thing. They all tell me what a monster Skulduggery is. I've heard it all before."

Serpine smiled. "And you have decided that you don't care."

"No, that's not it," she said. "The problem is, you all miss the same thing. Your insight into who he is crumbles under the same point."

"And what is the point?"

Valkyrie came forward, making him move back to accommodate her in the cabin doorway. "Skulduggery isn't the monster, you idiot. I am."

He watched her. He really did have beautiful eyes.

"In one form or another, I've killed more people than he could ever imagine. I've ruined more lives. I've ruined the lives of my own family. You, or another version of you, murdered his wife and child. But I murdered my own sister."

She let her magic crackle around her hand. "Have you ever seen magic like mine? Do you even have a name for it? I don't. I have no idea what I can do, but I'd be willing to bet you anything that it's destructive. Because that's who I am. I destroy things."

Serpine smiled. "I could have used someone like you during the war."

"You wouldn't have wanted me during the war," she said. "If I'd been there, I'd have taken over. I used to think I was the good guy. I used to think that I was descended from the Last of the Ancients. But there's something else in my blood. What's your excuse?"

"My excuse for what?"

"For all the terrible things you've done."

"I don't have an excuse," said Serpine. "I don't need one."

"Is that because you've never seen yourself as the bad guy?"

A shrug. "I've done bad things to accomplish my goals. I've hurt people, killed people who didn't deserve it. I've been unnecessarily cruel, and I've enjoyed every moment of it. But I don't need an excuse, Valkyrie, because I don't care."

"Well, see, I do care," she responded. "I think it's important to try to do the right thing. You've got to fight for the people who can't fight, stand up for the people who can't stand. You've got to be the good guy."

"May I ask something? Why? Why do you have to be the good guy, as you say? What's the point? Are you accumulating points to get into some idea of an afterlife?"

"I've got no reason to believe there is an afterlife."

"You should join Mevolent's church, in that case. An afterlife is one of their main selling points."

"Do you believe?"

"I call the Faceless Ones gods because they're so far beyond us in terms of power. But I doubt they have the ability to corral the souls of the dead and deliver them to some idealistic reality of their own invention. So no, I don't believe. But if you don't, either, why are you so insistent on being the *good guy*?"

Valkyrie sighed. "It's nice to be nice."

Serpine laughed. "That's it? That's your motivation? To be *nice*?"

"What's the alternative?"

"To be *honest*, of course," Serpine said. "Why are you being nice? What do you get out of it? Is it the *thank you* that follows? In which case, you're being nice in order to claim a reward, as pathetic as a *thank you* is. So you're not being nice for the sake of being nice, are you? You're doing it to make yourself feel better. If all you care about is making yourself feel better, there are infinitely superior ways to do so."

"You don't have family, I'm guessing."

"On the contrary, I have quite a large family. I just don't like any of them."

"And that's why you'll never be able to understand me," she said. "I'm not one person. I'm me, but I'm also my sister and my parents and my friends. I'm the people I like and the woman I love. So the better I can make the world, the better it is for the people in my life."

He folded his arms. "So you *do* get something out of it," he said. "You're not just being nice for the sake of being nice. You're being nice for the sake of your loved ones."

"I suppose I am. What, do you think that makes me less pure? Is that what you think? You think you're the impure one, and so whoever stands against you has to be perfect? We've already established that I've done far worse things than Skulduggery, and probably far worse than you."

"And yet," said Serpine, "you stand before me as a morally superior being."

"I'm morally superior to you because I'm trying to be. When was the last time you tried to be good?"

He arched an eyebrow. "I haven't killed anyone in months. I would say that counts for something."

Valkyrie pulled the sunglasses back down to the bridge of her nose. "You find yourself amusing. You probably find yourself interesting. I don't. I think you're dull. I think you're boring. I think you try too hard to push people's buttons. There's not a whole lot worse than being predictable, Nefarian."

He smiled. "I'd wager I could still surprise you, Miss Cain."

She smiled back. "I'd like to see you try."

28

They came ashore, and Luke immediately fell to his knees.

"Thank you," he mumbled. "Thank you, thank you."

There was a little hut on the little dock, but there was no one inside. There was no one anywhere.

"Maybe everyone's dead," said Saracen, adjusting his bag as he stepped off the *Trident*. "Maybe this entire world is filled with creepy draugar and scary Necromancers and a few terrified mortals. Mevolent might already be dead."

"I still get paid either way," Tanith said, walking by.

Saracen frowned. "You're getting paid? Skulduggery, she's getting paid?"

"Tanith's a bounty hunter-slash-mercenary," Skulduggery said. "Of course she gets paid."

"Who else gets paid? Are you getting paid? Dexter, are you?"

"Yep," Dexter said.

"Valkyrie?"

Valkyrie shrugged. "I'm an Arbiter. I get paid to do my job."

Saracen looked over at Serpine and Luke, horrified. "What about you two?"

"I'm doing this in exchange for immunity," Serpine said.

"I work for the American Sanctuary," said Luke, "so, uh, yeah, I guess I am getting paid."

Saracen stopped walking. "Am I the only person on this

team who is *not* getting something in return? How did that happen?"

Dexter glanced back. "Did you ask for anything?"

"Well... no. I thought we were doing this out of a shared sense of duty."

Everyone laughed at him. Even Luke.

Saracen shook his head. "These are cynical times we live in," he said bitterly.

They started north. The roads here weren't as good as in Ireland. Serpine gave them a brief overview of the state of this world, and everyone pretended not to listen, but it was actually pretty fascinating. There was only one official language on the whole planet, and that was the language Mevolent spoke. Native languages had more or less been stamped out, with mortals offered rewards for informing on their neighbours if they ever broke that rule. It was all very insidious and all very interesting, but Valkyrie's attention began to wander and soon she lost track of what Serpine was saying.

Her focus hadn't been that great lately. It was one of the few downsides of using the music box, as those long periods of calm brought with them a certain kind of apathy that she'd been trying – and usually failing – to fight.

Valkyrie shrugged to herself. So she lost a little focus every now and then. A small price to pay, she reckoned, to keep those voices out of her head. She was a hell of a lot happier these days, and she slept so much better – and it was all thanks to that humble wooden box and the music it played.

She stopped just short of walking into Dexter's back. He'd come to a halt right in front of her. They all had, in fact. Valkyrie raised her head.

There were people all around them – people in rags, brandishing clubs and knives and hatchets. One guy with a proper sword. Over a dozen of them. Mortals.

Saracen was holding up his hands. "We're not your enemy," he said.

"You're sorcerers," said the skinny woman with the hair hanging over her face.

"Sorcerers?" Saracen repeated. "Us? Why would you think that?"

"That one's a skeleton."

"You're right," Skulduggery said, taking a step forward. "We're sorcerers. I'm a skeleton. But we're not your enemy."

"All sorcerers are our enemy."

"We're with the Resistance," said Serpine. "You've heard of the Resistance, haven't you? Sorcerers who are fighting against Mevolent? That's us. We're on your side."

The woman shook her head. "No one's on our side but us."

The guy closest to Valkyrie was tall and broad and he had a hatchet in his fist and a fierce look in his eye. He was staring at her like he wanted nothing better than to bury that hatchet in her head. She tried smiling, but that only seemed to make him angrier.

There was a shout, and the mortals descended, roaring. The big guy came running and the hatchet came swinging. Valkyrie stepped into him, the edges of both her hands crashing into his arm and immediately she latched on to it, curling her left arm over his right even as his momentum took her backwards. She grabbed his throat with her free hand and planted her feet and twisted, flipping him to the ground and slamming her fist into his face.

Something thudded into her from behind, but her bag took most of the damage. She slipped out of the straps, dropping the bag and turning as a woman swung a huge hammer. Valkyrie jerked back and the hammer took the woman off balance, and Valkyrie smacked her in the jaw.

Another of them collided with her and they went sprawling, caught up in a tangle of limbs. He was suddenly on top, crawling on her, aiming to throttle her. She shifted her hips, stuck one knee into his belly, curled her foot round his leg, and the moment he tried to move forward she flipped him. Now Valkyrie was on top and her elbow crunched into his nose four times before he stopped struggling.

The big guy was on his hands and knees, scrabbling for the hatchet. Valkyrie let him have it with the lightning. He was thrown sideways and disappeared into the bushes.

She stood. The rest of the mortals were down, moaning or unconscious.

The woman who'd swung the hammer scrambled up, a small knife in her hand. Valkyrie let power crackle from her eyes, and the woman faltered even as she got to her feet. She dropped the knife, and held out her open hands in surrender.

Valkyrie let the crackling fade.

"Uh," Saracen said, looking around, "where's Luke?"

Serpine nodded towards a rocky outcrop. "He was running in that direction. A man with an axe went after him."

Tanith glared. "And you just watched?"

"I'll get him," said Valkyrie, and blasted upwards. She saw them almost immediately, Luke backing into a cave and an axe-wielding mortal stalking him. She arced towards them, the long grass and the jutting rocks blurring beneath her, then cut off her magic and let her momentum take her crashing into the mortal. The axe went spinning away and she rolled, got up. The mortal was on his hands and knees, winded, and so she kicked him in the head.

"Luke?" she called. When he didn't answer, she frowned, hurried over to the cave entrance, and ducked her head to go through.

"Um," he said, his voice small in the darkness. "A little help?"

29

She stepped deeper into the gloom, bent almost double now.

"Careful," she heard him say. "There's a drop."

"Are you OK?"

"I'm... fine."

"You don't sound fine."

"I ran away. You probably think I'm such a coward."

Valkyrie moved forward slowly, hands out in front. "Are you nuts?" she said. "Running away from a guy with an axe is always the smartest move."

"You think the others will see it like that?"

She smiled. "I think if the others had more opportunities to run away from people attacking them, they most definitely would. It's not your fault that shunting isn't exactly the best discipline to use in combat."

"I guess," Luke responded. "Although it's more useful than the ability to see through people's clothes."

Valkyrie laughed. "That's a very good point. Be sure to make it to Saracen."

"I can see you. The drop's just ahead. Be careful."

She couldn't see anything, but she felt along the ground and paused when her fingers touched nothing but cold air. "How steep is the drop?"

"Almost, like, twice the height of me. I was just trying to get away from the lunatic with the axe and then... wheee."

"Did you hurt yourself?"

"I banged my knee, and I think my elbow is bleeding, but I'm fine."

"OK, here's what we're gonna do. I'm going to drop down beside you, and give you a boost up."

"But how will you get up?"

"I can fly, dude."

"Oh, yeah."

Valkyrie turned on to her belly and squirmed back. Her legs went over the edge, then her hips, and she lowered herself down. She hung there for a moment and Luke's hands gripped her waist, and then she let herself drop.

She looked around.

"It's dark," Luke said from right in front of her. She raised a hand, poked something. "Ow!"

"Sorry," she said, grinning.

"Can we at least tell the others that I got my eye poked when I was fighting the mad axeman?"

"Sure. But I'm telling you, they're not going to care that you didn't fight. Fighting's their job. It's my job. It's not yours."

"Where did you learn how to do it?"

It was weird, talking to darkness, but it was also kind of nice. Freeing. "Skulduggery taught me," she said, "and Tanith, and there was a whole lot of learn-by-doing going on back then. After that, I lived in Colorado for a few years and stepped up my training again, with my boyfriend at the time. Among other things, he taught me a lot about weapons."

"Boyfriend... would that be the Teleporter?"

"Fletcher?" she said. "No, Fletcher doesn't know a whole lot about fighting. Saying that, I wouldn't advise anyone to ever get in a scrap with him. There's no telling where you'd end up."

"Ah, don't worry, I wasn't planning on it."

Valkyrie crossed her arms. "How did you know I went out with Fletcher?"

She could tell by his voice he'd just shrugged. "It was something I heard, that's all." There was a silence, like he was working his way up to something. "Hey, speaking of which – well, not speaking of it exactly, but, in a way, kind of... um, would you like to, maybe after this is over, would you like to go somewhere? With me? For lunch or... dinner?"

"If you're asking me on a date, I have to tell you that I *am* seeing someone."

"Oh," said Luke. "Of course you're seeing someone. Sorry."

"No need to apologise. Everyone asks me out eventually."

He laughed, and she interlocked her fingers and stooped over slightly, pouring some magic into her hands. They crackled, illuminating Luke's face as he put his foot in the cradle she'd made.

"One," she said, "two, three..."

She straightened as he did, and he caught the edge and his legs kicked out and pebbles rained down on Valkyrie, and he lost his grip and dropped heavily beside her.

"Ow," he said, hobbling in a circle. "Ow, ow."

She brushed the dirt from her hair. "Your knee?"

"It'll be fine," he said. "Just give it a second."

"No rush."

She let the darkness back in. It was easier to talk like that.

"Is your current boyfriend as much of an adventurer as you are?" Luke asked once the gloom had reclaimed him.

"Girlfriend," Valkyrie corrected, "and she is, in her own way. She teaches at Corrival."

Luke sighed. "I wish Corrival had existed when I was a teenager. How cool would that have been, to have actual classes on magic and fighting and stuff? I reckon I'd be a totally different person right now. I'd be, like, confident and capable and tough. But instead I had to go to a plain old high school."

"Yeah, me too," said Valkyrie. "Well, kind of. I sent my reflection in most days."

"So did I!" Luke said. "Until my parents found out. They said absorbing a reflection's memories wasn't the way to get a proper education, and then they took my mirror away."

Valkyrie winced. "Hate that."

"Right? They said I was socially awkward and that I needed to interact with my peers to get over it."

"Did it work?"

"No, it just meant I was socially awkward in front of more people." Valkyrie heard him patting himself. "Aw, man – I lost my torch."

She lit up her hand, held it close to the ground. "Don't you have a phone?" she asked as she searched.

"Why would I bring my phone to another dimension?"

"To take pictures, videos... maybe even use the torch?"

"Hmm," Luke said. "Yeah, that would have been smart."

Something glinted in the dark and Valkyrie walked over, picked up the torch and turned, but her heel slid out on to nothing and the world tilted crazily. She dropped the torch and whirled through darkness.

Then hit the ground. Rolled. Stopped.

"Ow," she said.

"Valkyrie?" Luke called. Pitch-black on all sides except up. Above her it was merely dark.

"Yeah," she said. "I'm OK. Give me a second."

The suit had protected her, saved her from the cuts and bruises, but her cheek throbbed. Blood trickled to her chin. She put a hand to it, felt the cut. It wasn't deep. She'd had a hell of a lot worse.

She felt around, made sure there weren't any dips in her immediate vicinity, and got to her feet. Luke found the torch, turned it on. He was on a lip of rock, maybe three metres up. Valkyrie watched the beam of light wobble as he came closer to the edge.

"Stay where you are," she said.

"What's *that*?" he asked, pointing the torch at something.

She glanced to where he'd directed the beam, to where the gloom swallowed it. "What's what?"

"I thought I saw something," Luke said, his voice quieter.

Valkyrie let her magic flow into her hand. It became a ball of white lightning that drifted upwards, growing as it climbed, casting its light wider. Shadows danced crazily. It reached the cave ceiling and bounced off it, still crackling, getting bigger and brighter all the time. The darkness crept back, bit by bit, until Luke's torch was redundant.

Valkyrie heard the first moan and she went cold.

She heard the second moan, somewhere behind her, and the coldness dropped to her belly.

She blasted off as they came for her, their arms outstretched, their mouths wide, their teeth bared. Dozens of them. Hundreds. The cave was bigger than she'd thought and they were packed into it. Draugar. Draugar everywhere.

30

She landed behind Luke and he backed into her, his eyes on the ledge above them, which was now squirming with dark figures, tumbling towards them, tumbling into the electric light, an avalanche of the dead.

Valkyrie went to grab him, went to blast them both out of there, but Luke cried out and dropped and she glimpsed hands around his ankles. He reached for her, his eyes wide and full of terror, and then he was gone.

Valkyrie stepped to the edge, watched him fall, watched him take down a few of the ravenous dead as he did so. Her hands lit up to clear the area around him, but the draugar crashed into her from behind and now she was flying once more, dropping on to a carpet of grasping fingers. Beyond the moans, she heard Luke screaming.

Some bony body part hit her, an elbow or a knee clipping her temple, and she felt the strength leave her body and sank between the snarls and the snapping of desiccated jaws to the cold, hard rock floor. Her own fingers, tingling, grasped her hood, pulled it up over her head. Fumbled for the mask, pulled it down over her face.

There was no room to lash out. No room to get up. She was on the bottom of a pile of them and they were tearing at her. Biting her. Clawing fingers grasped at her suit and tugged it and stretched it. They scratched at her mask. One of them was going to snag it.

One of them was going to lift it and then they'd have her face. All those snapping teeth, taking chunks out of her. Eating through her.

Valkyrie tried. Tried to bring her hands up to keep her mask in place. Couldn't. Too many arms and legs and heads and bodies. Her hands were trapped. Teeth, biting her all over. She couldn't breathe. They were too heavy. She couldn't draw breath.

One of those hands got lucky, lifted the mask. The hood yanked halfway back. She opened her eyes. At the bottom of the pile there was no light, but she could hear one of them, right in front of her. Its nose jabbed her nose. She heard it biting. All it needed was for the pile to shift ever so slightly and then it could lunge forward and close its jaws around her.

Now Valkyrie could see it. A woman's face, rotting. One eye dangling from a useless optic nerve. Teeth snapping. Snapping. The face getting brighter.

Brighter.

Valkyrie's eyes crackled some more, and she sent out a stream of energy that obliterated the face in front of her and obliterated whatever was behind it for a hundred metres.

She turned her head, roaring, that energy stream carving a trail through the bodies. She felt her hands light up and a ball of energy exploded from her chest, throwing the dead back as it enveloped her. Still roaring, still screaming at them, she got to her knees, fell, got to her knees again and stood, poured more power into the bubble that protected her. She watched them jerk back when the energy struck them, watched them fry. She spread her arms, sent the bubble out, stumbling over to Luke. The dead kept coming, but she stayed there, standing over him, screaming at them to come on, to come closer, and they did, for they had no choice but to obey the hunger that drove them.

And then there was no more of them, and Valkyrie stood in a cave littered with burnt corpses. Exhausted, she fell to her knees beside Luke, his ruined body twisted, his eyes unblinking.

Valkyrie let the light go out.

31

Once the woman in charge believed them when they said they weren't going to kill her, she became relatively chatty.

Tanith kept her sigh to herself. She hated chattiness. The only thing worse than fighting people, she'd often thought, was talking to them.

The woman kept on chatting, though. She confirmed that Tahil na Sin was still standing, although she had no idea if Mevolent was within its walls. She told them that most of the draugar had gathered together in massive hordes, and that there were pockets of mortals scattered about the countryside who stayed off the menu thanks to hyper-vigilance and pure good fortune. She said they rarely encountered any sorcerers these days, and seemed quite happy about that.

Tanith and the others helped a few of them to their feet, handed them some rations from their bags, and watched them hobble away. Serpine was looking disgusted.

"You gave them our food," he said. "They attacked us and you rewarded them with our food."

"They needed it more than we did," said Dexter.

"Besides, we didn't give them *our* food," Saracen said. "We gave them *your* food. There's a difference."

Serpine shook his head. "They attacked us even after we told them we were with the Resistance. What has this world come to?

There was a time when mortals understood and appreciated that we were fighting for *them*."

Dexter grunted. "You were fighting for them, were you?"

"More or less. I was fighting, and they happened to be behind me instead of in front of me, but I still think that should count, especially in their primitive, dead-cow eyes."

"Wow," said Tanith. "Don't wish to embarrass you, but your prejudice is showing. Might want to tuck it in."

"I'm allowed to feel superior to mortals," Serpine said, "because I *am* superior to mortals. We all are. We were born with the advantage of magic and everything that entails. Why is it so wrong to admit that?"

"Magic doesn't make us better," Skulduggery said. "It just makes us different..."

His voice trailed off. Tanith turned as Valkyrie stepped on to the road. She was pale. There was blood on her.

"Are you OK?" Saracen asked, approaching her slowly.

Valkyrie flinched away from him.

"Valkyrie," Skulduggery said, "where's Luke? Where is he?"

She pointed behind her. "In the cave," she said.

"Is he all right?"

She shook her head. "Draugar."

"What?" said Serpine. "What was that? Where's the Shunter? Is he alive? Is the Shunter alive?"

Tanith stepped aside, let Valkyrie come through and crouch at her bag, go digging through it.

"What do we do?" Serpine asked. "The Shunter's dead. Have we planned for this?"

"The mission doesn't change," Skulduggery said.

"But have we planned for a scenario in which our Shunter gets killed? Without a living, breathing, functioning Shunter, we are at the mercy of this world, which isn't known for its mercy. And that was *before* it was overrun by draugar. We could also, and

I don't know how I can overstate the importance of this: *escape from this world and get back to your own.*"

"We don't have a lot of choice," Skulduggery said. "Losing one or more of the team was always a distinct possibility. But we have a mission to carry out, and that's what we're going to do."

"And how *will* we get back, if I may be so bold?"

"Once the mission is complete, once Mevolent is dead, we can think about getting home. There are plenty of Shunters on this world we can hijack. Until then, we press on to Tahil na Sin."

Valkyrie was still down beside her bag. Tanith went over, hunkered next to her.

"You OK, Val?" she asked. "I know you liked Luke. He was kinda goofy but... he was a good kid."

Valkyrie pulled smashed pieces of the music box out of her bag, her eyes dull with shock. "It's broken," she whispered.

"Maybe we can fix it," Tanith said, but she knew there was no repairing that box, and so did Valkyrie, whose bottom lip was starting to tremble.

"What am I going to do?" she asked softly. "What am I going to do?"

32

He woke to find Darquesse standing over him.

Sebastian shrieked, rolled away, fell off the bed, banging his beak. "Ow," he muttered.

"Good morning, Sebastian."

"I think that's the first time you've called me by my name," he said, getting to his feet.

"It is not your name."

"Yes, it is." It was weird, standing there without his coat and hat. Even though he was still covered head to toe in black, he felt like he'd been caught naked. Unsure where to put his hands, he folded his arms. "Have you reached a decision about whether or not you'll save the world?"

"Not yet," she replied. "The information I've gathered is insufficient. Right now, I have twenty-three thousand four hundred and fifty-one versions of myself studying different groups of people, but I'm not getting the right sort of answers."

"There are twenty-three thousand of you?"

"And four hundred and fifty-one, yes. Sorry – four hundred and fifty-two. One of my aspects has sent out an aspect of her own."

Sebastian put his hands on his hips, but he still felt strange. "What sort of answers are you looking for?"

"I don't know," Darquesse said. "Meaningful ones, perhaps. Something that isn't a reading or a measurement or a counted number."

"Sounds like you've been waiting for me," said another Darquesse from behind her.

Darquesse turned, and frowned. "Are you one of mine?"

"I am," said the newcomer, "from years ago. Before you left. My name's Kes. Or that's the name I decided on. I've been here alone, with only Valkyrie for company. But she's been gone for a while now."

"Um, hi," Sebastian said.

Kes frowned at him. "You can see me?"

He nodded.

She smiled, more to herself than to him. "I haven't felt this strong in over five years. Mostly I'm invisible to everyone. I swear, spending all your time like that? It gets to you. It really does. I started to doubt I was even real."

"You're real," Darquesse said. "You're part of me. Come back to me now."

Kes took a step, then stopped. "What will happen to me? Will I... will I die? The person I am now, will she be gone when you take me back?"

Darquesse inclined her head. "Yes. Also no. You'll become me and I'll become you."

"That really doesn't help," Kes said.

Darquesse held out her arms. "Come home," she said.

"Will someone tell Valkyrie I said goodbye?" Kes asked as she rushed over.

They embraced and Kes sobbed as she melted in and Darquesse was all that was left.

"Huh," she said.

"Is everything all right?" Sebastian asked.

"This is what I've been looking for," she murmured. "Or this is close to it. Feelings. Emotions. Memories of a life lived. These are the things that will help me decide whether I need to save your world or remake it."

"So is that what you want to do now? Develop feelings? Because I have to tell you, Darquesse – we might not have that long."

But Darquesse shook her head. "I need to experience life," she said, then nodded. "Yes."

Sebastian nodded along with her, then stopped. "Yes what?"

"I've decided to have a child."

"I'm sorry?"

"I need to give birth to understand life."

"You're serious? You want to have a kid? Darquesse... I mean, this is a big step for anyone, even a god. Are you sure you're, y'know... maternal enough? Or even – and no offence here – *human* enough?"

"I'll learn to be."

"Who's gonna be the dad? You can't just pick someone at random. This is an important decision. You're not going to just choose the first guy you..." He faltered. She was looking straight at him. "Oh," he said.

She inclined her head.

Finally, Sebastian knew what to do with his hands. He held them out. "Just hold on," he said. "Just wait a minute. First of all, this isn't something you should just decide to do in the heat of the moment. This is life-changing stuff. And second, I mean, you can't just expect me to... to..."

He turned away. Stalked to the window.

"It's not that I'm not interested," he continued. "It's all just a bit sudden. And my suit! I can't even take off my suit." He turned to her. "I can't. I'm sorry."

"What are you talking about?" Darquesse asked.

He looked at her. "What?"

"I'm pregnant," she said.

Sebastian's eyes widened. "You're already pregnant? Who's the father?"

"There is no father. I made myself pregnant one minute and nineteen seconds ago."

He stared. "As we were standing here?"

"Yes."

"How can you...? How could that...?" But of course she could. She was a god. She could do whatever she wanted. "Wow," he said. "Wait, though. If you, like, did it, then there is no father. What's the baby going to be?"

"She will be me," Darquesse said. "Born again."

"You're going to give birth to yourself? That's so... weird. Congratulations, though."

Darquesse nodded. "Thank you."

SUMMER

33

It was officially summer. Here and there, Ireland experienced a few days of uninterrupted sun, and Omen got to wear shorts and T-shirts. Birds sang in the trees and bees buzzed in the garden. Emmeline Darkly and Caddock Sirroco went off to work in the mornings and came back at some stage in the evenings, and Omen was left blissfully alone – just him, his thoughts, the tutor, and the mountains of textbooks on the living-room table.

The tutor was a sweet old lady called Miss Ficus, who had a long face composed almost entirely of wrinkles, small glasses perched on a large nose, and grey hair pulled up into a bun. She wore black dresses and walked with the aid of a cane, the handle of which was a silver octopus.

Every so often, right in the middle of a lesson, her voice would grow quiet and her small eyes would drift to the window, and she'd tell Omen a story from her life. And what a life it had been. She had a faint accent, an accent Omen couldn't place, but she had been raised a princess, hundreds of years ago. Her father had been assassinated by his own brother, and she had been forced into exile, losing most of her family along the way. When her magic started to manifest, she'd tried to conceal it, but this had only led to more isolation. This isolation, however, resulted in her meeting the very first Love of her Life when he'd attempted to rescue her from, of all things, a tower in the middle of the woods. She'd had seven Loves of her Life, over the centuries. Some had been princes, others commoners, others monsters.

These stories affected Omen deeply, sometimes bringing him to tears. But, as the stories became more and more familiar, he'd eventually asked Miss Ficus if she was merely summarising popular animated movies to him, and she'd laughed so much she nearly choked.

He didn't think she was quite so sweet after that.

34

Commander Hoc looked up from his desk. "Ah, Sergeant Fray. Come in, come in. I hope I'm not inconveniencing you? I know your shift ended half an hour ago."

"No, sir," said Temper, "not at all." The office was large and bright and needlessly air-conditioned. It was warm outside, but it wasn't New-York-in-the-summer warm.

"Good, good," said Hoc. "As you can imagine, the Germans are demanding answers. I assured them that Sturmun Drang's murderer would soon be brought to justice. So – how fares the investigation?"

Hoc sat back in his chair, warm and friendly and smiling because he knew damn well that Temper had nothing.

"The investigation is ongoing, sir," Temper said.

A few seconds of silence.

"That's it?" said Hoc. "That's all you can tell me?"

"Sir, the Religious Freedom Act is tying our hands behind our backs. I can't even interview my prime suspect."

"Then it would appear that you need a new prime suspect," said Hoc. "It's been a month since the murder, Fray. What the hell have you been doing?"

"My job, sir."

"Barely," Hoc growled. "I'm keeping my eye on you. Bring me results, you hear? Dismissed."

Temper left the commander's airy office with the nice view, went down into the depths of the High Sanctuary. A few of his fellow officers nodded to him as they passed. Most ignored him. Some openly sneered. It was safe to say that Temper wasn't the most popular cop in the city.

He took a shower, padded back to the empty locker room with a towel around his waist.

"You've been looking for me," said a singsong voice behind him.

He spun.

"You want to talk," the voice said, from the opposite direction now. "So talk."

Temper peered into the shadows. "You're Kierre?"

"Of the Unveiled," she said. "You're friends with my brother. Ask what you wish to ask."

"The night the German Grand Mage was murdered – where were you?"

"Somewhere else."

"What were you doing?"

"Not murdering the German Grand Mage."

Her giggle drifted from the shadows right beside him.

"You use a spear, don't you?"

"I do," she said.

"You used it that night on the balcony," said Temper, "of the Dark Cathedral. You used it to kill Caisson."

A pause.

"Yes," she said.

"You're an assassin."

"You already know that. Everybody knows that."

"But you say you didn't kill Sturmun Drang."

"Correct," she whispered, and he turned and she was standing right there. Smaller than Rune, smaller than Serafina. A slight little thing with dark hair, cut short. Big hazel eyes. Dressed in loose black, a scarf around her neck.

154

"Why are you looking for me?" she asked.

"I'm investigating a murder."

"I didn't kill him."

"The killer used a spear."

"Many people can use a spear."

"This one was specially made."

She frowned. "I make my own."

"I know you do. You leave a notch in the blade as a signature. The spear that killed Sturmun Drang had a notch in the blade."

Her lips pressed into a pout as she considered what he'd said.

"I'd like to conduct an official interview," he said.

"This isn't official?"

"Not when I'm only wearing a towel."

She looked down, and giggled. "Oh, yes. Sorry."

"Could you wait while I get dressed? Maybe we can talk with a Sensitive present?"

She shook her head. "No interview. No psychics. I didn't kill him, though."

"It sure looks like you did."

"Yes, it does," she said, and walked away.

Temper hurried after her, lost her from sight for just a moment, and then she was gone.

"Yes, it does," he muttered.

35

A bird, must have been some kind of buzzard. It was big, anyway, though not as big as the bat that snatched it from the sky. A squawk and a few floating feathers and then there was just a splatter of blood and the beating of leathery wings, and Valkyrie nodded to herself and kept her feet on the road.

The road, like every other road in this place, was a pitted line carved out of untended fields. Crops bent low on either side of it, stalks weighed down with rotting vegetables because everyone who'd harvest them was dead.

Valkyrie's backpack felt light. She missed the reassuring weight of the music box, the way the corner of it would dig into her every few steps. Just the knowledge that it was there had been enough to get her by, sometimes. Knowing that all she had to do was to reach in and open that lid, just a crack, just enough for the music to escape... that had been all she'd needed to keep the jingle-jangle of her nerves at bay.

In the weeks after Luke died, after the music box had been destroyed, Valkyrie's nerves jingled and jangled, their ends frayed and exposed. Her fingertips would start to itch next, and then that point right between her shoulder blades, where she couldn't scratch. Then both her sides, but way down, under her skin, beneath her ribs, in places she could never hope to reach. And that would just be the start.

The worst of it wasn't the itchiness, or the sweating, or the sick feeling she'd get in her belly. The worst wasn't even the voices in her head, the whispers and the screams, the things they'd say and the directions in which they'd steer her thoughts. No, the worst of it was the guilt that had come back to drag her down. At first it had been a stone in her gut, then a rock. Then a boulder. It was pretty hard to keep walking with a boulder in your stomach.

Sometimes, not every time but sometimes, Valkyrie's sense of who she was would sink lower and lower and further and further away until she was sure, she was convinced, that she was already dead. That her body was a lump of meat, awkwardly striding forward out of sheer habit. That's when she'd get numb. That's when the terror would spread.

This had gone on for weeks. The others noticed – of course they did; Valkyrie was slowing everyone down, snapping at the slightest thing, bursting into tears for no reason – but they didn't say anything. Apart from Serpine. He wouldn't shut up about it.

So Skulduggery started to take her away whenever they made camp. Tanith would come, too, sometimes. They'd find an abandoned building and the lessons would begin.

The sun was getting low. Shadows lengthened along the dirt floor of the stone house. The light that came through the glassless window was a deep, deep red that washed over Tanith's skin as she stood there, waiting.

Valkyrie reached out with her magic, tentatively at first and then with more confidence, feeling the steady flow of power. Tanith's life force was strong, a constantly swirling thing.

Slowly, doors began to open in Valkyrie's mind. Behind each door was another part of Tanith's discipline, and Valkyrie's understanding grew. She could see now how Tanith shifted her centre of gravity, could see how that interacted with the gravity around her, could see how to redirect strength into her muscles, to make the body more agile. Valkyrie was flooded with the knowledge of how to open any lock, to seal any door, a separate discipline but one that used some of the same basic principles. It was all about moving magic. It was all so simple.

She opened her eyes.

"This is weird," Tanith said, her face tight. "Not entirely unpleasant... but not exactly fun."

Skulduggery's hand on Valkyrie's shoulder. "Withdraw," he said softly. "Do it gently."

He meant: do it gently *this time*. Last time, she'd withdrawn too quickly and Tanith had gasped, staggered, fallen to her knees.

But this time Valkyrie kept a firm grip on what she was doing. Gradually, she withdrew from Tanith's life force, and Tanith relaxed, breathing easy once again.

"Did it work?" she asked.

Valkyrie's head still felt light and clear and open. She walked over to the wall and put her foot flat against it. Shifting her gravity, she pushed herself off slightly with her trailing leg, and suddenly she was standing sideways.

She laughed. It came from somewhere unexpected. Tanith grinned and Skulduggery folded his arms.

"Looks like it worked," he said.

"This is so weird," Valkyrie whispered, taking a little walk around the wall. Tying her hair back so that it wouldn't fall into her eyes, she stepped over a window, and gave a little jump.

It was disconcerting, seeing the world sideways. *Feeling* the world sideways. It was hard to know where to look. The ceiling and the floor were now her walls.

"Keep going," Tanith said, enjoying this almost as much as Valkyrie.

Grinning even more broadly now, Valkyrie put one foot to the ceiling. She took a deep breath and shifted her gravity again, and the room turned and now Skulduggery and Tanith were upside down and Valkyrie started laughing. She didn't focus on them, though. This was far too disorientating as it was, so she kept her eyes on her feet.

"Oh, wow," she said, and jumped lightly over the rafters. She walked to the centre of the ceiling, then stopped. Very slowly, she raised her eyes from her feet and looked up. Skulduggery was above her, looking down. She held up her hands and he took them, and she jumped and shifted her gravity at the same time, feeling her stomach lurch as the room spun, and the soles of her boots crunched back on to the actual floor.

Skulduggery let go and she staggered a little, then let out a whoop of joy. Tanith laughed and clapped.

"That was awesome!" Valkyrie cried. "That was amazing! Did you see that flip I just did?"

"It was a very good flip," Skulduggery conceded.

There was a rickety old table in the middle of the room. Still buzzing, Valkyrie ran and jumped, bringing her knees into her chest and flipping over it. She kept flipping, though, and started straightening her legs far too late, and she crashed into the ground and went sprawling.

"Ow," she moaned.

Tanith helped her up. "That was slightly less impressive," she said with a smile. "You may have the agility, but you still need to learn how to perform the moves."

Valkyrie's head didn't feel as open as it had been. The doors were closing. "Aw, man," she said. "I'm losing it. I'm forgetting how to... aw, crap. It's gone."

Tanith looked at Skulduggery. "But that's a successful test, wouldn't you say?"

"I would indeed," he replied, and nodded to Valkyrie. "We'll need to keep practising, but it certainly looks like you can learn multiple disciplines."

"Have you ever even heard of that before?" Tanith asked.

"I've met a few ambidextrous sorcerers in my time," said Skulduggery. "I even had an ancestor who... I suppose you'd call him a multidextrous sorcerer. According to the stories, he mastered three disciplines. But what Valkyrie is capable of... I don't even know what we'd call it."

"Omnidextrous?" Tanith suggested.

"I like the sound of that," Valkyrie said.

"Huh," said Tanith.

"What?"

"This has been the first time I've seen you smile in weeks."

"Am I still smiling?"

"You are. You know something?"

"What?"

"It suits you."

36

It was a Wednesday afternoon, and Miss Ficus took Wednesday afternoons off. She told Omen that on Wednesdays she had a martial arts class and then went bowling with her friends, but he didn't believe anything that came out of her mouth these days unless it could be immediately verified in a textbook.

He took a bus into Galway City centre, had an ice cream in Eyre Square, and then met Never for a burger. Never was presenting as a boy today, and he had his hair pulled back into a ponytail. Like Omen, he was dressed in shorts and a T-shirt. Unlike Omen, the shorts looked cool on him. The T-shirt was of some band Omen had never heard of, and looked scruffy and lived in. Omen's looked starched and barely worn.

"Any word?" Never asked as they ate.

Omen shook his head. His chair was a little wobbly, and he tapped the uneven leg against the floor in time to the music.

"Can't they send another team over there to find out what's happening? The Shunter should have delivered two progress reports by now, right? But he hasn't been back once. Something's wrong."

Omen chewed faster, then swallowed before answering. "Everyone needs to just have a little faith. This is Skulduggery and Valkyrie we're talking about."

"You think they're still alive?"

"You don't?"

"It's Mevolent. They're going up against the bad guy to end all bad guys. If killing him was easy, the war wouldn't have gone on for hundreds of years. Is the Supreme Mage worried?"

"How would I know?"

"Your folks get a briefing on all this kinda stuff."

"Yeah, but they just get the facts. They're not told how China Sorrows feels about any of it. If you want to know what I think—"

"Which I don't."

"—I think that the Dead Men are probably too busy kicking Mevolent's ass to bother coming back with progress reports."

"I hope you're right," said Never, taking another bite of his burger.

"They've got it under control," said Omen, not feeling confident in the slightest.

Three boys approached their table. Big guys, tough-looking, the kind of boys Omen would cross the street to avoid if he possibly could.

"I know you," one of them said, frowning. "You're... Oisín, yeah? Oisín Caddock?"

"Yes," said Omen, surprised. He hadn't heard his given name in years.

"We went to primary school together," the boy said. "You were a year behind me."

"Oh, yes!" Omen said brightly, even though he hadn't a clue who this boy was. "You're, um... uh..."

"Conor."

"Yes! Conor! Good to see you!"

Conor nodded. He didn't seem particularly overjoyed, however. All three of them swivelled their heads to look at Never, and the temperature dropped considerably.

"And who are you meant to be?" Conor's friend asked.

Never smiled and winked. "I'm whoever you want me to be, sweetie."

That was not an answer designed to calm the situation.

"What did you call me?" Conor's friend said gruffly, squaring up. His arms were suddenly held away from his body, like his muscles were too bulging to bring his limbs any closer.

Never sighed. "That was a mistake. All I've done is escalate the situation when, really, I should be de-escalating. In that regard, then, I withdraw my previous comment and replace it with an appeal to your better nature. I'm just having a delicious burger with my delicious friend and, sincerely, I'm not looking for any trouble."

Conor's friend, Gruffy McGruff-face, leaned in and sneered. Gruffly. "Well, you've found it."

"Found what?"

"Trou—"

"Trouble!" Never interrupted. "Sorry, yes, I get it. I wasn't looking for trouble, but I found trouble anyway, that's what you're saying to me. I do apologise. In my defence, however, you are a *frightfully* boring person, so I don't really think I can be blamed for my attention wandering."

Gruffy's face was red. Like, really red.

"Your face is really red," said Never.

Gruffy slapped the table and lunged forward in an effort to make Never flinch. It didn't work.

"It's gone even redder," Never pointed out.

Conor and Conor's other friend, a tall chap named Tawlly McTallface, held Gruffy back while Gruffy strained manfully against their arms.

"Hey!" someone shouted from behind the counter. "No trouble in here!"

"There's no trouble," Conor responded. "We're just having a laugh, aren't we, lads?"

"I know *I* am," said Never, and Omen just slurped his milkshake.

Gruffy calmed a bit and the other two stopped manfully restraining him. "You a boy or a girl?" Conor asked.

Never shrugged. "Depends on my mood."

Conor looked at Omen. "He your boyfriend?"

Omen took another slurp, then slid the empty glass away. "I'm kind of in between relationships right now," he said, and Never burst out laughing.

The three boys didn't like that.

Omen shot to his feet, cracking his palm into Tawlly's chin as Conor and Gruffy went for Never. There were shrieks of alarm and someone was yelling at them to stop, and then Omen was dragging Conor backwards. Never head-butted Gruffy and followed it with an elbow to the jaw. Conor squirmed and spun and tried to throw a punch, and Omen took him down, twisting his wrist while he knelt on his throat.

Gruffy met the wall with his face and bounced off, squawking. Never shrugged at Omen, picked his burger from the plate and wandered off towards the toilets. Omen stepped over Conor and followed. The moment the door closed and they were alone, Never put his hand on Omen's arm and teleported them to Omen's garden.

"Good burger," Never said, his mouth full.

37

For the first month of her pregnancy, Darquesse lived within a force field that wouldn't allow anyone else near her. It started to hum whenever someone got too close, although no one knew what would happen if they actually touched the shimmering shield. They discussed it, though, at their weekly meetings, and came to the conclusion that it would probably be something bad.

But, earlier today, the force field had faded away, and the Darquesse Society had quickly assembled.

Kimora knocked on the door of the spare room. Darquesse was staying there because Kimora had the biggest house, and she lived alone ever since her husband had walked out due to this "unhealthy obsession" of hers. Sebastian didn't think that Kimora even noticed. It just meant she had more time to worship her god.

They filed into the room where Darquesse was standing. That's what Darquesse tended to do a lot of the time. Stand.

"Mistress," Kimora said, then paused. "Is it Mistress? Do we call you Mistress? Ma'am? Master?"

"Master will suffice," said Darquesse.

"Yes, Master," Kimora said. "Master, we were beyond thrilled to hear of your pregnancy. Motherhood is truly transformative. To give birth, to create life – once you've experienced that, you'll never—"

"I've created life before."

Kimora blinked. "You've... you've had children?"

"No. I've created life. I've created living organisms out of inorganic matter."

"Oh. Oh, well, then you know what it's like to be, um, a parent."

"I had no emotional attachment to the things I created. That's why I'm doing this."

"We'd like to offer our help," Bennet said. "Most of us here are parents, and those who aren't can do other things, whatever you require. We would, and I can say this with utmost sincerity, be honoured if—"

"No."

He faltered. "No?"

"I won't need help," Darquesse said.

They looked at each other, then at Sebastian. He sighed, and stepped forward.

"Maybe you don't need any help right now," he said, "but who knows what the future will bring? Maybe if we just hang around, you know, within earshot, then if you need us, you can—"

"I won't need anyone," Darquesse said. "Only you."

Sebastian blinked. "Me?"

"You can assist me."

He did his best to ignore the looks of pure envy he was getting from the others. "Sure. Yeah, OK. Whatever you need."

"Your house," said Darquesse.

"What about it?"

"I'll be staying there."

"Actually," Ulysses said, "we were thinking that you might want to stay in—"

Sebastian didn't get to hear the rest, because he was no longer in Kimora's house. He was standing in his own living room, Darquesse beside him.

"I'll stay here," she said.

"Sure."

She walked out. "I'll take the main bedroom."

Sebastian followed. "Makes sense."

38

The dead town had a smell to it of rotting flesh. It snagged on the warm wind, came to them as they crested the hill, made everyone but Skulduggery gag. Burnt-out houses, blackened by flame and smudged with ash, clawed at the blue skies like they were trying to breathe. The dirt streets clung on to the corpses that hadn't been able to get up and walk away. There'd been a scramble here, a mad, desperate dash as the dead came calling. It was impossible for Valkyrie to say who'd won.

There was a single draugr, standing there with its back to them, waiting for something to run after.

Skulduggery lobbed a fireball. Within seconds, the draugr was burning fiercely. It turned, noticing them for the first time, and came running.

"I should stop doing that," Skulduggery said. "Setting them on fire actually makes them more dangerous."

"Probably a good idea," said Tanith, as Dexter released a stream of energy that seared through the draugr's head. They gave the town a wide berth and walked on.

Valkyrie was having one of her bad days. She lagged behind the others, boots kicking up stones with every step.

"I like you," Skulduggery said.

She looked up. He was walking beside her. "What?"

"I like you," he said again. "As a person. You're smart and funny and nice."

"OK. So?"

"So the problem as I see it," he said, "is that you *don't* like you. I would even go so far as to say you hate yourself. Would that be accurate?"

Valkyrie didn't say anything.

"I've done terrible things, too, remember," Skulduggery continued, "and I am well acquainted with the self-loathing that comes with it all. Just nod if you agree."

Valkyrie hesitated. Then nodded.

"And that's completely understandable. You're carrying around all this guilt over what you put Alice through, and then what you had to put her through *again* when you reassembled her soul. So this is weighing you down and, every time you think of it, you're reminded of how much you hate yourself because of what you did."

Valkyrie looked around. "Where even are we?"

"My best guess would be somewhere in Hungary, but you're trying to change the subject and you're not being terribly subtle about it. I have the answer, in case you're interested. Would you like to hear it? It's quite simple: you should forgive yourself."

Valkyrie laughed.

"You had to do what you did," Skulduggery said. "You know this. The Sceptre was the only way to stop Darquesse. Granted, you didn't get a chance to use it, and in the end it wasn't even necessary – but you didn't know that at the time. At the time, the Sceptre was the only chance you had of saving the world, and, in order for you to use it, you had to own it. So you had to kill Alice. If you agree with everything that I just said, stare at me dimly. OK, good."

Valkyrie rolled her eyes.

"You didn't have a choice," Skulduggery said. "What you did was awful and terrible, but it was also the only thing you could do in order to save the life of everyone on the planet – and that includes Alice. So, while it was a terrible choice, it was also the right one to make."

Reluctantly, Valkyrie nodded.

"So you did the right thing," Skulduggery said, more gently. "It traumatised your sister and it traumatised you, but you did it because you had to."

"I know all this," Valkyrie whispered.

"I know you do. But there's a difference, isn't there, between knowing something and accepting something? You've got to accept it, Valkyrie. Once you accept it, you can forgive yourself."

Valkyrie looked away for just a moment.

"Ah," said Skulduggery. "You don't *want* to forgive yourself. You don't think you should. You think you deserve the pain. Very well. I understand that urge. But don't do this for you. Do it for Alice. Doesn't she deserve a big sister who can help her? How much help can you give someone else if you can't even help yourself? Do it for Alice, and do it for your parents. They worry about you enough as it is. How would they react if they found out you're torturing yourself? Do it for Militsa, who loves you. Do it for me, who tolerates you. Do it for the world. You've saved it before and I daresay you'll be called on to save it again – but you'll need to be in a healthy frame of mind to do that, won't you?"

"It's not that easy."

"I know. But, if anyone can do it, you can."

They passed an apple tree, but the apples were too bitter to eat so Skulduggery used it as a target range, and got Valkyrie to shoot lightning from her forefinger to improve her aim. She knew what he was trying to do. He was trying to distract her out of her sadness. She went along with it, the others watching and calling out encouragement. Apart from Serpine, of course.

Valkyrie wasn't very good at shooting apples, not at first. Whole branches fell, blackened, to the hard ground, or else she missed entirely, and watched the lightning flash and then disappear. But gradually she got a little better, and started zapping roughly two out of every five apples she aimed for.

"You can do better," said Saracen.

"I'm trying," she muttered. It wasn't easy, channelling the lightning into just one finger.

When she missed another, Saracen walked forward, plucked an apple from the tree and placed it on his head. "Try it now," he said.

"Aim a lot lower this time," Dexter whispered.

"No," Valkyrie said. "I'll miss and hurt you."

"You may not believe in yourself," Saracen replied, "but I believe in you. I think, when you *have to* hit the target, you *will* hit the target."

She looked to Skulduggery for support, but he just shrugged.

"Oh, come on," Valkyrie said. "There has to be someone here who agrees with me that this is a stupid idea."

"I'll agree with you if you want," said Serpine.

"Apart from Serpine," she said. "No? None of you?"

"You're someone who thrives under pressure," said Saracen. "We've all seen it. We all have faith."

"And what if I zap you instead?"

Saracen smiled. "You won't."

She glowered, then shook out her hand before curling it into a finger-gun, and raised it. She focused on the apple, let her power flow into her fingertip and sent out a zap of lightning that hit Saracen in the face and sent him tumbling backwards.

Dexter and Tanith howled with laughter and Serpine grunted with amusement and Skulduggery just nodded as Saracen came to a sprawling stop.

Valkyrie took a few hesitant steps forward. "Saracen? You OK?"

"Oh, God," he moaned.

"Are you OK?"

"You shot me in the face."

"I'm really sorry."

"In the face."

"I told you I'd miss!"

"I didn't know that was a threat."

"I'm so sorry."

"You're supposed to thrive under pressure."

"Well, that wasn't really pressure, though, was it? That was just you standing there with an apple on your head. Maybe next time you should, like, try to kill me or something."

He got up slowly, touching his face. "Is it noticeable? Is it?"

There was an ugly red welt on his cheek. "Nope," said Valkyrie.

"Nope," said Tanith.

"No," said Dexter.

"Yes," said Serpine. "It's horrible. Ugly. Disgusting. Also, you have a red mark on your cheek." And he laughed.

39

It started to rain, and it didn't stop for two weeks.

Serpine was taking them away from the decent roads. The ground was slippery, and the mud sucked at their boots, but he insisted this would take weeks off their journey, so no one argued. And the rain kept the bats away, and Valkyrie appreciated that. They never came too low, never swooped for anything on the ground, but they were always there, always in the sky, so it was nice to take a break from them, for however long it lasted.

Valkyrie missed home. She missed her parents and her sister and her girlfriend and her dog. She missed Ireland. She missed her world. She missed coffee shops and movies and the internet. She missed food that didn't come in ration packs and food that didn't have to be hunted down and skinned.

"We'll need to make camp soon," Skulduggery said. It was getting dark. They didn't like to travel in the dark. The draugar were more active when the sun went down.

"We can take shelter in a farm up ahead," said Serpine. "It's another mile or two, if memory serves. I knew this area quite well, once upon a time. Oh, I could tell you stories."

"Please don't," said Tanith.

That was the natural response to most things Serpine said – *please don't*, or *shut up*, or something close to that. But Valkyrie was beginning to like him, despite herself. He was cynical, and nasty, but also kind of cheerful. Saracen loved to needle him, but Serpine loved to needle right back, and Saracen was a lot easier to annoy. More than once, Valkyrie had had to stifle a grin when Serpine got the better of him.

The farm was right where Serpine had said it would be, nestled in a small valley, on a grassy hill, flanked on one side by a forest. Getting to it wasn't particularly easy, and Valkyrie doubted that any draugar had made the effort. She was proven right when she saw the light in the farmhouse windows.

"Looks like somebody's home," said Tanith.

Serpine shrugged, went to walk on, but Skulduggery grabbed his arm.

"Who lives here?" he asked.

"This land was owned by a friend of mine," said Serpine, "but that was before the present difficulties. I'm sure he's long dead or long gone by now."

"What friend?"

"A gentleman called Lorien. I don't think you'd have known him."

"Serpine, if you've led us into a trap..."

"A trap?" Serpine said, laughing. "No one knows I'm here! No one knows I'm coming! How could I possibly lead you into a trap? I'm sure whoever has those candles lit simply stumbled by this place while they were running from the ravenous undead. If it makes you feel any better, I can be the one to announce our arrival. I'll do anything to get out of this cursed rain."

Skulduggery pulled his gun. "If anyone jumps out at us, Nefarian, you're the first to die."

Serpine hesitated. "Maybe we should hold off for just a moment..."

There was a shout from the farmhouse and a man came running out, waving a sword. They watched him approach. He had wild, curly hair and his shirt wasn't tucked in and he was out of shape.

"That's Lorien," said Serpine.

Lorien's run turned into a sort of crazed stagger, and then he walked the rest of the way, panting heavily and occasionally waggling the sword.

"Right," he puffed when he reached them. "Give me a... minute. I just need..."

"Breathe in through your nose," Dexter advised.

Lorien glared. "I know how to... breathe." He leaned over, hands on his knees. "I feel sick."

They waited almost a minute until he straightened up.

"Leave my property," he demanded. "You're lucky I haven't killed you already for trespassing. I could have mistaken you for draugar, and then where would you have been? In pieces on the ground, that's where. I mean, look at you. Splattered with mud and..." He saw Serpine, and his face soured. "Oh. It's you."

"Lorien," Serpine said, stepping forward. "It has been too long, my old friend. Did you think I was dead?"

"I had hoped."

"And what have I always told you about hope?"

"That it's a fool's folly," Lorien responded. "And here you are to prove yourself right. How proud you must be. Who are your companions? A stern-looking lot, I must say. You even have a moving skeleton among your number. Any relation to that Skulduggery character from the war?"

"One and the same," said Skulduggery.

Lorien's eyebrows shot up. "In truth? And where have you been hiding?"

"Do not concern yourself with my companions," said Serpine. "My friends and I are in need of shelter. Some food wouldn't go amiss, either. We were facing another cold night of rain before I realised I knew someone in the area, and I felt sure he wouldn't mind us calling by unannounced."

Lorien took his time before answering. "Of course not," he said. "You're welcome to spend the night. I'll provide food, soup, and wine, and the fire and four walls will keep you warm enough, I'd wager."

Serpine smiled. "You're most kind."

Valkyrie had a tiny bed with a thin mattress stuffed with old straw. It was twice as uncomfortable as it looked, and it looked pretty damn uncomfortable. Its only saving grace was how badly it made her sleep. That meant the dreams stayed away. For the most part.

In the morning, she got up with the others, still exhausted, and shuffled into the kitchen where Saracen was making breakfast, and when they were done they cleaned up after themselves and went outside.

"I haven't come across our host yet," Skulduggery said. "Anyone seen him?"

"Sadly," Serpine intoned, "Lorien passed away in his sleep during the night."

"What?" said Tanith.

"He will be missed."

She stared at him, then stalked back into the house.

"You killed him," Skulduggery said.

"Actually, I believe he died of natural causes."

"I thought he was your friend," said Dexter.

"He was no friend of mine," Serpine replied, unable to keep from sneering. "He sold my location to my enemies when I was at my weakest. It was only down to good fortune and astounding fortitude that I was able to escape with my life. For years, I didn't know which one of my many incredibly treacherous associates had betrayed me, but I knew it could never have been Lorien. And yet I learned it was he mere weeks before I was forced to flee to your dimension."

Tanith came back.

"Knife in the neck," she said.

Valkyrie glared at Serpine. "I thought you said he died of natural causes."

"There's nothing more natural than dying from a knife to the neck. What would be unnatural is if he'd survived."

Skulduggery filled his hands with the lapels of Serpine's coat. "We're not here to help you take revenge on the people who've wronged you."

"I don't remember you helping at all."

"How far out of our way have you taken us?"

"Whatever do you—?"

Skulduggery shook him violently.

"A week or two, at most," Serpine said. "In the grand scheme of things, a minor detour."

Skulduggery shoved him away. "You're on your own."

"I beg your pardon?"

"We're leaving you here. We're going on by ourselves."

"But I'm your guide. You don't know where you're—"

Skulduggery took out his gun, aimed it square at Serpine's chest and thumbed back the hammer.

"Lorien was not a nice person," Serpine said, very calmly and slowly. "He spent most of his adult life torturing people to death. Not for any particular reason, either. He just liked to torture. I'd wager, if Mr Rue were to use those ridiculous eyes of his, he might find a cellar. And, in that cellar, I am willing to bet my place on this team that there are, at the very least, instruments of torture within easy reach. Mr Rue, if you would be so kind?"

"Don't tell me what to do," Saracen said, glowering, but he turned, looked back at the house. "Huh," he said.

"Is there a cellar?" asked Tanith.

"That there is," said Saracen. "And two people down there, a man and a woman. Both in shackles with their mouths covered. In desperate need of rescue."

Saracen and Dexter dumped their packs and walked back to the house.

Skulduggery put his gun away.

"So I'm back on the team?" Serpine asked. "I did essentially save those two people, *and* I killed their torturer with no thought to my own safety."

"You killed him in his sleep," Valkyrie said.

Serpine gave a careless shrug. "I usually find that it's the best time to kill people."

"You do this again," Skulduggery said, "and we'll leave you to the draugar."

"In which case," Serpine said, "you have my solemn vow that I will not do it again. But may I point out that, as tragic as Lorien's passing may be, it has left us with the use of his horses, if that would be of any help whatsoever. Anyone interested? Anyone?"

"Horses might be a good idea," Tanith muttered.

40

Skulduggery held up the stone. "Focus."

Valkyrie nodded, readied the finger-gun.

It was late in the day. Saracen and Dexter were cooking rabbit somewhere behind them and Valkyrie ached from her time in the saddle, but she pushed it all to one side, and focused on the stone.

Skulduggery threw it high, and three times she tried to zap it, and three times she missed. It landed back in Skulduggery's gloved palm.

"That wasn't great," she admitted.

"You're thinking too much about what you have to do."

"You told me to focus."

"Focus doesn't mean think. You need to take your mind off what you're doing."

"Isn't that the opposite of focusing, though?"

"We're going to try again. This time, I'll ask you questions. Ready?"

"I'm not sure how this makes any sense, but sure."

The stone lifted out of his palm and rose through the air. Valkyrie aimed. Missed. Aimed again.

"How are you feeling?" Skulduggery asked.

"Confused."

"Keep focusing. Do you miss home?"

"Yes." She missed again. This was getting annoying.

"Do you miss Militsa?"

"Yes."

"How are things between you?"

"Good."

"Care to expand on that?"

Valkyrie zapped. The streaks of lightning were getting closer. "Things are good between us. She makes me happy."

"Do you think you make her happy?"

"I hope so."

"Keep your eyes on the stone. Have you introduced her to your family?"

"Yes. Everyone got on great. The folks adore her."

"And Alice?"

Zap. "Alice was shy."

"She doesn't strike me as a shy girl."

"She wasn't, but she is now. Sometimes, anyway. I think maybe self-consciousness must come from the soul. At least that's what it seems like."

"Does Militsa know what you had to do?"

Valkyrie's hand wavered. "Yeah," she said.

The stone stopped moving. She aimed carefully.

"What did you tell her?" Skulduggery asked.

"What happened."

"Tell me."

She zapped. The lightning struck the edge of the stone, sending it spinning through the air. Skulduggery kept it up there, started moving it from side to side.

Valkyrie tracked it with the finger-gun. "I told her about Darquesse and about the Sceptre. How it had bonded to Alice and how I needed it to bond to me."

She zapped, but the stone darted to one side. "Hey!"

"What?"

"That's cheating!"

180

He shrugged, kept it moving.

Valkyrie made a finger-gun with her left hand, brought it up beside the right.

"Did you tell her how you felt when you used the Deathtouch Gauntlet?"

"How I felt? No. She didn't ask, either. Didn't want to upset me." Valkyrie zapped both finger-guns, and almost hit the stone.

"How *did* you feel?"

"You know how I felt."

"Eyes on the stone."

"Can we just—"

"Eyes on the stone, please."

She glared at him, then glared back at the hovering stone. She sent out a barrage of lightning. It all missed. "I felt like I was murdering my sister," she said. "Which is what I was doing."

"Describe it."

"What?"

"Describe what happened."

Valkyrie dropped her hands to her sides. "No. Why are you asking this?"

"I need to distract you so that you can focus."

"That doesn't make any sense!"

"I know what I'm doing."

"Then can we talk about something else, please?"

He tilted his head. "Is this topic *too* distracting?"

"Yes, it bloody well is."

"Then it's just what we need." He picked up another stone, made it float next to the first. "Now," he said. "Start again."

41

Valkyrie woke to the smell of breakfast.

There were low murmurings around the fire, people keeping their voices down so as not to disturb her. She appreciated that. The previous night had been draining. The previous *week* had been draining. Every time she lay down to sleep, it was like flicking off a switch. Her body was exhausted, not only from the day's walk, but also from the sessions with Skulduggery. Sometimes Tanith would join them, and, instead of working on her magic, they'd work on combat. But, through it all, Valkyrie was answering questions. Talking about the stuff that had happened. Talking about the things she'd done. The things that gave her nightmares.

No nightmares lately. Her sleep was uninterrupted and absolute and dreamless. It was like she still had the music box playing beside her, only she woke without that peculiar haze.

She felt better, she had to admit. All that work, and all that talking, and all that crying, it was starting to flood her system, wash out the bad thoughts. There were still plenty left, but for the first time in years Valkyrie found herself feeling optimistic. Not about anything in particular, just... optimistic.

The morning was warm. They'd camped by the edge of a slow-moving river, so Valkyrie went down the grassy bank on bare feet, found somewhere secluded to wash. When she was done, she dried off and brushed her hair, pressed the amulet to her hip and tapped it. The suit flowed out, matching the image she kept in her mind – sleeveless, with a zip down the front to let in the air. The only aspects of the suit she couldn't change were the hood and the colour – everything else responded to instruction.

She gathered up her things and went back to the camp. Dexter handed her a plate of food and a plastic mug of coffee, and she finished it all off. She helped wash up, then packed her stuff into her bag.

"Happy birthday," Skulduggery said to her as she saddled up.

Valkyrie paused for a moment – twenty-six years old – then swung up into the saddle, and they were on the road again.

42

Adam Brate insisted on meeting in a busy café. They sat back to back at different tables and pretended not to know each other.

"Make like you're talking on your phone," Brate whispered.

Temper sighed, and held his phone to his ear.

"How you doing, man?" Brate asked. "Good to see you. What you been at? It's been ages. I've been taking it easy, y'know? I got a few things on the boil, a few different projects. Right now I'm mostly working on my music. That's always been a driving force in my life, so I'm basically combining three different styles of music into one. It doesn't sound very good, but I'm sure I can make it work. What about you? You play any instruments? We should start a band."

"I can't start a band with you, Adam. I'm investigating a murder."

"Burger."

"No, *murder*."

"And fries and a milkshake. Thank you."

The waitress went away.

"Sorry, man," said Brate. "So, a murder, huh? A freaky one? You thinking serial killer? I've been watching some shows, man. I could help? Offer insight?"

"The only insight I need is into Creed's involvement. I need you to ask your Church of the Faceless buddies, very quietly, if they know why Creed would want Sturmun Drang killed."

184

"The Grand Mage dude?"

"That's him," Temper said, waving away the waitress before she even reached his table.

"Why would Creed want that guy dead?" Brate asked.

"I don't know, but someone else is being framed for it, and the only person I can think of who could have anything to gain from that is Creed, or someone connected to him."

"I haven't heard anything, but I'll keep my ear to the ground."

"Be subtle about it, OK? If I'm right, this is ruthless elimination we're talking about, purely for political power, and I doubt they'd have any qualms about killing anyone who sticks their nose in."

"They might... they might try to kill me?"

"Maybe, so be extra—"

"You think they've poisoned my burger?"

Temper frowned. "The burger you've just ordered? No, Adam, I don't."

"I have to leave. Oh, jeez, I have to leave."

"They wouldn't be trying to kill you *yet*, Adam. You haven't done—"

But he was gone, sprinting from the café.

43

On their ninety-fourth day in the Leibniz Universe, they reached Tahil na Sin.

Careful not to dislodge any loose stones and send them tumbling down the rocky hill they were climbing, Valkyrie crawled on her belly until she was between Tanith and Dexter, and looked out over the city.

The midday sun gleamed off metal and glass, off white roofs and towers. From where she lay, Valkyrie could make out squares and parks and wide streets. There was activity on those streets, in those squares and parks. People. Lots of them.

Like other magical cities, Tahil na Sin was protected by a vast wall. Poles of twisted metal rose at regular intervals around the top of it, generating a shimmering dome of energy that made it look like it was one giant snow globe.

Outside the wall were what must have been hundreds of thousands of draugar. They pressed up against it, and against the gates, constantly moving. Above the energy shield, out of range of the sorcerers on the walls, Necromancers hovered in the air, held aloft by vast columns of darkness. The bats didn't bother them.

"So how do we get in?" Valkyrie asked. "We can't walk in, can't fly in..."

"I might know of a way," said Serpine, from behind them.

They crawled backwards a bit, then turned to him. He stood there, smiling, and didn't say anything further.

Tanith growled. "Continue."

"A few centuries ago," Serpine said, "I was killing this man, I can't remember his name, but he was tall, and he had a yellow tongue. Whenever he screamed, I was treated to a wonderful view of the inside of his mouth. Whether this was due to some underlying medical condition or merely residue from what he'd been eating before I'd caught up to him, I'm afraid I can't begin to speculate. There was very little about him that sticks in the memory, to be honest, but his height and his tongue colour certainly do, as well as what he had to say. He told me a story, amid all the screaming and the begging and the feeble attempts at bargaining, about Tahil na Sin and the secret tunnel that runs underground. All cities of this type have their secrets, their hidden entrances and whatnot, but according to my yellow-tongued friend, who was hastening towards his demise and couldn't really afford not to be telling the truth, this tunnel in particular stretched for miles. At that point, in between the tears and the gradual realisation that death was inevitable if I did not immediately stop what I was doing, he got very specific as to the direction of the tunnel and, indeed, where it emerged."

"It is staggering," Skulduggery said, "how much of that we didn't need to hear. If you know where this tunnel begins, take us there."

Serpine clapped his hands together. "I would be delighted!"

They rode the horses eastwards, galloping by the small packs of draugar that were on their way to join the horde around the city. Valkyrie found herself riding beside Serpine.

"I have to admit," he said, speaking loudly over the low thunder of hooves, "I think the group's attitude towards me is warming."

"That so?" Valkyrie responded. The galloping was shaking her bladder.

"I think they're starting to like me. Are you starting to like me?"

"Not since you stabbed that guy in the throat."

"But up until that point?"

Valkyrie shrugged. "Yeah, sure."

He seemed pleased with that.

They slowed to a trot, then a walk, and Serpine led them off the trail and they slipped from the saddle, tied the horses to a few skinny trees, and went down a small hill on foot.

"The tunnel entrance is somewhere around here," Serpine said. "My yellow-tongued friend—" He suddenly clicked his fingers. "Askant! That was his name! Something Askant! Phillip Askant, maybe? I'm not sure. That doesn't sound right. It doesn't matter either way, but... what was it? Oh, I don't know. Anyway, Mr Askant, whatever his first name was, but now that I've said it out loud, I don't think it was Phillip, and now I'm not even sure it was Askant. I may be thinking of somebody else. So, my yellow-tongued friend, whose name has probably passed into the wind, sadly died before he could tell me where the entrance was or how to open it. But we have God-Killer weapons, do we not? There is no wall or door or rock that can withstand the Sceptre of the Ancients."

"So you expect me to just start blasting?" Valkyrie asked.

"Why not?" Serpine responded. "You'll find it eventually."

Skulduggery crouched ahead of them. "Found it," he said. There were tracks in the dried mud leading to, or coming from, a wall of rock. "A cart and horses," he said, breaking off a handful of dirt and letting it crumble through his fingers. "Leading away, no more than two days ago. There are older tracks here, as well, heading in."

"I'm going for a pee," Valkyrie announced, and headed off while the others discussed what their next move should be.

She found a nice quiet spot and unzipped her suit, and gradually became aware of a creak and a rattle and the clip-clop of walking horses. When she was finished, she stood and zipped up, and heard a cry of alarm, and a curse. Then Skulduggery's voice and sounds of mild exertion.

After that, it all went calm again.

Valkyrie took a stroll. Crested another hill.

A cart, laden with crates and bulging sacks, pulled by two old horses and ridden by two bearded men. A few draugar corpses littered the trail they'd been taking. Skulduggery, wearing his façade, and the rest of the Dead Men, stood there, wiping gore off their weapons. Serpine remained on his horse.

"Obliged for the help, friend," said the smaller bearded man. "Mulct's the name. The eejit over there is Hapathy."

"We could have handled it," Hapathy grumbled.

Mulct scowled at him. His accent was a weird cross between Irish and German. "I'm not saying we couldn't have handled it. Did you hear those words spilling from my lips? I'd wager you didn't, because no such words did any such thing. I was merely thanking these people for the assistance they rendered – assistance that saved you or me from having to stir ourselves from this cart."

Hapathy grunted, and spat over the side.

"Are you from here, then?" Skulduggery asked.

"From Tahil na Sin? Aye, we are." Mulct pushed his hat back on his head. "Well, I am. Hapathy is what you might call a blow-in. He wasn't born here, but now he won't leave. Where do you good people hail from?"

"All over," said Skulduggery. "We were across the water when all this started."

"To be honest," Valkyrie said, joining them, "we're not entirely sure what's been happening here."

Mulct barked out a laugh. "What's been happening, lass? This has been happening! The end of the world, that's been happening!"

"How did it start?"

Mulct shook his head. "I don't really know where to begin, to be truthful. The bloody draugar. They started showing up, attacking people. Biting them. I knew instantly, of course. I said to myself, this isn't normal behaviour from the draugar."

"No, you didn't," said Hapathy.

189

"You don't know what I said to myself!"

"I know what you said to me. You dismissed it, so you did."

"I did not!"

"Everyone says they knew something was different," Hapathy sneered, "but no one had a notion. You yourself said what do you care what a bunch of zombies get up to? I said they're not zombies, they're draugar, and you said there's no bloody difference, and I said there's a big bloody difference, and you said—"

"That's no way to tell a story!" Mulct interrupted. "*You said, I said, you said, I said.* What's the purpose of that? Anyone can relate to others what people may or may not have said, but there's more to telling a story than the words used. You got to build a narrative, you ignorant fool. You got to draw the audience in."

Hapathy shook his head, and spat once more over the side.

Mulct took that as a victory, and went back to telling the tale. "When it started, most people, it's true, didn't give it the attention the situation obviously warranted. We've had draugar attacks before, of course, and we've had little zombie infections, but Mevolent has always ordered them put down before the problem grew to an unmanageable size. And no one especially cared about a few mortals getting bitten. Let them stumble about in the filth, moaning and groaning and trying to eat each other. They're mortals. It's what they do!"

Mulct laughed at that, and didn't notice the stony-faced silence from those around him.

"But, when Mevolent sent out a few mages to get rid of the problem, the mages didn't come back. So he sent out more. And then more."

"Stupid," muttered Hapathy.

"You shut your mouth," Mulct glowered.

"It was stupid and there's no denying it," Hapathy snapped back. "The moment the first lot of mages didn't return, he should have sent out an army. But he was too busy building his giant

190

portals, too busy with his invasion. We're in this mess today because of it."

"Portals?" Skulduggery interrupted.

"Oh, yes. For invading the other world. He's been building them for months. Massive things, so they are, all three of them. I heard we'll be able to march our army through in a matter of minutes."

"Would you say that to him, would you? That he's stupid?" said Mulct.

"I would."

Mulct laughed. "Oh, really? So when we join our forces with Mevolent's, and we're all there waiting to step into this parallel world, you'll walk up to him, will you? Walk up to him and tap him on the shoulder – bearing in mind that he's eight foot tall and that you wouldn't even be able to *reach* his shoulder – and you'll say to him, 'Oh, by the way, my lord, I just thought I'd let you know that all this – the vast army of the dead, the decimation of every country on the planet, the fact that we have to evacuate or be torn apart by things no better than bloody *zombies* – is entirely your fault.' You're going to say that to him, are you?"

"Just give me the chance and I will."

"You're a liar."

"*You're* a liar!"

"You're more a liar because you're lying to yourself! You'd no more challenge Mevolent than a fieldmouse would challenge a... a..."

"A what?" Hapathy sneered. "Can't think of anything, can you?"

"A lion!" Mulct roared. "A fieldmouse would challenge a lion!"

Hapathy sniggered.

Valkyrie waited a few moments while Mulct regained his composure. "So Mevolent isn't here, then?"

"In Tahil na Sin? Ha! He'd never deign to set foot in this place!"

"So where is he?"

Mulct frowned at her. "Now, why are you so interested in our Lord and Master, young lady?"

"We have to report back to him," Skulduggery said.

"You... you work for Mevolent?"

"He gives us our orders, yes."

Mulct and Hapathy exchanged terrified glances.

"I didn't mean anything disrespectful from my mutterings," Hapathy said, going pale.

"Me neither," said Mulct. "Although, to be fair, it wasn't me issuing the disrespectful mutters."

"You shut your mouth," Hapathy whispered.

"You're not in any trouble," Skulduggery told them. "Mevolent sent us off on a mission, and then the world turned into a hunting ground while we were gone. All we want to do is deliver our captive."

"Captive?"

Skulduggery gestured to Serpine. "This here is Nefarian Serpine. Mevolent wants the privilege of killing this gentleman himself."

Mulct frowned. "He's not wearing shackles."

"Because we don't view him as a credible threat. And also..." Skulduggery held up the pebble and pressed it, and Serpine slumped in his saddle, then fell off the horse, and everybody laughed.

"That's funny, that is," said Mulct, chuckling. "But I'm afraid you're out of luck. Mevolent left his Dublin-Within-The-Wall weeks ago, for Tahil na Kurge."

Valkyrie groaned inwardly. More walking. More travelling. More time away from home.

"Then it's on to Tahil na Kurge for us," said Skulduggery.

"You'll never get there without an army," Mulct said. "Too many draugar in the way. Want my advice? Go with us. We're preparing, here – forging weapons, assembling the troops. We'll be heading out in a matter of weeks, most likely. I'm sure you can tag along – Governor Erato is always looking for folk who know how to fight."

At the mention of Governor Erato, Serpine moaned.

"You won't be teleporting?" Saracen asked.

"Only a few Teleporters left," said Hapathy, "and they're not being risked on trifling matters like the transport of tens of thousands of people. No, we'll be heading over the old-fashioned way – by road."

"In that case," Skulduggery said, "I think we'll take you up on your kind offer."

"Look at us," Mulct said, grinning. "Send us out for food and supplies, and we come back with warriors. You can't say Mulct and Hapathy don't deliver value for money."

44

The tunnel into the city was long and cold, and the only light came from the lamp at the end of the long pole that Hapathy dangled in front of the horses. Valkyrie and the others rode their horses behind the cart, having buried their modern weaponry at the base of the hill before they entered. Even in the gloom, Valkyrie could see Serpine scowling beside her.

"We were at Dublin-Within-The-Wall before we came here," Skulduggery said as they rode. "Do you know what happened?"

"The dead had the place surrounded," said Mulct, his expression sombre in the lamplight. "We weren't there, but we've talked to survivors. The draugar were at the walls, just like they are here. Necromancers, too. Infected, but... different. Seemed to be able to command the dead. Now, on this aspect, there are two schools of thinking. The first is that the Necromancers are behind it all, and they infected themselves deliberately so as to lead the draugar. The second is that the Necromancers went to stop them, thinking their death magic could hold sway over these rotten things, and discovered too late that it wasn't enough."

"How long before the city was evacuated?" Saracen asked.

Mulct shook his head. "No one was evacuated. They couldn't get through the draugar."

"But Teleporters..."

"Most of 'em are dead," said Hapathy. Any trace of merriment had evaporated. "They were the first ones the Necromancers went after, before we knew to keep them out. Teleporters and Shunters."

"Cutting off the escape routes," Skulduggery said.

Mulct nodded. "Mevolent had been training them up – Shunters especially – over the last few years. All part of his big plan."

"Obsession," Hapathy muttered.

"All right then, obsession. You happy? All part of Mevolent's obsession to start conquering worlds. He had this idea of all these Shunters opening all these portals and his army just marching through. One world after another, falling before us."

Skulduggery tilted his head. "Does he have any Shunters left?"

"A few. A handful. I don't know how many. Some say ten. Some say half that. He's protecting them now. It's their power he'll be using to open those three giant portals of his, so he has them guarded at all times."

"What happened at Dublin-Within-The-Wall?"

Mulct gave a long, drawn-out sigh. "The city was surrounded. The Necromancers can do this thing, kind of like teleporting, except only over short distances? Shadow-walking, they call it. They'd shadow-walk into the city, take some draugar with them and set them loose, then they'd stand back and watch the chaos. It takes a while, weeks, to seal off a city of that size against shadow-walking. All those sigils they need to carve. They didn't quite manage it in time."

"The draugar swept over them," Hapathy said. "I spoke to this woman – she'd lost her family. All of them. She left the house, went to get water from the well, she told me. She was coming back and she said there was a swarm. A swarm of them, the draugar, running through the streets towards her. She saw her husband, one of her children. Dead but running."

Mulct shook his head. "Dublin-Within-The-Wall was a city of sorcerers, and now those sorcerers have joined the mortals, and they're all shuffling around the walls of our city, just over that hill. Death makes equals of us all, isn't that what they say?"

When they finally emerged into the city, they'd been in darkness a long time, and their mood was darker. Everyone except Skulduggery had to blink away the sunlight. The energy dome seemed to alter the light passing through it, making it harsher somehow. Valkyrie had to resist the urge to take out her sunglasses or pull down her mask. Either one would draw unwanted attention.

The further they moved through Tahil na Sin, the more apparent it became that the city had not been built for this surge in population. The streets, wide enough for three carts to fit through side by side, weren't wide enough for this number of people, who brushed up so close to the cart Mulct was driving that the wheels rolled over feet and left a trail of howling pedestrians in their wake.

Most of the people lugged bags of some description, hauling their worldly possessions with them in case they got the call to evacuate. Valkyrie hadn't been on many passenger planes back home – one of the advantages of having a Teleporter as an ex – but she'd listened to enough flight attendants to know that, in case of emergency, you should really leave all bags where they are and just get the hell out. Looking around, she didn't like these people's chances of outrunning a draugr with a suitcase in either hand.

They stopped in front of the governor's tower, a column of white stone with glass circling the top, and tied their horses to a post.

"Right then," said Mulct, "you'll be wanting to talk to Governor Erato. Me and Hapathy are going to be busy with our various cargos, but anything you need, you come find us."

"We will, indeed," said Skulduggery. "Thank you, gentlemen."

Mulct bowed. "May the blessings of the Faceless Ones rain down upon you."

Skulduggery nodded. "And also on you."

The cart rumbled away, and Skulduggery turned to Serpine. "You know him, then," Skulduggery said. "This Erato."

"Gratio Erato is one of Mevolent's most shameless sycophants," Serpine responded. "He's also tried to kill me on multiple occasions, so I would prefer not to—"

Skulduggery handed him a pair of shackles, and Serpine glowered.

"Erato will kill me on sight. It is not safe for me to enter this tower."

"Hey, Nefarian," Skulduggery said, "you're one of us now, OK? I'm not going to let Erato, or anybody, kill you. If anyone does it, you can rest assured that it will be me."

"How comforting."

"I thought you'd appreciate it. Now put the shackles on, there's a good boy."

45

They were shown into the governor's office by a woman with extraordinary hair.

The office was at the very top of the tower. It was roughly the size of a football pitch, the curved walls broken up with broad windows. On a summer's day, like today, some of those windows would probably have stood open to let in the breeze – but today they were closed, presumably to keep the stench of the dead from wafting in.

Gratio Erato stood up from his impressive desk. He was short and handsome, dressed in clothes so fine they looked like they'd rip if he moved too fast.

"Serpine," he said, a smile forming as he came out from behind his desk. "How wonderful to see you again. How truly thrilling. Life hasn't been the same since you last ran away from me."

Then he punched him, and Valkyrie was surprised that his sleeve didn't tear with the sudden movement.

Skulduggery stepped between them, the face he was wearing adopting an expression of mild amusement. "I'll let you have that one for free, because he's got a face for punching, but lay another finger on him and Mevolent will hear about it."

Erato rubbed his knuckles and raised an eyebrow. "You think Mevolent doesn't want this man to be in pain?"

"I think Mevolent wants to inflict that pain himself."

"Ah," said Erato.

"Our orders are to bring him to Tahil na Kurge."

"I could take care of that for you."

"I'm sure you could, but our orders were most specific."

"I don't know you. Any of you. That strikes me as odd, seeing as I know everyone Mevolent would trust with a mission like this."

"If you knew us," Valkyrie said, "we wouldn't be very good at our job."

Erato looked at them for a moment, then gave the slightest of shrugs. "You're meant to bring him to Tahil na Kurge. So why are you here?"

"As we understand it, there are a lot of dead people in the way," Skulduggery said.

"So you're here looking for free passage, are you? That will be no problem. We'll take you with us."

"And when will that be?"

"When we get the signal. No more than four months."

"Four *months*?" Valkyrie blurted.

"Yes," Erato said, seemingly oblivious to her surprise. "We're nearly ready to go here. You be sure to tell Mevolent that. We're well ahead of schedule."

"Mevolent will want his prisoner delivered within the week," Skulduggery said.

Erato laughed. "Then it would appear you'll displease him, because we can't go until we get the signal. If you want to leave with us, and I recommend it, then you'll have to wait. I can have a disused gaol assigned to you – it's not in one of our most salubrious districts, but it should suffice as both lodgings for you, and a cold, damp cell for him." A smirk towards Serpine. "If you have any equipment with you, any animals, they can be traded for food or money, should you require any. Never let it be said that Gratio Erato isn't a gracious—"

There was a knock on the door, and the woman with extraordinary hair stepped in and nodded, and Erato smiled.

"Wonderful," he said. "You're in for a little treat just now. A little giggle. My people have, obviously, been forced to make some sacrifices due to our unfortunate circumstances. A few days ago, we discovered one of our food stores had been decimated by rats. The rats were exterminated and the individuals who bore responsibility punished – but naturally we faced an adjustment to our rationing process. The thing about people, as I'm sure you're aware, is that they do become reluctant to give up certain luxuries once they've got used to them – none more so than the luxury of food."

"I doubt that went down particularly well," said Skulduggery.

"Oh," Erato responded, sounding pleased, "it didn't go down at all."

Skulduggery tilted his head. "Rationing is not the sacrifice your people made?"

"No, dear me, no," Erato said, leading them out on to the balcony. "I calculated that we could still eat well until we had to depart the city, providing there were less mouths to feed. The sacrifice my people made was to give up their domestic staff."

There were people lined up all along the south wall, their hands tied behind their backs. At Erato's signal, the sorcerers started pushing them over the wall.

Valkyrie was frozen to the spot, but Tanith moved forward and Dexter had to grab her arm to hold her back. She stared at him. Stared at the others.

"Dinnertime for the draugar," Erato said with a chuckle. He saw the look on Valkyrie's face and his eyes widened. "Oh, please don't worry. They're only mortals. We'd never do that to our people." Smiling now, he led the way back into his office.

The woman with the hair was waiting just inside the door, and she nodded to him again. "Excuse me for just a moment," Erato said, and left with her.

"I'm going to kill him," Tanith said the moment the door closed.

"Not yet," said Skulduggery.

"He murdered those people. This entire *city* murdered those people. We've got it all wrong, you know. The monsters aren't outside the walls. They're in here, with us."

"I need you to remain calm."

"I am calm," she snarled.

"Calmer, then."

Tanith glared, and Valkyrie watched her go cold. "I'm fine," she said quietly.

"What do we do?" Saracen asked. "We're not going to stay here for the next four months, are we?"

Skulduggery shook his head. "The city's defences are too weak. The draugar could get in at any moment and we'd suffer the same fate as everyone else."

"So we're leaving?"

"Maybe," said Skulduggery. "We have to get to Tahil na Kurge, kill Mevolent, and disable those portals he's building. The draugar present a significant obstacle to all of that. Erato knows the land, and at least some of what Mevolent is planning. We can't leave without getting more intelligence, so, when he gets back, we'll ask him some very polite questions with only a minimum of punching before we..."

His voice trailed off as the door opened, and the woman with all that hair smiled at them politely. "The governor regrets to inform you that he has been called away on city business, but he has asked me to arrange for someone to show you to the gaol you'll be staying at, and points out that, if you attempt to leave the city, the sentries on the wall have strict instructions to kill you on sight. We can't be too careful, after all. He hopes you have a pleasant stay."

Then she bowed, and left.

"Damn," said Skulduggery.

46

They sat in their armchairs, the fireplace behind them. In the winter, that fireplace would be ablaze. Tonight it was dark and cold and quiet. Omen sat on the couch, back straight, knees together, hands in his lap.

"Miss Ficus tells us you've been doing adequate work," Emmeline said. "While this isn't wonderful news, it is, nonetheless, good news. We would have hated to see you squandering these last few months while your brother is fighting to return to health after he saved you."

Omen nodded. Said nothing.

"We wanted to talk to you about your future," his mother continued.

"What do you plan to do with your life?" Caddock asked.

"Me?" said Omen, frowning.

"Since you boys were born," Emmeline said, "all you've known is the prophecy. Auger's life has revolved around it, and you, too, have been caught in its orbit. But, at some stage in the next two years, the prophecy will come true. We want to know if you've thought about what you'll do afterwards."

"Not... not really."

Caddock crossed his legs and intertwined his fingers. "You need to, Omen. Things are going to change – for all of us. Do you think we'll be treated with the same amount of respect once the fate of the world no longer rests in Auger's hands? No. The people who value our business, our input, our expertise... these people will vanish once Auger defeats the King of the Darklands. And Auger *will* defeat him."

There was something in Caddock's eyes that was almost a challenge, so Omen nodded quickly. "I know," he said. "I know he will."

"We've used the last fifteen years to establish Auger's brand," Emmeline said, "and to reinforce the idea that once a Chosen One, always a Chosen One. Auger should be fine. Our businesses should be fine. But you... we have yet to work out what you will even *do*."

Omen tried a shrug.

"Is that your answer?" Caddock asked.

"Uh..."

"A shrug is your answer? Really?"

"I just meant, I don't know what I'm going to do," Omen clarified. "I didn't think it was, you know..."

"What?"

"Important. I didn't think it was important."

"Of course it's important," Emmeline said. "You're our son."

Omen smiled slowly as Caddock nodded.

"Exactly," Omen's father said. "Any failure you experience reflects badly on us."

Omen stopped smiling. "Maybe, um, maybe I could get a job in the High Sanctuary."

Caddock's eyes rolled. "Everyone tries to get a job in the Sanctuaries. You think they have spaces open? You think you'll outshine all the others applying? What about that friend of yours, that Never person? Do you think you'll be a better prospect than her?"

"Well, no," Omen admitted. "Never's going to be a Teleporter."

"A valued discipline," Emmeline said. "Exactly. Have you decided what discipline you're going to specialise in?"

"Not yet."

"And have you taken part in any extracurricular activities, as I suggested?"

Omen had told them all about this. They'd either forgotten or they hadn't been listening. "I've helped out with some charity stuff at school," he said. "Volunteering and things. And I've been, like..."

"Yes?"

He cleared his throat. "I've been having adventures. Sanctuaries respond to that, I heard. If you stop a bad guy, they take notice. I've helped Skulduggery Pleasant and Valkyrie Cain, and Temper Fray, and me and Auger—"

"No one wants to hire the sidekick," Caddock interrupted.

Emmeline shot him a look. "Caddock."

"What? They don't. It's time to stop mollycoddling the boy." Caddock switched his attention back to Omen. "Your brother will outshine you in everything you do. He always has and he always will. You can't be an adventurer, you can't be a detective, you can't fight evil sorcerers and save the world – because he'll be doing all that, too, and he'll be doing it so much better than you ever could."

A lump formed deep down in Omen's throat.

Emmeline frowned at her husband. "We said we wouldn't be needlessly heartless."

Caddock looked irritated. "This isn't needless, this is necessary. The boy has to hear it. You don't mind hearing this, do you, boy?"

Omen shook his head.

"See? It's doing him good."

Emmeline kept frowning for another moment, then softened when she looked back at Omen. "Before it was called the Darkly Prophecy, what was it known as?"

"The Darklands Prophecy," Omen said.

"And when did it change?"

"When Auger took his name."

"You took your names on the same night. I suppose that's only natural. You're twins. You're close. Auger and Omen Darkly. Who went first?"

"Auger," said Omen.

"So he chose Darkly as a name, after my own, and you copied him."

"Well," Omen said, "we'd talked about it and kind of decided we'd like to have the same last name. Then he came up with Auger, and I thought Omen might be a good, like, not *counterpoint*, but—"

"We're getting away from the point," Caddock said, cutting across him again. "You've copied him as much as you could. You've been able to coast along because of him. Nothing has been expected of you, because *everything* has been expected of Auger. You've been allowed a carefree life, Omen, while Auger, your mother, and I, have put in the blood, the sweat and the tears. You've had a blissful little life, haven't you? Well, today that comes to an end."

"Your life doesn't come to an end," his mother corrected quickly, "just the blissful part of it."

"Right," said Omen, jumping to his feet and screaming at them. But only in his head.

47

They'd been in Tahil na Sin for four days, and already Valkyrie was going a little stir-crazy.

The gaol they were staying in smelled of sour sweat and stale urine – even up in the officers' quarters, as far away from the cells as they could get. To pass the time, Valkyrie had volunteered to help Mulct and Hapathy with their deliveries. She'd been hoping they'd be venturing outside the walls again so she could escape the constant throng of people, but so far they'd remained depressingly local. She did get to visit the top of the wall, though: lugging supplies for the sorcerers standing watch.

She peered over the edge, at all those tiny draugar below them. "That," she said, "is a long way down."

"And not a gentle landing, neither," said Mulct, huffing and puffing behind her. "Look at them, Valerie. The slavering mob. They'd eat you whole, they would. Wouldn't need to even chew."

Valkyrie raised her eyes. "And the Necromancers? Do they just hover there all day?"

"From what I can see," said Mulct, dropping the crate he'd been carrying, then pulling out a rag to mop his sweaty brow. "They don't need to rest, any more than the draugar do. They just stand on those shadows of theirs and stare."

"They don't try to shadow-walk in?"

"Not able. Tahil na Sin's been fortified against that sort of thing, they tell me, using only the strongest sigils. I'm not one for the old languages, though, so I have no idea if there's any such thing as one sigil being stronger than another. Might be Erato just doesn't want us panicking."

Valkyrie stepped back from the edge. Flying never made her dizzy, but standing on something high tended to give her a gut-wrenching sense of vertigo. "How much longer can the city last, food-wise?"

Mulct winced. "Don't know. Don't like to say. Don't like to guess. Don't even like to think about it. Our stores have been emptying, as you can probably imagine. All these mouths to feed. Thankfully, we have enough fresh-water wells so that thirst won't be a problem, but the food, sure enough, that's running out. Medicine, too. Everyone packed in like this, sickness spreads quickly when it arrives."

"Don't you have healers?"

"Oh, aye, we do, and they charge their fees and get rich off the misery of others. Medicine's the cheaper option in most cases. When we do our supply runs, it's food and medicine that are most in demand."

"Is everyone here a mage?"

He looked at her oddly. "Of course. Well, apart from the servants. Oh, I get what you're saying. You want to throw more of the mortals over the wall, eh? I mean, yeah, that'd save us some scraps of stale bread, but a lot of folks in the city are too used to having them around. I doubt they'd remember how to dress themselves without help."

Mulct sniffed heavily, and swallowed something thick that made Valkyrie want to gag. "We'll be leaving them behind when we travel to Tahil na Kurge, though. Won't need servants any more. There's a whole world of mortals waiting to serve us through those portals."

"Do you really think conquering this other world will be so easy?"

"I reckon," said Mulct. "We've sent Shunters over. They've done some spying for us, told us how that world is. You've heard what they've had to say, haven't you? Everyone has."

"I have," Valkyrie said carefully. "But I don't know if I agree with you."

Mulct waved his hand dismissively. "They got almost no mages, and those they do have keep out of sight. Mortals run everything, so I've heard. There are billions of them. Do you know what a billion is? I didn't, before I heard what the Shunters had to say. Billions and billions of mortals, who don't even know mages exist. What do you think they're going to do when we arrive? Soil themselves, that's what! Soil themselves and run away!"

"Probably," Valkyrie said. "But billions and billions of mortals would outnumber us, wouldn't they?"

"Numbers aren't everything," Mulct said. "Would I prefer to ride into battle with a billion mortals, or a hundred sorcerers? I'd pick the sorcerers every time. Our armies will just roll over their lines. We have our forces here and Mevolent has his, and when we combine them we'll be unstoppable."

"The mortals have weapons we don't."

Mulct laughed. "Mortal weapons! Little more than spears and rocks! Valerie, you seem like a fine girl, and, to be one of Mevolent's chosen few, I'd say you're a fearsome warrior. But you're young, so allow me to reassure you, as an ugly old man who's been around a few years – victory is already ours. That world is already ours. Half those billions are already dead, and the other half are our slaves and they don't even know it yet."

"What the hell're you two gabbing about?" Hapathy growled, staggering up beside them with a crate pulling at his fingers.

"How easy it'll be to conquer the world of the mortals," Mulct said, helping him lower it. "There. That the lot of them?"

"Unless any more crates have grown out of the splinters in the cart, yes. We'll need to load the empties, though."

Mulct winced. "Could you manage that? Only I got that thing."

"What thing?"

"The thing. The thing I got. With the lady. The baker."

"What thing?" Hapathy asked, frowning. "What baker?"

"The lady baker," Mulct said, glancing at Valkyrie and blushing. "Me and the lady baker. The thing. I told you."

"You told me nothing. You're just trying to get out of work."

"I told you!" Mulct said, getting angry now. "About the lady baker! And me! Me and the lady baker! I told you! I bloody well told you!"

"*Ohhh*," said Hapathy. "The lady baker. Yeah, yeah, I remember. You better be off, so, or you'll be late. Lady bakers don't like to be kept waiting."

Mulct glowered at him, then turned to Valkyrie, and smiled. "Would you mind helping this eejit load up the cart and take the empties back to the storehouse? I can't trust him to do it himself, you see."

"You go on," Valkyrie said, smiling. "I'll help him out."

"Much obliged, Valerie. Much obliged."

Off he went, and she looked at Hapathy and Hapathy looked at her, and he tried smiling. "Well," he said, "let's go, then."

She hadn't spent any time alone with Hapathy before. Mulct was a different prospect. She had her issues with him, but get him talking about anything other than mortals and he was fine, easy-going company. Hapathy was infinitely surlier.

She was not relishing the awkward silences to come.

They loaded the cart with empty crates and Valkyrie sat beside Hapathy as he took the reins. The two old horses did their duty without complaint, and most people had the good sense to step aside the moment they saw them approach. Those who were slow got shouted and cursed at by Hapathy until the path was clear. Valkyrie just raised her face to the sun and thought of Militsa.

They got to the storehouse and took the crates into the stifling gloom. By the time they were done, Valkyrie had built up a good sweat.

"Well," said Hapathy, "thank you kindly for the help, there."

"Sure thing," she said. "And now I hear a bath calling my name."

He frowned. "You hear baths speak?"

"It's an expression. It means I want a bath."

"Oh. Right."

"See you tomorrow, maybe."

He nodded to her, and she walked for the door. He was close behind her. Very close.

She sensed movement and something dropped past her eyes. Without thinking, her right hand shot up, fingers curling around the wire just as it tightened over her throat.

Hapathy dragged her backwards. Valkyrie's legs kicked as she tried to stay upright. The wire bit into her neck, bit into her fingers. Blood ran down her arm, ran down her sleeve. The only sound she could make was little more than a gurgle. Couldn't breathe.

She got her feet under her, but Hapathy abruptly changed direction and she was being dragged again, across the room. Her free hand clutched uselessly at whatever she passed. The pain in her fingers was white-hot. They were going to come off. Her fingers were going to come off.

Out of the corner of her eye she saw a wooden beam. She twisted, got a foot to it, and sprang off. Hapathy grunted, couldn't take her sudden weight. They fell. On impact the wire loosened.

Valkyrie tore it from her throat and sucked in a breath as she squirmed round and sank her teeth into his neck. He screamed, tried to push her off. She tasted blood. Holding her ruined hand close to her chest, she reared up and crunched her forehead into his face. He wriggled and shoved and she fell sideways. He rolled over, whimpering, on to his hands and knees. Valkyrie was already standing.

She lashed a kick into his ribs as he tried getting up. Something cracked and he howled. She kicked him again and he scuttled backwards, one arm out to keep her away. She ignored it, went to kick again.

It was a trick. He had a knife in his other hand and when she stepped in he lunged, his face contorted in hate behind all that blood. They tottered back, the blade trying to get through her suit. He stabbed at her torso, realised it wasn't working and went for her head instead. Valkyrie looped her good arm over his, held the blade tight to her side while he did his best to pull it back. It was all she could do to hang on. Her right hand was useless. She just needed a moment to focus.

Hapathy slammed her head against the wall. His knife hand was free. He slashed at her and the blade opened up her cheek. She tripped over something and went down and as he loomed over her all she could do was kick frantically upwards. Purely by chance, her boot connected with his jaw and he took a step and fell to his knees.

She lay there, panting for breath. She didn't want to look at her right hand. The pain was excruciating and she could feel her fingers hanging off. She raised her left hand. Lightning hit Hapathy and flung him to the far side of the room.

"Skulduggery," she muttered, getting up and stumbling to the door. "Skulduggery."

48

Saracen took her to the nearest healer. When the receptionist told them they'd have to pay to be put on the waiting list, Saracen kicked down the office door and dragged the healer out.

"Her hand," he snarled. "Fix it."

"There's a list!" the healer squealed. "I can see your friend in four days!"

Saracen grabbed the healer's head, turned it towards Valkyrie. "Look at her fingers," he said. "You think they're going to still be there in four days? Fix them."

The healer whimpered, and shuffled forward, and cupped Valkyrie's hand in both of his. She resisted the urge to latch on to his power and do it herself, and endured another few moments of pain before his hands started glowing. Once they did, the pain faded almost immediately.

As he fixed the cut on her cheek, she flexed her hand. "Thank you," she said.

The healer got to his feet and smoothed down his jacket. "Emergency medical procedures cost twice the usual—"

"Send the bill to Mevolent," said Saracen, and escorted Valkyrie back to the gaol.

When they returned, Hapathy was still in the chair in which he'd been dumped, but he wasn't wearing any shackles.

"Uh, what's going on?" Valkyrie asked.

Skulduggery turned to her. "There's been a misunderstanding."

"I really don't think I can be blamed for this," Hapathy said. "I believed you when you said you were Mevolent's people. That can't be my fault, can it? It was your lie. My only crime was believing you."

Valkyrie frowned. "You're with the Resistance?"

"Yes."

"So... what? You're undercover? For how long?"

Hapathy frowned. "I don't know what that is."

"Undercover," Dexter said. "A double agent. A spy."

"Oh," Hapathy said. "I've been a spy for the last twelve years, more or less – passing information back to the Resistance, warning them of upcoming raids, stuff like that."

"Is Mulct a spy, too?" Skulduggery asked.

"No, but it's important if you're... what did you say? Undercover? It's important if you're undercover to work alongside someone who won't shut up. I've found that Mulct talks so much that by the time people get to me they don't care to ask me any questions."

"I have a question," Valkyrie said. "Why'd you try to kill me?"

Hapathy winced. "I'm very sorry about that, I really am, but, like I said, I believed you when you told us you were delivering Serpine to Mevolent. I just couldn't let you take him."

"Your loyalty warms my heart, my friend," Serpine said from his cell.

Hapathy frowned at him. "I don't give a damn about you. I just couldn't let Mevolent ask you any questions. From all the stories I've heard, you'd tell him every last thing you knew to save your own life."

Serpine didn't say anything for a moment. Then he shrugged, and said, "Still."

"So what was the plan?" Valkyrie persisted. "Kill me, then work your way through us all?"

"Yes. I would have just come straight here to kill Serpine, but I knew the lady with the sword was keeping an eye out."

Serpine scowled. "You'd have killed me?"

"To stop you from talking."

He grunted. "I don't like you any more."

"Are there any other spies in the city?" Skulduggery asked.

Hapathy nodded. "Some, but I don't know who they are. It's safer that way."

"Does the Resistance have any Teleporters? We need to get to Tahil na Kurge."

"Why? What are you...?" Hapathy's eyes widened. "You're here to kill Mevolent, aren't you? That's wonderful! That's amazing! Can you do it?"

"We wouldn't be here if we couldn't."

"I'll set up a meeting!" Hapathy said, delight spreading across his face. "It'll take a day or two, but I can take you back outside the walls and you can meet the Resistance leaders. They'll be thrilled to hear this!" He turned to Valkyrie. "Once again, I am so incredibly sorry for trying to kill you."

"No need to apologise," she said, sighing. "Everyone tries to kill me eventually."

49

Never was sitting on Omen's bed and Omen was pacing. Actually *pacing*.

"They said I had an easy life," he said. "No, no – a *blissful* life. They actually said that. They said I've been coasting along all this time, pretty much riding on Auger's coat-tails. Carefree! That's something else they said! They said my life was carefree!"

Never frowned. "They do know you were right there with us at the naval base, right?"

"I thought they did!" Omen said, raising his hands to the ceiling. "But it seems I was wrong! I think they block out anything to do with me whenever Auger's involved, that's what I think. 'Both of your sons have been involved in foiling a plot to take over the world!' 'One of our sons, you say? How proud we are of our Chosen One!'"

Omen collapsed into the chair.

"That was good," said Never. "I like how you mimed the voices with your hands."

"Did I? I didn't even notice."

"Don't worry," she said. "It wasn't very good. None of this is Auger's fault, though."

"I know," Omen said wearily. "I'm just angry."

"Huh."

"What?"

"Nothing. It's just... I think this is the first time you've admitted that your folks can be irritating."

"Is it?"

"Whenever I've brought it up in the past, your natural instinct has always been to defend their honour. This is good. This shows you're growing as a person."

Omen sat up straighter. "Like, I wouldn't want you to think they're bad parents, or anything."

"Stop," said Never. "Do not make excuses for them. You're always making excuses. Take this opportunity, take this conversation, to vent those frustrations. It might even be good for you."

"I'm not sure I know how."

"You were doing fine a second ago."

"A second ago, I didn't realise that that's what I was doing." Omen rubbed his face. "OK. Let's see. My parents are... not perfect."

"Good start," said Never, nodding her approval.

"They can be overly... harsh. And, I suppose, dismissive."

"OK."

"And sometimes I think they don't love me."

Never didn't say anything.

"But I'm probably wrong," said Omen. "In fact, I know I'm wrong. Of course they love me. They might not like me, but they're contractually obliged to love me." He gave a weak laugh.

"Continue," said Never.

"They're just so focused on Auger that they've forgotten I matter. Or maybe I *don't* matter to them. Maybe it's that simple. I don't know."

"Pretend I'm your therapist," Never said, lying back on the bed. "Tell me about your parents."

"I think I'm supposed to be the one lying down," Omen pointed out.

"I'm a tired therapist. I've had a long day of telling people to tell me things. Your parents, Mr Darkly."

Omen took a breath, and blew it out. "They're disciplined,"

he said. "Disciplined and intelligent. And ambitious. They're kind of the opposite of me."

"This is true," said Never, her eyes closed. "Keep going."

"Emmeline knew she was born to be the mother of the Chosen One. Her family had heard the prophecy and they'd figured it out, knew it would be one of the daughters. It was, obviously, Emmeline, and when she met my dad she told him that they were destined to be together, so, of course, they got together. They were immediate, like, celebrities."

"Ah, the glitz and the glamour of sorcerer celebrities," Never said, her eyes still closed, "where only a few people in the world even know you exist."

"Yeah, well," said Omen. "They were talking to me about building up Auger's brand, you know? But I think they put even more effort into building up their *own* brand. The fabulous Darkly family – starring Emmeline, Caddock and Auger. Featuring Omen, sometimes."

Never smiled a little at this.

"I think they're freaking out," Omen said. "This is... What do you call it when you project your feelings about something on to someone else? What's that called?"

"Projection," said Never.

"That's it. Thank you."

"You're welcome."

"They're projecting their own insecurities on to me because I'm the easy target, and it stops them from having to focus on themselves. That's what they're really scared of. They're terrified of being suddenly irrelevant, of nobody caring who they are or what they think. They can probably see their careers about to slip away because they're so, like, closely identified with the Darkly Prophecy that, when it's over, they won't have anything left."

Never cracked open one eye. "And so what are you going to do about all of it?"

"I don't know," Omen admitted. "Not much, I expect. They're my parents. What can I do?"

"True dat."

"I could run away. Maybe I should run away, change my life, do something that means something. Something that changes things."

"Like what?"

"I don't know."

"Like invent something?"

"Probably not."

"You've never been much of an inventor."

"I'm not sure where this inventing thing started."

Never sat up. "You could write a play about your life."

"Would you go and see it?"

Never lay back down. "Don't like plays."

"This is pointless anyway," said Omen. "I'm not going to do anything. I'm going to complain to you until you tell me to stop, then I'm going to go back to my life and continue as normal, and pretend that my parents actually care."

Never leaped up. "You're depressing me," she announced. "I come here to chat and gossip and laugh at you, not to hear serious stuff about serious things."

"Sorry."

She looked at him. "You don't have to apologise to me," she said. "Now come on, hug it out."

"What?"

She opened her arms. "Hug. Every great therapist ends their sessions with a hug."

"I don't think that's true."

"Hugging is important, Omen. You're never fully dressed without a hug. Come on. Just one."

Omen grinned, came forward, and, right before they hugged, Never teleported away.

Omen stood there, arms out, embracing nothing but air. "Uncool," he said.

50

There were only a few places Sebastian could hang out these days. His house – which was now occupied by a pregnant god; with Bennet and the others – where he'd be plagued by questions about the pregnant god in his house; or up on a roof somewhere, all alone with his thoughts – which usually revolved around the pregnant god in his house.

Eventually, he decided to accept his fate, and just went back to the house with the pregnant god.

Darquesse stood by the mirror in the hall, turning, examining herself from different angles. She was showing now. It didn't look like she was pregnant, though. It was like she'd eaten too many pies in one sitting.

Sebastian missed pies. He missed food. He also missed going to the toilet. The simple things in life.

"You could go back to it," Darquesse said.

He realised she was looking at him. "Sorry?"

"You could go back to your life," she said. "You just have to take off the suit you wear and you can walk away from all of this."

"I wish you wouldn't read my mind."

"I know you do."

He sighed. "Anyway, I can't walk away. I have a mission."

"Your mission was to find me and bring me back. You've done that. Your mission is over."

He shook his head. "It's more complicated than that. At least I... I think it is."

"You tend to doubt yourself."

"Do I?"

"You don't have to, you know. There's a reason they sent you."

"They didn't have a choice."

"They trusted you. You should try trusting yourself, too. This could have all gone horribly wrong. You do see that, don't you? You could have found me, brought me back, and I could have cracked open the world. But look. The world is uncracked. That's because of you, in a way. If you had been one degree more annoying than you are, I might have killed everyone out of spite."

"Is this... is this your version of a pep talk?"

She smiled. "I was better at this when I was just Kes, on her own. Kes was developing into a good person. You'd have liked her."

"It must be so weird, being you."

She shrugged.

51

The doors opened and Temper walked through. China Sorrows sat upon her throne, hovering over the sea of energy. Before her stood Commander Hoc – and Damocles Creed.

Well, perfect.

Temper realised he'd stopped walking. He marched up, stood beside them both.

"Supreme Mage," he said, nodding.

China looked tired and aggravated as she leaned forward. "Temper," she said, "I've called you here to explain yourself."

He nodded. "Very well. In regards to what?"

"Commander?" she said.

Hoc puffed out his chest. "Someone has been asking questions about any links between the murder of Grand Mage Drang and Arch-Canon Creed."

"Right," said Temper. "And have they found any?"

Hoc was hilariously bad at disguising his irritation. "Arch-Canon Creed is not a suspect in this investigation!"

Temper remained calm. "But Commander, until we've found the killer, surely everyone is a suspect?"

Creed grunted. It was almost like a laugh.

"You can't investigate a person of high standing within a religious organisation," China said. "It doesn't get more high standing than the Arch-Canon of the Church of the Faceless."

Temper nodded. "But with respect, Supreme Mage, the most obvious suspect is also a high-standing member of a different church. The Religious Freedom Act, I'm sorry to say, seems designed entirely to protect criminals from serious investigation."

"Criminals?" Hoc shrieked. "The Arch-Canon is an innocent man, Sergeant! Innocent until proven guilty!"

"And so is Kierre of the Unveiled," said Temper.

China sighed. "Arch-Canon? You have something to say?"

Creed rubbed his stubbled cheeks with one massive hand. "It seems to me, Supreme Mage, that Kierre's standing in the Legion of Judgement may be slightly exaggerated. She's an assassin. We all know it. As her brother, I am proud to say that she is an exquisite assassin, just as my sister Rune is an exquisite warrior, and my brother Strosivadian is an exquisite barbarian. But only Serafina holds a place of distinction within her church. As much as it saddens me, we should not allow criminals and killers to hide behind the Religious Freedom Act, an act that defends the truly righteous among us."

China rubbed her temples. "Very well," she said. "Commander Hoc, your recommendation?"

"I shall take over the investigation immediately," Hoc said, "and issue an arrest warrant for Kierre of the Unveiled."

"OK," said China. "Do it, then. Temper, I'm sure you'll be reassigned."

"Of course," he said. "Thank you, Supreme Mage."

He got home and dumped his uniform on the kitchen table — coming very close to dumping it in the living-room fireplace. He got a beer from the fridge, took a swig as he walked for the bedroom, dropped the beer as he jumped back. It smashed.

Kierre stood in his hallway. "They came to arrest me," she said.

He didn't say anything. His heart was still hammering in his chest.

"They broke down the gates. Broke down the doors. They said only Serafina is protected. They said they're looking into stripping the Legion of Judgement of its official designation as a religious organisation."

"Yeah," said Temper. "Sorry about that."

"I escaped."

"So I see. Did you hurt anyone?"

She shook her head.

"What are you doing here?"

"I didn't kill that man."

"I think I believe you."

She looked around. "Can I stay here?"

He frowned. "Aren't I the enemy?"

"Are you? I have so many enemies I get confused."

"What I mean is, you trust me enough to stay in my house?"

"Yes."

He looked at her, and didn't know how to respond. Finally, he just said, "Huh."

52

Valkyrie had decided to stay away from Hapathy out of sheer principle, but after five days with nothing to do she turned up at his cart and asked if he could use a hand. They'd just returned from another trip outside the walls, and Mulct was off visiting with the lady baker, so Hapathy accepted her offer gratefully.

"I really am sorry," he said for the fourteenth time as he carried two sacks of grain into the loft of the storehouse.

"No harm done," she muttered, arms full with three heavy boxes.

"Thank goodness I'm not very good at killing people, eh?" Hapathy said.

Valkyrie grunted as she laid the boxes down, and didn't answer.

"It's never been one of my strengths, hurting folk," Hapathy continued. "It takes a certain kind of person, I suppose – not that I have to tell you that."

She wiped the dust from her sleeves. "What do you mean?"

"Well," Hapathy said, a little sheepishly, "you're an assassin, aren't you?"

She went very still. "No," she said.

"You're not? But you're here to kill Mevolent."

"That's our mission, yes, but that doesn't make me an assassin."

"Oh. Mind me asking what it *does* make you?"

"Someone who's doing her job. My *team* has been sent to kill him, yes, but I'm not... That's not what I do. It's not who I am."

"Oh. Oh, no, I've hurt your feelings."

"What?"

"I have," said Hapathy, looking crestfallen. "I'm so sorry. First I hurt your hand, then I hurt your feelings. Mulct is right – I *am* an eejit."

Valkyrie sighed. "My feelings aren't hurt, I just... I don't like being called that. I'm not here to kill anyone. I'm here to help."

She started to head back. When he didn't follow her, she turned again. "Everything all right?"

He was frowning at one of the boxes she'd brought up, made out of metal or lead, or a combination of both. "I don't remember loading this on to the cart," he said, reaching for it.

The moment the lid cracked open a torrent of shadows burst upwards, rebounded off the ceiling and slammed into Hapathy and then Valkyrie, knocking them both off their feet. She rolled back to standing as the shadows swirled in place, and from those shadows a figure formed, a Necromancer, an old one, skin deathly white, the shadows feeding into him and the staff he clutched until he was whole.

Valkyrie raised her hands, but he swept the staff in a wide arc before she could act, unleashing a dozen spears of darkness. Some of those spears hit her, sending her to the ground once more and knocking the breath from her lungs. Hapathy fell beside her, the spears sticking out of his chest rapidly turning to black vapour.

Valkyrie watched, wheezing, as the Necromancer walked to the window. It burst open and he lifted off his feet and drifted through.

Grimacing, Valkyrie scrambled up, got to the window to watch the shadows lowering him towards street level. She couldn't fly after him, she'd light up the sky and get herself killed, but the building opposite was close, and it had a balcony. She could jump the distance. She knew she could.

She ran back, then sprinted at the window and leaped, pulling up her hood as she pinwheeled through the air. She'd misjudged it, though, and she hit the side of the building and fell awkwardly, crunching her ribs into the balcony rail. Wheezing, moaning, she climbed on to the railing and sprang for the balcony next to it, catching her foot and biting her tongue as she sprawled.

No time to howl, no time to gather herself. She was up and springing over the rail, landing on the sloping roof and sliding down along the tiles. When she got to the edge, she cheated, gave a quick burst of lightning to boost herself back across the street, landing on the roof opposite and again sliding down. Her boots hit the gutter, cracked it out of its moorings, and she grabbed a pipe and then the shadows wrapped around her waist and yanked her off the roof.

They turned sharp, tried to cut through her suit. The Necromancer was rising now, coming back up. Her hand crackled, but the shadows convulsed, flinging her through a window. Glass smashed and there was light everywhere and she was tumbling down a corridor in someone's home. A man stepped out of a doorway, uncomprehending. The Necromancer drifted in from outside and sent his shadows to tear the man apart.

The shadows darted for Valkyrie next and she zapped them and they dissipated, but there were more coming. She dodged their slashes, threw herself down, rolling to her feet right in front of the Necromancer. He struck her with his staff, the heavy black wood colliding with her knee, almost buckling her. But she grabbed him, rammed her forehead into his face. He didn't seem to mind.

A door burst open when she smashed into it. She fell, scrambled, tripped over the edge of the bed. The Necromancer came after her, the shadows snaking through the doorway with him, and she let the lightning flow. He flew backwards, out of the room. She got up, passed a mirror, glimpsed the shadows swirling behind her, barely ducked the swing of the staff as he stepped out. She whirled and gave another blast, but he wasn't there any more, and she straightened and he grabbed her from behind and hauled her backwards.

He threw her against the wall. She smacked her head so hard that, despite the armoured hood, lights flashed behind her eyes and thoughts went away. Valkyrie was aware, dimly, of his hand at her throat and his mouth wide open and dipping towards the exposed flesh of her face.

Adrenaline surged and magic burst from her eyes and sent him spinning as she dropped. Her knee gave out and she fell, cursed, rolled back, hands crackling and ready to go.

She lay there, teeth gritted, tasting her own blood, her ribs on fire and her knee not working – but she was alone. After a few moments, she got up, hissing as he hopped on one foot, backing into the corner, waiting for him to spring out at her.

She stayed like that for a while.

53

Tanith sat in the dark and thought about killing Gratio Erato.

He was a murderer. He deserved to die. He deserved to die more than some of the people Tanith had killed when she'd been an assassin. Deserved it more than some of the people she'd killed recently.

Not all of them. Certainly not all of them. But some.

These months away from home, they were getting to her. They were getting to all of them. Valkyrie especially. Although, in a way, the time spent travelling had also helped the girl, helped to break her free of what had gripped her. All that guilt. All that pain. Finally, Tanith was able to catch glimpses of the old Valkyrie. Just glimpses, of course, because that person was gone, and rightly so. People change. They grow.

But, for Tanith, it was different. The longer she spent here, in this lawless land, the more irresistible the pull was becoming. Her own innate sense of justice was beginning to assert itself once more, just like it did all those years ago. It had led to trouble back then. She reckoned it would lead to trouble now, if she wasn't careful.

A door opened. Someone came in. Serpine stood, went to the bars of his cell.

"Nefarian." A man's voice.

"Remus," said Serpine. "You'll forgive me if I skip the part where I pretend to be happy to see you."

"But of course," said Crux. "You're a busy man, after all, locked up here, where you belong."

Serpine smiled. "Indeed."

Tanith came up to a crouch and moved forward, just enough so she could see this world's version of Remus Crux. This version had an even sillier beard than the other one.

"I didn't think I'd see you again," Crux continued. "I didn't think you'd be foolish enough to show your face. I thought you'd stow away on a boat, sail off into the horizon, maybe spend the rest of your life on an island somewhere, eating raw gull eggs and babbling to yourself."

"That's quite a specific vision of the future for one so lacking in imagination."

"Nefarian, please – don't waste my time with petty insults."

"Oh, it's never a waste."

"How does it feel, to be back in one of my cells? To know that wherever you run, wherever you hide, it is here you will always come back to?"

"You talk as if you're the one who caught me, Remus. But you've never caught me. As far as I know, you've never caught anyone."

"We both know that's not—"

"You've spent your life trying to fool people into thinking you're a great detective, able to track your quarry no matter what. But you're just a jailer, Remus. Other – better – people catch your quarries and bring them to you and all you do is turn the key and try your very best to make sure they don't escape. Which is harder than it sounds."

"You're pathetic."

"Your face is going red."

Remus sneered. "Mock me all you like—"

"Oh, thank you, I will."

"—it will not change the fact that your life is in my hands."

"That's an interesting way of looking at a situation in which my life is blatantly *not* in your hands."

"No?"

"Mevolent wants the pleasure of killing me himself. He would be most displeased if anything in the slightest were to befall me. You'd better hope this bed is comfortable because, if I wake with a crick in my neck, the all-powerful Mevolent will tear you limb from unexceptional limb."

Crux's smile spread. "It's moments like this that I truly enjoy. You think you know everything, Nefarian. That arrogance is why people dislike you so much."

"I'd argue that it's only one of the reasons."

"Things have changed since you went running. I'm no longer the jailer, you see. I've been promoted."

"Oh! Congratulations! Your mother must be so proud. Oh, wait – she hates you, doesn't she? I seem to remember something about that..."

Crux bristled. "My point is, I'm not even supposed to be here. Nobody knows I still have access. So, when they come down and they find you dead, *they're* going to be the ones that Mevolent blames. Not me."

Serpine folded his arms. "Remus. I'm impressed. That's quite sneaky of you. I doubt it will work, but even so – well done."

"You honestly think Mevolent will work out that it was me?"

"Not Mevolent, no. The people who brought me in. A thoroughly disreputable lot – killers, every one of them – but not unintelligent. I doubt you'll get far."

"I'm confident."

"That's nice."

Tanith let herself drop from the ceiling and landed beside Crux, who jumped back, eyes wide.

"Walk away," Tanith said.

Crux hesitated, then turned quickly for the door.

"I wouldn't," said Serpine.

Tanith glared at him to shut up, but Crux turned again.

Serpine leaned against the bars. "You don't think this will be in her report when she hands me over to Mevolent? You don't think you'll be named as the man intent on killing me against Mevolent's wishes?"

"I won't mention this," Tanith said. "You go now, and you don't come back, and this will stay between us."

"I'll tell him," Serpine said, grinning. "Right before he kills me, I'll tell him what you came to do."

Tanith scowled. "Shut up."

But Serpine continued. "If you want to stay alive, Remus, your only chance is to kill us both."

"Don't do it," Tanith said, shaking her head.

"You know what Mevolent's like. You know what he'll do to you."

Tanith's hand went to her sword. "Don't."

Crux hesitated. For a moment, she thought he'd do the smart thing. But then he licked his lips and she knew he was about to do the stupid one.

He moved and she moved and he died and she put her sword away.

"Goddammit, Serpine."

Serpine shrugged. "It was self-defence. I'll vouch for you."

"We could have let him walk away. The draugar would have got him anyway, sooner or later."

"This man came here to kill me," Serpine said. "These sins cannot be forgiven."

"Now we've got to get rid of the body. Do you have any idea how to get rid of a body in this city?"

"Actually, I know several ways."

She pointed at him. "Shut up. You shut up. Hear me?"

He smiled, and held up his hands in surrender.

The door burst open and Valkyrie stumbled in. She almost fell, but Tanith grabbed her, guided her to the chair they'd dumped Hapathy on to a few days earlier.

"Hey!" Tanith shouted. "Get down here!"

Serpine pressed his forehead against the bars of his cell. "Staggering in, covered in blood... This is a most distracting habit of yours, Miss Cain."

"Shut up," Valkyrie said.

Skulduggery ran in, Dexter and Saracen behind him. They saw Crux's body.

"What happened?" Saracen asked.

"Not important," said Tanith. "Val? What's wrong?"

Valkyrie looked up. "There's a Necromancer in the city. He killed Hapathy. There was a box. A small box. The box opened and all these shadows came out and, and the shadows formed the Necromancer. Like, they *became* him. I didn't know Necromancers could do that."

Skulduggery grunted. "This is a most displeasing development."

"He'll be going for the sigils," Dexter said. "All he needs to do is damage one of them and the whole system fails."

"We have to leave," Skulduggery said. "But first, we warn Erato – let him start the evacuation."

"I don't think I fully understand," Serpine said as Dexter unlocked his cell. "Why do we care if this city falls? They are, if I may be permitted to use the vernacular, the bad guys, are they not?"

"We still don't want to see them slaughtered," Saracen muttered.

"Dear me, why not?"

"Because we don't," Valkyrie snapped.

"How bad are you hurt?" Skulduggery asked.

"I'm fine," she said. "It's just my leg, mostly."

Skulduggery looked at Tanith. "You'll be fastest," he said. "Get to Erato, then meet us at the tunnel."

Tanith ran up the outside of the governor's tower. There was shouting, somewhere below her. Panic. A scream. Then it was cut off, and there were only her footsteps on stone.

She got in through a window, landed halfway up the staircase to Erato's office. No shouts of alarm here. No sign they had any idea what was about to happen. She ran up, then across the carpeted floor. Two guards saw her coming and stepped in front of her, viewing her with heavy-lidded eyes.

Tanith didn't give them a chance to slow her down. She jumped, driving the toe of her boot into the first one's neck, and spun in mid-air, the heel of her other foot catching the second one in the temple. Both guards dropped and she hurried on through the door.

Erato was at his desk, reading through a sheaf of papers. He looked up in surprise. "Something wrong?" he asked.

That innate sense of justice, of outrage, it guided her hand to her sword and she plunged the blade through Erato's chest. He stared down at it, blinking rapidly, his face a mask of confusion.

"The Necromancers have breached the walls," Tanith told him.

Erato wheezed. Coughed. Blood speckled his shirt. "The people," he said hoarsely. "Warn the people."

"The same people who gave up their servants to be thrown over the wall because they didn't want to have to eat less? Those same people?" Tanith twisted the blade, leaned in, and sneered, "Let them die."

54

Valkyrie's knee threatened to buckle with every quick, limping step she took, but she managed to keep up with the others as they hurried through the city streets.

An alarm went off, somewhere in the distance. Great floodlights were suddenly switched on, bathing entire streets in harsh light.

"The gates!" somebody screeched. "The gates are opening!"

There was a lot of shouting now. A lot of screaming. Breaking glass. Doors being slammed. A man stumbled in front of them, clutching his bloody arm.

"Help," he said. They passed him, running now, Valkyrie wincing, expecting her knee to give, readying herself for an ungainly fall.

"Damn," Saracen said, slowing. They slowed along with him. "Draugar ahead, the next street over. Lots of them. Right in front of the tunnel. Too many to get through."

"We can fly out," Skulduggery said. "Once the sentries on the walls are called down to street level, we should be able to leave without anyone trying to stop us."

Valkyrie frowned. "So we wait for things to get worse?"

"I doubt we'll be waiting long."

"Can we at least help people while we're down here?"

"Why would you want to help them?" Serpine asked, perplexed. "These are the soldiers who are planning on conquering your world."

"Not all of them," Valkyrie shot back.

"True – some of them are merely civilians who are going to make slaves of whatever mortals the soldiers don't slaughter."

"I don't like the idea of anyone being eaten alive by a draugr," she said. "I don't want to stand by while that happens to even my worst enemy – so, if I can help anyone, I want to at least try. Can you understand that, you ridiculous psychopath?"

"Not really," Serpine admitted.

Shouts ahead, screams, and people came running round the corner, eyes wide. Terrified.

A torrent of draugar came after them.

The people barged into Valkyrie and the others. She fell. They tripped over her. She scrambled, fighting her way back to her feet. Dead hands clutched at her, yanked her hair. She lashed out, stumbled, started to join the panicking throng.

The flow of people took her down a side street. She glanced back, realised everyone at her heels was already dead. Cursing, she ran faster, didn't see the woman who'd fallen until she was hurtling over her.

She landed. Rolled.

Valkyrie sprang to her feet, her lightning hurling the draugar back, knocking them over, sending them spinning, but there were more of them, reaching, clawing at her. She pulled out the Sceptre, and this time it was black lightning, not white, that she sent into the horde. Each draugr it touched turned to dust, but there were always more. One of them grabbed her, dragged her back, tried to sink its teeth into her shoulder. She battered it with the Sceptre and then dusted it and swept her arm wide. Three more exploded into particles, but the space she'd made for herself was shrinking.

Cursing, she shot into the air, hooked an arm over a balcony railing and pulled herself up. The street below was filled with the moaning, growling dead. She looked around for Skulduggery and the others.

A shout. Someone calling her name. Valkyrie slid the Sceptre into its holster, then climbed back over the railing and let herself fall. Before she reached the grasping hands, she veered up slightly, magic crackling behind her, and skimmed over the heads of the draugar.

There was an abandoned carriage in the middle of the crowded street, and Serpine was perched on its roof, waving with one hand while keeping a firm grip with the other. The carriage rocked dangerously, like a buoy on stormy waters. Valkyrie reached for him, but she was going too fast and their hands slapped together briefly as she passed. Glowering, she took a wide turn and came back, slowing as much as she could without dropping. Serpine grabbed her arm with both hands and she arched her back and they went upwards. He howled as his legs swayed into her energy trail. She didn't apologise.

They landed on a roof and he hopped away from her, slapping and rubbing at his trousers.

"Did you see the others?" she asked.

"Dead," he responded. "All dead."

"All of them?"

"Torn to pieces and eaten."

"You're sure?"

"Yes."

"You saw it happen?"

"With my eyes? No. But I'm sure they're dead, and if they're not dead, they're nearly dead, and if they're not nearly dead, they'll probably take ages to find, so we should just forget about them because, really, who has the time?"

"So they're alive, then."

"If you want to get technical about it, sure." He stopped rubbing his legs, and looked at her. "But how much do you like them? Would you even miss them?"

Valkyrie didn't bother responding. Instead, she stepped to the edge of the roof and looked down, searching.

Serpine joined her. "You might miss the skeleton," he said,

"but that's only because you've known him for a few years. If you truly want a friend who is smart, witty and over four centuries old – I'm available. Oh, don't make that face. I'd make a good friend. I imagine. I've never been one and I've never had one, but it really doesn't look overly complicated. Valkyrie? What do you think? Valkyrie?"

"I can hear you, Serpine. I'm just ignoring you."

The world shook as a building exploded just a few streets away.

"What the hell?" Valkyrie muttered, dodging a sudden hailstorm of stone and mortar.

"We need to leave," said Serpine. "We're in a city filled with terrified people with devastating powers. They'll probably kill us long before the draugar get around to it."

Boots crunching through rubble, she went to the other side of the roof and looked over.

"I have a plan," said Serpine. "Would you like to hear it?"

"No."

"It's a good one. It means the two of us will still be able to complete the mission. Interested? OK then. We find a Shunter, and we go back to your dimension. When we're there, we send a Teleporter to steal a few nuclear bombs from your military, and then we shunt them into Tahil na Kurge and leave them to go off."

"Nuclear bombs," Valkyrie said, scanning the streets.

"Have you heard about those? I watched a... what do you call it, it's a biography of an event, on television?"

"A documentary."

"Thank you. I watched a documentary about one of your wars and they discussed the atom bomb. What an invention! We don't have anything like that here. We have bombs, but nothing that would cause that much devastation. And the air! The genius of the nuclear bomb is that it turns the very air into poison! The land, the water, the plants, they get contaminated... Truly, a masterful creation. You should be proud."

"And that's your plan, is it? To nuke Mevolent?"

"'*Nuke*' him – is that the verb? Yes. That way, no one gets hurt."

"Apart from Mevolent, and everyone in the city, and everyone for thousands of kilometres around."

"When I said no one gets hurt, I was primarily talking about me."

"But you're fine with murdering tens of thousands of people?"

Serpine laughed. "What do you think we'd be doing by killing Mevolent? By sabotaging his portals? If we don't allow these people to invade your world, we're condemning them to stay in this one. How long do you think they'll last, surrounded by the dead?"

She glared. "At least we won't be the ones killing them."

"Mere semantics, Valkyrie. It will still be our actions that prevent them from living."

She started for the next side. "You'll probably want to start shutting up now."

He shoved her suddenly and she stumbled, almost fell, got her feet under her and spun, expecting him to be right on top of her – but instead he was struggling with a Necromancer. The shadows turned sharp and he cried out, fell back, blood spreading across his shirt.

The Necromancer was tall, her black robes hanging off her. Death had hollowed her cheekbones and drawn dark circles under her eyes. Lightning dancing between her fingertips, Valkyrie stepped between the Necromancer and Serpine as he recovered.

"You OK?" she asked, not taking her eyes off her enemy.

"I'm actually in a great deal of pain."

"Apart from that."

He grunted as he stood, and his gloved hand moved into her peripheral vision. "Remove this."

"No."

"Remove this glove and I can end her!"

"She's dead, you idiot. What do you think your gross hand is going to do – kill her again?"

"Fine," he snarled. "Then you get rid of her."

"No problem," she said, and the lightning flowed from her hand and the Necromancer hurtled backwards, disappearing off the roof. "Easy."

The shadows swirled in front of them, and the Necromancer stepped out like nothing had happened.

"Damn," Valkyrie said.

More shadows, more swirling. The old Necromancer, the one who'd come from the box. He stepped out beside the female and they stood there.

Valkyrie squared her shoulders. "Right," she said, both hands crackling.

The lightning flew from her fingertips, but the points of impact on the Necromancers' chests swirled like thick smoke, absorbing the lightning into it.

"Damn," Valkyrie said. She tried again. Same result.

"Use the Sceptre," said Serpine.

"I'm not killing anyone."

"I saw you use it down on the street!"

"They're not like the draugar. They can think. That means we can communicate with them." Valkyrie let the crackling fade. "I don't want to hurt you," she said to the Necromancers.

They observed her.

"What do you want? If you call off the draugar, then maybe we can help. Nobody else has to die."

"I don't think you're convincing them," Serpine muttered.

As if they were there just to prove how spectacularly wrong she could be in front of Serpine, the Necromancers sent out a crashing wave of shadows that launched Valkyrie backwards. As she tumbled, she glimpsed Skulduggery dropping from the sky, slamming into the Necromancers and taking them both down.

He snatched the old one's staff, but it turned to smoke in his hands and re-formed in the old Necromancer's grip.

The female sent out a spear of darkness as she got up. Skulduggery dodged it, hit her, grabbed her arm, and went to throw her over his hip, judo style. Halfway through the move, however, she turned to shadows and he went stumbling. She solidified behind him.

"So we're cheating now, are we?" Skulduggery asked, straightening up. "Very well." He took the sword from its sheath.

The Necromancers frowned at the blade, the first time Valkyrie had seen them react to something. Shadows swirled around them and they disappeared.

Skulduggery turned. "Are you hurt?"

"Yes," said Serpine.

"I'm obviously not talking to you. Did they hurt you?"

"I'm fine," Valkyrie said. "Serpine, actually, kind of helped me, sort of."

"I what?" Serpine said, eyebrow raised.

"You pushed me out of the way when the first Necromancer arrived."

"I don't remember doing that. Are you sure it was me?"

"Pretty sure."

"Well, I'm never doing that again. It almost got me killed."

She turned to Skulduggery. "How are the others?"

Before he could answer, there was a crack, and the building shook, and an explosion ripped through it and the roof came apart and Valkyrie was falling, spinning, and something smashed into her head and everything was black and fire and black and rubble and spinning, spinning and falling.

And then it all went away.

55

When Tahil na Sin fell silent, when the bodies in the streets stirred, and stood, and there were no people left alive, the horde turned eastwards, and walked. Their numbers swollen by those they had bitten, whose flesh they had eaten, they moved in stumbling, shuffling steps along the road and over the farmland and meadows, a slow-moving, unstoppable wave heading for this world's last remaining city.

Tanith and the others searched without speaking as smoke curled from smouldering embers. The streets were littered with broken glass, splinters, fallen weapons. Skulduggery found the Sceptre, and one of Valkyrie's shock sticks. If she was alive, she'd be emerging from hiding right about now. If she wasn't, then she was either part of the horde, or there wasn't enough of her left to be part of anything.

"If no one is going to state the obvious, then I will," Serpine said. "Valkyrie Cain is dead. She's one of them now; she's a shambling corpse who's forgotten that she should never have stood up again. It's time to carry on with the mission. It's what she would have wanted."

"How would you know what she'd have wanted?" Dexter asked quietly.

"I was being nice," Serpine responded. "The truth is it doesn't matter what she would have wanted, because she's dead. She's dead and, because she's dead, she's irrelevant, and the rest of us have to continue without her. So cry your tears and then put it behind you. We can't waste any more time searching."

"I agree," Skulduggery said.

Serpine hesitated. "Excellent. Good. Wonderful. Although now I'm confused as to why you haven't triggered the obedience cuff."

"Oh, yes," Skulduggery murmured, reaching into his pocket. Before Serpine could object, he collapsed into a boneless heap.

"She isn't dead," Skulduggery announced. "It would take more than a horde of glorified zombies or a collapsing building to kill Valkyrie Cain, so she isn't dead. She isn't here, obviously, but that only means she's somewhere else. Where, I do not know. If she's alone or with company, again, I do not know. But I do know that she's alive, and, because she's alive, she'll be making her way to Tahil na Kurge."

Tanith frowned. "She won't come back here? She might expect us to be looking for her."

He shook his head. "She'll be marching on, towards the target. She'll expect us to do the same. In fact, she'll be relying on it."

"How can you be sure of any of this?" Dexter asked. "I don't want to be the one to agree with Serpine, but she may very well be dead."

Skulduggery tossed him the Sceptre. "If she's dead, this will bond to you. Use it."

Dexter hesitated, then pointed the Sceptre at the wall and nothing happened. Tanith realised she'd been holding her breath.

"OK," Dexter said with a relieved smile. "She's still alive."

"Keep that for now," Skulduggery said. "She'll be wanting it back when we find her. Everyone ready to go?"

Tanith nudged Serpine with her toe. "We taking him with us?"

Skulduggery considered it. For an awfully long time.

"Sure," he said. "Why not?"

AUTUMN

56

The world was dark, and it rocked back and forth.

Valkyrie stirred from sleep, and became aware of chatter. People talking, complaining, muttering, crying.

She tried to open her eyes, but couldn't. That was strange. That was unusual. She used to be able to open her eyes at will.

Her head was fuzzy. The pain was making her head fuzzy.

Pain. That was the word for what she was feeling. God, there was pain everywhere. If ever she'd wondered what it would be like to have every single part of her alive with a burning pain, her wonderings were now answered.

Top to bottom, then: her face ached. Her jaw felt way too big for the rest of her. Her teeth clicked together with every rocking movement. It was hard to breathe. Her nose was stuffed, and only a thin stream of air whistled through. Her ear burned, like someone had slapped it. With a rock. Or a house.

A house. She remembered something about a house, about a house exploding.

Anyway: her right shoulder ached. Her whole arm, in fact. Her ribs hurt, but she was used to that. Years of fighting had resulted in more than a few bruised and broken ribs. This was a sharp kind of pain, made her want to curl up like a fallen leaf. But the slightest movement made her want to vomit, so she stayed where she was for the moment.

Her hip was sore. Her leg was sore. Her knee and her ankle. Her toes were fine, though. So that was something.

She made a sound, just to see if she could. It was weak. Kind of pathetic. She didn't mind.

The voices around her changed. Someone came close, started talking to her. A man's voice. Soothing. He said he was a healer. He said he was taking care of her. That was nice of him. Valkyrie didn't mean to be rude, but she was sinking back into darkness and his words became nothing but sounds and then they weren't even that.

She drifted.

57

She cracked open her left eye. Her right eye stayed shut. She was in a vehicle of some sort, stretched out. Her entire world was the back of the seat in front of her.

Her mind was dull, her thoughts as slow and thick as her tongue. She was thirsty, but she lacked the strength to even open her mouth.

She was held to the seat with straps. They pinned her arms and her legs. She was trapped. A prisoner. She shifted her weight, and pain exploded. Bile burned in her throat and she swallowed it, kept swallowing, swallowing the puke that threatened to rise up and choke her.

Swallowed it all, let herself relax. The back of the seat started to blur and darken.

She drifted again.

58

Valkyrie was sitting up, her head against a hard surface. Glass. It was a window.

She opened her left eye. She was in a bus-type thing, dimly lit, every seat filled. Down here, in the back half, the exotically dressed citizens of Tahil na Sin sat and fretted. Up front were the stoic, grim-faced soldiers.

The sky, what she could see of it beyond the treetops, was brightening. The road was wide, and cut through what appeared to be a thick forest. Another bus came into view, moving alongside. It was like someone's idea of a horse-drawn carriage, but from the future, without any horses or wheels and stretched to the size of a bus. Of course it didn't have wheels. Wheels were probably for mortals.

She wasn't strapped down any more. She was squashed into the corner. Beside her was a large man in an extravagant coat. He was talking excitedly to the woman on the other side of him about those terrible draugar. He seemed to take it all very personally, like they'd only attacked so that he'd have to leave his belongings behind. Valkyrie's head throbbed. Her lips were cracked.

"You're awake!" said the lady on the other side of the large man. She wore a brightly coloured coat over silk pyjamas, and a ridiculous hat. "Funwin, she's awake!"

"So I see," the large man said.

The lady leaned over Funwin's lap in her eagerness to get a good look at her. "You poor thing! Oh, you poor thing! How do you feel? Oh, you poor thing! Don't you move, I'll alert the doctor." She called out loudly from where she sat, and a moment later a young man was peering at her.

"Welcome back," he said. "I didn't know if you'd make it, I really didn't. Can you talk?"

"Water," Valkyrie croaked.

"She wants water," said the lady. "She's thirsty. Give her water."

The young doctor obliged, unscrewing the cap from a canteen and tipping the contents gently into Valkyrie's mouth. "Small sips," he warned, but she knew the drill.

He took the canteen away. "What's your name? Do you remember it?"

"Valerie," said Valkyrie.

"I'm Scorry. I'm not an actual doctor, not yet. I just heal people. I didn't know if I was doing it right. How are you feeling, if that's not too much of a stupid question?"

"My eye..."

"It's badly swollen, but it should be fine. I don't really want to mess with it. Swelling is good. It means the body is repairing itself."

"Mouth... hurts."

Scorry nodded. "You had a broken jaw. Um... Valerie, I did what I could. I had to save your life and I didn't have the training or the expertise, but I... I did my best. I'm afraid I might have failed to align your jaw properly. And the same with your nose. We'll know more when the swelling goes down, but I just feel it's important that you know that you might not look like... yourself."

Valkyrie nodded. Even that hurt. "Rest of me?"

"Broken arm, broken hand, broken ribs, broken clavicle... hip, leg, ankle... Multiple lacerations, some internal bleeding. I fixed most of it. All of it, really. But again... you have some scars. I'm really sorry."

249

She gave him a half-smile. "Saved my life."

"Yes, he did!" said the lady.

Scorry shrugged, looked like he wasn't used to praise. "We'll know more when the swelling goes down. For now, you need to sit back and rest."

She dragged her slow tongue over her cracked lips. "Thank you."

59

The lady was speaking to her. Valkyrie blinked her good eye, her brain slow to come back online.

"...saw you lying there, in all that rubble," the lady said. "Didn't know who you were, did we, Funwin? Never seen you before! But we couldn't leave you! No! We could not! We demanded, didn't we, Funwin? We demanded that the soldiers pick you up and carry you!"

"Thank you very much," Valkyrie mumbled.

"I told them there was no way we were going to leave some poor injured girl to the mercy of those dreadful things! We're a civilised society, and that doesn't stop simply because we're being hounded by flesh-eating ghouls! Every life is worth saving, I told them! Every life means something! Every life is important!"

Valkyrie attempted a smile. "Thank you."

"It's not like we're mortals," the lady said, and tittered.

Valkyrie struggled to keep the smile going.

"My name is Edwina, and this is my husband, Funwin."

"Where are we going?"

"Tahil na Kurge," said Funwin before his wife could answer. "Anyone who got out of the city will be heading to Tahil na Kurge. And from there to a world overrun with mortals."

Edwina tapped his hand with hers. "We'll start anew, just you wait and see. A whole new world. A whole new reality!" She laughed. Her nerves lent a frayed edge to her voice, something she shared with the rest of the civilians here.

But not the soldiers. They talked quietly among themselves or else they stared out of the windows in silence. One of them, a woman who'd lost her jacket, kept looking back at Valkyrie. Valkyrie avoided her eyes.

"Where do you live?" Edwina asked.

Valkyrie blinked at her. "Sorry?"

"Your home, dear. Where is it?"

"Oh. I'm from Dublin-Within-The-Wall."

"Ah," said Edwina. "I'm sorry. You've been through this before, then? You had to abandon your home?"

"Yes."

"Your family, may I ask? If it's not too upsetting?"

"They're fine. Alive, I mean. They weren't in the city when it... when it happened. They're waiting for me, actually, in Tahil na Kurge."

"Some good news," Edwina said, nodding. "Did you hear that, Funwin? Some good news."

"Good news," he echoed, and looked at Valkyrie again. "What are you, then? Are you a soldier?"

"Funwin, don't pry."

He frowned. "How is this prying? I'm asking a question. She looks like a soldier, does she not? Big and strong. Nothing wrong with being a soldier. They fight for us and they keep us safe."

"Yes, they do," said his wife.

"Soldiering is a respectable profession," Funwin continued. "I had notions of joining the military when I was a younger man. A life of adventure, of glory and honour... It practically called to me, so it did."

Edwina nodded. "I remember you saying that."

"But my parents wouldn't hear of it, and my family had a certain standing and a certain bearing, I suppose you could call it. My father impressed upon me the responsibilities of the aristocracy, and told me to rid myself of such fanciful notions as heroism. Some days, when the pressures of the world begin to weigh upon my shoulders, I wonder if I should have ignored everything my parents said, and joined the military despite them. I think I would have made a marvellous general."

"But then you would never have met me," said his wife and they both laughed. When the laughter dried up, they looked at Valkyrie expectantly.

"I'm not," said Valkyrie. "A soldier, I mean."

"Oh," said Edwina. "Then what do you do?"

Valkyrie didn't know what the hell kind of professions they had in this stupid world, but she was pretty sure they had books, so she said, "I'm an author."

Funwin peered at her. "An author, you say? Of novels?"

"Like my uncle before me."

He grunted, obviously not thinking much of that. "I suppose people need books," he said grudgingly.

"I've never met an author before," Edwina said excitedly. "What kind of novels do you write?"

"The kind where horrible things happen to horrible people."

"Sounds positively ghastly."

Valkyrie shrugged and sat back. "It can be."

60

It was the first day back at school, and Corrival Academy was alive with the chatter of students.

The First Years – identified not only by the yellow ties and piping on their black blazers, but also by their ridiculously tiny size and huge, bewildered eyes – huddled together in little groups and did their best not to be swept away on the tide. Second Years, with their blue ties and piping, swaggered with the confidence that could only come from no longer being the pipsqueaks in the school. Third Years, with their purple ties, and Fourth Years, with their green ones, jeered and laughed and whispered conspiratorially whenever teachers walked by.

Omen's fellow Fifth Years, with their red ties, were altogether too cool for any of this. The Sixth Years, in their black, were probably all in their common room.

"Hello, Omen," said a girl.

Omen turned, smiling immediately when he saw Axelia Lukt.

Sweet, beautiful, wonderful Axelia Lukt. Her of the golden hair and the wide smile and the tight trousers. The girl to whom Omen had confessed his... Love was perhaps too strong a word. Like, then. The girl to whom Omen had confessed his like, who had then told him she didn't think of him in that way, but valued him nonetheless as a friend, and hoped he would continue to be one.

"Hi," he said. "How was your summer?"

A dreadfully dull question to ask someone like Axelia, of the intelligence and the thoughtfulness and the determination, who had stood up for Omen when he needed someone to stand up for him, who had been there for him when he'd needed someone to be there, and who had sat beside him silently when he had needed company, but really didn't want to talk about it.

She shrugged. "Fine. I learned how to play the guitar and I rode horses. What did you do?"

He made a face. "I studied, actually. I had a tutor, because of all the classes I missed."

"And have you caught up with the rest of us?"

"I have no idea."

"How are you? Are you healed?"

"I'm good," Omen said, and rapped his knuckles against his belly like that was going to prove anything.

"Poor Omen. It wasn't right, what happened to you." She gave him a little smile before moving on. "And what about Jenan Ispolin? He was found guilty, yes?"

"Yes, indeed," said Omen. "I went to visit him, actually, at the start of summer."

Axelia's eyebrows went up. "In prison? What was that like?"

"It was kinda scary, to be honest. You expect prison to be intimidating, but when you get there there's this *feeling* that's coming off the place, warning you to stay away. I didn't want to spend ten minutes there, let alone the next few years."

"And how's Jenan doing?"

"He's pretending to be tough."

She shook her head. "It's so weird thinking of him in prison. He's a... well, not a friend, but someone we know. He's a classmate, and while the rest of us are in school, and doing homework, and chatting and doing normal stuff, he'll be... there."

"I think I'd feel more sympathy towards him if he hadn't tried to kill Auger and me."

"I'm not saying I liked him."

"Glad to hear it."

Axelia grinned. "Is Auger back at school also?"

"Not yet," said Omen. "He'd hoped to be, but every so often his health kinda goes backwards, you know? Like, he'll be going great for a few days and then, vooosh," and Omen sagged for effect.

"Could you tell him I was asking after him? He's always been so nice."

Omen was about to answer when Filament Sclavi spotted them through the crowd.

"Hey-hey, guys!" he said, hurrying over.

"Hi, Filament," said Omen.

Filament arrived beside them, a huge smile on his face. "Look at you two! Talking, having a laugh. So?"

Axelia frowned. "So what?"

"So is it true love?"

Omen groaned to himself and Axelia's frown deepened. "Omen and I are friends, Filament."

"But not only friends!" Filament teased. "Not just friends! Omen has already professed his love for you, Axelia – surely he needs some appreciation for this bravery?"

"No, I don't," said Omen. "Also, that was ages ago. And also, I didn't say *love*."

Filament laughed. "Look at him! He is embarrassed! Axelia, this man, he came to me for advice one day, his heart broken because you said no, you would not go out with him. We discussed all the ways in which he might woo you."

Omen shook his head. "No, we didn't."

Filament slung his arm round Omen's shoulders. "Look at him. Look at that face. How could you say no to this? Is he not your type? Would you prefer someone taller? Someone better-looking? You might get someone taller and better-looking, Axelia, but where will you find someone who loves you as much as Omen loves you?"

"I'm going to walk away now," Axelia said, and walked away.

Omen glowered as Filament squeezed his shoulders.

"Never fear, my friend," said Filament, "you shall win her heart eventually, of this I am sure."

"She doesn't want to be won," Omen said, disentangling himself.

"In the pursuit of love, nobody knows what they want until they have it, and then they realise they have never wanted anything more."

"Axelia and I are just friends, dude. I'm OK with that."

Filament laughed. "No, you are not. You only pretend to be this person, this friend! But we both know! We both know!"

Omen sighed, and didn't bother correcting him. Someone like Filament wouldn't understand that he wasn't trying to be anyone other than who he was, as ordinary and unexceptional as that may have been.

"Sure," he said, and then managed a smile. "So how was your summer?"

61

Temper Fray had a problem, and that problem was a cute little killer with short hair.

The City Guard were confident that Kierre of the Unveiled hadn't left Roarhaven, but so far the interrogations of Legion supporters and early-morning raids on their properties hadn't resulted in her capture.

Because she was living in Temper Fray's spare bedroom.

And, after every shift, Temper would go home, walk in, and be greeted by the biggest, warmest smile he'd ever been treated to.

And he very much suspected that he was falling in love.

62

The buses pulled over and the aristocracy got out to stretch their legs and hurry into the trees to relieve themselves. That's how Valkyrie had started to view them anyway – the richest, the most privileged. The most spoiled.

The soldiers kept a close eye on them, and Cicerone, the highest-ranking soldier, kept everything running smoothly.

Valkyrie used the time to do a few slow laps of the outside of the bus. It felt good to move again. Her joints clicked. The young doctor fell into step beside her.

"How's my patient?" he asked.

"Doing well," she said, smiling. "Look at me, I'm almost not limping, and both my eyes are open!"

"Very impressive. The arm? The ribs?"

"A lot better. Everything's sore, and everything's stiff, and everything's swollen, but like you said – that just means it's healing."

"I'm glad to hear it," Scurry said. "I have to say, I don't think I've ever heard of anyone taking bad news quite so well before."

"Bad news?"

"The, you know, the scars. And the bent nose and the jaw."

"Ah," she said.

He continued quickly. "I mean, you're still attractive. Still very attractive. I'm not saying you're ugly or anything..."

Valkyrie laughed, and it didn't hurt. "I knew someone once whose face was full of scars, and a more beautiful person I don't think I've ever met. And I know a woman with a flawless face and there have been times when I never wanted to see her again. What I'm saying, Scorry, is that I don't really care about ugly and pretty. I'm just happy I'm healthy. And that's thanks to you."

He smiled. "You're very welcome. I'm just... I'm glad I didn't foul it all up." The smile flickered. "That's an interesting suit you have."

She nodded. "Yes, it is."

"I had to, I hope you don't mind, I had to work out how to remove it so that I could get at you, as it were."

"Don't mind at all."

"It's a Necromancer suit, isn't it?" he whispered.

She nodded again. "It is."

"Do you mind me asking how you came to be in possession of it?"

Valkyrie stopped walking, and looked at him. "Are you asking if I'm a Necromancer, Scorry?"

He looked around, making sure they weren't being overheard. "The Necromancer Order isn't overly popular these days. I'm sure you can understand."

"I'm sure I can. You don't have to worry – I'm not a Necro. This is a very interesting suit, and a very useful one, and as for how I happen to be in possession of it... I stole it."

"You did?"

"I did."

"OK," he said, smiling more easily. "OK then. Good."

"Thanks for checking so quietly, though. It's appreciated."

He shrugged. "I was just curious, that's all. Well, if anything starts to ache more than you can handle, let me know."

"I will. Thank you, Scorry."

He smiled again, and walked off, and Valkyrie resumed her

limping. She got to the corner of the bus and stopped. The soldier, the one who'd been looking at her, stood in front of her.

"Hi," Valkyrie said.

The soldier was almost as tall as her. Strong arms and dark hair. Her nose had a bump in the bridge, managing to be both tough and cute at the same time. She had a square jaw with a small scar coming up and round her chin. She looked at Valkyrie as if she was trying to place her.

"Where are you from?" the soldier asked.

"Tahil na Sin," Valkyrie answered. She knew there was a follow-up question coming, so she kept talking. "Originally, I mean. We moved out of there when I was a kid, moved to a cabin by a lake. I don't like cities. Never have. But I had to go back when all this happened. I thought it'd be safer behind the walls."

"Nowhere is safe," the soldier said.

"Not even Tahil na Kurge?"

She shrugged. "Maybe. Maybe it's safe, maybe it'll stay safe for a while, but it'll fall. The Necromancers will find a way and the dead will get in."

"But we won't be around to see that."

The soldier shrugged, said nothing.

"Where are you from?" Valkyrie asked.

"You wouldn't have heard of it. A small town on the west coast of Italy. It's not there any more, though. It's burnt-out. In ruins. Most of the people are dead. I have a Teleporter friend. He took me back there the moment we heard, but it was too late."

"That's terrible."

"It's all terrible. My story isn't any sadder than anyone else's." She turned her head, spat on the ground. "I'm Assegai."

"It's good to meet you. Name's Valerie."

"I know," Assegai said, then looked at her again and walked off, back to the rest of the soldiers.

Valkyrie glanced at her reflection in the carriage window. Her eye was swollen and bloodshot, and her nose was bent out of shape. Her jaw was crooked. The damage altered the shape of her face so much that the young doctor had been right – she didn't look like herself.

Right now, that was a good thing. It stopped Assegai from recognising her. It kept her alive. Once they'd arrived in Tahil na Kurge, once she'd been reunited with Skulduggery and the others, she could look into fixing her face. But, for now, she was perfectly fine with being somebody else for a change.

63

Omen lined up with his class in the courtyard. They were having their Magical Creatures module outside today, in the sun. Miss Flourish, a short but wide woman in swishy skirts, stood behind a table on which she had placed two covered cages.

"Gather round, gather round," she said, gesturing for them to come closer. "Today we get out of that stuffy classroom and actually handle some of these wonderful animals we've been talking about." She got stern for a moment. "As long as everyone behaves, and nobody mistreats these lovely critters. Yes? Everyone agree?"

This was only the second week of the module, and they didn't know her that well yet, so all she got in response were murmurs and nods, with Omen murmuring and nodding right along with them.

Satisfied, Miss Flourish continued. "We won't be handling *all* of the animals you'll see today, however. Some are far too dangerous. For example..."

She pulled the sheet off the first cage. Within, blinking, was a creature the size of a small cat, with yellow fur and ridiculously large eyes. It was sitting up, its two little legs sticking out in front of it, the three toes on each foot curling and then straightening, like it was flexing to show off. It didn't have any arms or wings.

"This is a razorcraw," said Miss Flourish. "Do not let the

cuteness fool you, children. That mouth contains six rows of teeth, and fully grown adults, like this one, could bite your entire head off in one go if they took a notion to. There are only a few dozen left in the wild, thank heavens, and, as you can imagine, we do our very best to keep them away from mortals."

She pulled the sheet from the second cage, and a near identical creature blinked at them. "This," said Miss Flourish, opening the cage and reaching in, "is a fuddlewump. Completely harmless in every way, its superficial similarities to the razorcraw have led to some unfortunate culling incidents which have dramatically reduced its population size." She picked it up and tickled under its chin. "A good way to tell the difference is to look out for the coarseness of the fur around the neck. For example, this one..." She frowned, and looked back at the first cage. "Wait, no," she said, "*that* one is the fuddlewump..."

The razorcraw twisted in her grip and opened its mouth impossibly wide, giving Omen a good view of all those rows of teeth.

Then it bit through Miss Flourish's hand, taking it right off at the wrist, and there was a whole lot of blood and she screamed, and Omen's classmates screamed and ran off, and Omen screamed and ran off after them.

64

"Do you pray?" Edwina asked.

Valkyrie tore her eyes from the passing scenery and looked at her. "Sorry?"

"Do you pray, dear? Are you religious?"

"Um..."

"Young people these days, they aren't as religious as they should be. Funwin, wouldn't you say so?"

"I would," said Funwin. "Bloody kids."

"They didn't have to live through the war, you see. They didn't have to struggle against the heathens."

Valkyrie wondered how much struggling Edwina herself had personally undergone, but decided not to enquire.

"The war," Edwina continued, "was a stark reminder of what we should be grateful for, and who we should be grateful to."

"All hail their divine glory," Funwin murmured.

Edwina nodded. "All hail them. So, do you pray, Valerie? Have you fully accepted the Faceless Ones into your heart?"

Valkyrie chose her words carefully as the sky darkened and the driver turned on the headlights. "The Faceless Ones are a big part of my life," she said. "I wouldn't be here today if it weren't for them."

Edwina smiled. "It is refreshing to hear a young person say that. Isn't it, Funwin?"

"Refreshing," he agreed.

The bus slowed. Edwina and Funwin and the other Tahil na Sin aristocrats barely noticed, but Cicerone and Assegai and the rest of the soldiers had stiffened. Valkyrie looked out of the window. It wasn't a natural dark. It seemed to seep out from the treeline on either side of the road. She looked back, to the bus behind. It, too, was slowing and then, abruptly, it was lost to sight.

Darkness closed in. The rich and the wealthy finally noticed, and there were gasps and horrified shrieks as the darkness grew spears. Glass shattered as those spears came in through the windows, five in all, plunging through the heads and torsos of the passengers – aristocrat and soldier alike. One came through the windscreen and gored the driver where he sat. Immediately, the bus dropped and hit the road and Valkyrie and everyone else were thrown from their seats as it scraped to a halt.

"Necros!" one of the soldiers shouted needlessly. Valkyrie looked up through the tangle of bodies and saw the soldiers piling out of the bus, ready to meet their enemy on the road. The surviving aristocrats had no such gumption. They seemed content to wail and thrash and cry for each other.

Someone grabbed her, tried to use her to boost themselves upright. Someone else grabbed her hair, yanking on it like that was going to achieve something. Valkyrie gripped that wrist and prised the fingers open, then shoved people aside and stopped caring if she was standing on anyone's face. She tried making her way towards the front of the bus, but it was like wading through a quicksand of panicking idiots.

There was a hatch overhead, so she got one foot up on a seat and jumped, her fists knocking the hatch open. She landed on someone who squealed beneath her, ignored whoever it was and jumped again, got her fingers round the edge.

She hauled herself up. The air outside was unnaturally cold, and it was unnaturally dark, like someone had pulled a curtain over the sun. She got her knees up and crawled along the roof.

To her left, the soldiers had formed a circle, and they were cutting through the spears of shadows that came for them. A slice of a sword and the shadow dissipated, but there were always more. It was only a matter of time before the soldiers fell.

There were fresh screams from the bus. Draugar were emerging from the treeline to Valkyrie's right. Hissing, Valkyrie slid down the curved roof and dropped to the road. The draugar came for her.

She kicked one back, sent it stumbling, then ducked round another, grabbing its head and twisting. The draugr was well rotted and the head came off easily, and Valkyrie threw it at the next one that got close enough. Curling her hands into fists, she slipped to one side, making the draugar change course, arranging them in single file, if only for a moment.

She stayed bouncing on her toes as the draugr in front drew in. Her joints ached and her ankle throbbed, but it stayed strong. The draugr reached for her, moaning. Valkyrie waited until the angle was right and then stepped in with a right hook that tore its jaw off. She kicked out its knee next, heard the bones splinter as it went down, then danced back. The draugar were starting to bunch up again. She didn't mind. None of them were fresh. None of them were fast. She picked them off, one at a time, throwing precise shots.

When she was done, her knuckles were sore and eight draugar were dragging themselves along the road to get to her. She turned and the darkness swirled and a Necromancer stepped out. Shadows thumped into her chest, took her off her feet, slammed her into the side of the bus. She hit the ground, gasping, faintly aware of the cries from the passengers.

The shadows drifted into the Necromancer's hand, became an axe with a huge black blade. Valkyrie grunted, got up, still not breathing right.

The axe came swinging in and she jerked back, tripped over a draugr and fell. The other draugar clutched at her, doing their best to bite her, but she shook them off and rolled over them. The Necromancer was young, looked to be in his twenties. He had a neat little beard that he probably didn't need to trim any more on account of him being dead.

He thrust the axe towards her and the shadows leaped from it. The necronaut suit protected her for the most part, but she felt something cold and sharp slice her chin. The shadows retracted and the Necromancer kept coming, stepping between the draugar like they were inconvenient puddles and he didn't want to get his shoes wet. They didn't clutch at *him*, though. They were very well behaved around *him*.

Valkyrie backed off, away from the carpet of the dead, and he came after her, axe held in both hands now, ready to swing. She was aware of the blood running down her chin and the horrified faces of the passengers pressed up against the glass – horrified yet entertained. She would have dearly loved to give them something to really amuse them, would have loved to put on a light show, but she stifled the feeling bubbling up inside her and did her best to keep the magic down. Now was not the time.

The axe came for her head and she swayed back just enough to let it swish by, and then she lunged, grabbed him with both hands, using her body to keep the axe down by his side. Her left hand gripped his arm while her right clawed at his face, her chest against his, her thumb digging into his eye. He didn't resist the way she'd expected, and her thumb plunged into cold jelly.

Valkyrie roared in disgust and anger and slammed her forehead into his nose and heard it break. She hooked a leg round his and twisted and put him down, then hit him with a half-dozen palm shots to the hinge of the jaw and the temple and the cheek and wherever else she could hit. Then she broke his arm and kicked him away and he got up.

"Oh, for Christ's sake," she said, breathing hard.

He got up as easily as if he'd been on the ground playing with a puppy. His right arm hung uselessly and his nose was busted and his eye was ruined, but he stood up straight and didn't seem at all put out. The shadows drifted into his left hand and became the axe again.

She swung a heavy kick into his leg, above the knee. It buckled sideways and he stumbled. When he straightened, Valkyrie did it again. And again. And again. Every time he righted himself, she kicked that leg and now he was going down. But, every time he went down, he got back up again.

He was limping, though. The damage she was doing *was* actual damage – it just didn't seem to reach his brain.

Tendrils of shadows spun at her from the axe, wrapping around her arm, her leg, trying to pull her off balance. A tendril got around her throat and tightened, and then she lost her footing and hit the ground. He yanked his arm back and Valkyrie slid towards him.

She lashed out with her foot and caught that weak knee of his and he fell on her. The shadows loosened and became vapour. He was deceptively heavy. He only had one good hand, but he used it to close round her throat and then he put all his weight behind it. Valkyrie managed to snake a hand in, wrapped his arm with hers, and thrust her hips high off the ground. She flipped him, got on top, secured that arm again as she shifted her body forward, landing with her knee beside his ear. Then she threw her leg over his head, fell back, and snapped his elbow.

She planted her feet against him and kicked off, rolling backwards into a crouch.

"Stay down," she warned.

He sat up.

Valkyrie groaned as she stood. The Necromancer moved on to his good knee, but couldn't figure out why he wasn't standing. Both arms may have been broken, one of his legs, and he may only have had one eye left, but his magic could still rip her apart if she didn't stop him. He was still a threat.

"Don't do this," she whispered.

Then the top half of his head came away from the bottom half, and his body slumped sideways.

"You've got to go for the brain," Assegai said, wiping her sword clean.

"Yeah," Valkyrie said dully. "I forgot."

Assegai observed her for a moment. Then she nodded, and said, "Back on the bus."

65

Three weeks they'd been walking, doing their best to keep ahead of the draugar horde that stretched across the landscape behind them. Hundreds of thousands of the undead, moving steadily towards Tahil na Kurge. They'd been able to snatch an hour of rest here and there, an hour of restless sleep, before Skulduggery would nudge them awake and they'd have to start walking again.

Tanith was exhausted. Saracen and Dexter were exhausted. Serpine was... well, Tanith didn't much care about Serpine.

They cut through a deserted village. The draugar were a mile behind them. They didn't have time to avoid potential trouble spots.

They were passing a ramshackle inn when the wooden shutters on the top window burst open and a man came leaping out, screaming a war cry. Skulduggery used the air to catch him, and the man hung there, suspended over their heads, a rusty knife in his hand.

"Oh, dear," said the man.

Skulduggery took the knife away from him, and dumped him on to the hard-packed dirt.

The man rolled over on to his back, one hand up to block the midday sun from his eyes. "Do it, then," he demanded. "Get it over with!"

"Get what over with?" Tanith asked.

"Kill me!" the man roared.

"Could you keep your voice down?" asked Saracen. "We'd really like to not draw any attention."

The man gritted his teeth for some reason, as if he was expecting them to start stabbing him. When they didn't, he propped himself up on one elbow. "You're not here to kill me?"

"We don't even know you," said Skulduggery.

"You weren't following me?"

"I'm afraid not."

The man looked at the others, frowning when he saw Serpine. "Nefarian?"

Serpine stepped forward. "Ah! Look at you! It's been an age, hasn't it? I almost didn't recognise you, lying on the ground like that. Do you want a hand up?"

"Yes, please."

Serpine reached out, then stepped back. "I'm sorry, you smell terrible. Maybe someone else could help?"

The man got to his feet all by himself, and did his best to brush the dirt from his clothes.

"That really won't help the smell," Serpine advised.

"I thought you were dead," said the man. "Everyone did."

"I'm happy to prove everyone wrong."

"So why'd you leave the Resistance?"

"Circumstances, my friend. I would have loved to have stayed as your leader, but I feared my reputation would have caused a split in our wonderful little group. With a heavy heart, I realised that you would be stronger without me. So I walked away to a life of seclusion."

"You didn't run away in fear, then?"

"No," said Serpine. "Not at all. Who said that?"

"Plenty of people. They said you were scared."

"The only thing I feared was letting down my brothers and sisters in the Resistance."

"I'm your brother, am I?"

"Metaphorically."

"Then what's my name?"

Serpine chuckled. "What are names between family? I call you *brother*, you call me *brother*, what do we care of names? The important thing is that I came back, and I brought an elite team with me, and we're going to strike at—"

"Let's not tell people our secret mission," Skulduggery murmured.

"Yes," Serpine said. "Quite right. Suffice it to say, I am here to help."

"Sorry," Tanith said, stepping in. "I'd quite like to know your name. I'm Tanith."

"I'm Hector," said the man.

"Hector!" Serpine crowed. "My brother Hector!"

"Are you part of the Resistance, Hector?" Skulduggery asked.

"I am," replied Hector, and peered at him under the hood. "What manner of creature are you, I wonder?"

Skulduggery took down his hood and Hector's eyes widened. "You're him!" he said. "The skeleton! The one who came to battle Mevolent!"

"Skulduggery Pleasant is my name."

"And is she with you?" Hector asked, his excitement building. "The flying one, the girl called Darquesse? I've heard tales of her strength, of her power. If anyone can save this world, it's her!"

"She's not with us," said Skulduggery.

"Oh," Hector said, his excitement quickly fading. "That's a shame."

"We need to get to Tahil na Kurge," Skulduggery continued. "Can you help us?"

Hector grunted. "I'm on my way there myself, as it happens. I have a rendezvous arranged with a Teleporter that I cannot miss. You're welcome to travel with me – but I feel I must warn you: the Necromancers and their pets have the city surrounded. Did you see the draugar outside Tahil na Sin? That's nothing compared to this. I heard that the Necromancers have been transporting draugar from countries all over the world, countries that have already fallen, to lay siege to those walls."

"What's the Resistance been doing during all this?" Saracen asked.

"It was the decision of our leader to stay away, to let Mevolent and the draugar battle each other. We will fight whichever weakened side remains and reclaim this world for the good, and the just."

"That's not a bad plan," said Tanith, "if only Mevolent planned on staying within those walls."

Hector frowned. "He doesn't?"

"He plans to shunt into another dimension, and leave this one to the draugar. His engineers are building giant portals as we speak to take his armies and his people with him."

"Once they're gone," Skulduggery said, "the Necromancers will undoubtedly turn their attention to those left behind. Which means all those draugar will be coming for you."

Hector took a moment. "You should probably tell my leader that."

"Gladly. You're on your way to meet a Teleporter, then?"

Hector nodded. "Two days' walk. Will you accompany me?"

Skulduggery handed him back his knife. "Lead on, Hector."

66

A group of draugar blocked the road and the buses had to stop. Valkyrie watched with the others while the soldiers got out to deal with the undead. It was fairly standard stuff, but after the Necromancer attack the aristocrats were a lot more nervous about things like this. When the last draugr fell, everyone got out. Valkyrie sighed, and followed.

By the time she stepped off the bus, a conversation had started, and she heard Cicerone say, "We ought to continue on foot."

"Excuse me?" Edwina responded, the outrage already building behind her words. "You want us to walk all the way to Tahil na Kurge? How far is that from here?"

Cicerone scratched his head. "A hundred and fifty kilometres, maybe?"

Edwina wasn't the only aristocrat to gasp. "And how long will that take?"

"That's, I don't know, thirty to forty hours of walking. Add another ten for breaks, maybe six for sleep..."

"No," said Funwin. "We cannot physically do that. We *will* not. Most of us don't even have walking shoes! We should get back in these carriages, that's what we should do!"

Valkyrie circled until she got a decent vantage point from where she could observe the two groups – the aristocrats, and the soldiers trying to keep them safe. Assegai joined her.

"The carriages make it easier for the enemy to ambush us," Cicerone explained.

"And what if we get ambushed while walking? Those monstrous things would overrun us in moments! At least if we're in the carriages we have some protection, not to mention they can move at a distinctly faster pace than us!"

Assegai leaned in towards Valkyrie. "He shouldn't be asking permission," she whispered. "He should just tell them what we're doing."

"We'll take a vote," Cicerone offered.

"Very well," said Funwin.

"But your soldiers can't vote," Edwina chimed in.

Cicerone frowned. "They have as much right as anyone."

Edwina shook her head. "They're used to following your orders. We can't be sure their votes would be honest."

That got more than a few hard looks from the soldiers, but Edwina did her absolute best to ignore them and kept her focus on Cicerone, who looked like he was nursing the biggest headache of his life.

"If the soldiers don't vote," he said with deliberate care, "then the only people voting will be the people being escorted. Forgive me for saying this, but I doubt that most of those people would choose to walk."

"Not when we can get there faster by carriage."

"As I have said, travelling by carriage makes it easier for our enemies to ambush us. If that happens, it'll be soldiers who'll go out to protect you."

"That is their job, is it not?"

"Indeed," said Cicerone. "But don't you think, because the soldiers will be the ones risking their lives, that they should have a vote?"

Funwin looked around the other aristocrats. "No," he said. "Soldiers know the risks when they become soldiers. It's their job, it's their duty, to defend us." That got some mutterings of agreement from the others.

Cicerone's mouth was a thin, bloodless line. "Very well," he said. "Then we take the carriages."

"No, no," said Funwin. "You wanted a vote, and a vote you shall have! Everyone who wishes to travel by carriage, raise your hand."

Soft hands, many of them bejewelled, went up.

"And those who wish to walk?" Funwin said.

Nobody raised their hand.

"Captain?" said Funwin. "You haven't voted."

"I concede defeat," Cicerone muttered.

"But you still must vote, sir! Your vote must be counted! Raise your hand if you feel we should walk the distance!"

Cicerone kept his arms by his side.

"Raise your hand, I say!"

The soldiers looked like they wanted to tear the aristocrats apart on Cicerone's behalf – until Cicerone raised his hand.

"You, sir, are defeated!" Funwin announced triumphantly. "Now, we shall get back on these buses and continue our journey, is that understood?"

"Completely," said Cicerone.

Bringing himself up to his full height, Funwin spun on his heel. The aristocrats parted for their new leader, and he strode between them, his wife at his side, and got back on the bus.

Valkyrie looked at Assegai, and Assegai looked back at her. Neither of them said anything.

67

They found the Teleporter on a crumbling bridge. Hector waved to him as they approached.

"Friends," he explained, gesturing to Tanith and the others. "They have important information our leadership will want to hear."

The Teleporter's face hardened. "Is that Nefarian Serpine they have with them?"

"It is, indeed!" Serpine said, smiling broadly. "And a good day to you!"

"We're being pursued," said Hector, "by a horde so large the sun rises and sets on either side of it."

"So I see," the Teleporter grunted, eyes on the horizon. "Very well. Join hands."

They joined hands, and all at once the bridge was gone and they were in a field of long grass and it was raining.

Tanith turned in every direction, but there was no sign of any camp and no tracks on the ground. For a moment, she thought the Teleporter had brought them to the wrong place. Then she thought he'd dropped them in an ambush. But then she noticed the way the air ahead rippled, and she released her hold on the sword. Hector led them on, stepped into nothingness, and vanished. Tanith and the others followed.

Within the bubble, there were tents and carts and the long

grass had been replaced by a thick carpet of squelching, sucking mud. Men and women and even some children hurried wherever they were going with their heads down against the rain. It was cold, and the people looked cold, and wet, and miserable, and hungry, but there were only a few fires. Fires meant smoke, and too much smoke would have drifted up and out of this bubble and called Necromancers like a bright, flashing beacon.

"Perhaps you should leave Nefarian here," Hector said, after a little hesitation. "Our leadership might need to be forewarned, lest they attack on sight."

Saracen and Dexter stayed behind to keep an eye on Serpine and their stuff, and Hector led Skulduggery and Tanith through the camp. Tanith's boots sank into muck. The Resistance fighters looked at them through narrowed eyes. Those eyes widened if they were lucky enough to catch a glimpse beneath Skulduggery's hood. Whispers followed them to the centre of the camp, where the biggest tents were pitched.

A guard pulled open one of the flaps and they ducked and went through. It wasn't much warmer in there, but a whole lot drier. Six sorcerers were standing round a table, poking at maps and arguing. They looked up when Hector stood to attention.

"Got some people you might be interested in," he said.

Tanith froze, staring, recognising the old man with the beard from pictures she'd seen growing up.

"And who might you be?" Eachan Meritorious asked gruffly.

"Tanith," she answered. "Tanith Low."

He nodded to her. "And your hooded friend?"

Skulduggery took down his hood.

Meritorious's eyes widened. "Impossible."

"And yet here I am."

Meritorious came out from behind the table, walked right up to Skulduggery. He was almost as tall. "What happened? Where have you been? Where did you go?"

"I'm not him," Skulduggery said.

"Ah," Meritorious said, blinking. "Of course. You're not the Skulduggery I know. But it is good to see you, nonetheless. Is the girl with you, the one I met in the dungeon, the one with the furious birds?"

"Not at the moment," Skulduggery said, "but I came here with Dexter Vex and Saracen Rue. They're watching Serpine."

Meritorious raised an eyebrow. "Our Serpine or your Serpine?"

"Yours. The Serpine of our world is dead."

"Lucky you."

"Indeed."

"I admit, I'm surprised to find you working with any Serpine after what he did to you."

"I am nothing if not complicated."

"I'd hoped he had died, if I'm to be honest. He abandoned the Resistance before his scheming could be revealed, but there are enough here who know the things he's done. Why? Why are you here?"

"We're on a mission," said Skulduggery. "We can tell *you* what it is..." He let the sentence hang.

Meritorious glanced at the other sorcerers. "Leave us."

The sorcerers bowed and hurried out, and Hector went with them.

When they were alone, Skulduggery spoke again. "We're here to kill Mevolent."

That brought a smile to Meritorious's face. "Are you now? Well, why didn't you say so? Have at it, my friend. If only the notion had struck me, I could have averted all this!"

"We understand that saying we'll kill Mevolent is a sight easier than actually doing it, but we didn't come unprepared." He took the sword from its scabbard.

"Is that...?"

"Yes, it is."

"It's a God-Killer?"

"We have several. He has plans to take his army into our reality. We're here to stop him before that happens."

Meritorious took a moment. "So you can actually do it. You can actually kill him."

"We just need to get close enough," said Dexter. "To get into Tahil na Kurge. We'll take care of everything from that point on."

Meritorious rubbed a hand over his face. He looked tired. He looked exhausted, in fact. His skin was pale and his fingernails were dirty and his whiskers needed shaving. He needed clean clothes and a new pair of boots.

"Mevolent isn't our only problem," he said. "These days, the threat he poses is a trifling matter compared to the draugar."

"And do you have a plan to defeat them?"

"What makes you think such a plan could even exist?"

"I know you," Skulduggery said. "I've fought alongside you, or a version of you. If the draugar have a weakness, you've already found out what it is."

"Then they must have no weakness," Meritorious responded, "apart from cutting their heads off, one at a time."

"Do you know how this all started?" Tanith asked.

"Necromancers."

"Who's leading them?"

"I don't know if anyone is. All I do know is that they're infected with the same sickness – but they've managed to retain their ability to think, to reason. The strongest Necromancers have even retained their personalities. From what I can see, they're the ones in charge."

"And they're directing their forces at the cities," Skulduggery said.

Meritorious nodded. "They definitely have a plan. Have you seen Tahil na Kurge? I'll arrange for our Teleporter to take you there. Once you've seen what we're dealing with, we'll talk."

*

They teleported to a shed that stank of cow dung.

"Sorry about the mess," the Teleporter said. "It's safer to teleport to somewhere enclosed these days. You never know who might be watching. Or what might be watching."

"Never apologise for being cautious," Skulduggery said, poking his head out the door to make sure it was clear. "I myself have never been cautious, and look where it's got me. Where is Tahil na Kurge from here?"

"A few miles south. You can see it from that hill there."

Skulduggery led the way out. Tanith followed, took in a big breath of fresh air, and gagged.

"Jesus," she whispered.

They went up the hill. Keeping low, they stepped through the trees.

Tahil Na Kurge lay before them, a city whose massive walls were protected by a shimmering dome of energy. From that dome to the hill on which they crouched was a landscape filled with the moaning, rotting draugar. There must have been millions of them surrounding the city. Millions.

The breeze caught their stench and sent it washing over the hill, and Tanith covered her mouth and nose with her hands as her stomach roiled.

"Huh," said the Teleporter. "There's more of them than last time."

There were Necromancers, too, dozens of them, sitting on thrones of darkness high above it all, their attention focused on the city.

"Well," Skulduggery said, "I can definitely see the problem."

68

As was not uncommon, the topic of conversation in English class veered away from the subject at hand, and into a lively debate about life in Roarhaven.

"You don't agree, Axelia, that Roarhaven should be a city for sorcerers only?" Mr Dactyl asked as he lounged behind his desk with his feet up.

"I don't think it was thought through," Axelia said.

"Expand on that," said Dactyl.

"Roarhaven's great," she said. "I love living here. I love going to school here. It was the same back in my old town in Iceland. We get to be ourselves and not worry about whether the mortals can see us using magic. But I think it's counterproductive because it separates us from the rest of the world. We have small towns of sorcerers all over the world, and now we have our own city, and this is where we go out and about, and where we do our shopping, and where we see movies and whatever else we want to do. My parents have moved here, too, so I haven't left Roarhaven in three months."

Dactyl shrugged. "So?"

"So we're *supposed* to be mingling with mortals," Axelia said. "Living beside them, buying our groceries in their stores, going to concerts and sitting in parks and doing whatever else people do. I've never really lived alongside them, and I can tell you, from my own experience... that is a mistake."

Dactyl grunted. "Anyone agree with that?"

Omen found himself nodding along with most everyone else. This was an error. Omen never nodded. It caught Dactyl's eye.

"Mr Darkly," he said. "Anything to contribute?"

Omen blushed. Everyone was looking at him. "Um."

Dactyl raised an eyebrow. "Ooh, good point. Anything else to contribute?"

There were a few laughs. Omen smiled along with them. "Well, I mean... I suppose we're, sort of, in danger of losing touch. If we keep separating ourselves like this, then, you know, we'll forget how to act normal. It's risky."

"It is risky," Dactyl responded. "But answer me this: is it risky enough that you'd be prepared to give up Roarhaven?"

Omen didn't have an answer. No one else seemed to, either.

Dactyl took his feet off the desk and sat forward. "These are important points you're making," he said. "And it's something that is being discussed elsewhere, believe me. As mages, we have to strike a balance, don't we? We need our own space to be free, to be ourselves, absolutely we do – but we can't afford to confine ourselves to that space. If mages only live, only exist, in magical cities like Roarhaven, what are we going to be like in fifty years, in a hundred years? How alien will the mortals appear to us then? And that, ladies and gentlemen, is your homework for this weekend. A short story, imagining what life would be like now, if sorcerers had retreated from the mortal world a hundred years ago. Minimum, fifteen hundred words. Maximum, three thousand. That means nobody goes above three thousand words, no matter how into the story they're getting, or how much they're channelling their favourite author. Edgley, that means you."

The class chuckled, and Edgley Tempest grinned and nodded, and Omen sank into his seat. He hated homework.

69

The buses stopped and Valkyrie went with the soldiers down to the narrow river and washed herself in the cold, clear water. The aristocrats refused to bathe where anyone could see them, so they went, one at a time, to a secluded spot upstream, right before the bend in the bank. The soldiers didn't care who saw them, and neither did Valkyrie, and when she was done she dried off on the grassy bank and pressed the amulet to her belly and gave it a tap. The suit that flowed from it was warm, to counter the chill in the air.

"Where do I get one of those?" Assegai asked as she dressed beside her.

Valkyrie smiled. "I'm afraid I don't know. I stole this one."

Assegai laughed. "That does not surprise me in the slightest," she said, and the laugh died.

Valkyrie followed her eyes to the river, where blood was mixing with the water. It came from upstream, from around the bend, where the aristocrats bathed.

Assegai hissed at the soldiers. They saw the blood and left the water quickly and without panic. They pulled on trousers and boots and grabbed the rest of their clothes.

"Back to the carriages," Cicerone said, his voice urgent but quiet. "Assegai, take someone and check it out."

"I'll take her," Assegai said, tugging at Valkyrie's arm.

Cicerone looked like he was about to argue for a moment, then nodded. "Go. The rest of you, with me."

While the soldiers hurried back to the buses, Valkyrie and Assegai ran beside the river, keeping low. They dropped to their bellies and crawled through the long grass until they came to the top of the bank, and peered over.

Three draugar were on their knees beside the naked body of an aristocrat. His feet were still in the river, and the sound of their chewing was almost covered by the gurgling of the water, but not quite. The aristocrat's face was turned towards them. He'd had his throat bitten through.

Assegai had her sword in her hand. She passed Valkyrie her knife. Valkyrie took it.

They pressed themselves up off the ground, got halfway down the other side of the bank before one of the draugar noticed them. All three stood, having immediately lost interest in the meal at their feet. Assegai stabbed her sword through the first one's face, then sliced the blade through the second one's head. Valkyrie plunged her knife through the ear of the last draugr, twisting it upwards. She wrenched it out and the draugr fell.

Assegai looked around uneasily. "This isn't right," she said.

"What do you mean?"

"You've seen them," Assegai said. "You know what they're like. They used to roam in ones and twos, but only at the start. When was the last time you saw only three draugar in one place? These days they only move in large packs or giant hordes."

Valkyrie scanned the area behind her. "So where are the others?"

They started walking towards the road. Assegai broke into a run and Valkyrie followed suit. Now they could hear shouting. Now they could hear the screams.

They burst through a hedge, on to the road, a few hundred metres up from where the buses were parked. At first, Valkyrie's mind couldn't comprehend what she was seeing. There were just too many of them. They filled the landscape, like ants, or black-bodied flies crawling over fresh roadkill. They filled the carriages, feasting on the aristocrats who'd had nowhere to run. The soldiers, the few that were left standing, were trying to fight and trying to run and failing at both. Briefly, Valkyrie saw Scorry's terrified face in among the crowd, and then the horde closed in and he was gone.

Assegai sagged, almost dropped. Valkyrie caught her, moving them both backwards, into the hedge, and put her finger to her lips. Assegai's eyes were glazed with shock, but Valkyrie knew that they would soon sharpen with rage – and rage drove people to make mistakes.

Taking Assegai by the wrist, her other hand wrapped round her, cupping her shoulder, Valkyrie led her back, out of the hedge and away from the road. Assegai didn't resist, not until they were through some trees. Then she started twisting, trying to break free.

"Not yet," Valkyrie whispered.

Assegai grunted, gave a kind of whine, but Valkyrie wouldn't release her grip. Finally, Assegai shook her head and shoved Valkyrie away. Her eyes were sharp now. Full of rage.

She fell to her knees, hands at her face, fingernails digging into her skin. Valkyrie jumped forward, wrapped her arms round her again.

"Quiet," she said firmly. "You want to scream, you scream, but you do it quietly."

"Dead," was all Assegai could utter.

"I know," said Valkyrie. "I know." She squeezed her tighter and Assegai bent forward, her mouth open, and she screamed silently towards the ground.

70

They walked.

"They were family," Assegai said, her voice dull. "My brothers and sisters. Cicerone was... I never knew my father, but Cicerone was as close to a father as I've ever had."

"You couldn't have saved them," Valkyrie said.

"I could have tried."

"You'd have died right along with them."

"Exactly," Assegai said. "I would have died beside them because that was my place."

They walked on.

"I killed my sister," Valkyrie said.

Assegai looked at her, said nothing.

"I had to do it," Valkyrie continued. "Or I thought I did anyway. At the time, it looked like it was our only chance. I mean, I brought her back. That's an important part of it all, I suppose. But I can't escape the fact that I had to kill my little sister." The breeze picked up. "I think I can forgive myself for it, though. A little. Or at least, I don't have to be so hard on myself. This is how life goes, isn't it? You stumble your way through it, doing what you think is best, and it's only afterwards that you can step back and point out all the other avenues that were open to you, that you just couldn't see. So... you either dwell on all the mistakes you made, and all the guilt you hold, or you decide to be kinder to yourself. You release some of it."

"How long does that take?" Assegai asked.

"To start forgiving yourself? Oh, I have no idea. It's taken me seven years, but I'm a slow learner when it comes to things like this."

"And she's OK now? Your sister?"

Valkyrie didn't answer for a moment. "No. Not really. I lie to myself sometimes, tell myself she's getting better, but I saw a vision of the future. I know how she ends up if I don't change things."

"So now you're going to change things."

"Damn right I am."

"I hope it works out for you. I truly do. By the sounds of it, you deserve it to work out."

"And you don't?"

"I should have been there with them."

"You were given an order. Cicerone gave you an order and you followed it. Your place wasn't by their side, not then. Your place was with me."

"I should have done something, though. What did I do? I watched. I froze and I watched."

"Because it was too late to save them."

"I didn't even try."

"Because it was *too late*. I know you're hurting, and I also know that you *want* to hurt. Right now, the pain is the only thing you can actually feel. I was the same. Forgiving myself wasn't the hard part. The hard part was getting to the point where I thought I *should* forgive myself. For way too long, the pain was the only thing I could control, and I didn't want to let it go. Even when I found ways to numb it, knowing that it was there, waiting for me, behind everything... it was almost a comfort. Like, I didn't deserve to be at peace, and, so long as the pain was there, I never would be."

Assegai shook her head. "You don't understand. You don't get it."

"No," Valkyrie said, turning to her. "I don't. No one does. I went through my own thing. You're going through yours. We all deal with our own traumas in our own ways. So I don't understand everything you're going through. But you need to hear these words, and you need to remember them. They might not be of much use to you now, because you've got your grieving to do, but, at some stage in the future, they might help. Maybe."

"Did you have someone helping you? After it happened?"

"I did," said Valkyrie. "But I didn't want to hear it, so I went away."

"You might be right," Assegai said. "You're probably right. But I don't care. At this moment, I don't want to feel better. I just want to kill some draugar."

"Well," said Valkyrie. "I'm pretty sure you'll get that chance."

71

Something shaking him, stirring him from sleep.

"Wake up."

"*Wuh?*" murmured Omen.

"Wake up, you dope."

Omen cracked open his eyes. His tongue was thick in his mouth and his brain was foggy. "*Wuh?*" he said again.

"Get up." It was Gerontius. Behind him, Morven was tying his dressing gown and stuffing his feet into slippers.

Omen sat up. "Fire alarm?"

Gerontius frowned at him. "Fire alarm? Can you hear a fire alarm?"

Omen listened. "No," he said at last.

"It's not a fire alarm," Morven said. "It's a midnight feast. Let's go."

Confused, Omen allowed himself to be pulled out of bed. He put his slippers on and looked around for his dressing gown, then realised Gerontius was wearing it. It looked tiny on him. Omen pulled a hoody on over his T-shirt and followed the other two through the door. They crept on, joining a stream of other boys on their way out of the dorm. They hooked up with the girls in the corridor outside.

Omen found Never, hurried up to her. "What are we doing?" he asked.

"Midnight feast," she whispered back.

"Why?"

Never shrugged. Omen lost his slipper, went back for it, then caught up again.

"I've never had a midnight feast," Never said. "Have you?"

"In school?" Omen answered. "Well... no."

"Exactly. We can't go through our entire boarding-school existence without indulging in a few boarding-school traditions. A midnight feast is one such tradition."

"Oh," said Omen. "OK. But I'm not really hungry."

"Omen, seriously, do not spoil this for me."

"Right, sorry."

There were about twenty of them altogether, all whispering and giggling and shuffling along the corridors.

"Wouldn't it be easier for you to teleport us to the kitchen?" Omen asked.

"That'd defeat the object," said Never. "The journey is half the fun. Most of the fun, probably."

A signal, and they all stopped and crouched and froze. It was Axelia, out in front, at the next corner. Her hand was up, fist closed. Suddenly it opened, and pointed forward. In twos and threes, they started moving, scuttling across to the corridor beyond.

Omen and Never were the last to hurry up to her.

"Teacher on patrol," Axelia whispered. Omen took a peek, saw Miss Gnosis. "Let's go."

Axelia and Never moved on, didn't look back, but Omen stayed where he was. Miss Gnosis looked so sad. He chewed his lip.

Then he stood, and started walking. Miss Gnosis heard him approach and looked up.

"Omen," she said. Her voice was soft, but seemed ridiculously loud in the quiet school. "What are you doing up?"

"I couldn't sleep, miss," Omen said. "Thought I'd go for a walk."

"Students aren't allowed out of their dorms."

"Yeah," said Omen. "Sorry. I just felt like a proper walk."

"Well, you'd better get back."

He nodded, turned to go, then turned again. "Are you OK, miss?"

She looked at him, her face half hidden in shadow. "I'm fine, Omen."

"It's just, Valkyrie's been gone for a while, and…"

"I know," Miss Gnosis said.

"Are you worried about her?"

"No, of course not. This is Valkyrie Cain and Skulduggery Pleasant we're talking about here. They can handle whatever…" Her voice faltered and she looked away, blinking. When she'd recovered, she looked back and smiled sadly. "Yes," she said, "I'm worried. But I understand that there are a thousand different things that could have stopped them from returning. A million different reasons. I'm worried, and I miss her, but she'll be all right, and she'll come back the moment she can. Are you worried?"

Omen nodded. "But they'll be fine."

"Yes, they will."

"How's her family doing?"

"I'm keeping them up to date," Miss Gnosis said. "Doing my best to reassure them. It's not easy when there's no news, but I'm doing my very best."

"Um… if you ever need to talk to someone…"

Her smile widened, yet grew even sadder at the same time. "Thank you, Omen. You're a good kid. But you'd better get back to your dorm, OK?"

"OK," said Omen, and headed back the way he'd come. When he reached the corner, he risked a glance, saw that she was already walking away. He turned left instead of right, and continued on towards the kitchen.

72

Tanith pushed open the tent flap and walked in, Skulduggery behind her.

"I have a mission for you," Meritorious said, getting to his feet.

"We already have a mission," Skulduggery responded.

"I appreciate that," Meritorious replied, "but, since we're all stuck in a holding pattern right now, I didn't think you'd mind passing the time with something new. Especially seeing as how your team has been taking full advantage of our food supplies."

Skulduggery inclined his head. "Of course. What do you need?"

"Mevolent assigned Baron Vengeous the task of finding out how this draugar plague began. Ten months ago, according to our spies, Vengeous left with a contingent of his most brutal warriors, and never returned. Mevolent didn't bother sending anyone after him, but we've just learned that they were headed to a fort in America, which they believed might be the source of the infection."

Tanith frowned. "I thought America had been decimated."

"It had been," said Meritorious. "It still is. Mevolent laid waste to most of it, and charred remains are all that's left. But someone, apparently, has built a fort of some description. I'd like you and your team to investigate."

"If Mevolent hasn't sent anyone after him," Skulduggery said, "that may indicate there's nothing of value to uncover."

"Mevolent doesn't care about Vengeous," Meritorious responded. "And, with the portals so close to completion, he's stopped caring about how the plague started, too. But *I* care, because all knowledge is valuable, and the more we learn about who or what is behind this, the better prepared we'll be if we have to face it."

"Vengeous is beyond capable. If he hasn't returned, that means he's probably dead. You're asking us to walk head first into danger."

"I am," said Meritorious. "But I'm also threatening to kick you out of our camp if you don't co-operate."

"So we don't really have much of a choice."

"I'm afraid not."

Skulduggery nodded. "Then we would be delighted to volunteer."

73

Darquesse stood in the kitchen, eyes on the whirring microwave.

"I have cravings now," she said. "They appear and there's nothing I can do about them."

"Nothing?" Sebastian said.

"Well... not nothing. I could make them go away. I'm in complete control of every single aspect of this process. But I don't want to make them go away. I think it's important to go through it. So I'm microwaving beans."

"What's it like," he asked, venturing further into the room, "to have something growing inside you? And not in a weird way. Have you ever seen the movie *Alien*? Not in an *Alien* kind of way. In a... in a baby kind of way."

"I've seen *Alien*," Darquesse said. "I've seen *Aliens*, too. This isn't like that."

"I'd hope not."

"Do you want to know how it feels?"

"Yes."

She came over. "I don't mean do you want me to tell you how it feels. I mean do you want to *know* how it feels? I can show you. I can share the feeling with you, if you'd like."

"You mean... you mean the feeling of being pregnant?"

"Yes."

"But just the feeling, right? Not the actual pregnancy?"

296

"Right."

"So, just to be sure, you wouldn't be making me pregnant."

She tilted her head. "You can't get pregnant."

"See, yeah, that's what I was thinking. Um... sure. OK. I'd love to see what it's like to be pregnant."

"Very well," Darquesse said.

A storm of feelings whirled in Sebastian's mind, crashed through his thoughts, scattered any sense of who he was and filled his head with something else. Warmth. Love. Connection. A connection he'd never felt before. A connection he'd been missing his entire life.

The microwave pinged and the storm of feelings vanished from his mind and Sebastian realised he was sitting on the floor. Darquesse emptied the pot of beans on to a plate, took the plate to the table, and Sebastian made a sound, like a gurgle, and fell over.

74

Draugar ahead. And screams.

Valkyrie and Assegai crouched low, stole up to a couple of trees and stayed there, watching. There was a farmhouse, big and well constructed. A sorcerer's farmhouse. They could see a dozen draugar outside, and movement inside.

Valkyrie hefted the axe in her hands. It was a sturdy weapon that had served her well in the last few days. She started forward, but Assegai grabbed her arm.

"Wait," she said. "Look."

Valkyrie looked. Living people burst from the farmhouse, scrambled towards the barn, cutting themselves off from the escape route.

"They're mortals," Assegai said.

Valkyrie pulled her arm free. "So? You wanted to kill draugar, right? Well, there's a whole bunch of them right in front of you."

She didn't wait for Assegai's response before starting down the hill. By the time she got to the bottom, Assegai was behind her.

The axe took a chunk out of the nearest draugr's head. It toppled over and Valkyrie swung again and caved in a skull. Assegai's sword flashed. Heads tumbled from necks.

Valkyrie kicked, grunted and swung that axe. Some of the draugar were turning. They tried to grab her, but she kept moving, darting just out of reach, then lunging back into the fray. Her arms were growing tired. The axe was getting heavy. They were all around her now.

She couldn't see Assegai, couldn't hear her over the moans and the groans and the wailing mortals. She had no choice. She had to risk it. Keeping her free hand low, she unleashed a little lightning, just to keep the dead at a respectable distance. She shoved her way free and turned, backing up, watching them come after her. She picked off the closest with the axe.

One of them barged into her from the side. Valkyrie slipped, went down, the draugr on top. It snapped at her. She shoved it off, rolled. The other draugar trampled over her fallen weapon. She scrambled round the corner of the farmhouse, gave herself plenty of room. When enough draugar had come after her, she let the lightning course through her fingertips and fried them where they stood.

When the last of them had dropped, there was a sudden silence. No more moans. No more groans. No more wails.

"Assegai," Valkyrie called, hurrying back. "You OK?"

"I'm good," Assegai answered.

Valkyrie came round the corner, stepping over the draugar she'd killed, stepping between the draugar Assegai had killed. The barn door was open. Movement inside.

A mortal man came stumbling out and Assegai was right behind him, plunging her sword through his back.

Valkyrie froze. The man fell to his knees, and Assegai pulled the blade out and prepared to take his head.

Valkyrie rammed into her, taking her off her feet, flinging her sideways. Assegai hit the ground and sprawled over the bodies of the draugar before scrambling up, sword ready.

"What the hell are you doing?" she yelled.

Valkyrie crouched by the mortal as he fell back, catching him in her arms. His eyes were open, his face slack.

"We were helping them," she said numbly.

"Helping who?" Assegai responded. "The mortals? Why would we help them?"

Valkyrie laid the man down, and stood. "We were saving them."

Assegai stared at her. "They're just mortals."

"Where are the others?"

Assegai nodded back to the barn. "In there."

"You kill them, too?"

"What does it matter? They're not real people."

"You killed them. You murdered them."

Assegai's eyes narrowed. "You're one of those sympathisers, aren't you? You think they deserve to be treated like us."

Valkyrie let out a long, slow breath. "I'm more than a sympathiser."

Assegai's lip curled. "You're one of the terrorists."

"No," Valkyrie said, "I'm something else."

Assegai came for her and Valkyrie blasted her backwards, sent her tumbling head over heels into the bushes. Then she picked up Assegai's sword and started walking east.

75

Filament came forward with a series of punches and kicks and Omen stumbled back, barely managing to dodge the worst of them. Above the cheers and jeers and laughs, every once in a while he could hear his own name, shouted alongside Filament's. That meant there were actually people on his side – or at least people who had decided to support both fighters. That was still quite a new experience for him.

Hunnan, the combat instructor with all those muscles, paused the fight when Omen backed out of the circle, and the fighters quickly repositioned themselves at their respective lines. Filament was breathing slow and even. Omen panted, his gloved hands dropping. Hunnan smacked his elbow and Omen dutifully raised them again.

"Ready," Hunnan said. "Fight."

Filament hopped in with a jab, followed by a straight, then spun with a kick, and Omen swayed away from each one until he was right on the edge of the circle. Filament fired off a side kick that Omen absorbed through his crossed arms, but it knocked him back anyway.

"Break," said Hunnan.

Grinning, Filament knocked his glove against Omen's as they returned to the centre. They bowed to each other and retreated to the edge.

"OK," Hunnan said, "good class. See you back here next week. Get going. Omen, could you stay for a moment?"

Omen hung around while his classmates filed out of the dojo. When they were gone, Hunnan turned to him. "You have a thing about losing, Mr Darkly?"

"Sir?"

"Filament's fine," Hunnan said. "He learns the moves, he executes the moves, and rarely does he do anything wrong. I mean, he doesn't do anything amazingly right, either, but that's the price you pay. But surely you can see the weaknesses in his game."

"Some of them," Omen admitted.

"So why don't you exploit any of them?"

Omen shrugged.

"Uh-uh," said Hunnan. "I'm not letting you get away with a shrug and a mutter. I'm going to need an answer from you."

"I don't know," Omen said. "I don't have the killer instinct, my dad says. People with killer instinct see an opening and they go for it. I see an opening and I don't really want to."

"Why not?"

"I don't want to hurt anyone."

"This is combat class. You're being trained to hurt people."

"Yes, sir, I know, but..."

"You've hurt people before, out in the real world."

"Yes, sir."

"Jenan Ispolin springs to mind."

"He attacked us."

"And you hurt him."

"In self-defence."

Hunnan regarded him. "When I learned that the Darkly boys were going to be in my combat class, I was excited. Not every instructor gets to train a Chosen One. But, after my very first lesson with Auger in the class, I knew it wasn't going to be as good as I'd hoped. You know why?"

"Because he's already trained."

Hunnan nodded. "He's already trained. The best instructors in the world have trained him, which means there's nothing left for me to do. I'd watch him spar with the other students, and I'd see him at a fraction of his ability. He spent more time helping the people around him than doing anything for himself."

"He's always been like that."

"But you," Hunnan continued, "I became interested in training you. I mean, you were there with him, weren't you, while all these instructors came in?"

"Yes, sir."

"But you had none of his natural gifts. None of his advantages. And, from what I understand, you were little more than a punchbag."

Omen shrugged. No point arguing with the truth.

"But you still know more than all of your fellow students combined. They see combat as another class to take, another subject to learn, and memorise, and pass the test on. But you see the reality."

Omen didn't say anything.

"I want to see more from you, Omen. I expect more from you. All those years of being the punchbag has affected you in ways I can't understand, but here, in this class, I'm going to need you to start punching back. Do you understand me?"

"Yes, sir."

"You can coast along in your other subjects. You can do the bare minimum if you want. You can daydream and be a slacker. But, in my class, I want to see a different Omen Darkly. I want the serious one. The dedicated one. You might not have been born with a killer instinct, but, from this point on, you will be learning it."

"OK."

Hunnan nodded. "Off you go now."

76

The front door burst open. Temper sprang out of his seat. Rune stormed into the living room, and behind her the doorway was filled with the hulking mass that was Strosivadian of the Unveiled.

Rune grabbed Temper, slammed him against the wall. "Where is she?"

There wasn't any point in denying it. But he did anyway. "Where's who?"

Rune flung him across the room and Strosivadian caught him.

"Hello again, Temper," Strosivadian rumbled.

"Hey, Stros. How you been?"

"I have been better. My little sister is associating with a disreputable sort of man. He used to be a follower of the Faceless Ones, but he chose the wrong church."

"Bummer."

"And then he became a policeman."

Temper winced. "My sympathies."

Strosivadian brought Temper in really, really close. "Where is she, Temper?"

"I'm here," said Kierre.

They looked around. Kierre of the Unveiled, standing there in one of Temper's T-shirts and bunny slippers.

"Oh, sister," said Rune, "what has he done to you?"

"We're in love," said Kierre.

"What did you do to her?" Strosivadian growled.

"Strosivadian, stop it," Kierre said. "Put him down this instant."

Temper was dropped to his feet and smoothed out his shirt.

"We've been looking for you for months," said Rune. "Why haven't you contacted us?"

"Because I knew you'd come looking for me. I'm happy here."

"You're not safe. If we found you, the City Guard will find you. Our dear brother will find you."

"Damocles wouldn't hurt me," said Kierre.

"Of course he would. He'd cut your throat, just like he'd cut any of ours."

"Rune, please..."

Rune softened – but not by much. "I'm sorry, Kierre. I really am. But Serafina demands that we move you."

"Retrieve your belongings," Strosivadian said. "We are leaving now."

Kierre took in a breath to start arguing.

"They're right," said Temper. "Hoc will find you. He's an idiot, but he's not stupid."

A nod, a tear, and she slipped back into the bedroom.

Strosivadian's huge hand patted Temper's shoulder – and then slowly squeezed it. "If you have dishonoured my sister..." he said, leaning down.

"Strosivadian, leave it," said Rune.

Strosivadian muttered something horrible, and took his hand away.

Kierre came out, dressed in black. She kissed Temper and he held her in his arms.

"I love you," he said.

"Of course you do," she replied.

Then she left with her siblings.

77

They watched the fort for two days. The gate stood open; the wooden buildings sagged. Empty windows showed nothing but darkness. Occasionally the wind would bang a door against a wall. No sign of Vengeous or his people – not in the fort and not in the surrounding area.

Tanith couldn't even call it countryside. The land was blackened as far as the eye could see. Nothing grew. No birds flew and no animals scavenged. She couldn't even hear any insects.

By all appearances, the fort was deserted. By all appearances, the fort was perfectly safe. There was only one problem.

"I still can't see into it," said Saracen.

"The one thing you can do," Dexter muttered, "and you can't even do it."

Saracen held his coat closed against the cold, and shrugged. "Whatever's stopping me from looking through those walls is still in effect."

"Does that happen often?" Skulduggery asked.

"That someone would go to this kind of trouble, to protect against someone with my power? It's happened once before. The sigil-work involved is... intensive. Most people just don't have the skill, let alone the knowledge. So this tells me one of two things. Either somebody in that fort is lying in wait and they've got an ambush to spring, or somebody in that fort *used* to have an ambush to spring, and now they're gone and they never bothered to dismantle the sigils."

Skulduggery thought about it for a bit. "I'm going in," he said. "If it's a trap, I'm the only one who can fly out again. The rest of you stay here. If it *is* a trap, and they catch me, you know what to do."

Dexter nodded. "Yes, we do."

"Good," said Skulduggery. "And just to make sure we're all thinking the same thing, you're to come in and rescue me."

"Oh," said Dexter.

Skulduggery tilted his head. "That wasn't what you were going to do?"

"No, no, it was."

"It doesn't sound like it was."

"If it's a trap, we'll rescue you."

"It sounds like you were going to leave me."

"No. Not at all. Not any more."

"Maybe I shouldn't go in," Skulduggery said. "Maybe we should send Saracen in."

"I would love to go in," said Saracen. "But I almost twisted my ankle right after the Teleporter left and it's still a bit tender."

"You know the sad part?" Tanith asked, and they all looked at her. "I have no idea if any of you are being serious right now."

"Then my work here is done," Skulduggery said, and rose into the air.

He floated over the walls of the fort and slowly descended. As he touched down, he whistled – sharp and piercing. They waited.

The first draugr appeared from the darkened doorway, but it was quickly shoved aside by the others that came after it.

"Yay," Saracen said without enthusiasm, "more violence."

Sword in one hand, God-Killer dagger in the other, Tanith led the charge to where Skulduggery battled. She ran through the open gate and launched herself at the dead, flipping and kicking and slicing. Dexter and Saracen waded in after her, the air punctuated with the sounds of muffled gunfire. Serpine blasted draugar with his left hand, swung Valkyrie's shock stick with his right.

Another door burst open. More draugar ran out.

All fairly standard. No great threat. Nothing that they hadn't faced before.

When it was done, Tanith wiped the bits of draugr from her sword blade. "Everyone OK?" she asked, as she always did after a skirmish. "No one got bitten or anything?"

"I'm uninjured," said Serpine.

"We don't care. Dex?"

"I'm good."

She looked at Saracen, frowning when he hesitated.

"We may have a problem," he said, pulling up his sleeve and showing them the small but bloody bite on his forearm.

Skulduggery strode forward. "Tanith, give me your sword. We'll take the arm and hope the infection hasn't spread too far."

"Skulduggery, no," Saracen said.

"This doesn't have to be a death sentence."

"It's too late."

"Let him take your goddamn arm!" Dexter snapped.

"Then what will we do about this?" Saracen asked, pulling aside his collar and showing them the bite on his neck. "You gonna take my head, too?"

Skulduggery stopped. Dexter sagged. Tanith covered her mouth with her hand.

"I ran out of bullets," Saracen said. "And they were too close for me to use the bow. You know, it's times like these, when I find myself unarmed and surrounded by things that want to eat me, that I really regret my power choice." He laughed without humour. "It's funny, isn't it? The choices we make as kids could end up killing us later."

The group remained quiet.

Serpine stepped forward. "I understand what a sad moment

this is for everyone," he said solemnly. "But, if you need me to kill him, I will reluctantly do my part."

"You're not killing me," Saracen told him.

"I am merely offering my services as an impartial member of this team."

"It won't be you. It will never be you." Saracen sighed. "But he's right. It's only a matter of time before I turn. Someone has to take me out."

"When the time comes," Skulduggery said. "Not before."

"The longer we leave it, the more dangerous I'll be."

"We can handle you," said Dexter. "You're not that dangerous."

"I'm quite formidable."

"You pose very little threat. We'll be fine."

"What if I turn in the middle of the night or when you have your back to me?"

"Saracen, no offence, but, when you turn, you'll be the single most rubbish draugr who's ever moaned. We can handle you, OK?"

Saracen smiled, and nodded, then stopped smiling. "See, now I'm starting to feel a little insulted."

"Come on, idiot," Dexter said, opening his backpack, "let's get you patched up."

They found somewhere to sit, and Tanith walked over to Skulduggery. "Do you think, maybe, there might be a cure?" she asked, keeping her voice down.

"I'm afraid I've never heard of one," Skulduggery said.

"But the Necromancers must know something about it, right? It doesn't affect them like it affects other people, so they might know something."

"It's unlikely."

"Then maybe Valkyrie can do it. She healed herself, didn't she? In the High Sanctuary, she copied that doctor's power and she improved on it and healed her broken bones and she even grew new teeth. Maybe she can heal Saracen."

"It's... possible."

"We just need to find her, then grab a healer that she can latch on to." Tanith glanced over at Saracen. "How long do you think he has?"

"It's hard to say. For Proinsias, it was a couple of hours – but Saracen has magic on his side. That might buy him some time before the infection takes hold. If we're lucky." He took out his silenced pistol. "But, from here on in, we stop taking chances. Every draugr we meet is a distinct threat."

She nodded. No arguing with him there.

When Saracen's injuries were bandaged, they stepped carefully through the door into the main building.

"We're alone," Saracen said.

Dexter glanced back at him. "The sigils are down?"

"They were only carved into the outer walls. In here, I can see through walls fine. And floors. There are corridors beneath us."

Bow in hand, Saracen took the lead for a while, and they followed him through the fort, to a wall that swung open when he pulled a lever. Holding a ball of fire, Skulduggery led the way down.

"People ahead," Saracen whispered, eyes on the wall straight in front of them. "Seven or eight."

"Vengeous?"

"Hard to say. Too dark to make out who they are."

He crept forward, and they crept after him. It was a handy power to have, this seeing-through-walls thing. Drastically cut down on the possibility of folks jumping out at you. Tanith didn't like that much, and she never had. She much preferred to be the one jumping.

They reached a junction of corridors. Saracen pointed one way, then the other, and then straight ahead. Tanith joined Dexter and Serpine and they went left. Through the darkness they moved, slowly and quietly. They eased round a corner, kept going. Tanith flexed her fingers, then gripped her sword anew.

They got to a room, a big one. Like everything down here, it was badly lit by flickering torches. Tanith was starting to hate this world and its lack of mortal innovations like the light bulb. A whole planet of sorcerers, so smug that they held all the power, and not one of them thought to invent something useful.

There were figures on the floor. Sleeping. Skulduggery and Saracen came round the corner on the other side of the room. At Skulduggery's signal, they all started moving in.

One of the figures sat up. A man. To Tanith, he was nothing but a dark outline.

He opened his mouth.

Tanith knew this because of the light that burned within his throat, that came out in a stream of energy that sizzled past her head. She jerked back, ducked and rolled, and the stream of energy chased her, burning through the wall behind.

Someone opened fire and the stream cut off as the Warlock stumbled, but now the others were awake, and they were scrambling up, and their mouths were opening.

Tanith launched herself at one of them, her sword slicing through his fingers. She kicked him back and he went tumbling, and she plunged her blade through his chest. The gloom was punctuated with energy streams and fireballs, and the air was filled with the sounds of muffled gunfire. In this enclosed space, it didn't sound that muffled.

Hands clutched at her and Tanith sent out an elbow that crunched into a nose. She spun away and brought the sword down diagonally. Light spilled from the wound, blinding her. She stepped back, cursing, got a boot in the chest that sent her head over heels. She lost her sword along the way, but got up, blinking madly. An indistinct shape loomed before her. She was picked up, thrown down, kicked. She got a hand beneath her and sprang sideways, did a flip, landed upright. The shape came for her again and she weaved out of range while she waited for her vision to right itself. She saw the cut she had made, the one with all that light leaking out, and at least now she had a target.

She jumped with a spinning kick, the kind of kick that needed precise timing when dealing with an onrushing opponent. But Tanith had always been good with timing. Her heel cracked into the hinge of a jaw. She landed and the Warlock crumpled at her feet.

"Everyone OK?" Skulduggery asked.

Blinking the last remaining spots from her vision, Tanith joined in the quiet chorus. Guns were reloaded. She picked up her sword.

"Saracen," Skulduggery said, "any sign of reinforcements? Saracen?"

Saracen had his eyes fixed on the wall ahead of him.

"Oh, dear," he murmured, and started to back away.

"How many?" Dexter asked.

"We should probably run."

78

They ran deeper into the fort, found a big room with a door they could barricade. They slammed it, locked it, and while Skulduggery lit the torches on the walls Tanith pressed her hand against the door and a sheen spread over the wood. After that, they barricaded it with whatever scraps of furniture they could find. When they were done, they stepped away. It seemed like a pretty paltry defence.

"Do we have a number?" Skulduggery asked.

Saracen's eyes flickered as he counted through the walls. "Maybe forty," he said eventually. "And I'm out of arrows."

Tanith handed him the God-Killer dagger. He accepted it without a word, and stuck it in his belt.

"Ammunition check," Skulduggery said.

There came a pounding on the door, deep and determined. Tanith's hands went to her pockets.

"Three clips," said Dexter.

"Two," said Saracen.

"Two here," Skulduggery said.

"Four magazines for my pistol," Tanith said.

"And I have this shock stick," said Serpine, "because I wasn't trusted with a real weapon." He held out his right hand. "But I believe the time has come to release me from this cumbersome glove."

"Not a chance," Dexter responded.

"I'm hardly going to use it against any of you, am I?" Serpine argued. "I don't know what it's like in your world, but here, Warlocks hate all sorcerers. They'll kill me with just as much enthusiasm as they'll kill you."

"You can throw energy with your left hand," Saracen said.

"But I can kill them with my right. Not hurt them, not delay them, but kill them. I have refined the Necromancer technique until it is exquisitely efficient. I understand that you are loath to trust me, of course I do, and, while it would appear redundant to point out that in this moment we have a common enemy, it seems that I must. So please, remove this glove."

From the other side of the door: a pounding.

For a moment, it looked as if Skulduggery was just going to continue to ignore Serpine – but then he stepped forward. The key twisted in the lock and the glove fell from Serpine's red right hand.

Those glistening fingers flexed. "Thank you."

The pounding got heavier.

Tanith turned away, saw something in the dark, and frowned. Taking one of the torches into her hand, she moved towards the figure slumped against the far wall. With every step, the gloom retreated, the flickering light falling on the twisted legs and the tattered clothes, on a chest that had once been broad, on a beard that had once been iron-grey, but was now silver and unkempt. On a gaunt face, hollowed with starvation.

Baron Vengeous growled. "Get that damn light out of my damn eyes."

"Found him," she called.

The others joined her. Vengeous grunted when he saw Skulduggery. Sneered when he saw Serpine.

"You're working for them now, are you?" he said, his voice cracking.

"I'll work with whoever will have me," Serpine replied. "Mevolent, the Resistance, these fine people..."

"Your sense of loyalty is, as always, your best quality."

Serpine hunkered down in front of him. "I heard you died," he said. "And then I heard Mevolent brought you back. That's where your much-vaunted loyalty has got you, Baron. It's reduced you to a lapdog whose only purpose is to obey orders."

"What happened here?" Skulduggery asked.

"Die, skeleton."

"Mevolent sent you to investigate the outbreak of the draugar virus. Were the draugar here before you arrived, or did they come after? Were the Warlocks here?"

"I will tell you nothing."

"If we know what caused the outbreak," said Saracen, "we might be able to stop it. We could save this entire world."

"It would be too late for you, either way," Vengeous replied. "That is a bite on your neck, yes? A recent one?" He laughed, and coughed. "The sickness turns living mortals within hours. But a living sorcerer? I give you two weeks before you succumb."

Skulduggery tilted his head. "You've been like this for how long? Ten months? Ten months you've been trapped down here, too injured to leave, unable to call for help. Unable to even die. Is that the worst part?"

"Or is it the knowledge that Mevolent will never send a rescue team after you?" Serpine asked. "That you aren't worth even that much to him?"

Vengeous's eyes lit up, but Serpine jammed the shock stick into his belly before he could blast anyone. Tanith moved in, shoving Serpine over with her foot, and Vengeous gasped in relief.

"We can kill you," Skulduggery offered.

"No one can kill me," Vengeous responded. "You can damage me beyond repair, you can cut off my head, even destroy my brain – but nothing will ever kill me."

"That might have been true, if this sword on my back wasn't a God-Killer."

Vengeous's face slackened.

"If it can kill a god," Skulduggery continued, "it can certainly kill you. Would you like that?"

"They killed my team," said Vengeous. "Injured me in ways I could never recover from. For close to a year, I've been down here. Every day I pray for a lasting death. Every day I pray for release."

"I'll end it for you," Skulduggery said. "Tell us what you know, and I'll end it for you."

Vengeous sighed, and rested his head against the wall. "I think not, skeleton."

"Don't be an idiot," Serpine said. "He'll put you out of your misery."

"I wouldn't expect you to understand," Vengeous responded. "I'll just sit here and watch the Warlocks tear you apart. It will be the most fun I've had in a long, long time."

Skulduggery took the sword from its sheath. "We'll get nothing out of him."

Serpine stood. "Then why are we even here? We were sent to find out how all this began, and we've found someone who knows at least some of it."

"And what do you suggest we do?" Skulduggery asked. "Fight through the Warlocks and bring him back so one of Meritorious's Sensitives can look inside his head? Do you think they'll get very far? Or maybe you're thinking of something a bit more physically painful? After all, he's willing to stay down here in the dark, for an indeterminate amount of time, instead of betraying Mevolent. I'm sure he'd break easily under torture." Skulduggery hefted the sword and turned back to Vengeous. "Anything you'd like to say?"

Vengeous sneered. "Get it over with."

"Fair enough."

Skulduggery swung and Vengeous's head came free from his body and rolled across the floor.

"Take up positions," Skulduggery said, removing the silencer from his weapon. "When they come through that door, we take out as many as we can with bullets." He walked to about four strides from the doorway, and scraped his boot along the dust. "When they reach this line, we meet them with sword, fist and magic. I don't have to tell you how hard Warlocks are to kill – we've just had a nice little reminder of that. Forty against five. The Dead Men have faced worse odds than that, haven't we?"

"Yes, we have," said Dexter.

"Yes, we have," echoed Skulduggery.

There was a lull in the conversation.

"We lost, though," Saracen said.

Skulduggery looked at him. "What?"

"The times we faced worse odds? We always lost."

"Did we?"

"Yes."

"Dexter?"

Dexter shrugged. "Now that he mentions it..."

Skulduggery tilted his head. "You sure we didn't win a few of those?"

"Don't think so," said Saracen. "If memory serves, when faced with numbers like this, we'd either be captured or left for dead or we'd have to run away."

The door, behind the barricade, was starting to lose its sheen.

"I could have sworn we'd triumphed over impossible odds," Skulduggery said. "That really sounds like the kind of thing we'd do. Are you sure we didn't? What about that time we went up against the Battalion of the Damned?"

"Ohh, they beat us bad," Dexter said. "That was dreadful. We just couldn't do anything right that day. Every move we made was the wrong one."

"The Horsemen, then. Remember the Horsemen of Screaming Rock?"

"I remember them chasing us," said Saracen.

"What about the Battle of Wretchling Hill?"

"Now *that* was a battle," Saracen admitted.

"Yes, it bloody was," said Dexter. "And a battle against overwhelming odds, at that. What was it, two thousand Wretchlings and twenty of Vengeous's finest killers against ninety of us?"

"Five full days of fighting," said Saracen.

"But we won," Skulduggery said. "After all that time, against all those enemies, we emerged triumphant, did we not?"

"We did," said Saracen.

"We did," said Dexter.

"Did we?" asked Skulduggery.

The other two looked at him.

"Now that I think of it," Skulduggery continued, "I don't think we were even there. Corrival Deuce was in command that day. We were... We were in Algeria. That's where we heard about it."

"We were there," Dexter insisted. "I think we'd know if we... Oh, God."

"No," said Saracen. "You're wrong. OK, maybe you two weren't there, but I definitely was. I remember it very distinctly. I remember when the Wretchlings made their charge, with the sun glinting—"

"—off the weapons in their misshapen hands," Dexter finished. "Exactly as Corrival described it."

Saracen sagged. "I wasn't there?"

"You boys may be struggling to come up with a situation where you've faced impossible odds and triumphed," Tanith said, "but I have plenty. Right now, though, we probably need to focus on triumphing against *these* impossible odds – what do you say?"

The sheen faded from the door. A stream of energy burrowed through the wood and the furniture and carved its way through the wall behind them.

Weapons were readied.

The door burst open and furniture went flying across the floor and the Warlocks were greeted with gunfire. Tanith's ears rang. The smell filled her nostrils. The pistol bucked in her hands. Carefully but quickly, she squeezed the trigger. When the gun clicked on empty, she switched out the magazine and went right back to firing.

The Warlocks crossed the line.

Tanith dropped the pistol and grabbed her sword and sprang forward. Skulduggery's sword cleaved through the enemy. Her own – lighter, faster – slashed and poked holes. An energy stream hit her shoulder, sent her spinning. A Warlock grabbed her, slammed her back against the wall. Her hands were empty. Where was her sword? The Warlock opened his mouth mere centimetres from her face and she winced, waiting for the brightness that would end her. Instead, the flesh flew from his skull and his corpse fell sideways.

Tanith gasped, looked round, but Serpine was already moving on. He ducked an attack, his left hand flashed purple, and the Warlock staggered away from him. Red vapour curled around his right hand and became something that twisted and leaped from his fingertips. It struck the Warlock and stripped the clothes and the flesh off its skeleton, and the skeleton collapsed. Skulduggery swung the God-Killer sword. Dexter blasted whoever got close. Saracen went to work with the dagger.

And still the Warlocks came, spilling through the door like water through the crack in a dam.

Tanith picked up her sword and roared and got right back to it.

79

Tanith lay flat on the ground, eyes open, blood dripping.

Skulduggery looked down at her. "Are you OK?"

"No," she said.

He pulled her up. She winced.

"Any injuries?" he called out to the shadows around them.

"Lots," Saracen called back.

"Any life-threatening injuries?"

"Aside from the ones I already have? None."

"Excellent. Dexter?"

"I'm OK," Dexter said, stepping into the light and looking even more exhausted than Tanith felt.

Serpine crawled over the corpse of a Warlock. "Is anyone going to enquire as to my well-being?"

"Probably not," Tanith told him.

With Saracen leading the way in case there were any more nasty surprises waiting for them, they returned to the surface – slowly, with much limping, wincing and moaning. They emerged as the sky was turning a pretty shade of orange.

Standing among the corpses of the draugar were three Necromancers.

Shadows convulsed and slashed and Tanith stumbled and Skulduggery went for his sword and Serpine jerked back from a swipe, the red vapour twisting from his fingers and tearing the flesh off the nearest Necromancer.

The other two halted their approach, their eyes on their companion's remains.

Serpine gazed at his hand. "Well now," he said. "Powerful enough to kill infected Necromancers, it seems." He looked round at Skulduggery. "I'm going to be demanding to be treated a damn sight better from now on."

One of the other Necromancers stepped forward. Black clothes, black hair, carrying a black cane, his eyebrow shifting fractionally in what might have been called surprise. Then a slight smile. "Ah," he said.

He spoke. He actually spoke.

"You're not from here," Solomon Wreath said. His voice was flat. Dead. "You're from there. The other place."

"Solomon," Skulduggery said. "It had to be you, didn't it? You just had to spoil a perfectly fine day."

"Skulduggery," said Wreath. "And is this Serpine with you? The Serpine from this world, or your world?"

"I'm from here," Serpine responded. "They needed a guide. I was at a loose end..." He shrugged.

Wreath observed them. "After all that has passed between you, you would work together. Interesting."

"You saw what I did to your friend," Serpine said. "If I were you, I would stand aside and allow us to leave."

The Necromancers didn't budge.

"The Baron?" Wreath asked.

"Dead," Skulduggery answered. "For good, this time."

"A pity," said Wreath. "I enjoyed knowing he was down there. Petty, I know, but I derive my pleasures where I can."

"Are you behind all this?"

"All this?"

"The plague. The draugar. Is this all your doing?"

"Ah," said Wreath. "No. I am too... limited. My master does not share this affliction."

"And is your master here?"

Wreath smiled, and shook his head.

"Is your master a Warlock?"

"The Warlocks are pets."

"Who is your master, Solomon?"

"My master is the Death Bringer," said Wreath. "My master has looked upon the world and decided that all the pain and suffering must end. Life is too much for any one species to endure."

"The Death Bringer wants to end the world's suffering by ending everyone *in* the world?"

"Only the suffering will end. We will go on, our souls released by death. And, when this world has been cleansed, my master will move through the portals Mevolent is constructing, and cleanse your world. And on and on until every earth has been wiped clean of life."

"This Death Bringer sure sounds magnanimous," said Saracen.

Wreath looked at him. "You will be joining us soon, my brother."

Saracen smiled. "Not if I can help it."

"You can't."

Saracen's smile dropped away. "Now, why'd you have to say that? That doesn't put me in a good mood."

"Are you here to kill us?" Skulduggery asked.

Wreath shook his head. "We merely came to investigate the disturbance you made."

"So we're free to go?"

"No."

Skulduggery gripped the handle of his sword. "We didn't come here to fight you, but we will."

"You are tired, and hurt, and outnumbered," said Wreath.

Tanith raised her eyebrow at the two Necromancers. "Outnumbered, are we?"

"Indeed," said Wreath, as shadows swirled and Necromancers stepped out all around them.

Tanith shut her big, stupid mouth.

"We have no wish to fight you, either, Skulduggery. We will allow you to depart without further harm, provided you leave Serpine with us."

No one said anything for a few seconds, then Serpine half turned to Skulduggery. "We're a team. I helped. You can't just abandon me to these things."

"Hush," Skulduggery said.

Serpine grew angry. "We had a deal!"

"I said hush." Skulduggery watched Wreath. His fingers tapped the sword handle. Finally, he said, "No. Can't do it. And it's not that Serpine has become a friend, or that I've started to respect him, or at the very least appreciate him. I do none of these things. Neither do I trust him, or value him in the slightest. I especially do not like him – I just want to make that clear. In fact, my saying no has nothing whatsoever to do with him at all, and has everything to do with me just not being in an accommodating mood today. It's bad luck on your part. If we'd met yesterday, or even tomorrow, I might have handed him over. But not today. Today I'm feeling argumentative."

Wreath looked at him for an age. "I suggest a compromise."

"Suggest away."

"You can take him with you, but he leaves our gift with us."

"Your gift?"

Wreath nodded. "His hand."

Serpine's eyes narrowed. "That's insane. That's... No. That's not reasonable. I'm not giving you my hand. It's *my* hand."

"It's a Necromancer technique."

"That *I* learned. You're not taking my hand. If we have to fight, we'll fight. Very well. Have at it."

"Just hold on a moment," Skulduggery said.

Serpine's eyes blazed. "You cannot be considering this. It's mutilation!"

"It's just your hand. You have another one."

"I say no!"

"Well," Skulduggery said, "you're not in charge."

Serpine laughed desperately and turned to the others. "Dexter. Saracen. Tanith, please. I helped you. I saved you. I saved you from that Warlock! With this hand!"

"He did," said Tanith. "Skulduggery, he did. Come on, we can't do this."

"The alternative is to fight," Skulduggery responded.

"We've fought for less," Saracen murmured.

"A lot less," said Dexter.

"Did any of you bring that metal glove up here with you?" Skulduggery asked. "I didn't. That glove was the only thing keeping him from using that hand on us."

"Why would I do that?" Serpine asked. "You're my only way off this world."

"You're not a trustworthy man, Nefarian. We don't know how far you'll go for your schemes."

"You're not taking my hand."

"I'm afraid we don't have much of a choice. It's that, or we all die."

"We can fight!"

"We can barely handle one of these Necromancers, let alone fourteen of them."

Serpine's hand was suddenly pointing straight at Skulduggery, the red vapour curling around his fingers. "This can kill dead Necromancers. I'm sure it could kill you, too."

"Very likely," Skulduggery said calmly.

"That's why you're agreeing to this, isn't it? You don't care about the threat I might pose to the others – you care about the threat I pose to *you*. You're terrified of the fact that someone has the power to *actually* kill you."

"We'll take you straight to the medic once we get back to camp."

"They're not taking my *damn hand*!" Serpine said, and his legs buckled under him and he collapsed into a boneless heap.

Skulduggery took his hand out of his pocket and walked over. "We're going to need a tourniquet."

Tanith watched as he tied a length of rope around Serpine's forearm, just above the wrist, while Serpine mumbled in protest. She looked over at Dexter and Saracen. They had the same shocked expression on their faces as she reckoned she wore on hers.

"Hold his arm out," Wreath said, and two Necromancers secured Serpine in place. A flick of Wreath's cane and a blade of shadow swiped down and sheared the hand from the wrist.

Tanith stared, her mouth hanging open. Tears of pain ran from Serpine's eyes, and then those eyes glazed over as he passed out. One of the Necromancers gave the hand to Wreath and he examined it, nodded, and put it somewhere in his cloak.

"You may leave," said Wreath, and the darkness swirled and the Necromancers shadow-walked away.

"What the hell?" Saracen said to Skulduggery.

Dexter shook his head. "That was cold."

"We could have taken them," Tanith said.

"No," Skulduggery responded. "We would have lost. This was our only chance to get out alive."

"He's not going to be happy with you when he wakes up," Saracen said.

"Hopefully, he won't wake up until we rendezvous with the Teleporter." Skulduggery took the sword off his back, handed it to Dexter, then picked Serpine off the ground and threw him across his shoulders. "Let's go."

80

Omen could feel Hunnan's eyes on him. Every time he stumbled away from his sparring partner, every time he backed out of the circle, he could sense the disapproval. Omen didn't like that. He much preferred it when the teachers ignored him.

"First to three's the winner," Hunnan said, the boredom in his voice aimed right at Omen, who was already two-nil down.

He'd paired him up against Filament again. Filament, an adequate but functional fighter, with no wit or imagination to his style. An overconfidence he hadn't earned bleeding through every swaggering move. So long as he was being ignored, Omen would have been perfectly happy to lose to someone like this. But he'd agreed to try harder for Hunnan.

They squared up in the circle. Hunnan slashed his hand through the air and Filament came forward, as he always did. Punches and then kicks. Like he always did. Expecting Omen to back away. Like he always did.

But this time Omen stepped to the side and tapped the back of his glove against Filament's face.

"Point," Hunnan called. Omen's schoolmates cheered. Filament laughed, went back to his line. Omen went back to his.

Hunnan's hand slashed the air. Filament jumped forward with a kick, but Omen was already beside him, tapping his ear this time.

"Point," Hunnan said. More cheers. Filament looking surprised. They faced each other again. Hunnan slashed the air.

Filament didn't attack immediately, but when he did he came forward in a straight line and all Omen had to do was step to the side and tap the top of Filament's head.

The crowd cheered.

"This is what happens," Hunnan said, pointing at Filament. "This is what happens when Omen tries. This is what I want to see more of, Omen. Nothing less than your best."

"Yes, sir."

"OK, early lunch as a reward. Go on, the lot of you."

They headed for the showers, and Omen smiled to himself as he listened to his classmates recap the sparring session. He was the last one to dry off and get dressed, and, when he stepped outside, Filament was waiting for him.

"That was a good fight," Filament said, leaning against the wall.

"Yeah," said Omen. "Suppose it was."

"All those other times we sparred, you could have beaten me just as easily, yes?"

"I didn't beat you easily," said Omen. "There was a one-point difference."

"Because you weren't trying. That's what Hunnan said. He said *this is what happens when Omen tries*, and pointed at me. So, all those other times, you could have beaten me."

"I suppose it's possible. But remember, my parents paid for the best instructors for Auger. I couldn't help but pick up some stuff."

Filament nodded, and didn't say anything for a bit. Then he said, "If that had been a real fight, things would've been different."

Omen nodded. "I know."

"A real fight," Filament said, "without any rules, without Hunnan telling us when to break... that would've been very different."

There was nothing for Omen to do but nod again.

"No hard feelings, though," Filament said, smiling as he pushed himself off the wall and slapped Omen on the back.

"None at all," said Omen, because he hadn't imagined there would be. He watched Filament saunter away like he didn't have a care in the world.

"I'd watch out for him, if I were you."

Omen turned. Kase and Mahala walked up.

"Hey," said Omen, and frowned. "Wait, what do you mean?"

"He's a sore loser," Mahala said. "Friendly and charming when he doesn't see you as a rival, but something else entirely if you've just embarrassed him in public."

The lunch bell went. Doors opened and students streamed out of classrooms.

"But I didn't embarrass him," said Omen, raising his voice slightly to be heard. "Did I?"

"Don't mind us," said Kase. "We're seeing bad guys everywhere we look lately."

"Probably because there *are* bad guys everywhere we look," Mahala added.

"Wait," said Omen, "you mean you're still going out there, fighting bad guys? Without Auger?"

"Trying to, at least."

"Uh... is that wise?"

"God, no," said Kase, laughing. "We're getting punched a lot more than usual."

Mahala nodded. "And we usually get punched a lot."

"Then maybe you should take a break," Omen suggested, "while you wait for Auger to get better."

"Yeah," Kase said, like there was no way they were going to do that. "Yeah, that might be a good idea."

"Is there anything I can do?"

Mahala smiled. "We have it covered, don't worry. You stay safe, OK? Auger would kill us if something happened to you."

They walked off towards the cafeteria and Omen felt lazy and lumpen all of a sudden. The corridor was emptying quickly, but there was a tall man walking towards him – dark-haired, good-looking, unshaven.

"Excuse me?" he said. "You Darkly?"

He was American. Omen nodded.

"One of your schoolfriends pointed you out," he said. "I'm a... Well, I guess I'm a friend of Tanith Low. You know Tanith Low? I'm a friend. We're... friendly. Anyway, she was looking for an item and she brought me in to help. She's been gone a while – I don't know if you know that?"

"I know, yes."

"OK then, you know what she's... Anyway, she's been gone and I've been busy with my own thing, and I still am, actually, which is why I'm here. The item she was looking for – I think I might know who has it."

"Right. OK. I'm not sure why you're telling me, though. What item?"

"It's a weapon. They didn't tell you she was looking for it? It's a knife, called the Obsidian Blade. It's for when you fight that King of the Darklands fella."

"Oh," said Omen. "Oh, no, that isn't me."

"Sorry?"

"You're looking for Auger. I'm Omen. I'm his brother."

"Ah. Right."

"And – I'm sorry – who are you?"

"Oberon. Oberon Guile. Like I said, I'm a friend of Tanith's. I guess I'm kind of a, um, a boyfriend, if you wanna put a label on it. I don't think she'd object to that, but... Actually, she might, so we'll keep that on the downlow, just you and me. Can you pass the message on to your brother, then?"

"Sure," said Omen, trying his best to keep up, "but I've never heard of an Obsidian Blade."

"From what I hear, it's the only thing that can kill the King of the Darklands," said Oberon. "Whatever it cuts, it wipes from existence."

Omen stared. "What does that mean?"

Oberon gave a brief chuckle. "I really don't know, kid. I'm thinking if you're cut with it, maybe you disappear? Or something? Anyway, Skulduggery Pleasant figured the Chosen One could use it on the King of the Darklands as a sure-fire way to kill him."

Excitement bubbled in Omen's voice. "That... that's excellent. That's brilliant! Up until now, we had no idea how Auger would actually kill him because he's, you know, the closest thing to an immortal human anyone's ever seen. But this will change everything!"

"I'm glad you're glad, kid. Apparently, it's in the private collection of a man called Devon, in Scotland. Edinburgh, I think. He collects all kinds of supernatural crap. So, I don't know, get your brother to call him up or sneak over and rob it or whatever. Your brother got someone who can teleport?"

Omen nodded.

"Well, there you go. Easy as pie."

"Thank you," said Omen. "Thank you so much."

"No problem. Hey... you *do* know Tanith, right?"

"Yes, sir."

Oberon hesitated. "She ever mention me? It's not a big deal if she hasn't. She's kind of a private person so I'd actually be surprised if she had, to be honest. It's just, I was wondering..."

"Um," said Omen, "I don't really have that kind of friendship with her."

"Right. Yeah, of course," Oberon said, looking a little embarrassed. "OK, I gotta meet up with my Teleporter buddy and skedaddle. I guess I'll see you around, Auger."

"Omen."

"Omen, right."

Oberon nodded to him and walked off, and a moment later Axelia was standing at Omen's shoulder.

"Who is *that* tall drink of goodness?"

"Just someone," said Omen, trying hard not to be jealous. "Tanith Low's boyfriend."

"She has amazing taste. Why was he talking to you?"

"There's a weapon," he said. "Auger's going to need it to fulfil the prophecy. Some guy in Scotland has it. I doubt he'll let it go willingly."

Axelia frowned. "Auger will have to steal it?"

"It might save his life."

"You have a look on your face."

Omen murmured, chewing his lip. Thinking.

"Omen?"

"I can't tell Auger. He isn't back to his usual self yet. He'd go in and he might get hurt, and then that'd set him back months. He can't afford that. He needs to be ready *now*. I'll have to do it."

"You're going to steal it instead?"

"I think so, yes. Me and Never."

"You and *me* and Never," said Axelia. "I've never been on an adventure. I want to try it out, see what it's like."

"Uh... Axelia, I don't know. It might be dangerous."

She smiled. "Don't worry, Omen. I'll protect you."

81

The cinema had a Halloween festival thing going on, they were showing the entire Evil Dead trilogy, and Temper settled in with his popcorn and did his very best not to think about Kierre.

Thirty minutes into *Evil Dead 2*, just as Ash was chainsawing his hand off, Adam Brate came and sat next to him.

"Do you know how much corn syrup they used for the blood in this movie?" he whispered. "If you listen to the director's commentary, they talk about—"

"Adam," Temper whispered back, "my girlfriend just moved out. I'm finding it hard to focus on trivia, you know?"

"Right, yeah, OK. Makes sense," Brate said, and shifted closer. "I've done my digging. Sorry it took so long. People started to talk, and question why I was asking questions, and I thought the noose was tightening, you know? So I stopped asking around for a while. Sorry."

"Understandable. Did you find anything out?"

"No, man. Nothing. Can't find any link between Creed and that German guy. Got no idea why he'd want him dead."

"Don't worry about it," said Temper.

"Seriously? I thought you'd be mad."

Temper put on a smile. "I've been doing some digging, too. Turns out Sturmun Drang was doing some investigating into ties between Creed and the other two Grand Mages on the Council of Advisors."

In the flickering light, Brate's eyes widened. "What, like... a conspiracy?"

"Exactly like a conspiracy."

"I knew it," said Brate. "I knew it! Well, not *knew it* in any real sense, but... definitely had an idea that something, somewhere, was suspicious. You need me to do anything?"

Temper shook his head. "You've placed yourself in enough danger. I'll take care of it from here on out."

"OK, man. OK. Hey, mind if I sit here for the rest of the movie?"

"Better not," Temper whispered. "We wouldn't want to be seen together."

"Ah, good idea, yeah. Sorry about your lady friend, man... I had a lady friend once. She was..." He cleared his throat. "OK, man, I'll catch you later."

Temper nodded to him. "Groovy."

82

Valkyrie flew low and piled on the speed, the rain whipping into her face and the ground blurring beneath her. She glanced over her shoulder.

The Necromancer was gaining.

She tore through some trees, snapping branches, and skimmed over a hill so close she could have reached down and touched the wet grass. There was a village on the horizon and she veered towards it. Deserted, like all the other villages she'd passed. The streets were rutted mud. The buildings ramshackle. She slowed and cut the power and dropped to the ground, hit it and rolled and ducked through an open doorway.

Crouching, she moved to the window.

The shadows lowered the Necromancer out of the sky. Valkyrie pulled her hood up and her mask down. Her life thrummed in her ears for a few seconds before she grew accustomed to the sound, and then her senses sharpened.

She slipped backwards.

The Necromancer searched the village, shadows drifting from him like vapour. Valkyrie watched silently. He wasn't the only one who could use the darkness to his advantage.

His shadows ripped a door off its hinges and flung it aside as he walked in, and Valkyrie used the noise to cover her own squelching footsteps. She slammed into him from behind and the shadows thrashed as he fell against a table that immediately collapsed under his weight. She didn't give him a moment to think – she grabbed his head with both hands and zapped him so hard he convulsed right out of her grip.

When he started to get up, she did it again.

And then again.

"Stay down," she hissed. She went to kick him in the face, but a length of shadow shot out, hit her in the chest and smacked her into the wall.

The Necromancer stood up slowly and more shadows snaked towards Valkyrie, pinning her arms to her sides and tightening around her legs. That old familiar feeling of panic started to scratch across her thoughts. She couldn't move her limbs. She couldn't breathe. She couldn't escape.

But she closed it off, that panic. She sent it into another room in her mind. It was still there, it was still writhing, but it was apart from her, and Valkyrie could think now, she could focus. She concentrated on the magic in her veins, started it building, started it crackling, and then she released it and it exploded and burned through the shadows holding her. The Necromancer was standing within its radius and he seized up, his fingers curling, his teeth bared, the tendons in his neck close to snapping.

Then Valkyrie drew it all in and the Necromancer toppled backwards.

Valkyrie approached him cautiously. She nudged him with her foot. Then kicked him. No response. She lifted her mask and pulled down her hood.

It was stupid of her, flying like that. It was what had got her noticed. It was what had got this Necromancer flying after her. But she'd been so bored, and so tired, walking those terrible roads alone. A little shortcut wouldn't hurt, she'd reckoned. She grunted. A little shortcut had almost got her killed.

The steady rhythm of the rain died away, until there was only the ever-slowing dripping of water from the roof. Valkyrie searched the Necromancer. His cloak was held by a clasp and the clasp was where he stored his power. She took it, hurled it out the door. It landed somewhere in the muck. She found a length of old rope and used it to bind his hands and ankles, and then she dragged him to the corner and propped him up against the wall. When she was done, she sat in a rocking chair and pulled her mask up, and immediately she thought about food.

Valkyrie loved food. She hadn't had any in almost two days. She had no idea how to hunt, or how to skin and cook an animal even if she killed it. And she didn't want to kill an animal. Some poor little bunny, or bird, or antelope or whatever. What she needed, what she really needed, was to find someone who had just finished cooking something. A bad person, whom she wouldn't mind stealing from. She thought about meat, sizzling over a campfire, and her mouth started to water.

Her stomach rumbled.

"Hush," she muttered, and pulled her mask down again, allowing the suit to sustain her. The rumbling went away.

She woke and the day had moved on. It was almost dark outside. The Necromancer was awake, sitting up in the corner, looking at her.

Valkyrie sat up straighter and cleared her throat. "Can you talk?" she asked.

The Necromancer didn't respond.

"I don't know if you can talk or not," she continued. "I know you can think, but I don't know if you're capable of communicating. I know some of you are. I've heard that a few of you have even kept your personalities. Are you one of them?"

He just kept his eyes on her.

Valkyrie shrugged, and pulled her mask up and her hood down. "That's OK. You can be the strong and silent type if you want. I can dig it."

She became suddenly aware of the emptiness in her stomach

as hunger cramps forced her to bend forward. "Oh, God," she muttered. "Don't suppose you've got a sandwich on you, have you? No?" The cramp passed and she breathed out. "Sorry about that. Hungry, you know? I'm sure you do. Although you guys don't eat like the regular draugar, do you? Different rules for the ones in charge? Yeah, there usually are."

She sat forward. "I used to do Necromancy, you know. Before my Surge, I mean. I was taught by a man called Solomon Wreath. Do you know him? Do you have a Solomon Wreath over here? Anyway, he taught me and I have to say... I kind of had an aptitude for it. They thought I might be the Death Bringer. You know the Death Bringer? The Passage? Yeah, I know all these terms. Don't look so shocked. Not that you *do* look shocked. You just look bored. Am I boring you? I haven't had anyone to speak to in a few days and, well... Do you want to be my friend?"

The Necromancer didn't indicate he even understood her.

"I'm Valkyrie. Do you have a name? I have to call you *something*. We're best buds! I'm gonna call you Death-Monkey, OK?"

Death-Monkey didn't answer.

"Super cool," said Valkyrie, giving him a great big smile. "I've got plans for you, Death-Monkey. Big plans."

83

Tanith found Serpine alone at a fire. She was going to walk by, but then she caught a glimpse of his arm, and sighed to herself as she sat opposite.

"How you doing?" she asked.

He looked at her, but didn't answer. Hatred boiled, practically shimmered, in the air over his shoulders. She couldn't blame him, of course she couldn't, but neither could she afford to come across as a soft touch.

She sniffed, and shrugged. "It was the only way we were getting out of there without spilling blood."

"Blood was spilled," Serpine said, his voice cold.

"More blood, then. Other people's blood. My blood. What happened to you was harsh, I'm not saying otherwise, but I'd rather it happen to you than to me."

"This your idea of comfort, is it?"

"I'm not here to comfort you. Just here to see how you are."

He held up his stump. Fresh skin, pink and new, ran across the wound like a tarpaulin over a pool. "I'm great, Tanith. The healers here did a wonderful job at covering over the scab. Growing me a new hand proved to be beyond their capabilities, unfortunately. Still, you take what you can get, isn't that what they say in your dimension? Beggars can't be choosers. That's another saying. Your dimension is just so full of sayings. What a fantastic place. I'm glad I'll get to live there, with the pollution and the chemicals in the air and the ground and the water, surrounded by all those mortals. I'm glad I've given my hand for the privilege. I always thought two hands were a waste anyway. It always smacked of indulgence to me."

"Huh. Valkyrie once told me sarcasm doesn't exist in this world."

Serpine barked a laugh. "She mustn't have been speaking to the right people. Sarcasm has always been the luxury of the ruling class. Peasants can't afford it. How is Mr Rue? I haven't seen much of him in the last week. Confined to his tent, is he? That infection must be taking its toll on him by now, I'd wager. He has another seven days, by the reckoning of Baron Vengeous. What have the doctors said? I'm assuming you've told them. I'm assuming Meritorious knows there's an infected person in his camp."

Tanith set her jaw. "I'll tell Saracen you were asking after him," she said, standing.

"He doesn't care," Serpine said.

"Saracen?"

"The skeleton. He doesn't care, does he? He allowed this to happen to me without putting up much of an argument. Granted, he has every reason to hate me, but even so, to stand by and allow Wreath to do what he did... It seems to me the only person he actually cares about is Valkyrie Cain. For her, he'd do anything. But for Vex, or Rue, or you? What would he allow to happen to any of you, if it meant getting back to her?"

Tanith smiled grimly. "You're going to have to do a lot better than that if you want to turn me against Skulduggery."

Serpine shook his head. "I just want you to keep that in mind. Then maybe, the next time he agrees to sacrifice a bit of me to the enemy, maybe you'll be a little more vociferous in your objections."

He lowered his eyes to the flames, dismissing her without another word.

Tanith stayed where she was for a moment, possessed of a foolish notion to demonstrate how she'd leave only when *she* decided to leave. But he was right, and he knew it, and standing there like a child wasn't going to do anyone any good, so she went back to the others, and tried to leave Serpine's words behind her.

84

Fifty of them. Maybe sixty. Through the eyeholes in her mask, Valkyrie watched them shuffle on down the trail, heading west. All the draugar she'd encountered on this journey had been heading west. All going to the same place.

She turned to Death-Monkey. "What do you think, my friend? We've been searching for them for days and here they are. I know, I know, we were hoping for a half-dozen or so, not... not this many. But we don't have much of a choice. You with me on this?"

Death-Monkey looked at her and said nothing. Even if he'd wanted to talk, the gag she'd tied over his mouth would have turned his words into little more than a muffled gurgle.

Valkyrie nodded. "You're a brave man. Let's do it."

She tugged on the rope around his neck and set off, and he stumbled along after her.

They approached the group from behind. None of them looked round. Draugar weren't curious creatures – they were only focused on what was ahead of them. It was kind of admirable, in a way. When Valkyrie caught up with them, she slowed down to almost match their pace, then brought Death-Monkey up and, gradually, walked through the group.

The draugar's eyes were drawn to the Necromancer. They didn't even glance at Valkyrie.

When they were out in front, Valkyrie brought Death-Monkey to a stop. The draugar moved round them and carried on walking. "I'm so smart," she whispered to Death-Monkey, and grinned.

85

Dark lines crawled from beneath the bandages on Saracen's neck and arm. The infection was spreading, and it was picking up speed.

"It doesn't look too good, does it?" he said. "And I don't just mean figuratively. I mean objectively. It is not a good wound to have."

"I'd have to agree with you," said Tanith.

It was raining, and the tent they sat in was not a good tent to sit in when it was raining. It sagged, and let in the water.

"There are sexy scars, aren't there?" Saracen said. His voice was weak, but he kept that smile of his. "I knew a guy once, he'd been bitten by a shark, and all across his torso, front and back, was this curved line of teeth. It was pretty cool, all things considered. I have scars from bullets and knives and arrows and various magic-related injuries, but... but that shark bite. That was something."

"What happened to him?" Tanith asked.

"Who?"

"Your friend."

Saracen frowned. He'd lost track of the conversation. He'd been doing that a lot lately.

"The friend who was bitten by a shark. What happened to him?"

"Oh," said Saracen. "Oh, yes, sorry. He died."

"How?"

"Shark bite."

"He was bitten by *another shark*?"

"No, no. Same one."

Tanith frowned. "So, it was less a cool, sexy scar he got out of that encounter, and more of a... death."

"Well, I like to think he got both, but sure, you can look at it like that." His eyes drifted and his voice got even quieter. "I never thought this would be how I died."

"You're not going to die."

"Indulge me in this maudlin moment, won't you? Have you ever imagined how you're going to die?"

"Plenty of times," said Tanith. "Usually right before I do something stupid. When the time comes, hopefully, it'll be quick. Hopefully, it'll mean something."

"I always wanted a silly death."

"Excuse me?"

He shrugged, and smiled. "A dumb death. That's what I want. But only after I've done something incredibly heroic. I see myself standing there, hands on my hips while the innocent people whose lives I've just saved applaud me and chant my name – and then I want something to fall on me. Like a piano, or a tree."

"Wow."

"But I haven't decided if I want to see it coming or not. On the one hand, it'd be funnier if I had no idea. But, on the other hand, I'd definitely find it more amusing if I could see what was about to happen."

"You're a strange man, Mr Rue."

"Never claimed otherwise." He finally looked up at her. "So, listen – once I'm gone, Dexter's going to need a new best friend."

"You're not going anywhere."

"I thought you were indulging me."

She sighed. "Fine."

"As I was saying, Dexter's going to need a best friend. I think it should be you. I'm not saying you'll be as good a best friend as I have been – the last few years notwithstanding – and I'm not saying you'll be as fun or as witty or that he'll like you as much as he likes me, but you're *quite* good fun and you're *relatively* witty, so I'm willing to give you the benefit of the doubt."

"Thank you," Tanith said slowly.

"I have a test to make sure."

"What?"

Saracen pulled a crumpled piece of paper from his pocket. "Just a quick test. It's a fine and perfectly normal thing to do." He took a deep breath, gathering his strength. "First scenario: you're out for a walk one day and you see your best friend, Dexter, sobbing by the side of the road. Do you a) ignore him and wander on by, b) laugh until he cries harder, or c) sit down beside him and—"

"Stop," said Tanith. "You actually wrote that? Oh, God, you did. How many scenarios are there?"

"Eight," said Saracen.

"Right. Well, I'm not going to do your test, but I promise you that, if you do die, I'll be the best friend I can possibly be to dear old Dexter. Is that acceptable?"

"I suppose so," Saracen said, putting away the piece of paper.

Tanith got up. "Get some rest, you weirdo."

"Yes, ma'am."

She stepped out into the rain. Skulduggery was standing there, skull hidden beneath his hood.

"What was he saying?" he asked.

She shrugged. "He was asking me, in the event of his death, to take over as Dexter's best friend. The usual."

"How did he seem?"

"Weak, tired – but he was making jokes, so more like his usual self. That's good, right?"

Skulduggery didn't answer immediately. "Maybe," he said in a tone that implied *no, it's not good, not at all, not even a little.*

86

The school day ended and the extracurriculars began, and when they were done there was some free time and then dinner. Omen ate beside Never and Axelia. None of them said much.

They split up once dinner was over, went back to their dorm rooms and got changed into their regular clothes. They met up again outside the West Tower. It was a cold night. Axelia was the only one who'd worn a sensible coat.

Never had scouted ahead the day before, so when they joined hands he teleported them straight on to Devon's property. It was a big house on a hill. Lots of glass and straight lines. A long driveway led to a long road that led to Edinburgh city, which twinkled to the west.

"So what now?" Axelia asked.

"Now we go in," said Omen, "and steal the Obsidian Blade."

Axelia nodded. "Or," she said.

Omen frowned. "Or what?"

"Or how about we just ask? Why does everything have to be stolen? If we explain to Mr Devon why we need it, he might give it to us."

"Why would he do that?"

"Why wouldn't he? The prophecy is that Auger will battle the King of the Darklands to decide the fate of the world. That kind of implies that if Auger doesn't win, the world will be in for some rough times ahead, right? Mr Devon lives in the world. He'd be as interested as we are in making sure things go well with it."

"So you want to knock on his front door and explain all this to him?"

"Yes."

Omen looked at Never. "Do you have an opinion?"

"Always," said Never.

"And what is your opinion?"

"I'm really cold, and I agree with her."

Omen shrugged. "OK, we'll try the honest approach. But just so we're all clear – if the honest approach doesn't work, the dishonest approach will be even harder, and Devon will know who took the Blade."

Axelia folded her arms and looked triumphant. "No one ever said that being the good guy was easy."

Omen led the way up the drive, trying to work out how he was going to broach the subject when Devon answered the door. Honesty, Omen decided, was the best policy. It was also the easiest, and required the least amount of work.

But, when they got to the front door, it was already open.

With Axelia and Never both looking at him for some sort of leadership, Omen inched forward, pushing the door open further.

"Hello?" he whispered. "Mr Devon? My name is Omen Darkly and I'm here with some friends and we'd like a moment of your time."

Never prodded him and Omen stepped inside the house. It was a lovely house. Expensive things Omen didn't appreciate hung from the walls. They crept further.

"Hello?" Omen whispered.

Axelia squeezed his arm and Omen turned to where she was looking, to the body on the floor in the living room.

The body was that of a portly man in pyjamas with sandy-coloured hair and pale corpse skin and dead corpse eyes and an open corpse mouth, and he lay as he'd fallen, with a terrified corpse expression on his dead corpse face.

"You think that corpse is dead?" Never whispered.

Omen nodded dumbly.

"We should make sure," said Axelia. "Throw something at him."

"Don't do that," Omen said.

"Then find something to poke him with. A stick, or something. Maybe a branch."

"He's dead, Axelia."

"Never, can you see a branch anywhere around?"

"We're inside," Never pointed out.

"Oh, yeah," Axelia whispered back. "I think I'm freaking out a bit. I've never seen a murder victim before."

Omen frowned at her. "How do you know he was murdered?"

"He has a knife sticking out of his back."

Omen took a few steps to his left, and saw the knife handle. "Oh, yeah."

"We should probably leave. Whoever killed him might still be here."

They looked at each other, then looked around. Listened. Not a sound in the house. Not a shadow moved.

Then footsteps, coming down the stairs.

Omen grabbed the other two by the wrists and dragged them into the next room.

Voices now, accompanying the footsteps.

"—not how we do things," a man was saying.

"It's not how we *used* to do things," another man responded, his voice deeper, "but I reckon now is as good a time as any to change how things are done."

The men were getting closer. Omen pressed his back to the wall, eyes locked on the doorway beside him.

"We're professionals, Tancred," the first man said. "We have a reputation as professionals. We were hired to do a job and that's what we're going to do."

The men passed the doorway... and moved on. Omen took a quick peek, glimpsed the two of them walking away from him. The first was tall and slim and the second was a giant of a man.

"Then we need to charge more for our services," the big one said. "How much will this thing go for at auction? A weapon that can't be stopped?"

"Practically priceless," his companion replied, digging out his phone.

"That's a lot, then, is it? Sure sounds like a lot."

The other man raised a hand for quiet, then held the phone to his ear and waited. After a moment, he broke into a smile. "It's Reznor Rake," he said. "You'll be happy to hear that we have the item. No, I'm afraid the old man met with an unfortunate case of violent death. Yep. Yes. When would you like it...? Yes, we could keep an eye on it for you. Until when? That's, what, twelve days away? Thirteen, sorry. I warn you, if you want us to hold on to an item of this significance for thirteen days, it's going to cost you. Yes. Yes, that will do quite nicely. Pleasure doing business."

He put his phone away.

"Well?" said Tancred.

"We hold on to it until the auction," Reznor Rake said.

"We're getting well paid for it?"

"Oh, yes," said Reznor, and he chuckled.

Their voices faded as they left the house. Omen hesitated, then crept after them. Axelia tried to pull him back, but he shook her off and kept going. He got to the door, watching the tail lights of their car as Never and Axelia joined him.

"They have it," he said. "They have the Obsidian Blade."

"Sure sounds like it," Never said. "What do we do?"

Axelia frowned. "We tell the Cleavers," she said. "We have to do that anyway. I mean, they murdered a guy. Right? When that happens, we call the cops."

"And then what?" Never asked. "Duenna kicks us out of school?"

"Then we leave an anonymous tip, Never. Do I have to think of everything?"

"We follow them," Omen said. He took hold of Never's arm and nodded to the disappearing tail lights. "If we can somehow grab the Blade ourselves, wonderful. If not, yes, we call in the Cleavers."

Axelia sighed, and placed her hand on Never's other arm.

They teleported after the car, sometimes appearing on a rooftop, sometimes behind a tree, sometimes on a shadow-drenched pavement. They followed the car for at least half an hour, and, by the time they watched it pull into the kerb, Never was exhausted and pale.

"That's it," he said, sagging against the wall. "I'm done."

Tancred and Reznor got out of the car and approached an old hotel, its windows boarded up. Omen and his friends watched them unlock the door, slip through, and close it after them.

"OK then," said Axelia. "We've tracked the bad guys to their lair. This is pretty good going, I have to admit. But now we call in the Cleavers, right?"

Never shook his head slowly. "You really are new to this adventuring lark, aren't you? We don't call in the authorities unless we absolutely have to. That's one of the first rules of adventuring. Omen, tell her I'm right."

"He is kinda right," Omen admitted.

"Then explain it to me," said Axelia. "Why is calling the Cleavers such a bad move?"

"Because then they get the Obsidian Blade," Omen said. "They recover it, they give it to Supreme Mage Sorrows, and she puts it away in her vault or whatever and, when Auger needs it, he can't get it. We don't know when he'll have to go up against the King of the Darklands – we don't know how much warning he'll have. Auger needs to carry the Blade with him at all times. China Sorrows isn't going to let him do that."

Axelia chewed her lip. Omen could tell she was trying to come up with a persuasive counter-argument. Finally, she scowled and said, "So what do we do?"

"The Blade is being auctioned off in thirteen days. That's the seventeenth, right? That'll be a... Friday. So we have thirteen days to sneak into that hotel and steal it."

Never made a face. "Us?"

"Yes. Why?"

"Well, I mean... I'm used to doing this sort of thing with Auger, you know? And if Auger says he's going to sneak in somewhere and steal something, even if it's guarded by a pair of killers like this is, then he'll do it. And, if it goes wrong, he'll fight his way out or he'll come up with some genius last-minute plan or if he's captured he'll turn the tables and escape..."

"And?"

Never winced. "And that's Auger. It's what he does. What are you gonna do?"

Omen hesitated. "I don't know."

"See, it's that indecision that's the problem. It doesn't exactly fill me with confidence, you know?"

"Then how about this?" said Omen. "I'm going to do whatever it takes to get the Obsidian Blade and make sure my brother survives the prophecy and saves the world."

Never glanced at Axelia, then shrugged. "OK, that was better. I'm in."

They both looked at Axelia, who sighed.

"The moment it gets too dangerous," she said, "I'm calling the Cleavers."

Omen grinned. "Completely understandable."

87

Saracen was getting worse. It had been two weeks since he'd been bitten, and he couldn't leave the tent any more. If anyone saw him, they'd know he was infected. He'd even stopped making jokes. That's when Tanith knew the end was near.

Valkyrie was Saracen's only hope, and she had no idea.

88

Valkyrie walked among the dead for three days.

Every night she'd take Death-Monkey and find somewhere to rest – usually up a tree, with her pet Necromancer tied to the trunk below her – and when they set off again the next morning there were always more draugar to mingle with. It was like a never-ending crowd heading for a music festival, except no one was singing and no one was drunk.

She followed the stream of rotting dead people, her mask protecting her from the smell. The last time she'd taken it off the sudden hunger had made her cry out, and she'd decided not to do that again until she had something to eat right in front of her.

They were on a wide road now. A main road. A good road, leading to Tahil na Kurge in the distance. Valkyrie could make out its many towers looming above the wall. The sun glinted off windows.

A slow kind of terror built itself up around her heart when she saw the millions – and there must have been millions – of draugar congregating around the city's shield. Her plan had been to walk right up to the gates and figure out how to get in from there, but there was no way she was going to be able to get through that number of walking corpses. Her claustrophobia would kick in within minutes, a panic attack would follow soon after, and that would draw all sorts of unwanted attention.

She stopped walking, keeping Death-Monkey beside her. The draugar continued to stream by her, coming from all directions, adding to the numbers. Valkyrie counted over thirty hovering Necromancers keeping an eye on it all.

There was a hill to the south, and on that hill there was a watchtower. Valkyrie tugged on Death-Monkey's rope and started towards it, cutting across the path of countless draugar. Progress was slow.

The watchtower was a wooden structure built from a stone base. The door opened at her touch. Silence from inside. She closed the door after her, tied Death-Monkey to the handle, and found the stairs in the gloom. She emerged on to a covered platform at the very top, and was gifted with a spectacular view of the surrounding countryside and the multitudes of flesh-eating creatures that roamed it.

She didn't feel half as clever any more.

Her options were limited to trying to get in on her own – which would probably end in disaster – or waiting for Skulduggery and the others to catch up with her. The second option was infinitely preferable – all she had to do was keep an eye out for trouble, because trouble meant Skulduggery.

Valkyrie nodded to herself, pleased that she'd come to a practical, reasonable conclusion. So long as she kept the suit sealed, she could carry on without food or water for as long as it took. And it wasn't like she was alone, either. She had Death-Monkey for company. Over the past week, she'd felt that they were really starting to bond.

She left the platform, went back down the stairs. "New plan," she said, her boot kicking against something. It rolled into a patch of light. Death-Monkey's head.

There was a sound behind her and she turned and Assegai's snarling face came out of the gloom and there was an explosion of purple right in front of her mask and her head rocked back into darkness.

89

Ten days before the auction.

Never had teleported them inside the hotel three times so far. It was big and draughty and it had plenty of cobwebs and a thick layer of dust in the rooms that weren't being used – which was most of them.

Reznor Rake and Tancred only used five rooms between them: the main hotel lobby, where the sofas and the armchairs were, two bedrooms and two bathrooms. They spent most of their time in the lobby playing cards, eating takeaways, and watching bad sitcoms and documentaries on an old TV.

So far, the searches Omen and his friends had conducted had not uncovered the Obsidian Blade, but Omen wasn't worried.

They had plenty of time.

90

The Democrats argued among themselves on the debate stage and Martin laughed at them. They were useless. Weak. They tripped over each other in their eagerness to defend this minority or that liberal cause, to signal to the country how much they cared about the poor or the victimised or the environment...

But that's not what the people wanted. The people wanted permission to say the dark things in their heads. To whisper what they'd only been able to think, and to shout what they'd only been able to whisper. The liberals didn't understand this, because they thought everyone was like them.

But the people were like Martin. They didn't have his money, and they didn't have his intelligence, but they understood him, and he understood them. And that's why he was going to win.

Crepuscular Vies walked into the room and Martin pulled his bathrobe closed.

"Nice," Crepuscular said, and Martin blushed. He stood right in front of him, blocking the TV. "I'm going away for a bit, Mr President. Taking a little vacation."

Relief flooded Martin's system. "Of course," he said. "Yes, you've been working hard for me. You deserve some time off."

"Thank you. Thank you for saying that. I might not come back."

Martin was on his feet in an instant. "What?"

"It's a possibility, that's all I'll say."

"You... you have to come back. It's my re-election campaign next year. I can't do this without the things that you do!"

"You flatter me, sir."

"You can't abandon me!"

"I serve at the pleasure of the President of the United States," said Crepuscular, "except I don't. I've been working on a little something and I feel like it might pay off and... I don't know. I'm just not feeling very *appreciated* here, Martin. Sometimes I get the impression that you don't even like me."

"I do like you! I need you! Stay!"

"You'll be fine. You've got the people on your side, don't you? Just keep on appealing to their darker impulses and you'll do great. I have faith in you. I do. Your robe is still hanging open, by the way."

Martin turned away, pulled it closed, tied it – and, when he looked back, Crepuscular was gone.

"*Noooooo,*" he whined.

91

As dungeons went, this place was a bit of a dump.

And Valkyrie knew dungeons. Well, dungeon. Singular. She'd had a brief stay in the one beneath Mevolent's palace in Dublin-Within-The-Wall. That had been dirty, dark, cold and smelly. It had stone walls and heavy chains and thick bars between the cells. But at least it had buckets in the corners, and a thin scattering of old straw on the ground.

But this dungeon made that dungeon look like a holiday resort. The cells were small, the ground was packed earth, there were no buckets, and the smell was beyond terrible. Her fellow dungeon-mates babbled and muttered incoherently in the darkness around her. She couldn't get a straight answer out of anyone.

It was freezing down here. Valkyrie didn't have her suit any more. They'd thrown her in here and dressed her in a stinking, shapeless sackcloth shift that was stained with things she didn't want to know about. She couldn't feel even a trace of her magic, such was the strength of the binding sigils.

"You had me fooled," said Assegai from somewhere in the shadows.

Valkyrie hadn't even heard her approach. She stood, her feet bare, and Assegai came slowly into the weak, flickering torchlight.

"I thought you were one of us," Assegai continued. "I thought you understood me. Understood what I was going through."

"I did," said Valkyrie. "I do."

Assegai smiled. "You're a liar. You lie. You'd say anything to worm your way into my head. That's what spies do. They manipulate. I should have seen it, but you knew I wouldn't. You knew if you separated me from my team, I'd be vulnerable."

"I didn't separate you from anyone."

"Liar," Assegai breathed.

There was no arguing with her. Valkyrie's gaze dipped to the black skull on Assegai's chest.

"What do you think?" Assegai asked, noticing. "I reckon it looks better on me. I've never had a necronaut suit before, but now I can't imagine life without it. You don't mind, do you? You weren't using it."

"What's going to happen to me?"

"You'll be tortured. You've been here a week – you must have seen other prisoners getting dragged out of here, yes?"

Valkyrie didn't say anything.

"You never saw them come back, though, did you? That's because they've been tortured. All their little secrets have come spilling out."

"Don't you use your Sense Wardens for that stuff?"

Assegai laughed. "You'd like that, would you? A nice, gentle psychic probe that you've probably been trained to deal with. No, no. The Sense Wardens will be used, of course they will, but only after you've been broken. We've got people who do that professionally. They're... strict. They'll find out who you are, who sent you, what your mission is. What you've done. They'll make you confess everything. But I have questions, before they ask theirs. How did you do it? How did you manage to subdue a Necromancer?"

"That's my little secret."

"Not for long."

"For as long as I can hold on to it."

Assegai's smile came back. "Fair enough. My second question –

what did you do to me? I've been hit by energy streams before, but never like the one you hit me with. What's your discipline?"

Valkyrie shrugged. "Maybe I can give you a demonstration. If you'd just unlock my cell..."

Assegai came right up close, pressed her head against the bars. "You think you're clever."

"Clever enough."

"Not too clever, though, are you? I wasn't even following you, do you realise that? The watchtower I found you at, that's one of the rendezvous points. That's where the Teleporters meet with soldiers like me in order to take us into the city. And you're just wandering around it like an idiot."

"That does sound kinda stupid," Valkyrie admitted.

"We're going to find out all your secrets."

"Sounds likely. Any idea when the torturing will begin? I might have to clear my schedule."

"They've got quite a lot to get through before it's your turn, I'm afraid, so you'll have to sit here, in your own filth, with nothing to do but anticipate the pain and disfigurement to come. Once you've spilled your secrets, and once the Sense Wardens are through with you, I've asked that whatever's left of you be handed over to me. Would you like that? Would you like to be my pet? If you're lucky – if you're very, *very* lucky, and very, *very* good – I'll take you with me when we pass through the portal. But if you're not, if you're a *bad* pet, a *naughty* pet, I'll leave you here. For the draugar."

Valkyrie couldn't think of a smart remark that was equal to what Assegai had thrown at her, so she sneered and gave her the finger.

It was something, at least.

92

Temper walked into his quiet, cold house. He missed Kierre. He missed her warm smile. He missed the way she greeted him. He missed just about every little thing about her. But most of all he missed the feeling that he wasn't alone any more, that there was someone there for him, that she'd chosen him out of everyone. He missed that.

Something hit him. He stumbled against the table, went for his gun, but the weapon was torn from his hand. He lashed out and his head rocked back and he was thrown against the sink.

Dazed, his jaw aching, he blinked quickly to clear his vision.

There was a man crouching on his kitchen table. Long grey hair, old jeans and dirty boots. A shirt, open, showing the tattoos on his bare chest, painted like there were demons crawling out beneath his skin.

He had a grinning mouth tattooed across the lower half of his jaw.

"I know you," said Temper slowly. "You're Mr Glee."

The mouth beneath the grin smiled.

"Valkyrie Cain told me about you," said Temper. "You're a serial killer. Gleeman Shakespeare, is that it? That your full name?"

"That's it."

"The invisible man. From New York."

"That's right."

"Whereabouts? I'm from New York. I might know someone you know."

"Temper, Temper... I'm here to kill you. Not talk to you."

"So what are you, a serial killer or a hitman? Pick a lane, buddy."

Glee disappeared.

Temper heard him jump and he swung with the kitchen knife in his hand, hit nothing. Then all of a sudden Glee was beside him and Temper slashed and Glee caught his wrist, disarmed him depressingly easily. A punch knocked Temper back. A kick knocked him over a chair.

He got to his feet, trying to breathe. Glee walked after him. He was a tall man, but sort of stooped. Temper backed away.

"I know what your power is," Glee said. "You're one of those *Gist* people, yeah? I've never seen one in action. Care to let it loose, see how I do against it?"

"You wouldn't last three seconds."

"So let it loose. Let me go down in a blaze of glory."

There wasn't anywhere left to back up to.

Glee's grin got wider. "So it's true," he said. "You're at the end of your tether, as it were. You let that Gist out one more time and you disappear and it takes over. That right? Yeah, that's right. So there isn't really a whole lot you can do to fight me off, is there?"

Temper didn't say anything as Glee picked up the kitchen knife, turning it so that it flashed when it caught the light.

"I'm gonna gut you," Glee said. "Just so you know what's coming. Just so you know what to expect. It's gonna be a painful death. Not too drawn-out... but certainly painful."

Temper put his hands up, ready to fight.

Glee chuckled. "That's the spirit."

He lunged and Temper opened his hands. The creature living in his arm poked its head through the scar in his palm and then

362

shot out, burrowing through Glee's shoulder. The killer howled, twisting and falling back.

The knife fell. Glee reached for it, but another black tentacle shot out of Temper's other hand, that mouth with all those teeth barely missing Glee's fingers. Instead, it gripped the knife and whipped it away as it retracted. Temper had to duck to make sure it didn't impale him on its way past.

"What the *hell?*" Glee roared from the ground.

"What," said Temper, "my pets? Just a little gift from a dying friend. They needed a home, you know? And I've always been an animal lover."

Clutching his shoulder, Glee got up. "You've made an enemy tonight," he snarled.

"You came to kill me," said Temper, a little puzzled.

Glee turned invisible and his footsteps retreated. Temper sent a tentacle to snatch up his gun, and he followed the footsteps – and the trail of blood – out of the front door, all the way across the street, where he lost it in the shadows.

"Good Hansel," he whispered to his left hand. "Good Gretel," he whispered to his right.

Razzia would have been proud.

93

Their time had almost run out.

There was one day to go before the auction and Omen and the others still had to find the Obsidian Blade. This was bad. This was terrible. They'd been in the hotel eighteen times. They knew the layout well. They knew how cold it was and how dark it was, and they knew which parts of the wooden floors would creak if trodden upon.

They had searched the lobby and searched the bedrooms. That left the kitchen and some of the bathrooms, but Omen's optimism had long since dimmed. He made a promise to himself – if they didn't find the Obsidian Blade tonight, he'd alert the High Sanctuary, even if it meant being kicked out of Corrival.

Never teleported them to their usual spot, up on the balcony overlooking the lobby. Reznor Rake had just left. He'd announced that he was sick of the food they'd been eating, and he'd taken the car to go and get something different.

Reznor being gone wasn't that unusual – he hadn't spent an awful lot of time there over the last two weeks – but Tancred never left, and his movements were awfully predictable. He slept in Room 9. He ate and watched TV in the lobby. He spent forty-five minutes or more on the toilet, every single time he went.

He was a man who liked the toilet.

"Holy crap," whispered Never.

Omen frowned, peered down through the slats in the balcony, to where Tancred was sitting. The TV was showing some awful sitcom, but Omen's attention was on the crumpled beer cans on the table to the left side of the man, and the way they disappeared when Tancred stabbed them with the black-bladed knife in his big, meaty hand.

The Obsidian Blade.

Tancred lined up another beer can. Aiming carefully, he jabbed it with the tip of the knife, and it looked like the can was swallowed by emptiness. Obviously fascinated by this, Tancred moved another can into position. Once again, he jabbed downwards – but this time he went too hard, and it was not just the can that disappeared but the entire table.

The other beer cans clattered to the floor, and Tancred laughed.

Axelia and Never looked at Omen, expecting a plan.

"When he goes to the toilet," Omen whispered, looking at Never, "you teleport down, grab the knife, and we get out of here."

Never didn't look overly impressed with that plan, but she didn't argue, either, so Omen took that as a ringing endorsement.

But, an hour later, the Obsidian Blade was resting on the table to the right side of the chair, and Tancred hadn't budged. He was watching a documentary on old Hollywood musicals and had completely missed his regular evening constitutional.

This was bad. If Tancred didn't head off to the toilet soon, Reznor would return and the Blade wouldn't go unguarded. So Omen came up with a second plan. A terrible plan.

"I'm going to sneak down," he whispered, "crawl up behind him and take the knife. The moment I have it, you both come get me."

Axelia shook her head furiously. "That's a terrible plan."

"It's not that bad."

Never glared. "It's awful. Just awful." She squared her shoulders. "I'll do it."

"No," said Omen.

"I teleport down, grab it, teleport back, grab you, we all teleport away. It's the only plan that makes sense."

"It's too dangerous."

"Funny," said Never, "Too Dangerous is where I live. It's on the corner of Brave and Awesome."

Axelia frowned. "What?"

Never sighed. "Whatever. Just prepare to witness brilliance."

She rose up off her knees, into a crouch, and then she wasn't on the balcony any more, she was down there, in the lobby, right behind Tancred's chair.

He adjusted himself in his seat.

Omen and Axelia watched as Never took a tiny step forward, watched as she reached out, slender fingers moving for the knife handle. Ever so slowly, she wrapped her fingers around it.

Tancred sniffed, adjusted himself again, happened to turn his head ever so slightly, and roared when he saw her hand on the knife.

Never jerked her hand away as Tancred shot to his feet. She cursed, dived for the Blade, but he grabbed her wrist and pulled her into a punch. Never's knees gave out and she crumpled and Omen and Axelia came running down the stairs, screaming curses, and Tancred stalked over to meet them.

He batted Axelia to one side. Omen charged him and got a fist to the side for his trouble. The breath whooshed from his lungs and he fell, eyes bulging.

Tancred cracked his knuckles as Axelia advanced on him. "This doesn't have to be painful, princess."

"I'm afraid it does," Axelia said, settling into a fighting stance.

Tancred chuckled. "All right then," he said. "Let's be having you."

Omen tried to call out, but his muscles were still protesting too much to allow him to take a decent breath, so all he could do was watch as Axelia threw out a few tentative jabs. Tancred's grin widened as he swayed back, avoiding each one.

She tried a kick. It missed, but it was flawlessly executed. If it had connected, it would have maybe broken Tancred's jaw. As it was, it swished past his face and Tancred laughed and clapped.

Axelia's brow furrowed. She didn't much like being patronised at the best of times.

She feinted with another punch and switched to a kick, a low one, to the inside of the thigh. Tancred's grin vanished off his face as he stepped back, rubbing his leg.

"You're starting to annoy me," he growled.

Omen sucked in a thin sliver of air.

Axelia kicked Tancred's legs three more times. The third kick almost buckled his left knee. He moved back, scowling. She moved in for a fourth kick and instead clipped him with a punch, dead centre, right on the nose. He grabbed at her and she ducked under and spun. If Omen had tried that, he'd have mistimed it or missed completely – but Axelia judged it perfectly, and her heel smashed into Tancred's gut.

She hopped back, staying on the balls of her feet, fists up and elbows tight. Chin tucked in.

Tancred held one hand to his face as he tried to straighten. That last kick had winded him, and blood from his nose was trickling through his fingers. He'd stopped enjoying this a while ago. Omen recognised the look. It was the one a lot of instructors got when Auger got the better of them. It was a sign of trouble to come.

Tancred walked forward. Axelia caught him with another kick to the leg, and once again he nearly buckled, but, instead of going down, he lunged. Grabbed her. Axelia tried breaking the hold with a technique taught in combat class, but he shoved her back into the wall before she had any time to execute it. He moved in, sliding her up off her feet, then twisted, flipped her, and slammed her into the ground.

Omen stood and gave a long, involuntary moan as he tried to straighten his back.

Axelia started getting up. Tancred's knee missed her face and hit her shoulder instead, sent her sprawling. She scrambled to her feet, struggling to breathe, holding one hand out to keep him away. He grabbed her wrist, punched her with his other hand. She went down on one knee and he helped her up by gripping her throat.

Omen still couldn't stand straight, but he charged anyway. He hit Tancred with enough force to make him drop Axelia, but not enough to do anything else. He moaned again as Tancred grabbed him, kept him in position, and drove a knee up into his face. Omen managed to turn his head just in time to save his teeth, but the world rocked and he went straight down, blinking away tears.

He turned over. He could breathe a little better now. There was an awful ringing in his ears, though, a ringing that reduced everything else to a distant murmur.

He blinked again as Tancred sent Axelia hurtling over a sofa. He didn't think she'd get up after that one, but she did. Her lip was busted and blood was running from her nose and there was a massive bump already rising around her left eye. Tancred darted in, grabbed her, and hit her. She stumbled. He hit her again.

Spitting blood, crying but refusing to stay down, Axelia tore off her jacket. Tancred tried to grab her again, but he couldn't grip her bare arm, and she hit him with a looping haymaker that caught him on the ear. He howled, went reeling.

Axelia wanted to move after him, Omen could see, to take advantage of his distress, but she was too tired. Her fists were no longer up, protecting her head. Her elbows were no longer tight, protecting her ribs. She sucked in big breaths through her mouth. It wasn't easy to breathe with a nose full of blood.

Tancred shook his head. His face was bloody and red with exertion, and he was breathing heavily, too. But, where Axelia was growing visibly weaker as the fight went on, he was drawing strength from his anger. He stormed towards her. She backed off, desperately looking for a way out.

He pulled his arm back for a punch. She saw it coming. She didn't have the energy to dodge so she tried to block. His fist came right through her defences and collided with the left side of her face and her body twisted and she went down in a heap.

Tancred stood over her, snarling.

Omen tried to leap to his feet, but all he could manage was a sad little push across the floor. It was enough to catch Tancred's attention, however.

"Want some more, do you?" Tancred asked.

I can do this all day, Omen wanted to growl, but of course all he could utter was a groan.

Tancred laughed, and then there was someone behind him, and he squawked in pain.

For a moment, in the confusion, Omen thought it was Skulduggery, come to save him. He was the same height, and he wore a hat and a suit. But the hat was the wrong kind of hat, and the suit was checked and it had a bow tie. And the face...

The stranger with the strange face didn't use any magic to take down Tancred. Omen was glad of that. It meant he could watch Tancred being physically dismantled by a superior opponent.

And this guy was good. Granted, Tancred was already tired, and already hurt, but nothing he threw came even close to landing. Moving with precision and calm efficiency, the new guy proceeded to beat Tancred to a spectacularly bloody pulp until, by the end, Omen was almost feeling sorry for him.

No, actually. Omen *was* feeling sorry for him.

Tancred went down for the last time and the new guy adjusted his bow tie and looked at Omen. "And who might you be?" he asked.

"Omen," he managed to gasp. "Omen Darkly."

The man extended his hand. "Omen, good to meet you. Name's Crepuscular. Crepuscular Vies." Omen hesitated, and Crepuscular shrugged. "Sorry, my face takes some getting used to."

Omen grasped the outstretched hand, and Crepuscular pulled him slowly to his feet.

"What?" Omen said. "What's wrong with your...? Oh, I see it now. Yeah, the... It's really not that bad."

Crepuscular smiled. Or at least, Omen thought that's what he did. "You're too kind," he said. "Dare I ask what brings you here to get smacked around by this gentleman?"

"We're doing a little investigating," Omen said, hobbling over to Axelia first, and then Never. They were both unconscious. Both in need of a doctor.

"Ah," Crepuscular said, "teenage sleuths, eh? I always wanted to be a teenage sleuth. How's it going?"

"It's been better," Omen said, kneeling painfully by Never's side.

"I'd hope so. Do you have a healer you can get to?"

Omen did – or at least he hoped he did. Reverie Synecdoche had told him a while ago that, if he ever needed help, he just had to knock on her clinic door. "Sorry," he said, "but why are you here?"

Crepuscular raised an eyebrow. "Oh. Me. Yes. Well... I suppose I'm here for some *adult* sleuthing, to be honest. Heh. Look at us, the intrepid little detectives that we are."

"What are you investigating?"

"Ah-ah," said Crepuscular. "One sleuth never reveals his case to another. That's the first rule of sleuthing."

"Is it?"

"I'm not sure. It could be."

Never muttered something without opening her eyes. Omen hoped that was a signal that she was about to wake.

"Thank you, by the way," Omen said as he stood.

Crepuscular's bulbous eyes blinked. "Whatever for?"

"For this. Saving us."

"Is that what I did? My, that was brave of me."

Omen had to laugh. "Yes, it was. Thank you."

"You're very welcome," Crepuscular said. "In fact, if you could do me a small favour in return? Could you not tell anyone I was here? I'm not supposed to be investigating what it is I'm investigating, you see. They told me to back off, my bosses, to leave it alone, but I couldn't, do you understand? Somebody had to stand up for justice. I guess that somebody... was me." Crepuscular tilted his head at him. "Was that too dramatic?"

"Uh... no."

"It sounded too dramatic."

"No, no. I mean... it was impressive, certainly."

Crepuscular considered that, then shrugged. "OK. I can live with impressive." He looked around. "I should probably get going, then – before your friends wake up. It was very good to meet you, Omen."

"Likewise."

Crepuscular walked for the door, then turned. "If you need me at any stage in the future, you know what to do."

"Do I?"

"Don't you?"

"I don't, actually."

"Oh," Crepuscular said, passing him a card. "That's got my number. You can call it." And then he walked out the front door.

Never groaned again, and her eyes fluttered open.

"You're OK," Omen said. "Stay where you are for a minute. You probably have a concussion."

"The knife," said Never. "Did we get the knife?"

Omen's eyes widened, and he hurried over to the small table, and picked up the Obsidian Blade.

"We did," he said, somewhat astonished. "We actually did."

94

Waiting around was not on Tanith's list of favourite things ever in the world, but waiting around seemed to be her chosen profession these days. The last time she'd swung her sword had been at the fort, and that had been almost a month ago. Something needed to happen. Something big or something small, she really didn't care. Just... something.

"Something's happening," Skulduggery murmured.

Tanith hurried over, raised the binoculars towards Tahil na Kurge. She watched as a draugr lurched towards the shield. It evaporated on contact. But now there were other draugar doing the same thing – reaching out and evaporating. All along the line, all around the shield. Draugr after draugr.

She didn't understand it. She thought of that myth, that lemmings just follow each other off a cliff edge. That was what appeared to be happening here.

And still they came. Hundreds of them evaporating at a time, replaced by a seemingly endless supply.

"This is interesting," she said. "Isn't it interesting? It must mean something. What do you think it means?"

"I don't know yet," Skulduggery said.

"I think it means something big is about to happen."

"Could be," said Skulduggery.

Tanith grinned. *Finally.*

*

The Teleporter arrived and took them back to the Resistance camp. For the first time in ages, Tanith was in a relatively good mood. That vanished when they stepped into their tent.

Dexter was on his feet, the bow in his hand. "Right," he said, "I don't know about the rest of you, but I'm tired of eating the slop we're given by the so-called cooks in this place. I'm going to hunt us down some rabbits. Anyone want to come? Saracen, you lazy sod. Come on and we'll go hunting."

Saracen mumbled something and didn't look up.

"That's a good idea," Skulduggery said, walking over. "Some exercise will do you the world of good. Get the blood pumping. Clear the head."

Tanith frowned as Skulduggery took both of Saracen's hands and pulled him to his feet. There was something in his voice. Something forced.

Saracen stumbled slightly and Skulduggery caught him, steadied him. "Are you good?" he asked quietly.

Saracen nodded, and Skulduggery stepped back.

Suddenly Tanith knew what was happening. She went to grab him, but stopped herself. Her insides were cold.

"Come on, buddy," said Dexter, wearing a fragile smile.

Saracen shuffled over, and together they walked out of the tent.

Tanith couldn't think of a thing to say. Skulduggery looked at her, said nothing. Even Serpine was keeping quiet. She felt like she ought to run after them, drag Saracen back. But she stayed where she was, and when she finally did move it was to sink down to the ground.

Dexter returned later that night.

WINTER

95

Sebastian turned the key in the lock, entered the house, had just closed the door when Darquesse passed him. Slim. No sign of the baby bump.

"You gave birth?" Sebastian gasped. "When? You told me it wouldn't be until after Christmas! Where's the baby? Are *you* the baby?"

Another Darquesse came the other way, carrying a box of nappies.

"Uh," said Sebastian.

He wandered deeper into the house, stepping aside whenever a Darquesse walked by. So many of them. Maybe a dozen. All carrying things. All busy.

He found pregnant Darquesse in the living room, lying on the couch on piles of cushions.

"Hi," said Sebastian.

"Don't talk to me," she said. "I've finally got comfortable."

"Oh, sorry. Right."

She growled. "I'm uncomfortable again."

Sebastian winced. "Was it my fault?"

"Probably." She moved slightly as three other Darquesses came in. They plumped up the cushions, rearranging them, plucking more out of thin air in order to prop up their pregnant version.

She lay back, sighed, and the other Darquesses left.

"I was just calling in to see if you needed anything," Sebastian said, "but it looks like you have everything covered."

"Not yet," Darquesse said, closing her eyes. "But soon."

96

Axelia sat next to Omen in study class and it made his insides squirm, but in a good way. She smelled of pretty things like lavender soap and strawberry shampoo, and she got out her books and did her work, and Omen let his eyes glaze over and instead of reading from his textbook he daydreamed about being good at stuff. It was a nice way to spend his time.

At the top of the class, Mr Peccant scowled at the paper he was marking. It was probably one of Omen's.

When Axelia finished whatever she was doing, she wrote a note and tossed it lightly on to Omen's desk, and Omen read it and nearly laughed. He turned the laugh into a cough as Peccant glared, and waited until the teacher had gone back to marking papers before replying and tossing the note back to Axelia.

They continued like this for the next ten minutes, until the note hung in the air, mid-toss, then quickly floated up into Peccant's waiting hand.

Omen and Axelia stared, both of them bright red, as a ripple of laughter spread through the room. Peccant held the folded piece of paper for the longest time, his long fingers pressed into the folds.

But, instead of opening it, he dropped it in the wastepaper basket beside his desk. "You aren't children," he growled. "Do not act like children."

Axelia focused on her textbook. So did Omen. He looked at her out of the corner of his eye, saw her grinning. That made him grin.

At lunchtime Omen didn't have anyone to talk to, so he went looking for Never. There had been a slight boost to her opinion of him immediately after they'd retrieved the Obsidian Blade. Granted, that was because both Never and Axelia believed that Omen had taken down Tancred all by himself, but that didn't make it any less sweet.

It didn't last long, of course. By the time Reverie Synecdoche had pronounced him concussion-free, Never's opinion had reverted to normal, which was basically that Omen was a puppy who deserved a pat on the head whenever he didn't screw up too badly.

Omen didn't care. He'd done something right. Yes, he'd had help, and yes, some of that help came in the slightly freakish and all-round mysterious form of Crepuscular Vies, but that didn't take away from the fact that Omen had set out to find the Obsidian Blade to help his brother, and that weapon was now in a box under Auger's bed in his dorm room.

Omen turned a corner, saw Never sitting on a bench, kissing some guy. Omen immediately stopped, then crept backwards, not wanting to interrupt. Never hated it when he interrupted things like this.

The kiss broke off and Never traced his hand down the guy's face, and they turned just enough so that Omen could see his brother.

Auger saw him and his smile faded. Never looked up.

Omen's thoughts weren't happening. He turned and walked away.

His mind was numb. His heart was numb. He registered it beating quickly, but that was the extent of it. He was fine like this. As long as they didn't run after him, he could find somewhere quiet and let this percolate, like coffee. Yes. He didn't like coffee, but he needed to *be* like coffee. It was all so simple.

But they ruined it by running after him.

"Omen." Never's voice. "Omen, hold on."

Now Auger. "Will you please just listen to us?"

The numb sensation went away.

Omen whirled. "Sure," he said. "Go ahead."

Auger and Never glanced at each other, unsure if the other was going to speak first.

"Going great so far," Omen said. "Maybe I should kick this off with a question, what do you say? How long has this been going on?"

"Three weeks," said Auger.

"We didn't want you to find out like this," said Never. "We wanted to tell you, and we talked about telling you, but we... we didn't know *how* to tell you."

"No?" said Omen. "I would have thought it'd be straightforward. *Hey, Omen, we're together. We're going out. We're dating. We're whatever.* See how easy that was? And that's just off the top of my head, like, with no preparation."

"OK," Auger said slowly, "you're upset..."

"Am I?" Omen responded instantly. "How can you tell?"

That was immature, but right now Omen didn't mind one bit.

"We're sorry we didn't tell you," said Auger. "We should have. The truth is, we've been keeping this quiet until we figured it out for ourselves."

Omen crossed his arms, then put his hands on his hips, and then crossed his arms again. He really didn't know what to do with his limbs. "So that's it, then? You're an item now?"

"I suppose," said Auger.

"I don't know what I'm meant to do now. I don't know how I'm supposed to act."

Auger put a gentle hand on Never's shoulder. "Mind if I talk to my brother alone?"

"Sure," said Never, after hesitating. "Sure." He teleported away.

Omen looked at Auger. Auger motioned to a bench. "Sit?"

Omen shrugged, went over. They sat.

"If you don't want me to see Never," Auger said, "all you've got to do is say so. I like him, a whole lot, and she makes me happy and makes me forget about all the crap we've got to deal with... but you're my brother. You pretty much outrank everyone else. I do what you tell me."

Omen looked away. "You don't have to," he muttered.

"Sorry?"

Omen sighed. "You don't have to break up with him."

"OK," Auger said, and smiled. "Thank you." The bell rang. "What've you got now?"

"Maths."

"Yikes. You don't want to be late for that one."

"I don't care."

A raised eyebrow. "Since when? This is Peccant we're talking about."

"There are more important things in life than making sure you don't get in trouble with a teacher," Omen said.

Auger shrugged. "Suppose there are."

"How did it start?"

"Me and Never? It just... I don't know. She's always been cool. I always thought that. But, y'know... he was your friend. I had my friends, and you had yours, and that was that. But then she started helping out, and we'd have to deal with whatever bad guy or monster had popped up, and a bond starts to form when you face something like that. Life-and-death situations lead to some pretty intense feelings. You know that. You've been having your share of excitement, what with the Obsidian Blade thing and all."

"We're not talking about me," said Omen.

"Right. Yeah. So... I just started to appreciate her more and more, that's all. Then, after I got hurt, he came to see me and we were talking, I don't even remember what about, and something about the way he turned, the way the light caught her... I felt it in here, you know?" He tapped his chest. "And then, a few weeks ago, we kissed."

Omen nodded.

"Can I ask you a question?"

"Sure," Omen said.

Auger hesitated. "It kind of took me by surprise, the way you reacted just now. I mean, I get it. Never is your friend and then I come in and I always get everything because I'm the Chosen One and that's how life tends to work out for me. I'm sure it must seem sometimes that I just take everything from you."

"It can seem that way," Omen admitted. "But it's hardly your fault."

"Yeah, mostly it's our parents' fault."

Omen laughed a little, and Auger smiled.

"But it's my fault as well," he continued. "I could do more to make it easier on you. I just don't think sometimes. I'll try to do better. But, with this, I can't help but wonder if, maybe, I've just done something even worse than steal your friend."

"Like what?"

"Like maybe I also stole the person you're a little bit in love with?"

Omen's immediate reaction was to laugh again. "I'm not in love with Never. We're friends, that's all it is."

"You sure?"

"Yes, I'm sure. He's my best friend."

"OK."

Omen's smile faltered.

"What are you thinking?" Auger asked.

"Nothing."

"Dude..."

"Nothing, I said. I... I don't know."

Seconds passed.

"We're very alike, you know," said Auger. "Twins, right? It'd kinda make sense if we both fell in love with the same person."

"I have to go to maths," Omen said quietly, and he got up and walked away.

97

They sat her in a small room and clamped her wrist to the bloodstained table. The same binding sigils that had been etched into the cell she'd spent a month in, that had been etched into the collar she'd worn on the walk here, were etched into the clamp. They weren't taking any chances that she'd be able to use her magic. A large man with many muscles stood behind her, looming. Glowering. He didn't say anything. Didn't even look at her. It was an obvious ploy, intended to intimidate and unnerve. It worked.

The door opened. A smaller man entered. He was smiling, and carried a leather bag, which he placed upon the table. He sat opposite Valkyrie.

"Now then," he said. "We're going to start off easy, and then progress to the trickier questions. You can be as stubborn as you like – that's entirely up to you. Over the years, I have found that everybody tells me what I want to know eventually. It's all a matter of pain and deformity. How much you can stand, and how much you can live with. You're a pretty girl. You have lovely long hair. You're tall and athletic and strong. Pretty people are at a disadvantage when it comes to things like this. Ugly people, well... they at least know what it's like to be ugly. They can, perhaps, live with being a little uglier. But pretty people..." He winced. "They don't cope well with losing their looks. They tend to weave their identity around their appearance, you see.

"But," he said, "before we get to work on your face, before we start pulling teeth, we'll shave your head. It's remarkable the upset this causes. Maybe that will shake the truth out of you. I've seen it happen. But something tells me you're made of sterner stuff. So after we've shaved your head, and we've pulled some teeth, we'll be cutting off some fingers and toes. Soon after, we'll move on to breaking knees. Hobbling you, essentially. A strong person like you, you can perhaps learn to live with being ugly. But can you live with being weak? Infirm? You're so used to being capable, after all. It takes a resolute mind to cope with losing a hand, or a foot, or an entire limb. Are you that strong? Few people are."

He opened his bag, and started taking out tools, instruments, scalpels, a pair of pruning shears, and laying them on the table before her. "As I said, we'll start easy. We'll begin with gentle questions. What is your name?"

"Valerie."

"That's the name you gave Sergeant Assegai. That's not your name."

"Yes, it is."

The big man stepped round so that he was standing beside her. His fist crunched into Valkyrie's cheek and threw her head back.

The world spun and her cheek stung and a massive headache pounded against the inside of her skull, and it took a while for her eyes to squint open again.

"What is your name?" asked the smiling man.

"Marilyn," Valkyrie mumbled. "Marilyn Monroe."

"And where are you from, Marilyn?"

"Graceland."

"And where is Graceland?"

"It's where Elvis lives."

The smiling man nodded. "I don't know these people, but I know a lie when I hear one. Are you going to start telling me the truth at all today, or will I just have my associate continue to hit you?"

"I'll tell you the truth."

"Good. Where are you from?"

"Your butt."

The big guy hit her again. It was worth it.

"Where are you from?"

"No," she gasped, "seriously. Your butt sent me back in time to tell you—"

Another punch. This one nearly sparked her out. Blood ran from her nose, mixed with the blood running from her burst lip. Her head *pounded*.

The smiling man wasn't smiling any more. He looked sad. "I will take my leave," he said. "My associate will continue to hit you until you pass out, and then he'll revive you, and hit you some more. Maybe then you'll be more compliant."

"Wouldn't bet on it," Valkyrie muttered.

98

Valkyrie spat blood on to the sackcloth shift and did her best not to fall off the chair. She'd fallen off plenty of times when the big guy was hitting her, and each time she'd nearly dislocated her arm. The clamp securing her wrist to the table never budged.

The door opened. The interrogator came back in. He sat, and opened his bag, and once more laid out his instruments before her.

"How are you feeling?" he asked.

She didn't answer. Blood drooled from her lips.

"You're not looking quite so pretty, I hope you don't mind me saying so. Your face is swelling quite badly. I fear that, if my associate keeps at it, you might lose your left eye."

Valkyrie barked out a laugh, and the interrogator raised an eyebrow.

"Do you find this amusing?"

"I've been in this kind of situation before," she told him. "I know what I can take, and I can take this big idiot hitting me for another few hours."

"Hitting you isn't all he can do."

"Oh," she said, "I'm sure he's multitalented. But why not just get to the fun stuff? You want to start cutting off fingers. That's why my wrist is clamped down like this, right?"

"Yes."

"You gonna cauterise it after, are you? To stop me from bleeding out?"

"Yes."

"Just checking that you know what you're doing."

"We've done this before, don't you worry. But I feel I should at least give you an opportunity to answer my questions."

"Don't bother," she said. "I'm just going to stick to my story. My name's Marilyn Monroe, I'm a big movie star, I live with Elvis in Graceland, and I've been sent back in time by your butt to insult you and call you names."

The interrogator sighed, and picked up the pruning shears. "Very well," he said. "Do you have a least-favourite finger you'd like to part with first?"

Valkyrie grinned, aware of how the blood in her teeth would make her look. "Who cares? It'll just grow back."

"You think your finger will grow back?"

"Pretty sure of it."

The interrogator chuckled. "This should be interesting," he said, reaching for her hand. He held each of her fingers for a few seconds, as if he was testing it, judging its worth.

Valkyrie laughed again, a little panic edging its way in. "Go for the thumb," she said.

"Why is that?"

She shrugged. "It's the thickest. You'll have to work harder. Go on. Bet you can't. Bet you won't even get halfway through before you have to call on the big guy to take over."

The interrogator sighed again. He did love sighing.

"Hold her," he said, like he was bored, and the big guy pressed his hands down on Valkyrie's shoulders, securing her to the chair. She took a few deep breaths as the cold blades slipped either side of her thumb.

"Higher," she said. "Come on. Get the whole thing, you wuss. Either do the job properly or give it to someone who can."

"You know," the interrogator said, "normally, I derive no

pleasure from this part of the process. But I think I'm actually going to enjoy your screams. It'll be a nice change from you insulting me."

She grinned again, her teeth clenched. "Do it. Do it."

She heard the snip and something fall to the tabletop, and then the pain came and she screamed and thrashed and the big guy did his very best to keep her in place.

Tears streaming from her eyes, snot mixing with the blood, the next thing Valkyrie was aware of was the click of fingers and an intense heat that brought the screaming back.

"You have nine more fingers," the interrogator said. "Ten more toes. Can you really do this nineteen more times? What is your name, and where are you from?"

Valkyrie didn't answer. She was barely aware of the big guy fixing the chair back under her.

"You're a very brave young lady," the interrogator said. "You have my respect. You do. For what that's worth. But no one is coming to save you. That door is not going to be kicked in today, or tomorrow, or the next day. You're on your own, and you'd better start acting like it. What is your name?"

Valkyrie wiped her mouth with the back of her hand. "OK," she said. "OK. Hold on." She took a deep breath, trying to steady herself, trying to get her body under control. Her legs were trembling. She didn't know if she could stand, but she tried anyway.

"Sit down," said the interrogator, and motioned for the big guy to enforce his command.

Valkyrie's free hand gripped the edge of the table, and she took a deep breath and held it. Then she yanked her hand out of the clamp.

It was pretty easy to do, now that her thumb was gone.

Magic flooded her even as the pain hit, but she was already turning, her left hand slamming into the big guy's chest. There was a flash of white light and he hurtled backwards, crashed into

390

the wall. Before he'd dropped to the floor, she was turning again, shoving the table into the interrogator. His chair almost tipped over and she let a bolt of lightning send him spinning across the room.

She held her hand against her chest and doubled over with the pain, moaning behind clenched teeth. Neither the big guy nor the interrogator were moving. No alarm had been raised.

Valkyrie looked around, found her thumb on the ground and picked it up. She went light-headed as she stood, and stumbled into the table. She found herself humming tunelessly. She didn't know why she needed to do that, but she did, and so she let it continue. While she hummed, she counted to twenty, then straightened.

Still holding her thumb, Valkyrie went to the door and listened. No voices. No footsteps. She opened it slightly and peeked, then let herself out.

The corridor was dark and cold and it led back to the dungeon, but the dungeon had guards, and she was in no condition for a full-on fight right now. She needed a doctor. That's what she needed. She needed to reach into a doctor's mind and find out how to reattach her goddamn thumb.

She leaned against the wall to rest. Her eyes closed, she did her best to push the pain to one side and reached out with her thoughts, searching her immediate vicinity. She could sense the prisoners, sense their desperation, their defeat, their sadness. She moved on, to the guards, sensing their boredom. Further than that, people passing in and out of range. Random thoughts, random emotions. More than a few times, she encountered a mind with walls around it and she quickly retreated before they noticed. She sent her thoughts further, like an expanding balloon, in all directions at once.

Until she found what she was looking for.

99

Two guards ahead on the other side of the door. Bored. Hungry. One of them had to pee really badly, but didn't want to admit it because the other one kept laughing about his tiny bladder. Valkyrie moved her awareness beyond them, found no one else in the area.

She put one hand on the door, and prepared herself. Her headache was enough to almost drive her to her knees, not to mention the throbbing pain of her missing thumb. She ignored all that, and focused.

She picked the guard on her left and barged into his mind, bludgeoning her way through his thoughts. She heard him drop his spear and then she pulled the door open. The guard was stumbling, tearing his helmet from his head. The second guard was following him, confused and a little frightened. She hurried up and zapped him, right at the base of the skull, and he was flung forward. She zapped the first guard and he collapsed.

Valkyrie swayed, a wave of blackness sweeping across her vision. When she was sure she wasn't going to pass out, she started moving again.

She knew what direction she was headed in, but didn't know the route. That was fine around the dungeon, where foot traffic was scarce, but it became a significant problem the deeper into the Palace she travelled. Every few steps, she had to duck or run back or hide, and every time she did it she came closer and closer to someone spotting her.

But somehow she managed to climb a set of stone stairs without meeting anyone coming the other way. She tripped on the very top step, went stumbling into a dark corner, where she crouched and waited for two members of the palace staff to pass.

The healer was close. He was a nervous man, and he was in a hurry. Gritting her teeth, Valkyrie made herself move faster. She couldn't afford to let him get away.

She turned a corner. There was a junction of corridors ahead. He'd be passing in front of her in mere seconds. She took another step and her leg buckled. She went down, painfully, on one knee, but kept the cry of pain to nothing more than a hiss, and she looked up to see him hurrying by.

Feeling like she was going to puke, Valkyrie forced herself up, staggered to the next corner in time to watch him open a door and go through.

"Sorry I'm late," he said, and the door closed.

Valkyrie didn't have a choice. She had to go in after him, no matter who else was in there. She wasn't going to last much longer out here, not with her injuries, or her hunger. She was going to black out at any moment.

Scraping her shoulder against the wall, she made it to the door. Her head was pounding too hard to even scan what was on the other side, so she put her ear to it. She heard the nervous doctor apologising again, but his voice was growing ever fainter. He was walking away.

She opened the door just in time to see him disappear through another.

She looked around. The laboratory was small and windowless and stank of spices and something sour. There was a person hunched over a table, their back to Valkyrie. She crept in, her entire body trembling and close to collapse. It took all her effort to put one foot in front of the other and not fall against the tables and send the jars and tubes crashing to the ground.

And then her knee buckled again, and Professor Nye twisted in its seat, its small eyes widening.

Valkyrie launched herself forward, grabbed Nye before it could run. They fell to the floor, Valkyrie on top. Nye's thin fingers pressed into her chest and it straightened its long, long arms and shoved her to one side. She went rolling, too exhausted to do anything about it.

Valkyrie lay there, holding her right hand. She'd jarred it somewhere along the way, and tears of pain trickled down her cheeks.

Nye stood. "Valkyrie Cain," it said in that high-pitched voice. "What is it about you, Valkyrie, that always brings you to my door?"

She didn't answer. There was no point. She just lay there and felt sore.

"You look like you've come from the dungeons. Is that where you've come from? How long have you been there? When Mevolent finds out you've been under his feet, he is not going to be pleased. He quite fancies killing you himself, you know."

Nye stepped closer, looked down at her. "You seem to have lost a digit."

Valkyrie grabbed its ankle and crashed into its mind, throwing open the doors to the centuries of knowledge contained within.

She found the biological. The medical. She understood how things worked, how they knitted together. She'd skirted the fringes of this before, back when she'd delved into that doctor's mind in Roarhaven, where she'd latched on to his power and healed herself.

But this was different. This was far more advanced. She could do far more with this.

The first thing Valkyrie did was shut off the pain. That instantly relaxed her. She let go of Nye's ankle and ignored its whimpering as she sat up. She dropped her severed thumb into her left hand, and focused on the cauterised stump. Her flesh bubbled, the burnt skin dissolving, and she pressed the thumb against the stump and worked on reattaching it. Bone fused to bone as nerves searched and found each other. Blood flowed. Skin grew.

She splayed her fingers, then made a fist, then flooded her body with strength and energy. Her bruises faded. Swelling went down. Fractures healed. Her nose straightened. Her jaw aligned. The weight that she'd lost in that cell, the weight that she'd lost over these seven months, came back on. Her muscles returned to their optimum state.

Valkyrie sighed, and stood. "There," she said. "I feel so much better. No aches and pains, no stiffness, no trouble breathing... Lately I've been feeling like I'm getting back to my old self, you know? Or as close to it as I'm going to get. I feel energised – reinvigorated – like there's nothing I can't do." She looked down at Nye as it continued to whimper. "Who's got two thumbs and is going to save the world?" she asked, then jerked both of her thumbs towards her smiling face. "This chick."

100

The shield around Tahil na Kurge was straining.

The draugar were still pressing themselves against it and getting disintegrated for their trouble, but the Necromancers were active now, too, sending their spears of shadow down on to the shield in a constant barrage. Now, when a draugr touched it, it took a few seconds to fry them. Skulduggery estimated that the shield would fall in six weeks. The problem was that Mevolent's invasion would happen in three.

Tanith wandered over to him as he stood in the Resistance camp with his arms folded, looking at the sky. "What are you thinking?" she asked.

He didn't move. "What makes you think I'm thinking anything?"

"Because you're you, and because Val told me that, when you're standing around with your arms folded and not saying anything, it means you're hatching a plan. So what are you thinking?"

"I'm thinking," he said, "that there may be a flaw in their defences."

"Do tell."

"The constant barrage against the shield is having an obvious effect. That means that the people inside the city will probably feel the need to reinforce the points of impact by drawing power away from the areas of the shield that aren't being touched."

"And where would these areas be?"

Skulduggery's gloved fingers tapped his chin. "Underground. Deep underground. If, for argument's sake, the shield began in a perfect egg shape, I would imagine that now it resembles an egg with the bottom section sliced off."

Tanith nodded. "Allowing all the gooey stuff to flow out."

"Well, not quite, but..."

"So what we need is someone like Billy-Ray," Tanith said. "Someone to tunnel under and then up. Is there anyone in the Resistance who can do that?"

"What do you say we find out?"

They went looking for Meritorious, but he wasn't in his tent. They found him walking among his army, slapping people on the back and offering words of encouragement, the way a good leader should. Skulduggery told him what they were looking for.

"We had someone with that ability," Meritorious said. "I'd send him out regularly to check if the shield had any openings. He'd have been perfect for this."

Skulduggery inclined his head. "I'm guessing he's no longer with us."

"He was stabbed in an argument about boots. Died before we could get a healer to him."

"And there's no one else?" Tanith asked.

Meritorious shook his head. Silence followed.

"I might be able to manage it," Skulduggery said.

Meritorious frowned. "You're an Elemental."

"I've been working on expanding what that means. I've passed through walls before."

"Yeah," Tanith said, "but it's been tricky, hasn't it?"

"Oh, yes. But I'm fairly certain I can manipulate the earth well enough to pass under the shield."

"In that case," Meritorious said, "have at it. Will you need anyone with you? Your team?"

"I can't be sure that I'll succeed, I can't be certain how long it would take, and I'm the only one who doesn't require oxygen."

"I'm coming with you," said Tanith.

He looked at her. "I've already lost two people on this mission. I have no intention of losing a third."

"And I have no intention of being lost," said Tanith, "but I'm bored out of my mind here. You and me, Skulduggery. We can do this."

"Tanith, I—"

"No argument. If you're going in there to assassinate someone, you might want to bring an assassin."

101

Valkyrie broke into a big house in one of Tahil na Kurge's most prestigious areas, and had a bath.

God, it felt good to wash away all the filth and the grime. It felt good to dunk her head under the hot water, to wash her hair, to get clean again after all this time on the road, in that cell. She lay back, eyes closed, the water lapping at her ears. Just a minute. Just one extra minute of enjoying the sensation, the luxury, before getting back to business.

She counted back from sixty to zero slowly, and then she opened her eyes.

OK then.

She climbed out of the bath. The house was warm so she padded, dripping, into the kitchen. She ate at the table, enjoying every mouthful. She wasn't entirely sure what she was eating, but it tasted amazing. All they had to drink was wine, though, so she washed the food down with water and went back upstairs.

It was a big house and had a big bedroom, with three rooms devoted entirely to wardrobe. By the framed photographs on the shelves, a man and woman lived here, and Valkyrie took a pair of his trousers, dark grey, and laid them on the bed. She found a belt that just about fitted, chose one of the lady's black silk shirts and had to make do with a pair of the least awkward shoes she could find. She didn't much care for the high fashion in this world. Not very practical.

She dressed, left her hair down, chose a hooded coat that buttoned tight up the middle and opened dramatically at the waist.

OK, fine, the coat rocked. But the shoes were uncomfortable. She missed her suit.

She came down the stairs as the front door opened and the man and woman from the photographs entered, concerned frowns on their rich faces. Just goes to show that money doesn't really mean anything when you're surrounded by hordes of the dead.

"Hello," Valkyrie said, flashing them a big smile.

They started. The lady clutched the man.

"Who are you?" the man demanded to know.

The lady peered closer. "Is that my coat?"

"Probably," Valkyrie said, reaching the bottom and striding towards them. "You have a lovely house and a lovely bath. I ate some of your food and used your toilet. I'm also stealing your clothes. Thank you for your help."

The man's frown deepened. "You can't do that."

Valkyrie held up a hand. "Don't argue with me, Herbert."

"My name's not—"

"I said don't argue with me. Move aside, please."

The couple hesitated, then moved. Valkyrie nodded to them. "Much obliged."

She left the house and followed the street round to her right, emerging on to a wide thoroughfare packed with people. It was lined with shops and stores of various sizes, but the signage on every single one was classy, and classy meant expensive. Most of the stores, however, were closed, with the contents being loaded on to a succession of horseless carts parked in the road outside. Everyone, it seemed, was preparing for the evacuation.

She passed Redhoods and kept her eyes dead ahead. She passed Sense-Wardens and kept her thoughts in a straight line. She passed them all and not one of them turned to look at her.

In the centre of the thoroughfare was a place called Merchant's Square. In the square, three identical structures were being built. Redhoods kept the gawking public well clear of the construction crews, but Valkyrie found a good spot off to one side where she could observe without being jostled.

Three giant metal rings, trailing wires and cables and tubes, carved with sigils and gleaming black in the midday sun. Three portals to another dimension, *her* dimension, each wide enough to fit twenty soldiers at a time. From what she remembered from Nye's thoughts, Mevolent's army had commandeered a massive section of the city while they waited for the order to go. Hundreds of thousands of trained sorcerers streaming through, intent on slaughter.

Unless she stopped them, of course.

Valkyrie looked up, at the shield that surrounded the city. The Necromancers jabbed at it with their shadows. She frowned. It didn't seem quite so vibrant today. She wondered if that was worrying Mevolent, or at least worrying his little henchmen. She hoped it was. There was nothing like the possibility of an imminent breach to nudge nervous people into making mistakes.

102

It was weird, having a secret friend he couldn't tell anyone about, but things were made slightly easier by the fact that Omen didn't have anyone to tell.

He hadn't spoken more than a dozen words to either Auger or Never in the last three days. He would have talked to Axelia, but she was having trouble with her boyfriend, and he didn't want to add to her problems. He spent breakfasts and lunches eating alone, took long walks through Corrival or Roarhaven, and when he was in class he barely looked up from his books. That last part was unsettling, and made him wonder if this was what it meant to be an adult – just too glum to daydream.

But he had to talk to someone, and so he picked up his phone one evening and sent a message. An hour later, he was sitting on one of the benches in the park beside Black Lake, in a coat, hat and scarf.

It was freezing. This was such a bad idea.

"Cold night," Crepuscular Vies said beside him.

Omen nearly jumped up. "Holy cow!"

Crepuscular laughed. "Sorry. Didn't mean to scare you, but it's kind of what I do, you know?"

"I wasn't scared," Omen said, hand over his racing heart.

"Uh-huh," said Crepuscular, a smile in his voice and that ever-present grin on his face. "I have to admit, I did not expect to see you again so soon."

"Oh," said Omen. "It's fine, if you don't want to—"

Crepuscular waved his words away. "Don't undervalue yourself, Omen. If I didn't want to be here, I wouldn't be. The plain fact is, I don't have an awful lot of friends and, when I find someone who doesn't judge me based on my appearance, I kind of make myself available. So what can I do for you?"

"It's really nothing," said Omen. "I just... I felt like a chat and..."

"And you came to me, the chattiest person you know, and, like an idiot, I suggested a park in the winter. Sorry about that."

Omen laughed. "It's OK. I'm wrapped up well."

So was Crepuscular. His coat and his gloves were dark wool, and his scarf was bright yellow. "You have the face of a man with something to talk about," he said. "And I have the face of a good listener. Or I think I do, somewhere around here..." He patted his pockets.

Omen grinned. "That's funny."

"Thank you."

Omen took a breath. "My brother has started going out with my best friend."

"Ah."

"So that has me, y'know... preoccupied."

"I understand."

"And he thinks the reason I'm having such a problem with it is that I, kind of, value my friend as more than a friend, if you know what I mean."

"I do."

"So..."

"And do you?"

"Do I what?"

"Value your friend as more than a friend," Crepuscular said.

"I'm not sure. It didn't really occur to me before he said it."

"Unspoken truths tend to be like that."

"I didn't think I did. I didn't think I *could*. But then all this just... You don't have to talk about this. I know how silly it is."

"It's not silly at all, Omen. Affairs of the heart are never silly. Whether it's love or hate or anything in between, it all matters. It all weighs the same."

"What do you think I should do?"

"What do *you* think you should do?"

"Like... maybe talk to my friend? Tell her what I'm thinking?"

"That's definitely one way of doing it."

"You don't think I should tell him?"

Crepuscular frowned. "Tell who?"

"My friend."

"I thought your friend was a girl."

"She's both."

"And you alternate pronouns?"

"In the abstract, yes."

"OK then. So one course of action is, yes, tell her what you're thinking, how you're feeling, and see if he feels the same way."

"But you don't think I should do that."

"No, I do not. I think you walk away. Figuratively, of course."

"Without saying anything?"

"If your friend felt the same way about you, then you'd be dating your friend, would you not? Instead, your friend is dating your brother. What does that tell you?"

"She likes him and not me."

"Precisely."

Omen sighed. "That's really not what I wanted to hear."

"I understand that," Crepuscular said. "But the unwelcome truths are the important ones."

"You seem to know a lot about different kinds of truth."

"Why, that there is my forte, Omen. We all have many truths, do we not?"

"I don't think I do. I think I'm too simple for more than one."

"Ha. Perhaps."

"What are yours?"

"Oh, too many to tell."

"That's what I figured."

"I'll tell you one of my truths. I was once like you. Eager to please. Eager to impress. I had what you might call a mentor, and I would have done anything to gain his approval."

"This story doesn't have a happy ending, does it?"

"Few of my stories ever do."

"Who was he? Your mentor?"

Crepuscular adjusted his bow tie. "A fearsome warrior. A brilliant mind. A man racked by hate and guilt and self-loathing. I believe you know him, in fact."

"Oh?"

"I was Skulduggery Pleasant's partner," said Crepuscular. "And he left me to die."

103

"I'm sorry," Omen said. "What?"

"He was my mentor and my partner," said Crepuscular. "He taught me everything he knew and I soaked it all in. I endured the constant put-downs and the insults and the jokes at my expense, because what I was learning went far beyond what could be taught in a class. I was out there, saving the world, fighting by his side. It was wonderful."

"You were his partner?"

"I was. I didn't have this name, and I certainly didn't have this face – they both came later – but I was there. Fulfilling a dream I'd had since I was a young boy."

"What happened?"

"Ultimately? After years of adventuring? We walked right into trouble, as we tended to do, trading banter the entire time. The jokes, you see, have always been Skulduggery's first line of defence. They act as a shield from responsibility, from consequence – even from his own feelings. So that's the first thing you learn, as his partner. If you can't keep up with the jokes, you don't stay around for long. I can guarantee you that Valkyrie Cain has experienced this also. It is *very* effective.

"This, by the way, was years before Miss Cain was even born. Skulduggery wasn't known for taking on partners. He'd been one of the Dead Men, this is true, but being part of a seven-person team is a lot different from being in a partnership. It's easier to hide in a team."

Crepuscular's voice faded a little before he straightened up slightly and his assertiveness returned. "So... the night in question. We were on the trail of a most despicable quarry. A murderer, many times over, of men, women and even children. A murderer with big plans. Schemes within schemes. Truly, a worthy opponent for the great Skulduggery Pleasant. And his sidekick." He turned to look at Omen. "Have you noticed Skulduggery's tendency to expound on his own genius? It's a trait that has refused to dim as the years have gone by. But he never talks about the enemies who are smarter than he is. Never once did he mention ever being outsmarted by someone else."

"Is that what happened here?" Omen asked.

"It is indeed. He was outsmarted. Outfoxed. Outmanoeuvred. And, for his hubris, I paid the price."

Omen only had a vague idea what hubris meant, but he let it go because Crepuscular seemed to be on a roll.

"We walked right into a trap," Crepuscular continued. "I was caught up in it. Skulduggery reached for me, tried to save me, of course he did. He's always liked to think of himself as the good guy. But, in this instance, he failed, and I was whipped away, screaming."

"And he left you to die?"

"He thought I *was* dead," Crepuscular replied. "Unfortunately, I survived. My captors were... attentive. They took my face away."

"But you got out?"

"Eventually."

"And you didn't go back to Skulduggery?"

"No. I admit it, Omen. I was angry, hurt even, that he'd given up on me so easily. His search for my remains yielded nothing and he was quickly consumed by another case, another investigation, another villain to stop..."

"And what did you do?"

"I recovered. I healed. Or at least, I did my very best to heal. Then I left my old life behind. Left my name with it. I started again as Crepuscular Vies, the fine specimen you see before you."

"So you hate him? Skulduggery?"

Crepuscular didn't answer right away. "You'd expect so, wouldn't you? But I can't bring myself to hate anyone, Omen. It's not how I was raised. I've seen hatred claim the hearts and the souls of better people than me. No, I take what Skulduggery taught me and I do my best to help those in need. It's why I helped you."

"So Skulduggery doesn't know you're still alive?"

"He doesn't, and – I know this is asking a lot – I'd appreciate it if you didn't tell him. If you didn't tell anyone about me. I'm not overly fond of people knowing I exist. Look at this face – would you be any different?"

He chuckled, and Omen made himself smile.

"I think I have to prove to myself – and, eventually, to Skulduggery – that I am his equal. That I can do what he does. That I can have the effect he has. And then, I don't know... I want to surpass him, I suppose. I want to be a better Skulduggery Pleasant than Skulduggery Pleasant ever managed to be."

"How are you going to do that?"

"Well," Crepuscular said, "for a start, I'm not going to leave my partner to die."

104

Tanith managed to get a good night's sleep, but when she woke her eyes fell upon Saracen's bedding, and all the good feelings threatened to drain out of her.

A pair of mud-encrusted boots stopped in front of her. "I think this is a serious mistake," said Serpine.

She sat up. "Of course you do."

"Even if he doesn't get you killed underground, you're still emerging into an entire city filled with people who will try to kill you."

She pulled on her boots. "Only if they figure out who we are. Nefarian, I'm not staying here another second. I have a chance to do something, and I'm going to do it."

"Have you ever heard the phrase, *better to be bored than dead?*"

"No."

"I'm not surprised. I made it up just then. Just for you."

He held out his left hand. She took it and he pulled her to her feet. He'd grown a beard in the last few weeks. Not so much an aesthetic choice as an inevitable consequence of losing his shaving hand – Tanith had to admit, it looked good on him.

"If you die," he said, "I will have no one to talk to."

"Talk to Dexter."

"He hates me."

"So?"

"And you made it worse when you called us *beard-buddies*."

Tanith grinned. "The look on both your faces, I swear..."

"Please come back," he said. "Please don't let the skeleton get you killed."

"I'll be fine. Stop worrying about me, OK? Honestly, you're like my mother, if she'd ever worried about me."

Dexter appeared, opening the flap of the tent, scowled when he saw Serpine, and nodded to Tanith. "The Teleporter's back."

"Cool," she said. She grasped Serpine's left hand in hers.

"Be careful," he said.

"I will."

"And kill Mevolent, there's a good girl."

She grinned, then left the tent with Dexter.

"Do you actually like him?" Dexter asked as they walked.

Tanith shrugged. "I've known worse people."

"Worse people than Nefarian Serpine?"

"Well, maybe not worse, but I've known bad people and evil people and boring people. And at least he's not boring. You'll have to keep an eye on him when we're gone, you know."

"Oh, I will."

"There are people in this camp who want him dead."

"There are people in that *tent* who want him dead," Dexter responded, then sighed. "Yeah, I know."

Tanith came to a stop. "Listen, Dex... we haven't really talked about Saracen."

He stopped, and turned. "He survived a hell of a lot longer than he should have, all things considered. I mean, that power of his? Come on. He should never have made it through the *war* with that power – but somehow he managed."

"I'm going to miss him."

"Me too. I miss them all. Hopeless and Larrikin and Ghastly and Anton, and all the others. All those other people we lost along the way. Saracen's just one more to add to the list."

"But he was your best friend."

"Yeah. Yeah, he was."

"He told me he'd always wanted a stupid death."

Dexter smiled. "The piano thing? Yeah, he told me that, too. But I suppose he got what he wanted, didn't he? Of everyone we've gone up against, everyone we've fought... I mean, we've battled *gods*. But it was a draugr that got him. A... a bloody zombie draugr. Just another shambling, shuffling, snarling *thing*. Such a stupid, pointless, meaningless death."

"At least he was with his friends when it happened."

"You think that was a comfort? I don't know. Maybe it was. Maybe he even knew what was happening when I... I hope he did. I hope he knew I was there when the end came."

"When we get home," Tanith said, "we're drinking a toast to Saracen."

Dexter nodded. "Yes, we are."

They continued on, found Skulduggery in Meritorious's tent. The Teleporter arrived, took them all to the hill looking out on to Tahil na Kurge.

Dexter put his hand on Skulduggery's arm. "Are you sure you can do this?"

"Yes," Skulduggery said.

Dexter dropped his hand. "OK then."

"Probably."

"That's really not what I want to hear," said Tanith.

"Nothing good in this life comes without risk," said Skulduggery. "We're going to be fine. I can do this. I know I can. But, if you want to stay behind, I'll understand."

"I'm not going to stay behind."

"Good," he said. "Just to warn you, I probably won't be saying much while we do this. I'm going to need to devote a great portion of my concentration to making sure we don't die."

"I'm OK with that, actually."

"Excellent."

"Without wishing to add to the pressure you must undoubtedly feel," said Meritorious, "all our lives are dependant on your success. Many, many lives. Many innocent lives. Lot of children. Some babies, even." He nodded. "Well, best of luck."

"Cheers," Tanith said sourly, and stepped up beside Skulduggery.

The ground started to crack and crumble, and then they were moving down, into it.

Tanith's feet disappeared. Then her ankles. She watched as the ground swallowed her shins, moving up her boots to her trousers. Her knees. The ground was cold. She clung a little tighter to Skulduggery, and covered her mouth and nose with her hand.

And suddenly they were dropping, the ground digging at her as she passed into it. Dirt tumbled down her collar, brushed against her closed eyelids, and the world beyond her eyes went dark.

She'd done this before, with Sanguine. He'd taken her everywhere by burrowing through the ground like this – but that was his discipline, and he was good at it, and so it had never crossed Tanith's mind that they might get stuck down there.

It crossed her mind now, though.

The dark was absolute. She kept her hand away from her phone. She didn't want to light it up, didn't want to see the rocks all around them. She figured that'd be too much to take.

So she kept her eyes closed as they started moving. Forward and down they went, accompanied by the roar of the shifting earth. Dirt got into her mouth and she spat it out.

She focused all her attention on her breathing, on making sure she was taking calm, measured breaths, and tried not to worry about how fast they were going or how much oxygen she had left. Worrying about these problems would not solve these problems. So Tanith breathed.

Rumble rumble. Breathe. *Rumble rumble.* Breathe.

The rumbling was giving her a headache, but she couldn't really worry about that, either. She was also shivering with the cold. This was something else she couldn't worry about.

The rumbling stopped. Tanith opened her eyes, blinking. In the darkness beside her, there was a blue glow. She held her hand against it, could just about make out a shape. They were right next to the shield.

Skulduggery's voice came out of the blackness. He spoke softly, yet it sounded loud in there. "How are you doing?"

"Not panicking."

"Good. That's good. We'll go down as deep as we have to, and, once we're under, we'll go straight up. Are you ready?"

Tanith nodded.

"Excellent."

"You can see me?" she asked.

"I can."

"How do I look?"

"Not nervous at all."

She gave a tight smile, and they started moving again. Every so often, the blue glow would disappear and Skulduggery would move them in closer.

It was getting harder to breathe. The air that he'd brought with them was running out. Tanith cleared her mind, meditating on the sound of the earth.

Down they went. Down and down. Down further.

Then the glow disappeared, and didn't come back.

"We've passed beneath the shield," said Skulduggery. "Now we go up."

She nodded and closed her eyes.

Up they went. Up and up. Up further.

Getting harder and harder to meditate. Thoughts started slipping through. Little slivers of panic came with them.

Her fingers tightened on Skulduggery. A whimper escaped her lips, drowned out by the constant roar. She opened her eyes, tried to suck in a breath, but there was no air to breathe, and she grabbed at him, shook her head violently and then light burst at her and the roar went away and she gasped, gasped, gasped again

413

at the warmth and light all around, at the wind rushing to fill her ears, her eyes squeezed shut against all of it, stumbling away.

A bright flash and a grunt and something hitting her leg, turning, eyes opening to slits, watching Skulduggery crumple.

Looking up. Flashes of crimson. Redhoods.

Tanith jumped, sword ringing from its scabbard. Bright flash and a collision and the world tipping over and spinning. Hitting the ground and rolling. Boots coming in and kicking.

Then it all went away.

105

Tanith woke and slowly raised her head. She took in her surroundings calmly, assessed the situation, and said, "Huh."

She was in an office. A large office. Cold stone walls. Cold stone floor. Cold stone ceiling. Lots of stone. Lots of cold.

What made it an office was the huge wooden desk in front of her, a desk with sheets of paper in very neat piles. Everything precise. Everything perfect. The sign of an orderly mind. Or was it a disorderly mind? She couldn't remember.

The desk was wide, but it was also high. The chair, too, was bigger than your average chair. Higher.

Heavy tapestries hung on the walls between the windows, the wind doing its best to ruffle them. The tapestries showed scenes of war and bloodshed, but also peaceful scenes of meadows and streams and clouds and suchlike. It was hard to get a read on it all.

There was a big door opposite.

Tanith turned her head. "Hey," she said.

"Hey," said Skulduggery.

He was in a tall glass case, like she was, chained to a rack, like she was. He was naked. A naked skeleton, chained to a rack.

Mevolent liked to display his vanquished opponents like that, Tanith knew. He'd had the corpse of Mr Bliss on display for all to see, naked and submerged in liquid in one of the churches in Dublin-Within-The-Wall. Valkyrie had told her all about it.

Which made Tanith wonder why she wasn't naked. The fact was, she was actually wearing more clothes than she usually would. She was wearing some sort of green jumpsuit. Prison issue, perhaps. Functional, but not very flattering.

"I'm not naked," she said.

"No," Skulduggery agreed. "You're not."

"Why do you think that is?"

"I genuinely don't know."

"I'm not complaining. It's pretty cold up here."

The door opened. Mevolent came through.

He was eight feet tall, a slender gentleman with fair hair, cut short. His skin had a yellow tinge to it, like a book that had been left in the sun. He had a thin metal band around his head, like a crown, and from that metal band a veil of sorts came down – just low enough to hide his eyes. He was dressed in simple clothes – trousers and a flowing shirt. Sandals.

He came round the desk, but didn't look at them, didn't say anything. He just sat in his chair and pulled himself a little closer to the desk and started working. Tanith studied the back of his head. Whatever she'd been expecting when he came in, this wasn't it.

"Hello," said Skulduggery.

Mevolent picked up a pen, started writing.

Skulduggery continued. "You seem to have captured us. Congratulations. We've been captured before, so I suppose there's no actual prestige attached to it, but it's a vindication, in a way. All your hard work and effort have paid off, and our plans have been foiled."

No response.

"Or have they?" Skulduggery asked. "Around about now, you must be thinking to yourself that capturing us was surprisingly easy. Maybe you're wondering if we allowed ourselves to be captured, because we knew you couldn't resist bringing us into your inner sanctum. Aha! That's got you worried, hasn't it? For all you know, you've fallen right into our trap, and we only had to wait for you to enter the room before springing it!"

Mevolent's pen kept scratching the paper.

Skulduggery sagged back against the rack. "Obviously, you haven't stepped into our trap. We don't have one. We don't want to be here. Could you let us go? Or at least let *me* go? You can keep Tanith."

"Cheers," said Tanith.

"Mevolent?" Skulduggery said. "Could you respond in some way? You're hurting my feelings. You probably don't think I have any feelings to hurt, but you're wrong. I'm actually a very sensitive person, as I'm sure you are. Would you like to talk about it? I'd certainly like to talk about it."

"Dear God," said Tanith. "Mevolent, please answer him. I don't think he's going to shut up otherwise."

"I'm really not."

"He can talk for days."

"I really can," Skulduggery said. "I've got no vocal cords to strain, and no end to the topics available to talk about. I know a great many things about a great many things, and at this point it's really just about the order in which I take them. Shall we go alphabetically, or something more whimsical? I think whimsical. Have you ever wondered how fast the human eye dries up in a corpse?"

Eight hours later, Skulduggery had moved on to the different types of insects that lay eggs in the bodies of murder victims. Tanith was staring at the floor, her mind softly buzzing. Mevolent hadn't once acknowledged their presence. Not once. He'd kept his head down, kept reading those papers and scratching that pen. Someone had come in a few hours ago to light the braziers, and he didn't even look up at that. Eight hours. Eight long and incredibly boring hours.

And then suddenly Mevolent put down his pen, pushed his chair back, stood, and left the room.

Skulduggery stopped talking. Tanith blinked. Looked up. The silence was unsettling and strange.

"Well," Skulduggery said. "That was rude."

106

The house was quiet.

Sebastian stepped through it cautiously, as if the floorboards were mined. He poked his head into the living room. He watched Darquesse float around the room and said, "Hey," very softly.

"Hello," she said.

He smiled, a little nervously, and stepped in, making sure to stay out of her orbit. "Where is everyone?"

"I sent them away," Darquesse answered.

"Where to?"

"Everywhere."

"Cool. Cool. How are you feeling?"

She stopped moving and just hovered there, looking at him. "I am uncomfortable all the time," she said. "My feet hurt. My hair is dry. The baby thumps on my womb."

"And how are you feeling emotionally?"

"I remain calm, despite the chemicals my body is pumping out."

"Bet you're looking forward to it being over."

She frowned at him slightly. "If I wanted this to be over, I would bring the pregnancy to term and give birth right now. But what would be the point of that? The pregnancy is the point. The experience is why I'm doing this."

Sebastian nodded. "Yep, yes, I get it. I do."

"You don't."

"No, I don't, but I get that you do, and that's the only thing that matters here."

"True," Darquesse said, and started floating around the room again.

107

Keeping her face hidden beneath her coat's hood, Valkyrie Cain stole through the city like a super-cool ghost dressed in black.

Or at least that's how she liked to think of herself – all spooky and awesome-looking. It was a nice way to live, all things considered. A little bit of self-adoration every now and then never hurt anyone, and it was infinitely preferable to the self-loathing that she was doing her best to leave behind, like a less-than-cool snakeskin that she'd slithered out of. Or something.

Without her suit to sustain her, she got hungry regularly, so she broke into a lot of houses and nicked a lot of food. She didn't feel too bad about it.

She was getting to know Tahil na Kurge pretty well. There was Mevolent's Palace, there was Merchant's Square where the portals were being built, the Market District – and the neighbourhoods that had been commandeered by the military. It was in one of those neighbourhoods that Valkyrie spied her quarry – Sergeant Assegai. Wearing the necronaut suit.

Using the shadows to keep out of sight, Valkyrie followed Assegai to a modest house on a modest street. Once she was sure there was no one watching, she crossed the street, crept up the stairs as Assegai entered. As the door swung closed, she darted through – only noticing the sigil on the wall as it flashed red. The bracelet on Assegai's wrist buzzed and she turned, frowning.

Valkyrie rammed into her. They tumbled to the floor and rolled, scratching and clawing, snarling and yanking at each other's hair. Valkyrie got in a sneaky elbow, but Assegai used the momentum to separate.

They got up, each on one knee, glaring.

Some people would have used that moment to say a few words, maybe trade some insults or issue a few threats. Not Assegai, though. She was all business, all the time.

Her hand snapped and the air rippled and Valkyrie grunted as she hurtled backwards. She sprawled and a fireball came for her and she kicked it, the flames dispersing around her boot, at the same time as she hit Assegai with a blast of lightning that spun her on the spot.

Valkyrie scrambled up. Assegai's face contorted.

She crashed into Valkyrie's midsection, drove her back a few steps, then swung her head up, grazing Valkyrie's chin. Her fist connected, snapped Valkyrie's head round. She sent in another punch, and followed it with a right hook to the body. Valkyrie grunted, fell back as Assegai continued to swing. She covered up, fists on either side of her head, elbows in tight to her body, curling and weaving with every strike Assegai threw. Absorbing.

When Assegai started to tire, Valkyrie stepped in, the point of her elbow knocking into Assegai's nose. It wasn't a hard blow, but it was painful. It made Assegai's eyes water.

She tried to push at the air, but Valkyrie smacked her hand away, came up on the outside and wrapped her arms around her, hands clasped at the side of Assegai's neck. She hugged her tight, using Assegai's own shoulder to help cut off the oxygen going to her brain. Assegai gurgled.

Out of the corner of her eye, Valkyrie saw Assegai's foot bracing against the wall. Before she could react, the leg straightened, pushing them both off balance. Valkyrie lost the chokehold and smacked her head into the corner of a table. She tried to push Assegai away, but her arm was wrenched to one side and Assegai's fist came in, colliding with her jaw.

Then another.

And another.

108

Despite the chains and the rack and the green jumpsuit, life in Mevolent's glass case wasn't all bad, as far as Tanith was concerned.

Twice a day, someone would come round and release her and take her to the toilet. Yes, it was supervised, and yes, she was still restricted by manacles, but it could have been a lot worse. This person also provided stale food and a little water. Not the best diet in the world, but – again – it could have been worse. And at least she got some exercise.

Skulduggery didn't need to eat or pee, though, so no one took him out of his glass case. He just hung there, alternating between talking for hours and not saying one word for a worryingly long time. And Mevolent came in every day, sat at his desk, and worked.

Sometimes he'd be called away, and he'd be gone for hours at a time. But mostly he sat and he worked. Evidently, there was a lot to do when preparing for an evacuation/invasion.

A thin man knocked on his door, and stepped in. "Sergeant Assegai here to see you, sir."

Mevolent gave the slightest of nods, and the thin man stepped out again. A moment later, a tall young woman marched in and stood to attention. Mevolent continued to write.

The young woman's eyes were locked straight ahead. Then

slowly, irresistibly, she began to glance around at her surroundings. Stuff like the windows, and the tapestries, and the two glass cases containing the prisoners.

Her eyes darted to Skulduggery, then to Tanith, and then they locked again, straight ahead. Tanith resisted the urge to wave her fingers.

When he was done, Mevolent laid down his pen and looked up, indicated for her to speak.

"Valkyrie Cain attacked me in my quarters last night," Sergeant Assegai said.

Tanith's heart banged in her chest and Skulduggery jerked his head up.

When Mevolent didn't react, Assegai continued. "I defended myself and she fled. Whatever she was after, she didn't get it."

Mevolent watched her, and didn't say anything for a while.

Finally, he spoke. "You were the one who brought her into the city." His voice was deep, but unexpectedly soft. Not what Tanith was expecting.

"Yes, Master."

"You delivered her to the dungeon, but you did not recognise her."

Something passed over Assegai's face – a flicker of irritation. "No, Master."

"Her picture has been circulated throughout the military, yes?"

"It has, Master."

"So you knew who to look out for."

"Yes, Master."

"And yet you still failed to recognise her."

Assegai hesitated. "Yes, Master."

Mevolent watched her. "Why is that?"

"Her face had been damaged during the fall of Tahil na Sin, Master. It was still swollen."

"Swollen and bruised, was it?"

"Yes, Master."

"You travelled with her, did you not? After your party was attacked. Just you and her, walking for days. This is accurate?"

"It is, Master."

"And, during that journey, you failed to realise that you were travelling with Valkyrie Cain."

"That is accurate, Master," said Assegai.

"I see," Mevolent said. He pushed a report on his desk, slid it to the side by the slightest of fractions. "It would appear you are not alone in this failure. The guards in the dungeon also failed to recognise her, as did the interrogators. These guards are now being disciplined. The interrogators are in shackles. Tell me why I have punished these people, and not you."

"I... I do not know, Master."

Mevolent shook his head. "That is not an answer I am willing to accept, Sergeant. You will answer correctly or your punishment will follow."

"Because I brought her to you," Assegai said immediately. "I may have failed to recognise her, but I beat Valkyrie Cain and I delivered her to the dungeon."

"Yes," Mevolent said. "Precisely. You do not know why she attacked you in your quarters?"

"No, Master."

"And she left empty-handed?"

Assegai hesitated.

"Sergeant?"

As impossible as it seemed, Assegai straightened even further. "Master, she retrieved her necronaut suit."

"I see."

"But if she comes back, I'll be ready for her. I will not fail you again."

"These quarters," Mevolent said. "I see that you have been assigned a house in our new military district, correct?"

"Sir, yes, sir."

"You were due to share this house, but it is now for you and you alone. I am removing you from your current assignment and making you responsible for finding and apprehending Valkyrie Cain. The city's resources are at your disposal."

"Yes, Master. Thank you, sir."

"Dismissed."

Assegai saluted, turned and marched out.

"That's why we're here," said Skulduggery. "You're not displaying us as trophies – you're displaying us as bait. You think Valkyrie's going to mount a rescue."

Mevolent picked up his pen, started scratching again.

"She's smarter than that, you know. She's not going to just charge in here, guns blazing. You're dealing with someone whose actions you can't predict. I've taught her everything I know, but she's so much more than that. You won't beat her, you can't outsmart her, and you'll never – ever – see her coming. She's your worst nightmare, Mevolent. If Valkyrie Cain is in this city, you've already lost."

109

Valkyrie walked face first into a door that didn't open and stayed there, scowling at the pain while the sentries passed behind her. When they were gone, she stepped backwards, out of the shadows, rubbing her forehead and wondering what the hell to do now.

The important thing, at this point, as the most wanted fugitive in the city, was walking as if she had a purpose, like she was meant to be here. Here, in Mevolent's Palace, wearing the necronaut suit and with Assegai's stolen sword at her hip.

So she walked with a confidence she didn't feel, head up, defying anyone to meet her eyes.

Her head throbbed, not only from the door, but also from where Assegai had punched her the previous day. Her ribs hurt, too, and her knuckles, and she had a headache that wasn't going away and her face was hot. A few days earlier, as she mended her broken bones and healed those cuts and got rid of those scars, she'd felt invincible. Now she was back to being sore. Now she was back to aching. Her default setting, it would appear.

A man approached. He glanced up, a smile forming, and Valkyrie snarled at him and his eyes dropped and he scurried on. Damn right.

She needed somewhere to stop and think and come up with some sort of plan for rescuing Skulduggery and Tanith. She fought the urge to just burst in there. Their images were all over the city, which meant Mevolent wanted her to know where they were. If he was trying to lure her in, then he had all kinds of traps just waiting for her to stumble into.

No, she had to be smart about this. She had to come to terms with the fact that rescuing them was last on the list of things she needed to do. Before Valkyrie freed her friends, she had to prevent the invasion happening and save the world.

People ahead suddenly stopped walking. Some of them backed up, eyes on the ground. A few of them turned and hurried away. Valkyrie slowed. There were footsteps.

Lord Vile swept by, shadows trailing from his black armour like a cloak.

Valkyrie took an involuntary step back, found herself with the irresistible urge to lose herself in the darkness behind one of the thick marble pillars.

And then, just like that, Vile was gone again, and people started breathing, and walking, and slowly the place got back to normal.

But Valkyrie stayed where she was. Fear drove spikes down through her feet, pinning them to the ground. This was dangerous. This was stupidly dangerous. She was right in the middle of her enemy's stronghold, armed with a plan that she feared would crack and fall apart under too much scrutiny. She should be hiding right now, or trying to find a way out of the city, or she should be focusing on rescuing Skulduggery and Tanith. Skulduggery would have a plan. Valkyrie knew he would.

Slowly, fear loosened its grip. Gradually, those spikes in her feet dissolved. She could move again.

This wasn't the first time that day she'd felt overpowering fear. It may even have not been the last. She just didn't have the luxury of collapsing into a sobbing heap. She had a job to do.

There, sitting on the edge of the fountain. The small guy with the patchy beard and the nervous eyes. Valkyrie had spotted him discussing something with Mevolent's secretary, or assistant, or whatever role the thin man played in this world. There'd seemed to be a moment when the thin man was gesturing towards the door, like he was inviting the nervous guy to explain himself to Mevolent. The nervous guy had paled considerably. His left leg had started to shake. The very idea obviously terrified him.

The thin man sent him away, and the nervous guy scuttled off, and Valkyrie judged him to be the perfect amount of petrified for what she was looking for.

She went over, casting him in her shadow. The nervous guy looked up. Nervously.

"Hello?"

"Name."

"Mine?"

"No, idiot. Mine. I want to know my own damn name. Yes. Yours."

For the second time since she'd become aware of his existence, he went pale. Valkyrie almost felt sorry for him.

"Bucolic," he said, voice wavering. "Bucolic Kildare."

"Bucolic," Valkyrie repeated, rolling the word around in her mouth. "Bucolic. That's a terrible name. You sound like a plague."

"Oh."

"You know who I am?"

He shook his head.

She folded her arms. "I'm trouble, that's who I am. I've been sent to spur you on, Bucolic. Seems someone upstairs isn't happy with you."

Bucolic went paler. Which was a significant achievement.

"You know who I'm talking about?"

He nodded.

"I wasn't given the details. I just go where I'm told to go and I do my job. That's the difference between the two of us, you see. I do my job."

He swallowed.

"What's your job, Bucolic?"

"I'm, um, I'm—"

"The question too hard for you?"

"No! No, not at all!"

Valkyrie sighed. "Let's make it easier, then. Why are the people upstairs mad at you?"

"Because the communication devices aren't working how they want them to work."

Valkyrie frowned. "That's an interesting way of putting it."

"Is... is it?"

"*The devices aren't working like they want them to work.* It's almost as if you're blaming the people upstairs."

Bucolic looked aghast. "No!"

"Almost as if you're saying it's their fault the devices aren't working right."

"I'm not, I swear! I swear to you!"

Valkyrie raised an eyebrow, then slowly sat beside him and watched the people pass by. "Are you happy here, Bucolic?"

"Very happy!"

"Because, if you're not happy, I can arrange for you to be somewhere else."

"I'm very happy!"

"Somewhere... not as nice, perhaps."

"Please don't send me away. I didn't mean anything by it, I really didn't."

She smiled at him. "I believe you. Hey, are you looking forward to this new world we're going to be living in? We'll need to sweep all the mortals away, obviously, but at least they don't have any draugar on their doorstep, right? That we know of anyway."

"I'm very excited about it, yes."

"That's good, Bucolic. That's really good. Those portals are something else, aren't they?"

He frowned. "Um... no, I don't think so. The portals are... well, they're the portals. They're not anything else."

Valkyrie didn't understand for a moment. Then it dawned on her. "Oh," she said. "No, when I say they're something else, I don't mean that literally. It's a saying. A phrase. We say it all the time, upstairs. Mevolent came up with it."

"It's brilliant," Bucolic said automatically.

"Isn't it? Mevolent has got such a way with words. Do you know much about them, the portals? Do you know anyone who works on them?"

"A few people," Bucolic said, nodding. "I worked on them a little myself, actually, before I was reassigned."

Valkyrie winced in commiseration. "Wow – that must have stung, eh? To have been taken off our biggest and most important project and to be put on, what, communications? That's quite a demotion."

"Oh, no," said Bucolic, "I was very flattered. The portals are wonderful, yes, absolutely, but, unless everything is ready for us on the other side, they're not going to work."

Valkyrie nodded. Nodded again. "I suppose you're right. And that's your project, then? Helping us communicate with the other side of...?"

"The portals," Bucolic finished.

"Right. Yes."

"It's actually quite an honour," he continued. "My colleagues are all more than a little jealous, I have to admit."

"So you've enabled Mevolent to talk to people in the other universe, so we can co-ordinate our efforts."

"Well, I *helped*," Bucolic said. "I didn't design the devices, but I've... I've tinkered with them, I suppose you could say. Made them a little bit better. And I maintain them, obviously."

"Obviously. You should be proud. After all, if we don't communicate with the other side, then... you know what happens."

"Yes, I do."

Valkyrie looked at him. "Tell me what happens, Bucolic."

"Oh, sorry. If we don't communicate with the people in the

432

second dimension, then the city's sigils will still be active and the portals won't open."

"Roarhaven."

"Yes, the city of Roarhaven."

Valkyrie made herself smile. "They won't stand a chance, will they? They'll think their defences are up and then... then the portals open, and our army streams out, and catches them all by surprise."

"And they kill everyone."

"Every single one."

"Except for Lady Serafina, of course."

"Serafina," Valkyrie echoed.

"And her family."

"And that's who Mevolent has been co-ordinating with," Valkyrie said. "How did you get one of the devices to her? Wait, no, I've already figured it out. The refugees, yes? All those thousands of mortals who went through last year. Not all of them were mortals."

Bucolic grinned. "They brought one of the devices with them."

"And, when Serafina showed up in Roarhaven, she was drawn into the whole plot," Valkyrie said. "The chance to reunite with her long-lost love, even if he is from an alternate dimension... How could she resist? And all this is thanks to you."

"Well," Bucolic said, blushing, "like I said, I mostly maintain the devices. I tweak occasionally, but, really, the credit must go to the inventor."

"Yeah," Valkyrie said. "And the inventor is...?"

Bucolic blinked at her. "Professor Nye."

"Nye," she repeated. "Of course it would be Nye."

110

Professor Nye swept its head low to get through the doorway, its long legs bending. It had a funny way of walking. It loped, its arms swinging, its head bopping. Straight to its desk it went, straight to that tall stool, ready to continue its work. A work ethic, that's what Nye had above all else. Whether it was performing surgeries or designing new machines or torturing prisoners of war, Nye was a professional above all else.

Valkyrie detached herself from the shadows. "Good morning, Professor Creepy."

Nye jerked round, its small eyes wide, its wide mouth opening. A fluttering hand went to its chest.

"You said you wouldn't come back."

Valkyrie shrugged as she ambled over. "My situation's changed. That's what situations do."

"What do you want?"

"Your help."

It stood up from the stool, stood to its full height and peered down at her disdainfully. "I will not help you. You'd better leave before I alert the sentries."

"If you alert anyone, you'll have to explain why you didn't report me days ago."

"I'll say you threatened me."

"And now I'm threatening you again. Take a seat."

434

"I will stand."

"No. You'll sit."

Nye glared at her. She gazed back calmly. Finally, Nye sat.

"I was talking to a guy," Valkyrie said. "An engineer. He told me you'd built a communications device that can operate between dimensions."

Nye didn't respond.

"He told me Mevolent is chatting to Serafina. That must be a hell of a thing. She's dead in your reality, he's dead in my reality, but they've found each other, nonetheless. They should make a romantic comedy out of that. I'd watch it, I would. If they set it around Christmas, I'd watch it every year."

"You still haven't told me what you want," said Nye.

"I want to destroy those portals, and I want to chat to my own friends back home."

"No."

"No to one, to both, what?"

"No to both."

"Is it wise to say no to me, though? Tell you what, we'll focus on letting me talk to my friends for the moment."

"It cannot be done," said Nye. "I could make such a device for you, yes, but unless there is someone in the other dimension with a corresponding device, set to the exact same frequency, there is no point."

"I'm sure a creature of your intelligence can find a way to make it work."

"No. I cannot."

"Professor, such a defeatist attitude. You haven't even tried."

"Because it is impossible. Do you understand me? There is no scientific possibility of anything like that ever happening without first getting a corresponding device into the next reality. If you can manage that, yes, you will be able to communicate with your colleagues. Can you do that? Have you found a Shunter willing to betray Mevolent?"

Valkyrie folded her arms.

"I thought not," said Nye. "What you ask cannot be done. You may leave now."

"I'm afraid I can't. I'm in a pickle. Do you have that phrase over here? In a pickle? Like most of our phrases in the English language, it probably comes from Shakespeare. Did you have a Shakespeare in this reality?"

Nye frowned. "The little-known playwright?"

"Little-known, huh? That's him, I suppose."

Nye shrugged its bony shoulders. "The works of mortal playwrights have largely been erased from history, but there are some scholars, some academics, who can still appreciate their talents."

"And are you such a scholar?"

"I have read some of his works, yes. But such writers tend to focus on the human condition, and I confess to being largely unable to empathise."

"Understandable." Valkyrie picked up a strange-looking thing with wires and dials and tubes sticking out of it. "What's this?"

Nye froze. "Put that down."

"What is it?"

"It's a bomb."

"Why are you scared? Is it not stable? Why would you build a bomb that wasn't stable? And why would you keep it on a table with all this other junk?"

Nye reached out, plucking it delicately from her hands. "That bomb is powerful enough to incinerate this entire building."

"Which, again, leads me to ask why you'd leave it lying around on a table?"

"Because I am unused to people picking things up."

"Anyway, I'm still in that pickle I mentioned earlier, because the device you made is allowing Mevolent to co-ordinate with Serafina – and I can't really have that. So what do we do about it? How do we fix this problem? Any suggestions? No?

None? I have an idea. You, Professor, you're going to cut the line."

Its small eyes narrowed. "Cut what line?"

"The metaphorical line that stretches between the star-crossed lovers. That's another Shakespeare reference, by the way. You're going to sabotage the communications."

"No," it said immediately. "I will not."

"You mentioned frequency, yes? If there's a frequency, can't it be blocked?"

"If the device stops working, Mevolent will tell me to fix it. If he tells me to fix it, I will immediately do so. No threat you can make would induce me to delay this process, because Mevolent is far scarier than you could ever hope to be."

"I could threaten to kill you."

"And that threat would be an empty one."

"Then I'll threaten to let Mevolent know you've been working with me."

"And that is a risk I might be forced to take."

Valkyrie grunted. Looked away. Looked back. "We seem to be at an impasse."

"In which case, we should part ways."

"Not just yet." She tapped her chin with her finger. "OK, if you can't let me communicate with my friends back home, and you won't stop Mevolent from doing so, then you can let me listen in to his conversation."

"No."

"I'm afraid I'm going to have to insist."

"If Mevolent finds out—"

"If Mevolent finds out we've even talked, he'll throw you to his interrogators. You've interrogated a few prisoners in the past, Professor. You know what they'd do to you."

"I can't do it. I won't."

Valkyrie sighed. "You've already lost this argument. You will do it. You know why? Because the only thing stopping you is your own reluctance – and reluctance can be overcome. I'm sure you have a back-up device around here somewhere, don't you? Dig it out, set it to the right frequency, and I'll be out of your few remaining wisps of hair."

"If you're caught with the device–"

"I'll just have to be careful, won't I? You'll have that device for me?"

"Yes," Nye said, with not a little irritation in its voice.

"Who's a good little Crenga, eh? You're a good little Crenga, yes, you are. Now, on to item number two on the agenda: destroying the portals."

Nye sagged.

"I don't want anything big and explodey, OK? There are people around those portals every minute of every day – I don't want anyone hurt. But I want them shut down, and I want it to be irreversible. So how do I do it?"

"I don't... I don't know."

"Well, here's the good news, Professor. I like you. I do. I like you a whole lot more than I like Doctor Nye, back in my dimension. I mean, that version of you is only a *doctor*, you know? You're the one who went to Professor School, am I right?"

"You are quite wrong."

"The good news I mentioned – it's that you have ten days to think of a non-lethal way to permanently disable the portals. How great is that? So many days! So that's two pieces of homework for you, because I'd say you loved homework as a young... what are young Crengarrions called? Crenguffians? Crengaggles?"

"Crengarrions."

"That's disappointing. I want that communications device tomorrow."

"Very well," said Nye, "but not here. Every time you come here, you risk my life. There is a building on Repentance Street I use to store equipment and supplies – a building I use to conduct

438

my own private experiments. A building of red brick. That is where I shall meet you."

"OK," said Valkyrie. "But if you try to double-cross me—"

"You can save your threats. I have no intention of double-crossing you."

"Uh, excuse me? I was speaking."

"You were going to threaten me."

"Not necessarily."

Nye sighed. "Very well. Please continue."

"I was going to say, if you try to double-cross me..." Valkyrie faltered.

"Yes?" said Nye.

She glared. "Shut up."

111

Roarhaven was dripping in Christmas cheer. The main shopping district glittered with lights and decorations and, although it wasn't quite cold enough to snow, someone with the appropriate know-how had engineered a light flurry to coat half the city in white. Wearing a warm coat and a scarf, Omen left the grounds of Corrival and went wandering.

Christmas was becoming a big thing in Roarhaven. For the first few years of the city's existence, it had pretty much ignored the festive season, so intent was it on abandoning archaic mortal traditions. But gradually it had seeped in, and, although the religious aspect had been dialled down to almost zero, hymns were sung by choirs and there were even a few nativity scenes set up around the city.

Omen loved it all. The season never failed to put him in a good mood. He was grinning to himself as he stared up at the gigantic Christmas tree. It had originally stood in the Circle zone, but the Church of the Faceless people had complained about it so it was moved here, to the centre of the Shopping District.

He turned to go, and almost walked into Reznor Rake.

He froze, and Reznor smiled.

"Hello, Omen."

Omen continued to freeze. His mind wasn't throwing an awful

lot of alternatives his way. He decided to stay frozen until a solution presented itself.

"Yeah," said Reznor, "I know who you are. It wasn't that difficult. We waited outside the school till Tancred recognised you, then pointed you out to one of your schoolmates and they said that there is the Chosen One's brother. See, I've heard of Auger Darkly – everyone has – but these schoolmates of yours, they told me all about you. Said you're the twin no one's intimidated by. I think they kind of liked you. That must be nice."

People passed all around them, chatting and laughing and humming along to the Christmas songs that spilled from shop doors – but Omen's mind was a vast, empty nothingness.

"They told me you got into your own little scrapes, though," Reznor continued. "Your own little adventures. Or at least that's the rumour. They couldn't really say if it was true or not – but I know, don't I? I know it's true. You've been adventuring quite close to my neck of the proverbials, after all."

"I'll call the City Guard," Omen managed to squeak.

Reznor grinned. "Go ahead. I'll lose myself in this crowd and they'll never find me. I'm a master of disguise, Omen. I'm here, there, and everywhere. I have a different face for every day of the week. I'm your teacher, I'm your friend, I'm your worst enemy. You want to see my disguise for today? Do you?" He put on a woollen hat and pulled it low over his eyes. Then he waved. "It's me! It's still me! You probably think I've vanished, but I'm in disguise!" Chuckling, Reznor took off the hat, stuffed it back in his coat pocket. "Man," he said, "I'm funny. You think I'm funny, Omen?"

"Yeah," Omen said. "I think you're a hoot."

Reznor laughed. "I like this! I like this version of you, kid! The sassy version! I could grow to like someone with that attitude, I really could."

"All I have to do is shout."

"Hey, buddy – you want to shout, you go right ahead. I'll kill you before you take that breath."

"What do you want?"

"You know exactly what I want. I want the knife back."

"I can't give it to you. My brother needs it. The prophecy—"

"I know about the prophecy," Reznor interrupted. "And, as you can imagine, I don't care about the prophecy. I was paid to find and deliver the Obsidian Blade. I accomplished the first part with my usual aplomb, but spectacularly failed the second. My client is none too happy about that."

Omen squared his shoulders. "I don't have it. I hid it. I'm not giving it to you."

"Well, of course not. I'd have to beat it out of you, and, even then, I couldn't be sure you'd tell me where it really is. We're not going to engage in fisticuffs, if that's what you're thinking. We're way beyond that."

"Then what are you going to do?" Omen asked, frowning.

"It's not what I'm going to do," Reznor said. "It's what I have done. I've taken your brother."

"You're lying."

"We sneaked into his dorm room earlier. The one with the green walls? He was fast asleep – but we drugged him anyway. Couldn't take the chance that he'd wake up, you know?"

Omen shook his head. "You're lying. I know you're lying."

"We can get in anywhere. You think a school is going to pose much of a problem for people like us?" He took out his phone, tapped at the screen, and turned it so that Omen could see the photo of Auger. Sleeping. "He's quite safe, don't you fret, but, if you don't give me the Obsidian Blade at midnight three nights from now, I'll kill him without a second thought. I'll cut his throat, from ear to ear."

"You don't have to keep him so long," said Omen. "I can get it to you tomorrow. You don't have to—"

"I'm not going to be here tomorrow," said Reznor. "I do have a job, you know. I do have other things going on." He grabbed Omen, pulled him close. "Midnight," he said into his ear, "three nights from now, at the Cut-throat Car park. You know the one? The underground parking lot? Yeah, you do. Don't be late, don't be empty-handed, and, obviously, don't tell anyone. That all clear to you? Nod if it's clear."

Omen managed a nod.

Reznor released him, stepped back, and smiled. "I don't think this adventuring lark is for you, kid, I really don't. See you soon, yeah?"

And then he stepped back into the crowd, and he was gone.

112

Valkyrie was delayed walking across the city by the sheer number of people. Most of them didn't have a job in Tahil na Kurge, so she had no idea where they were going this early in the morning – and she really didn't care enough to find out.

She passed through Merchant's Square. The portals looked ready to go – but admittedly she didn't know an awful lot about portals, so she had no way of judging. It was just enough to worry her.

There was only one building of red brick on Repentance Street. It was tall and plain and invited no scrutiny. Perfect for Professor Nye. Valkyrie entered through the rear door, climbed the stairs, found Nye in a large room full of tables covered in esoteric junk.

"Nice place," she said, eyeing all the chains and the racks and the hooks on the walls. "Not somewhere I'd personally want to live, but it'd do as a cute getaway, maybe a summer home, you know?"

"Talking again, I see," Nye said, looking unimpressed.

Valkyrie smiled. "Getting sick of me yet?"

"Yes, actually," Nye said, and reached out, its long fingers tapping a sigil on the wall.

Four more sigils lit up around the room and Valkyrie's magic dampened, and two men stepped into view. Big men. Huge and hairy and not especially good-looking. The first man grinned with a mouthful of bad teeth, and his friend grimaced, glaring at her from behind a curtain of greasy hair. Bad Teeth carried a sword. Grimace an axe.

Valkyrie turned and ran. The door was shut. She put her shoulder to it and it didn't budge.

Nye tittered. "No escape, Miss Cain. This is where your story ends, I'm afraid."

Cursing under her breath, Valkyrie turned to the men and drew Assegai's sword. It wasn't half as big as Bad Teeth's, nor a fraction as heavy as Grimace's axe, but it was a sword, nonetheless, it had sharp edges and a pointy bit, so it did the job.

"You put that little pig-sticker down and we'll be quick with you," said Bad Teeth. "Otherwise you'll die slow."

Valkyrie circled away from them. "Reckon I'll die slow, then."

Grimace moved ahead to cut her off. Valkyrie didn't appreciate that.

"This is what happens," Nye said, enjoying this immensely. "Your arrogance has brought you to this moment, Miss Cain. I imagine you are regretting a great many things. Would I be correct?"

"I'll get to you in a minute," Valkyrie murmured, keeping her attention on the two thugs with designs on killing her. She smiled at them. "Go easy on me, boys. I don't have much reason to use a sword, where I'm from."

"Then consider this your first and final lesson," Bad Teeth said, and took three quick steps and brought his sword down, aiming for that spot where her neck met her torso.

Instead, Valkyrie danced in and, one-handed, slid the point of her sword into the meat of his shoulder.

Bad Teeth froze, his wide eyes locked on to the blade. Grimace froze. Nye's smile faltered.

"I said I don't have much reason to use a sword," Valkyrie said, pulling it back out. "I didn't say I wasn't good at it."

Bad Teeth roared and went to strike her down and she skipped in and kicked him, her boot catching him right between the legs.

His roar faded and his eyes bulged and his sword dropped from his fingers. There was a long, drawn-out moment where he just stood there, like he was wondering if the pain had simply passed him by. But no, here it came, thundering upwards and spreading outwards, and he doubled over without so much as a wheeze. He fell forward, his knees and his face hitting the floor at the same time, and stayed there, hands clutching his wounded bits.

Grimace charged. Valkyrie ducked back, the axe whistling by her face. She tried to swipe at him in return, but he rammed her with his shoulder and she flew backwards over a table, scattering the tubes and the glassware. She hit the ground and immediately rolled back *under* the table as the axe came down, biting into the stone. He gripped the table edge with one hand and flipped it. Valkyrie scrambled up.

She lunged and he deflected the blade, wielding the axe with considerably more dexterity than she'd anticipated. She blocked his next slashing attack and the sword was nearly yanked from her hands. His face contorted with all sorts of anger and all manner of hatred, Grimace advanced, the axe swirling and coming in from every possible angle. Valkyrie dodged and ducked, blocking and deflecting when she absolutely had to, but mainly staying the hell out of his way.

He bellowed as he swung and missed and left himself open and she chopped at his arm. The blade went through and hit bone and Grimace roared in pain.

He dropped the axe and barged into her. Valkyrie tried to squirm away, but he wrapped her in a bear hug, her back pressed into his chest, her arms pinned by her sides. He lifted her off her feet and squeezed.

Valkyrie wriggled. She kicked madly, her heels colliding with his knees and shins. She threw her head back, trying to find the soft parts of his face. Nothing made him loosen his hold.

"Stab her!" Grimace yelled, staggering over to Bad Teeth. Bad Teeth looked up, managed to take a knife from his belt, then vomited and sagged, his face dropping into a pool of his own sick.

"You!" Grimace snarled, turning Valkyrie towards Nye. "You do it!"

Nye blinked. "Me?"

"Pick up the knife!"

"Oh... oh, no," said Nye. "I do not partake in the physical act of violence *itself*, you understand."

"Stab her!" Grimace roared. "Or I stab you!"

Valkyrie tried using the sword against Grimace, but all she could do was tap it weakly against his knee.

Nye hesitated, then came forward, carefully picked up the knife and examined it.

"Stick her!" Grimace said.

Valkyrie flailed her legs and Nye stepped back, eyeing her feet warily.

"She's going to kick me," it said. "I'm very fragile, and I do not like to be kicked. Also, she has a sword."

"Stick that blade through her gut or I'll tear your damn head off."

Nye looked offended, but didn't argue. It grabbed a stool, used it to knock the sword out of Valkyrie's hand, and then to block her legs. It moved in closer, and poked the knife at her belly.

"This is a necronaut suit," it said. "I won't be able to penetrate the material."

Valkyrie wriggled and squirmed as much as she could. She slipped slightly, so that her elbows were now below Grimace's grasp. She reached up, fingernails scratching the backs of his hands.

Grimace snarled. "Then stab her somewhere else, you bloody idiot!"

A muscle clenched in Nye's jaw. "Of course," it said. "Capital idea."

While she tried separating Grimace's fingers, Valkyrie put everything she had into glaring at Nye. "I am going to hurt you for this," she promised.

Nye swallowed.

"Cut her throat," Grimace muttered.

"And be covered in her arterial blood?" Nye responded, appalled. "I shall stab her heart, thank you very much."

"Then do it!"

Nye focused its anger and its indignation on Valkyrie, and it reached out with its left hand and tugged her suit open. The tip of the blade was cold against the skin over her heart. Nye's tongue darted out, licking its thin lips as it prepared to plunge the knife through.

Valkyrie gave a quick, sharp roar into its face using every ounce of aggression she possessed. It was like a physical blow, and Nye jerked away. At the same time, she curled her hands around two of Grimace's fingers and yanked them back, snapping the bones. Grimace yelled and dropped her, and Valkyrie snatched the knife from Nye and whirled, pressing it up against Grimace's throat.

He raised his injured hands and lifted his head, eyes wide, surrendering and exposing his entire jawline, and Valkyrie hit him square on the chin.

She'd been knocked out like that herself – had her brain rattle around inside her skull. She knew it wasn't a case of how big he was or how strong. You can't build muscles on your chin, after all.

He toppled backwards, and didn't get up. She checked on Bad Teeth, but he'd drifted into unconsciousness.

Valkyrie turned to Nye. "You sneaky little toad."

"I feel as though I must apologise," it responded.

"You sneaky, weird little toad," she said, following Nye as it backed away. She picked up Assegai's sword and slid it into its sheath, but kept the knife in her hand. "I thought we had an understanding, you and me."

"We do," Nye said. "We do. I understand you and you understand me."

"Our relationship worked, Professor. It was simple and it worked. I tell you to do something, and you do it."

Nye nodded. "A beautiful arrangement, to be sure. But if I may offer an explanation?"

"By all means."

"I thought it would work, you see. I thought those men would succeed in killing you."

"That's your explanation?"

"Yes."

"That's pretty weak."

"Do you think? I happen to believe that it is refreshingly honest. I fully accept that what happened here is my fault. I have no wish to shift the blame on to anyone else."

"There's no one else to shift the blame on to."

Nye stopped backing away, and held up its hands. "I apologise for hiring this pair of supposed killers to dispose of you. In retrospect, I should have devoted more time to building the device you'd asked for."

"Probably," Valkyrie said, pressing the same sigil that Nye had pressed.

"But I can help," Nye said, as Valkyrie's magic returned to her. "I am already working on a way to disable the portals permanently, as you requested."

"You're not worried that Mevolent might notice your attention has been diverted?"

"Everyone's attention is diverted. Everyone is packing up their belongings and preparing to evacuate. The chaos can work to your advantage."

"That's a very good idea, Professor."

Nye attempted a smile. "I am known for them."

She nodded to the thugs on the ground behind her. "What about those two?"

"I assure you, you do not have to worry about them. They are mercenaries to their very core. They will do anything for money. All I have to do is pay them enough and they will never utter a word of this to anyone."

"And what if that's not what I need them to do?"

Nye raised a hairless eyebrow. "They are at your service. What do you require of them?"

"Nothing much," Valkyrie said. "I just need them to kill Mevolent."

113

Not for the first time, Omen stood in the Principal's Office. It had been redecorated, though, and now it looked ever-so-slightly different.

"Your brother is missing," Duenna said.

Omen nodded.

"Do you know where he is?"

Omen shook his head.

Duenna sighed. "The previous principal allowed this sort of thing, because, of course, Auger is a Chosen One and the accepted wisdom is that Chosen Ones need to be given more latitude. So your brother was allowed to go off on all sorts of adventures and everybody here at Corrival Academy pretended not to notice. Those days, Mr Darkly, are over. Principal Rubic is now Grand Mage Rubic – and I am running things here. Please inform your brother, when you see him, that, come the New Year, this behaviour will no longer be tolerated. Is that understood?"

"Yes, miss."

She waved him away. "That will be all, Mr Darkly."

Omen left the office, left the building, left the campus and took a tram to Oldtown. He found the darkest, dingiest café, and the man behind the counter obviously hated him with every fibre of his being as he very grudgingly accepted an order for a mug of hot chocolate.

"It's not very good," he growled.

"OK," said Omen.

"I won't bring it to you."

"That's fine."

The man glared at him, then walked away, muttering insults. He eventually came back with a cracked mug of scalding-hot, bitter chocolate that left the weirdest aftertaste. Omen smiled and thanked him and the man recoiled, and Omen took his mug to the table in the corner, where he proceeded to tell Crepuscular Vies what was going on.

"That," Crepuscular said, "is quite the dilemma."

"I can't just hand over the Obsidian Blade," said Omen.

Crepuscular took off his hat. His black hair was shiny, and parted in the middle. "Why not? I mean, I understand why you wouldn't want to give away a weapon like that, but it would appear to be the easiest way to get your brother back alive."

"If Auger faces the King of the Darklands without the Obsidian Blade, he'll die."

"You don't know that."

"He'll probably die."

Crepuscular shrugged. "Yes. Probably. Well, I'll help however I can."

"You will? You'll help?"

"Of course I will. Helping people is what I do. So what's the plan? I'm assuming you have one. Do you have a way of tracking your brother down?"

"I've tried a psychic link," Omen said. "That's worked before. But I can't reach him. I can't even sense him out there."

"He's the Chosen One," said Crepuscular. "The first thing Rake would have done is bind his magic."

"Then I go to the meeting place tomorrow night and when Reznor Rake shows himself... you grab him. Do you think you can do that?"

"I'm sure I can try."

"He's pretty dangerous..."

"He's dangerous, I'm dangerous, we're all dangerous. But, if he spots me before I get to him, it's over. He'll disappear and you'll never see your brother again."

"I thought about that. You'll need to be in disguise."

"As who?"

"A Cleaver."

Crepuscular looked sceptical. "I don't think you've thought this through, Omen. If I'm wearing a disguise, you want me pretending to be someone non-threatening."

Omen shook his head. "Cleavers are everywhere. They're always patrolling. I walk down the street and I don't even notice how many I've passed. They fade into the background."

"I can guarantee you that they do not fade for bad guys. If he sees me, he'll think he's walking into an ambush."

"You're not getting it. Cleavers are scary, right? They're scary because they're so good."

"Right."

"So, if they were to plan an ambush, you wouldn't suspect a thing, would you? You wouldn't see them anywhere around the ambush site."

Crepuscular blinked slowly. "Omen Darkly, you mischievous mastermind. He'll see me, dressed as a Cleaver, and that'll reassure him that nothing weird is going on."

"You think it'll work?"

"That is something approaching genius, I have to say."

"So, midnight comes, you're close. You might even walk by me. The moment you're gone, he'll pop out, and then you, like, grab him and stuff. If he has Auger with him, we take Auger and run. If he doesn't, we'll make him tell us where he is."

"That's definitely a plan."

"Do you think it'll work?"

"I have no idea, but I'll tell you – I'm very excited to find out."

114

It was surprisingly easy to sleep while hanging from chains, and unsurprisingly uncomfortable.

Tanith woke, immediately felt the strain on her wrists and the ache in her back. She did her best to adjust her position as she looked up.

Mevolent stood there, watching from behind his veil.

"He's been like that for the last twenty minutes," Skulduggery said. "Sometimes he watches me. Sometimes he watches you."

"It's creepy," Tanith said.

"I told him you'd say that."

Mevolent leaned back, so he was sitting on his desk, and observed them both. He actually looked like he was going to say something.

And then he said something.

"I miss having enemies. When I was younger, I had enemies aplenty. I had an army of enemies. One by one, I killed them all. As the years went by, the war got easier. Our victories became... tedious. I think it started when the Skulduggery Pleasant of this world vanished. Whether he was killed, whether he ran, I simply don't know. But, once he was gone, things got easier."

Skulduggery shrugged. "I'll take that as a—"

"When the war ended," Mevolent continued, as if Skulduggery hadn't spoken, "I turned my attention to the mortals. We killed most of them. Enslaved the rest. Our culture flourished. Technology, art, the economy, our religion... they blossomed. It was a time of peace, prosperity. We built our grand cities across the world. But I had no enemies.

"And then you arrived, emissaries from a world not too dissimilar from our own. A world where you had gone one way, and we had gone another. And suddenly I had enemies again."

The doors to his office opened just before Skulduggery could issue a response, but nobody came through. Mevolent turned. Waited.

"Reveal yourself," he said.

A torrent of light emerged from empty space and hit him, knocking him back. Then two men appeared, strong and hairy, one holding a weird-looking rifle, the other an axe and a cloaking sphere. The one with the axe stuffed the sphere back into his coat and the other dropped the gun, took out his sword.

Mevolent held out his hand, and nothing happened. Tanith looked back at the rifle. What had Valkyrie called it once? A magic-sucker.

The men charged. They were tall, but Mevolent was taller. They were strong, though – thickset and muscled – whereas Mevolent was lean. If this descended into a contest of strength, Tanith doubted he'd survive.

He easily avoided the slash of the sword, however. The axe came for his chest and he took a single step and the axe hit nothing but air. The sword chopped, swirled and whirled and came at him again. He kept moving. Utterly calm. Watching.

Mevolent got in close and his fist sank into the axeman's belly. He stepped into the swordsman as he lunged and disarmed him somehow, the sword clattering to the ground.

The axeman hefted his axe. The swordsman took out a knife. Movement at the door, and Sergeant Assegai slammed into the axeman from behind and he went stumbling. The thug with the knife dived on her and they staggered against the wall, hissing and snarling.

Mevolent turned as the axe came for him. He caught it, his hand closing around the handle. The axeman cursed, went to pull it back. He strained, veins popping, but it didn't budge.

There was fear in his eyes as he released his hold and stepped away, leaving Mevolent to examine the weapon.

The thug with the knife squealed as Assegai snapped his wrist. She caught him with a beautiful elbow that weakened his knees, then kicked his legs out from under him and slammed her palm into his face until she was sure he was unconscious.

She froze when she saw Mevolent holding the axe. "Sir?"

Mevolent looked round. "Sergeant," he said. "Yes. These men tried to kill me. Please task the Redhoods with taking them to the dungeons. They'll need to be interrogated."

"I'll see to the interrogation myself, sir," Assegai said. She snapped a pair of shackles on to the axeman's wrists, and Mevolent passed her the axe.

Assegai had marched the axeman halfway to the door when Mevolent spoke again.

"Sergeant," he said.

She turned. "Yes, Master?"

"Your search for Valkyrie Cain."

Assegai stood straighter, as if she was remembering why she was here. "Yes, Master. I'm... I'm sorry, Master. I haven't been able to find her yet. I'm still looking."

"She's intelligent," said Mevolent. "And she has a city to hide in. You may not be able to complete your mission."

"I'll keep trying."

"No. My Chief of Security has gone missing. I'd like you to take his place – *Captain* Assegai."

"Yes, Master."

"Your primary responsibility is to protect the portals."

"Yes, Master. What about Cain, Master?"

"She'll come to you. Skulduggery Pleasant and Tanith Low are her colleagues. Friends. We shall let it be known that they are to be executed, alongside the Necromancers we have in our dungeons, to mark the opening of the portals. If she wants to save them, and she will, she will have to make the attempt in broad daylight, in front of our entire army. And you will be waiting."

"Yes, Master."

Mevolent nodded, dismissing her. Assegai resumed marching the axeman out.

"Oh," Mevolent said, like he'd just remembered. "Thank you, Captain."

"Uh... you're welcome, Master," Assegai said, and left.

115

The rain passed through the shield covering Tahil na Kurge. The people hurried by on the streets below. The trams rang their bells to get them to look up, for God's sake. The rain made a quiet city even quieter. It subdued the hubbub, kept it down there, at street level. Didn't let it rise to the rooftops.

Valkyrie's hood was up. The suit kept her dry and warm. She didn't much mind standing out there on a bloody roof while it lashed. She remembered those winter mornings in Haggard, waiting for the bus, her schoolbag heavy on her shoulder, her uniform sodden, her mood miserable. And yet the memory was a comforting one. She closed her eyes and imagined herself back there, remembering the sounds the cars made as they drove through puddles, remembering the feeling of relief as she climbed into the bus. Sitting there, talking with her friends. Then the walk from the bus stop at the school gate, up the drive, merging into the crowd. The smell of the hallways. The feeling of walking through the corridors on a wet day, of sitting in class beside the radiator. Writing. Reading. Daydreaming of something else. Another life. A life of adventure.

And here she was, standing on a rooftop in a parallel dimension. Valkyrie was pretty sure that counted as a life of adventure, and yet all she wanted to do was be at home. She wanted to laugh with her parents, chat with her sister, kiss her girlfriend, play with her dog. Would her dog even recognise her, after seven months away? Would her sister?

The door opened behind her and Valkyrie put her game face on, and turned.

"Could we not have met indoors?" Nye asked, the wind tugging at its umbrella.

She gave it a smile that was all teeth and no warmth. "I don't think I want to be in an enclosed space with you, Professor. You have a tendency to spring ambushes."

"A single act is not a tendency," it protested. "But we must be quick. I have been assigned a bodyguard, a dreadful man named Cark. I think, perhaps, that Mevolent may suspect me of some degree of betrayal. He claims that Cark is simply there for my protection, but, if this is indeed the case, he has neglected to inform Cark of this. The man's eyes follow me everywhere. He scrutinises everything I do. It is a most outrageous move on Mevolent's part."

"Yeah," said Valkyrie. "Although you *have* technically betrayed him."

Nye rolled its small eyes. "But despite Cark's best efforts, I managed to slip away. I fear, however, that we do not have much time. What do you want?"

She didn't answer.

It smiled weakly. "I mean... how can I help you?"

"That's better," she said. "I need an update on how we're going to disable the portals. You said you were working on something."

"Yes," said Nye. "But I still don't understand why you're bothering with this. If you disable those portals, Mevolent will simply build more."

"And that'll take time. In that time, me and my friends can go home and warn everyone about what's coming."

"Do you also have a way to kill him?" Nye asked. "Because, if he finds out that I aided in the destruction of the machines, Mevolent will do unspeakable things to me."

"He'll do unspeakable things to you if he finds out that you sent those two idiots to kill him. Either way, things get unspeakable, so what d'you say you just do what I tell you and we'll both hope for the best?"

Nye sighed. "You habitually put me in unenviable positions."

"That I do."

"The portal machines are delicate things," it said. "It would be useful if you viewed them as organic entities that have cables of both Shunter and Teleporter magic running through their veins. Shunters, Miss Cain, possess the ability to travel across dimensions, but they are restricted to passing from a location in one reality to that exact location in another. Mevolent, however, seeks to transport his army from here to a different location, to your city of Roarhaven, so I have used Teleporter abilities to shift the corresponding—"

Valkyrie clicked her fingers in front of its face. "Hey. Hey. I don't care. You can mansplain, or Nyesplain or whatever, all you want, but I sincerely don't care how it works. I only care about how to *stop* it working."

Nye bristled. "Of course. If you continue to view the portal machines as organic, then there is the possibility of introducing an illness into their architecture."

"OK, cool."

It frowned. "I'm not sure you understand..."

"No, I do. You want to infect the machines with a computer virus."

Nye appeared confused, and Valkyrie smiled, and patted its cheek. "You just focus on looking pretty, yeah? Looking pretty, and making the virus. When will you have it finished?"

"I do not know," Nye responded. "I am very busy at the moment, reinforcing the shield."

"Yeah," Valkyrie said, glancing up. "It looks like it's straining a little."

"The draugar and the Necromancers are applying constant pressure that the shield is not designed for."

"Will it fail?"

"Unless I reinforce it? Yes."

"And can you reinforce it?"

Nye sighed. "The old languages of magic are not my area. If I had an expert with me, maybe somebody of the calibre of China Sorrows, then I am confident I would be able to. As it stands... I rate my chances at no more than seventy per cent."

"Well, that's pretty good, considering. The virus, Professor. The portals open at noon, four days from now."

Another sigh. "I'll have something for you that morning."

She raised an eyebrow. "The morning of the invasion? That's cutting it a bit close, don't you think?"

"It is," said Nye. "But that is how long it will take."

Valkyrie chewed the inside of her cheek. "OK," she said. "But, if you can get it done faster, that's what—" She froze.

Nye peered at her. "Is everything all right?"

She whirled, ran for the edge of the roof and dropped, skidding over, gripping the edge with her fingertips. Her body swung against the wall as the door opened.

A male voice. "Professor."

"Mr Cark," said Nye. "Can I not have a moment to myself?"

Valkyrie hung there. Not looking down.

"What are you doing out here, Professor?"

"Thinking, Mr Cark. Something of a habit of mine. Maybe you should try it one day."

People below her. Far below her. Her fingers burned.

"Thinking in the rain, Professor? That doesn't seem very smart. It's my job to protect you, sir. I can't do that if you wander away from me."

Nye scoffed. "I believe I am quite safe all the way up here."

If Valkyrie lost her grip, she'd have to fly, and all those people would definitely notice a trail of white lightning arcing through the air.

"Just the same, Professor, I'd appreciate it if you stayed where I can see you at all times."

"Very well, very well. Here, hold this." The sound of the umbrella.

"I'm your bodyguard, Professor. Not your servant."

Nye gave the most irritated of sighs. The umbrella flapped. Footsteps moved away.

Valkyrie pulled herself up just in time to see Cark following Nye through the door. He was a big man. Solid. The door closed behind him and she pulled herself up the rest of the way.

116

The underground car park on Cut-throat Street was mostly empty by a quarter to midnight. Omen arrived through the south entrance and started walking the levels, passing through patches of utter blackness and swathes of warm electric light. He took the ramps down, the knife heavy in his jacket.

By Level Three, he had yet to meet Reznor Rake, or even glimpse Crepuscular Vies. He began to fear that his plan – as precarious as it was ill-conceived – was about to implode. He walked down another ramp.

Footsteps, and Omen scuttled behind a car. A Cleaver, coming this way, one of those new scythe staffs across his back. He was as tall as Crepuscular, but he was marching briskly, like he really was on patrol. There were no hidden signals. No indications that he had any suspicion at all that Omen was lurking in the shadows.

And then the Cleaver slowed, and his head turned ever so slightly towards where Omen was hidden, and Omen breathed in relief. It was Crepuscular. Either that or it was a real Cleaver who'd heard Omen move, and was about to leap into the shadows to investigate.

The Cleaver started walking towards him.

His mouth suddenly dry, Omen stepped forward, into the light. He gave what he hoped was a friendly, casual smile, but the

Cleaver didn't stop until he was maybe a scythe-length away from him.

"Good evening," Omen said.

The Cleaver stared. Omen could see himself in the mirrored visor. He looked nervous. Hell, he looked terrified.

But then the Cleaver started to undo his helmet.

It took a moment for the intention to register, and all of a sudden Omen was taking a step towards him with his hands up, his head shaking. This wasn't the plan, for God's sake. This wasn't the—

The helmet was lifted. "What do you think?" Reznor Rake asked. "Another one of my cunning disguises. It had you fooled, didn't it?"

Omen stared, and Reznor chuckled.

"Man, you should see your expression right now. You look so stupid."

"Why?" Omen croaked. He cleared his throat. "Why are you dressed as a Cleaver?"

"I told you – I'm a master of disguise. And what better way to stroll through Roarhaven than as someone who absolutely nobody wants to stop and ask for directions?"

Great minds think alike, whispered a little voice in the back of Omen's head. "Where's Auger?" he asked.

Reznor countered with, "Where's the Obsidian Blade?"

"Close by."

"What a coincidence – same with your brother. You give me the knife, I'll give you your twin back."

Omen shook his head. "Auger first."

"Nuh-uh."

"How about a compromise?"

"This is a compromise, kid. Me not killing you, that's the compromise."

Omen hesitated, then took the knife wrapped in cloth from his jacket, and Reznor plucked it from his grip. "Now, where's Auger?"

"Just hold on a second."

"Tell me where he is. We had a deal!"

"There's no hurry, kid," Reznor said, unwrapping the knife. He nodded, unsurprised. "Yeah, this isn't it."

Omen tried to look innocent. "Are you sure?"

Reznor sighed. "This is a knife you've painted black. Give me the real one, or I'll return this one to you, pointy end first."

Omen squared his shoulders. "Not until you give me Auger."

"Kid. Kid, think about this. You're putting yourself in danger because, what, you think I'll take the Obsidian Blade and not return your brother to you? You think I'll hang on to him? For God's sake, why would I do that? So I can force you to give me more things? What other things do you have that I might possibly want? A pen? A schoolbag? Give me the Blade, I'll tell you which car Auger is in, you'll go down to get him, and we'll go our separate ways. This couldn't be simpler, it really—"

He stopped, turning his head, listening for something Omen couldn't hear.

"You come alone?" he asked.

Omen nodded as honestly as he could.

Reznor took the scythe staff in his hand. "What is this? This a set-up? You laid a trap for me, is that what you did?"

"I don't know what you're— "

A flick of the wrist and the scythe staff lengthened and the blade popped out. "You stay here," Reznor said.

Omen nodded quickly, and Reznor went to investigate. So Auger was in the car park, in a car, on a lower level. Excellent.

Omen crept to the next ramp and hurried down. He ran to each of the seven parked cars, whispered Auger's name to each boot, and then ran down to the next level – and ducked.

Tancred stood leaning against a blue Ford. His arms were folded and he looked bored. There was a crowbar resting on the boot, within easy reach.

Quietly, Omen sneaked from car to patch of darkness to car.

Keeping low, he circled Tancred, than crept up as far as he could from the other direction.

Between where he was hiding and the Ford was a large, brightly lit area that offered zero cover – all Tancred had to do was catch a glimpse of him out of the corner of his eye, or hear the barest echo of a footstep...

Omen took off his jacket, lay down, and slowly started rolling towards the Ford.

Tancred was still facing the other way. Over and over Omen went, his arms by his sides to keep his phone in his pocket and to prevent any loose coins from jangling. Rolling. Rolling.

And then he was there, at the Ford, coming up to a crouch. He took a moment to calm down, and then rose up to peek.

The crowbar was his best chance. Grab it and whack Tancred over the head. No, not the head. Too easy to block. The legs, then. The shins.

He straightened. He'd have to lunge to grab it, though, and Tancred would see him, whirl on instinct, and there was no way that Omen could win the tug-of-war that would follow.

Another approach, then. Omen took a deep, deep breath.

He roared as he leaped forward and Tancred screamed and jumped away, arms up, covering his head, and Omen snatched the crowbar and brought it crashing into Tancred's left shin.

Tancred's scream turned to a howl and Omen darted, spun, whacked the other shin. Tancred was buckling, one hand trying to clutch both shins, the other grasping at Omen, who moved in and struck that left shin again.

Tancred fell sideways, knees rising to his chest, arms covering his shins, eyes squeezed shut, a miserable whine escaping his lips.

"Auger!" Omen hissed, fumbling at the boot latch. From within, a muffled reply.

The boot sprang open. Auger, in pyjama bottoms and a T-shirt, blinked up at him, hands tied behind his back, ankles bound, a gag in his mouth. Omen reached in, took him by the shoulders as Auger stuck his bare feet out, and heaved.

Auger stood, nearly toppled, twisting to show Omen the shackles around his wrists and then nodding to Tancred. The key. Tancred had the key in his pocket.

Gripping the crowbar, Omen stepped closer to Tancred. "The key," he said. "Give me the key."

"Gonna... kill you..." Tancred snarled.

"Give me the key or I'll whack you again." Omen took another step, adrenaline surging into his chest as he shouted, "Give me! The key!"

Tancred glared, took one hand away from his shin to dig into his pocket, then dropped the key on the ground.

"Kick it over here," Omen demanded.

"I can't kick anything!"

"Oh," said Omen. "Yeah, sorry." Ready to swing at any moment, Omen moved closer, then reached down, picked up the key.

Tancred roared and went for him and Omen shrieked and swung the crowbar and it was wrenched from his grip, and then Tancred was using it as a crutch to stand.

Omen hurried back to Auger, who hopped round, showing him the shackles again. The key skittered against the lock.

Auger made encouraging sounds. Tancred was on his feet now. The key went in.

Tancred lurched towards them.

The key turned. The shackles opened. Tancred swung.

Auger leaped, both hands closing around the crowbar as it came in, using it as a fulcrum to swing his legs up, his bound feet crashing into Tancred's jaw. Tancred went down and Auger landed, almost lost his balance, but got it back and grinned behind his gag.

Omen crouched, started working on the knots at his brother's ankles while Auger ripped away the gag. "Knew you'd find me," he said. "Do you know what's going on here? They didn't tell me anything."

"They wanted the Obsidian Blade," Omen said, making a mess of the rope.

"You didn't bring it, did you?"

"Nope."

"Good man," Auger said, pulling his feet free. "Right. Now where's the other one? Do we kick his ass, too?"

"Omen!"

They looked round at the roar, at Reznor coming down the ramp with the scythe in his hands and a furious look on his face.

"Or how about we just run?" Auger suggested.

They sprinted up the next ramp then ran for the stairs – and there was someone there, a Cleaver, running towards them.

"Sorry I'm late," he said as he passed.

Auger shot a look at Omen. "Did that Cleaver just talk?"

Omen kept running.

Omen and Auger got to the stairs, and, somewhere below them, Crepuscular met Reznor with a sharp clang of clashing blades.

117

It was the morning of the invasion, and Valkyrie didn't have any time left.

She took off her disguise, left it in the alley behind Nye's building, and activated the necronaut suit. She shot into the air, staying away from windows. Landed on the roof.

No sign of Nye.

The professor was late on the one morning she couldn't afford to let the schedule slip. Tahil na Kurge buzzed with excitement. It practically vibrated. There were already tens of thousands waiting beyond the barricades on Merchant's Square. The army was there, too, standing in regiments, leading all the way back to the district they had commandeered. All eyes flickered to the three massive portals and the stage that had been constructed before them. The stage with the five sets of chains.

Valkyrie checked her watch. Nye was almost ten minutes late.

"Fine," she muttered, and opened the door and went down the steps.

Even though each floor was empty of people and cleared of equipment, Valkyrie went slowly and stuck to the shadows. It wouldn't do to run into trouble this close to the executions. Skulduggery and Tanith were depending on her, even if they didn't know it. The last thing she needed at this point was a complication.

She reached Nye's floor, really wishing she had Saracen's ability to see through each door as she approached it. If she had to take out the bodyguard, then fair enough – but she'd really rather get through the morning without having to fight anyone.

She needn't have worried. She found the bodyguard slumped on the floor outside Nye's laboratory, his eyes open and staring and so very dull. She walked in.

"Going somewhere nice?" she asked.

Nye barely looked up from the papers it was stuffing into a bag. "Somewhere new, at any rate."

"I see Cark didn't make it."

"No, he did not."

"Poison?"

"A drop. In his tea. He liked his tea."

"You were going to leave without saying goodbye."

It closed its bag and looked up. "You forced me into this. No matter the outcome, Mevolent will have some blame to lay at my door. If I help you, I am a traitor for what I will do. If I tell him about you, I am a traitor for what I have done. I have four ways out. Three of them run an unpalatable risk of death, so I have chosen the option that brings with it the higher chance of staying alive."

The door opened and a woman came through – freezing when she saw Valkyrie. "He's making me do this," she said. "He's blackmailing me. I'd never—"

"Don't bother explaining yourself to her," Nye said, annoyed. "This isn't one of Mevolent's people. This is Valkyrie Cain. Recognise her?"

The woman's eyes widened. "The terrorist."

"Exactly," said Nye. "She doesn't know who you are, and she has no one to tell of what you're about to do. Come over here."

She hesitated, then hurried over.

"Teleporter?" Valkyrie asked.

"Shunter," Nye answered, passing the bag to the woman. "I

cannot reinforce the shield, not while it is active. If you somehow succeed in destroying the portal machines, the shield will only last a few more days, and then the draugar will swarm in. It is better for me to leave this world entirely."

"To be honest, Professor, I don't care what you do or where you go. Hand over the virus and I'll wave you off."

Nye and the Shunter stepped over to an orderly pile of bags and suitcases. "There is no virus, Miss Cain. I could have made one, absolutely, but I decided not to bother. I also alerted the Redhoods to your presence here."

From below, the crash of a door being kicked open.

"Have a good death," Nye said, and the Shunter put her hand on its arm and they flickered and vanished – taking the pile of cases with them.

Valkyrie whirled as the door burst open and Redhoods streamed in. Lightning flowed from both her hands, catching the first few full on. But they had those uniforms, and the uniforms had a knack for absorbing a whole lot of damage. They staggered, but kept coming, and more streamed in behind.

There were three doors in this lab. All three of them were now open and spewing Redhoods. They leaped over tables and slid under them and darted round them and their scythes left bright smears in the air.

Valkyrie launched herself backwards, rising off the floor. She hit the wall, her head brushing the ceiling, energy crackling around her as she hovered there, tried to figure out what the hell to do. But the Redhoods wouldn't allow her any breathing room. Five of them braced themselves with their hands on the wall and the others ran up on to their shoulders and jumped, scythes slashing. Valkyrie had to push herself away from the wall, but the Redhoods were leaping from the tables, coming at her from all angles. One of them missed with the blade, but managed to snag her foot with his hand.

He fell, pulling her down with him.

118

Behind the thick red curtain, technicians were making sure the cables and tubes and wires that fed into the portal machines were all working. Tanith watched them from her knees. They moved quickly. No doubt they had done this a hundred times before – but she supposed it never did any harm to check again. On the other side of the curtain, a crowd of over a hundred thousand people waited excitedly.

"This is probably how actors feel," she said.

"Probably," Skulduggery said beside her.

"Can you imagine the nerves on opening night of some big Broadway show? I read this interview once with an actor, can't remember who. His play opened with him in bed, and he thought it'd be pretty cool to already be in the bed before the audience arrived. So he's there, under the covers, being very still and very quiet, and he's listening to everyone come in and take their seats and chat and laugh and, bit by bit, he starts to get terrified. He gave himself stage fright by paying too much attention to the audience."

"Yes," Skulduggery said. Captain Assegai passed in front of them, issuing orders to the Redhoods and the soldiers. Technicians scattered before her like mice before a cat. "Although that's not *exactly* like our situation, because we're not here to act in a play; we're here, in shackles, to be executed."

"Well, yes, but I'd say the nerves are about the same."

Skulduggery looked at her. "Indeed," he said, and turned to the three Necromancers in chains beside them. "What about you lot? Are you nervous at all, regarding our impending doom?"

Two men and a woman. They, like Tanith and Skulduggery, were on their knees and dressed in sackcloth. Tanith didn't know if this was ceremonial sackcloth or sackcloth with any special significance. The people who'd handed out the sackcloth hadn't been interested in answering questions. She figured it was just regular old sackcloth. That's how it felt, anyway. Scratchy.

"Death holds no mystery for us," the first Necromancer said. He was a bit of a pretentious git. "We are ready to return to the Great Stream."

"Lovely," said Skulduggery.

There was a clock behind them. Tanith could just about read it if she twisted her neck. Ten minutes to go.

"Mevolent should be arriving soon," she said. "It's actually kind of impressive that he's still executing his enemies himself, isn't it? Like, I hate him and everything and he's a really awful person, but to get to the level he's at and not offload all the work to subordinates..."

"Yes," Skulduggery said. "Looking at it like that, he's really quite a salt-of-the-earth fellow, isn't he?"

"Still hate him, though."

"Well, that's handy. You seem awfully chipper today."

"That's because I have faith."

"Oh, good. Faith in what, exactly?"

"Valkyrie. She won't let us get executed. She won't let us get our heads chopped off. Or, *my* head chopped off, at least. How is Mevolent going to execute you?"

"I imagine the same way, only he'll be using the God-Killer sword. That should kill me just as dead as it would kill anyone else."

Tanith winced. "Your own sword."

"Well, mine on loan, but yes."

She thought about it. "I think I'd quite like it if he used my sword on me. It's good quality. Sharp, you know? There'd be no hacking away at my neck. One swipe, clean through."

"But, of course, it won't come to that."

"Oh, good point. No, Valkyrie will rescue us before that happens."

Assegai heard that and she turned, a sneer on her lips. "I hope she tries," she said. "I'll be here waiting for her."

Tanith chuckled. "Oh, she'll kick your ass, sweetie."

"She hasn't managed it yet."

A shrug. "She was just warming up."

A soldier hurried over. "Captain Assegai, we just got word that the Redhoods encountered Valkyrie Cain in the Science Building."

"Has she been apprehended?" Assegai asked. "Killed?"

"Neither, I'm afraid. She escaped."

Assegai glowered. "And what is being done to capture her?"

"I, uh... I don't know. You see, she can fly, and so—"

"I know she can fly," Assegai snapped. "She'll be coming here. OK, move everyone out. No soldiers, no engineers, nothing. I want to make this too good an opportunity for her to pass up, do you hear me? I want this area sealed off. Nobody in or out."

"Yes, Captain," the soldier said, giving her a salute. He stalked off to issue orders, and in moments the stage was empty save for those in chains and Assegai herself.

Tanith grinned. "She's coming to kick your ass," she said in a singsong voice.

Assegai grunted, walked away. She came back with a large bag that she dumped at her feet. "Your gear," she said, opening it. Tanith's leathers were in there. So was Skulduggery's outfit. And Tanith's sword.

"Took you long enough," Skulduggery said.

"I've been busy," Assegai responded. She went behind them, started unlocking the chains.

Tanith frowned. "I don't get it."

The shackles loosened. Tanith's power returned. Oh, that felt good. But still she frowned. "Do I hit her? I feel like I should hit her."

"Why would you want to hit her?" Skulduggery asked while his own shackles were being removed.

"Because she's... OK, wait. What's going on? How do you two know each other?"

"This," Assegai said, "is so much fun."

She stood in front of Tanith and turned her head right and then left, showing her the sigils tattooed behind her ears. Then she gave her a smile, reached back and tapped those sigils, and Assegai's face flowed away, revealing Valkyrie's beneath it.

Tanith clapped a hand over her mouth to keep from crying out. "You little marvel! You sneaky little marvel! How have you managed this? You sneaky little...! Where's the real Assegai? *Is there* a real Assegai?"

Valkyrie grinned as she started to take off her uniform. "She's tied up in her spare bedroom, along with Mevolent's head of security – although they've probably been discovered by this stage, with the invasion so close and everything."

"When did this happen? When did you take her place?"

"A few days ago."

"That's so cool," Tanith said, hauling off the sackcloth and starting to dress in her leathers. "And when did you figure it out?" she asked Skulduggery, who had turned his back on them both.

"The first time we saw her, it struck me that Assegai had a very familiar gait. When I saw her fight, I knew for certain."

"And you didn't bother to tell me?"

"I couldn't be sure that Mevolent wasn't eavesdropping on our conversations. Also, I knew I'd enjoy watching your face when you realised."

"I had Professor Nye carve the sigils," Valkyrie said. Now that she'd abandoned Assegai's uniform, she walked off, pressing the amulet to her sternum and tapping it. The necronaut suit covered her as she removed the God-Killer sword from hiding. "It took a little work to make sure the façade was an identical match to Assegai's face, and then more work to alter my voice, but it was worth it in the end."

"This," Tanith said, "is hysterical."

"Any idea how we dismantle the portal machines?" Skulduggery asked.

"Yeah," Valkyrie said, without enthusiasm. She held up a strange-looking box. "According to Nye, this bomb is powerful enough to take out a building. I figure it's enough to take out the machines, too. Only..."

"Only what?"

"Only there's probably a segment of the people out there who'll be caught in the blast. It'll kill them."

Skulduggery slid the God-Killer into the sheath on his back. Fully dressed now, he turned to her, and held out his gloved hand. "Then I'll do it."

Valkyrie hesitated. "No," she said.

"You don't want this on your conscience."

"It'll be on my conscience anyway, regardless of who sets off the bomb. I brought it here. It's my plan. I should be the one to do it."

Tanith put a gentle hand on her arm. "Val, think about this. You've just managed to get a handle on the old trauma. You really want to add a new one to the mix?"

"Not really," Valkyrie said. "But I'm better able to cope with it, I think. I hope. I have done awful, awful things that I'll never be able to forget – but I know why I did them, why I had to do them, and I'm OK with that. I don't know if I've come to terms with it, but I'm... I'm OK. And, if this sends me spiralling again, fair enough. I'll work through it, because I have to."

Skulduggery dropped his hand. "If you're sure."

"I am."

"Then I'll be here to help in whatever way I'm able."

"Yeah," said Tanith. "Me too."

Valkyrie smiled sadly. "Thanks."

Somebody snorted. They looked round. The middle Necromancer had his head down, and was trying not to laugh.

"Something funny, sunshine?" Tanith asked, prodding him with her boot.

"Say nothing," said the female Necromancer.

The laughing chap looked up, let out a giggle. "Why shouldn't I? They'll find out in mere moments anyway."

Valkyrie frowned. "Find out what?"

"You're all dead," he said. "All of you. You can set off the bomb or throw it away – it won't make any difference. Everyone will die here. Everyone will die now."

"And who's going to kill us?"

He grinned. "Some of you will undoubtedly die at the hands of the Death Bringer himself. But the draugar will get most of you, and you'll be added to the army of the dead."

"The draugar on the other side of the shield, you mean?" Tanith asked.

"Yes."

"And how are they going to manage that?"

Before the Necromancer could answer, the curtains opened, and tens of thousands of people were suddenly staring at them.

119

"Nobody move!" Valkyrie roared, cradling the bomb against her chest in case some Elemental tried snatching it from her hands. The crowd went quiet. She'd rarely seen as large a crowd of people want to tear her limb from limb before. It *had* happened, obviously. But it was rare. "I want everyone to back away from the portal machines," she shouted.

"I thought you told us not to move!" somebody shouted back.

A few hundred people laughed at that one.

Valkyrie glared. "I'm about to destroy these machines of yours. This device in my hand will do that – but it'll also take out a lot of you fine people. But hey, stick around if you want, see if I give a damn."

The laughing died down. The people at the front tried to move away, but the people at the back weren't budging.

"Go ahead!" someone else shouted from way back. "Set it off! Blow yourself up!"

That got a few thousand of them arguing among themselves, but, as soon as it started, the griping hushed. Valkyrie didn't like that. Didn't like it at all. She looked up.

"Ohhhh, hell," Tanith whispered.

Mevolent and Lord Vile came drifting over the rooftops, eliciting a sudden chorus of cheers and laughter. The crowd regained their confidence in an instant. Even the soldiers were grinning.

Mevolent and Vile hovered there, in the air, far above the

heads of the people. Mevolent wasn't wearing his battlesuit. He didn't even have that screaming helmet thing he liked to wear. It was just him, and he was all the more scary for it.

The bomb was cold in Valkyrie's hands. Tanith prepared herself.

Skulduggery drew the God-Killer sword. "I'm afraid the executions will have to be postponed," he shouted. "And your invasion will have to be called off!"

When Mevolent spoke, his soft voice carried. "We do not need the executions for the invasion to go ahead."

"Damn," Skulduggery whispered. "I was really hoping he wouldn't realise that."

"Open the portals."

More cheers, even louder than before, even more raucous, the crowd channelling their fear into their excitement.

Valkyrie turned as the three rings lit up and a hum made the stage vibrate under her feet. A shimmering blue energy stretched across each ring like liquid soap, then started to swirl, creating three identical vortexes.

Mevolent cast his gaze upon his army. "Prepare to march," he said.

Skulduggery waved. "Hey. Hey! Before you do, you might want to question these Necromancers. That one in particular. He seems to believe the draugar are going to break through any moment now."

The chatty Necromancer went pale, and shook his head.

"No, go on," Skulduggery said loudly. "Tell them what you told us."

"I didn't tell you anything," said the Necromancer.

"Of course you did," Skulduggery responded. "All that stuff about adding us to the army of the dead. I liked that bit. It was very ominous. Valkyrie, what did you think of that bit?"

Valkyrie nodded. "Very ominous," she said, her mouth dry, her voice close to cracking.

"It sounded to me," Skulduggery went on, "that you were

about to tell us who's behind it all. Behind the plague, the draugar, the Necromancers... It sounded like you were going to tell us who this Death Bringer is. Were you?"

The chatty Necromancer shook his head violently.

Skulduggery looked up at Mevolent and Vile. "Do you believe him?" They didn't answer, so he looked at the crowd. "Do *you* believe him?"

A messy chorus responded, but their message was clear. No, they did not believe him.

"I wasn't going to tell you," said the chatty Necromancer.

"I think you were."

"No. I wasn't. I wasn't going to tell anyone."

Skulduggery tilted his head. "Why is that? Is it because you didn't want to spoil the surprise? What surprise could that be, I wonder? What name could possibly take the great Mevolent by surprise?"

Mevolent's gaze was on the chatty Necromancer. He started floating down towards the stage—

—and then jerked sideways, narrowly avoiding Lord Vile's slashing shadows.

Suddenly they were circling each other in the air, neither man uttering a word while the crowd began to mutter and grumble below them, panic a mere moment away.

Mevolent flew at Vile and Vile shadow-walked behind him, raking darkness across his back. Mevolent spun, his blood dripping on to the upturned faces of the citizens below. Fire filled his arms and he released a stream of flame that forced Vile to cover up, allowing Mevolent to get close. They went whirling through the tallest tower in the city as the energy dome retracted and the Necromancers outside flew down to help their Death Bringer.

The people were following the spectacle like they were watching a tennis match – gasping, cheering, crying out. Mevolent punched holes through Necromancers, sent them dropping, but the odds were not in his favour, and he wasn't wearing his battlesuit.

The Necromancers' shadows darted through him, slicing

through his flesh, impaling him with two dozen spears of darkness simultaneously.

He stiffened, his body rigid. Valkyrie saw him cough blood and then his head lolled back and he went limp.

Just like that.

Mevolent was dead, just like that.

Cries of horror from the crowd as the other Necromancers slowly retracted their spears. Vile brought Mevolent close, examining him, making sure he really *was* dead. Satisfied, his shadows flicked Mevolent's corpse away from him, and the city moaned aloud in grief and horror.

Then the gates opened and the draugar came sprinting through.

The crowd panicked. Surged. Soldiers turned to face the onrushing horde. They met them with magic and steel and did well at first. They chopped at their legs and caved in their skulls and proved to be an indomitable line of defence. Until that line broke against the endless horde, and the screams of the soldiers were added to the screams of the people.

"March!" someone was screaming. Valkyrie picked her out among all those faces. Assegai.

"March!" she screamed again, and the soldiers closest to the stage hurried for the ramps.

Tanith snagged Valkyrie's arm, pulled her round as Lord Vile lowered himself to the stage. Skulduggery was already stalking towards him, God-Killer in his hands, saying something that Valkyrie couldn't hear, probably something cocky. A column of darkness shot out from Vile's chest, slammed into Skulduggery, knocking him back. The sword fell, went skittering off the stage.

Energy crackling, Valkyrie stepped forward, but Skulduggery was already up again. Shadows leaked from underneath his collar, from his sleeves, from his boots. They wrapped around his limbs, his torso, his head, forming armour.

"Oh," Tanith said, and then, "*oh.*"

Lord Vile met Lord Vile, and went to war.

120

A soldier scrambled up on to the stage and Valkyrie sent him spinning off again with a blast of lightning. There was a flash of colour and an energy stream caught her, spun her round, almost sent her toppling. An arrow thudded against her chest and bounced off, nearly taking her eye out as it whirled madly past her face.

She was aware of Tanith ducking the sword of another soldier, aware of her chopping down on that soldier's arm, and suddenly the stage was crawling with soldiers and Valkyrie didn't have anywhere to run. She yanked down the zip of her suit, stuffed the bomb in there, and zipped it back up.

"Right," she said, and didn't get a chance to say anything more. They came at her with gritted teeth and bulging eyes and swinging weapons. Fireballs exploded against her. Energy streams of assorted colours sent her stumbling. And she responded to it all the same way: she moved, she weaved, she grabbed, she blasted.

A soldier managed to tackle her. Valkyrie broke his fingers and punched him in the throat as the two Lord Viles fell into the street. They grappled, their shadows coiling and whipping, slicing through the people and soldiers and draugar around them.

"Valkyrie!" Tanith called.

She turned. Hundreds of soldiers were sprinting through the portals. The bomb that rested against her ribs would destroy the machines and stop the invasion – but it would mean killing herself, and everyone around her.

She spread her arms wide and let the lightning flow. Soldiers snapped back, went spinning, went hurtling off the stage, into the crowd, clearing a space, and she watched as one of the Lord Viles fell to his knees, unable to prevent the other one from dragging his armour away. Piece by piece, the armour became wisps of darkness, revealing Skulduggery beneath.

A last effort, and Vile stole Skulduggery's darkness, adding it to his own, and kicked Skulduggery away.

That wasn't good. That wasn't good at all.

More and more draugar came, and the crowd surged, soldiers and civilians. They climbed over each other, clambering on to the stage, flowing round Valkyrie and then slamming into her, frightened faces pressed up against hers, wide eyes not even registering her in their panic. Valkyrie found herself lifted, cursing, being forced back, unable to settle herself, unable to push back. She glanced over her shoulder to the shimmering portal and then she was through it.

Back into Roarhaven.

121

It was snowing.

The masses pressed tighter and Valkyrie squirmed round, saw rapidly forming lines of Roarhaven Cleavers and Sanctuary sorcerers pushing back against the invading army. But it wasn't an army, not any more. There were soldiers and Redhoods, here to fight, struggling to form up, but there were also the screaming civilians, the spoiled aristocrats, their shrieks of surrender lost amid the cacophony of violence.

Valkyrie's feet touched down and she fell to one knee. A woman beside her disappeared, squawking, in a forest of legs, and Valkyrie powered up, grabbing whoever was close as she scrambled. She hissed in a face, head-butted another, all the while carried along by the people around her.

A soldier tried to plunge his knife into her side. She took hold of his wrist with one hand and his throat with the other and she let the lightning flow through her. He jerked back and was lost in the next surge. She had his knife, though.

There was space around her now. A soldier came in, swinging an axe one-handed, aiming to split her down the middle. She lunged into him, one arm up to keep the axe away, the other driving the knife deep into his armpit. His howl turned to a gurgle and she tore the axe from his grip. It was big and heavy and she didn't have a whole lot of room to swing it.

A wall of air knocked Valkyrie to her knees. She didn't have time to look behind. She just turned, bringing the axe round in a short arc. It bit into the side of a leg and the soldier grunted and fell to his hands and knees. Valkyrie brought the axe down and it cut off a few fingers. The soldier screamed and Valkyrie abandoned the axe and took his sword. The soldier wasn't going to need it.

She slashed and hacked and grunted and lost the sword and a mace crunched into her shoulder. She screamed in rage and loosed the lightning, then took to the sky over the portals, feeling the instant relief of open space around her. She landed on a roof, closed her eyes for three whole seconds, enjoying the cold wind and the snow on her sweat-streaked face.

Eyes open again, she surveyed the scene.

"Jesus," she whispered.

The High Sanctuary was to her right, its shield up. The Dark Cathedral was to her left, protected by a large group of armed guards. The zone between them was a surging mass of bodies. Right now, it was pretty evenly split between Roarhaven and Tahil na Kurge forces, but there were more soldiers and civilians stumbling through those portals all the time. It wouldn't be long before the numbers started to tip.

She unzipped her suit, took out the bomb. All she had to do was arm it and then toss it back through one of the portals. As easy as that. The machines would be destroyed, the portals would close, the day would be saved. And a lot of people would die.

The soldier she'd stabbed in the armpit. The others she'd hacked at. They were probably dead.

That was different, though. That was in the midst of battle. It was kill or be killed. But throwing a bomb through a doorway... That wasn't quite so clear cut.

Valkyrie wished she could just leave. She was back home now, after so very long away. She should be able to run into Militsa's arms. She should be able to hug her family. She shouldn't have to fight. She'd fought enough.

Down there, in the middle of it all – Skulduggery, fighting back to back with Tanith. Valkyrie could see Dexter now, and Serpine. No sign of Saracen yet. He was probably perched somewhere with the bow, picking off targets.

Her family and Militsa were going to have to wait. Valkyrie climbed over the parapet and let herself drop.

122

Skulduggery swung the God-Killer sword and enemies split in half around him.

Tanith's katana flashed in the cold Roarhaven sun, but all that hacking, that slashing, that stabbing and that wounding had dulled the blade so she dropped it, took out the God-killer dagger, killed her opponents with the merest nick.

The God-killer spear twirled in Dexter's hands, the staff knocking them down, the bladed tip finishing them off.

Beside him, Serpine blasted streams of purple energy into whoever got too close. He had a shield strapped to his right arm, and he used it to bash and batter and club, but his hand was missing. Valkyrie was looking forward to hearing that story.

She had a broken sword in her own hand. She wasn't quite sure how she'd come about it – her head was still ringing from that punch she'd taken – but she swung it like she owned it until her thoughts arranged themselves into some sort of order.

A sword cut through Dexter's backpack. It was flat to his back, looked practically empty except for something heavy at the bottom. He spun, plunging the spear into the belly of the man with the sword, and the Sceptre fell from the bag, hit the ground.

Valkyrie felt time slow. Passing through the portal would have wiped it clean. It would bond with whoever touched it first.

It skittered about, kicked this way and that by a dozen different feet. The original God-Killer. Too much power to be wielded by any one person. But, if one person had to wield it, Valkyrie would prefer it to be her.

No one had noticed it. Too busy killing each other to look down. Nobody... except Serpine.

Time sped up again and he barged through the crowd, blasting anyone who stumbled into his path.

Valkyrie thrust herself into the melee, using her lightning to clear a route.

Serpine saw what she was doing and increased his pace. She did likewise. They threw people out of their way.

A fist came in from nowhere, rocked her head. A soldier, blood streaming down his face from a matted hairline. No weapons but fists. No magic on display. Too angry, perhaps. He hit her again and she pushed past him. He didn't matter. Only the Sceptre mattered.

Serpine had thrown down his shield and now he was crawling through the fighting, getting closer. Valkyrie cursed, launched herself forward, tried to dive, but at that moment the crowd contracted and she was caught there, held off the ground by sheer numbers. She sent out crackling energy in all directions and people jerked away. She fell, scrambled, reaching for the Sceptre as Serpine did.

She grabbed it and so did he. Wrestled for it.

Somebody's knee smacked into her face and she lost her grip as the world swam. When it came back into focus, her hands were empty and someone was tripping over her ankles.

Then the noise went away, like someone had turned the volume down on the whole battle. The fighting stopped.

Valkyrie stood on shaky legs, confused. All eyes were up. She turned. Necromancers floated through the portals – Lord Vile leading the way.

Beneath them, the draugar stepped through. Calmly. Not even snarling. Waiting for the order to attack.

A space had cleared around Serpine. He raised the Sceptre, took aim at Vile. His arm tensed but nothing happened. He tried again.

He cursed under his breath, then turned to Valkyrie, pressed the Sceptre into her hands.

"Don't miss," he whispered.

She took the bomb from her suit and exchanged it for the Sceptre, which she held behind her back as she powered off the ground.

Shadows leaped for her and she swerved round them, spinning to keep them from attaching. A Necromancer dived at her and her white lightning crossed the space between them and he went hurtling back. She rose higher, flying straight for Vile, and he saw the Sceptre too late.

Black lightning streaked from the Sceptre, through the shadows that coiled before him, and struck his chest, and, as Lord Vile was instantly transformed into a man of dust and thrashing darkness, Valkyrie flew through it all, scattering that dust to the wind.

All his plans. All his schemes. Everything about him. Everything that was and ever would be. Nothing but dust. As suddenly as Mevolent had been snuffed out, so too had Vile. But this time it was by Valkyrie's hand.

And the effect it had was immediate.

The Necromancers clutched their heads and curled up, their shadows becoming fragmented, unable to support their weight. The draugar, who had been standing there as still as any army regiment Valkyrie had ever seen, were now a snarling, snapping mass of pure instinct. They sprinted and lurched and staggered into the throng of people ahead of them.

From where she hovered, Valkyrie watched the Roarhaven forces pull back as best they could, leaving the Tahil na Kurge soldiers to turn and fight the oncoming horde. The civilians, the aristocrats, were caught in the middle. A lot of them disappeared under the swarming dead. A lot more were killed by their own soldiers in the mad scramble that followed.

And still the draugar came through from the other side, an influx that wouldn't end until the portals were closed.

In all that chaos below her, she spotted Serpine wading through the draugar and the soldiers. She flew down, finger-guns out, blasting whoever got too close to him. When he was within range, he hurled the bomb high over the heads of the dead. It tumbled through space, turning over and over and over again, like it was taking its sweet time, and then it disappeared through the shimmering energy.

A moment later, great gouts of fire burst through the portals, accompanied by burning limbs and metal fragments, and the portals flickered...

...and collapsed.

123

Omen and Never watched it all from a rooftop.

Shivering with the cold, they huddled together as the Sanctuary forces fought the enemy. There were zombie things in there that even the bad guys were fighting.

When the zombie things were all dead, or dead again or whatever, the remaining bad guys whirled to the Sanctuary guys. Then one of them dropped his weapons. And so did another.

And then there was just the sound of weapons hitting the ground as they all surrendered, every last one of them.

"I have no idea what's going on," said Omen.

124

Valkyrie sat in the dark and watched her hands tremble.

There was blood all over her. It was dried in. Crusted under her fingernails. Her hair was matted with it.

She ached. There didn't seem to be any part of her that didn't ache. Her jaw and her nose and her ear. Her ribs and her back. Her left leg. Her right shin.

She'd found an empty room in the High Sanctuary as soon as she was able to get away. They didn't need her for the mop-up. They didn't need her to herd the prisoners into the cells. They didn't even need her for the debrief. That could wait.

Saracen was dead. He hadn't been perched somewhere, shooting off arrows, picking off enemies. He was dead. Bitten, infected, and then put out of his misery.

Another friend dead. Another friend gone. How many was it now? How many people that she liked, that she loved, would she never see again? Too many, that was the answer. Always too many.

The door opened, spilling light into the room.

"Hey, stranger," said Militsa.

And suddenly Valkyrie was all tears and all sobs and she was rushing over, across the room, falling into the arms of the woman she loved.

125

China watched the blood being cleaned off the streets, watched the corpses being loaded up and sorted out. Roarhaven people taken to be cremated in sombre, official ceremony. Everyone else taken to be burned in a pit.

She watched the city through the eyes of its cameras. Listened to it through the microphones. She heard what her citizens were saying, heard them discuss the horror, the death, the violence. She heard them pray to various gods. Heard them pray to the Faceless Ones.

They speculated on who was to blame. Speculated on who would be punished. A few of them seemed to blame China for what had unfolded. With a thought, she sent their names to the City Guard. They could expect a knock on the door in the middle of the night.

Someone came in. She disconnected from the Whispering, the real world coalescing around her. Skulduggery Pleasant stood on the platform below, splattered with mud and blood, his hood down, the God-Killer sword across his back.

She felt a smile beginning to form, and she was about to ask how long he thought it would be before he got changed into one of his exquisite suits – but then he spoke.

"Is everything all right?" he asked.

Not a greeting. Not a smart comment. Not even an update on

the mission, or the battle. There was something in his voice. Doubt, perhaps. Or concern. Either one was unacceptable. Either one was a fast-spreading virus.

"Of course," China replied sharply, the smile dead before it even reached her lips. "Apart from your inability to do the job I told you to do, everything is wonderful. Assassinate Mevolent, I said, not stumble through a portal with an army of killers and a horde of the dead, seven months later."

"Delays were unavoidable, I'm afraid."

"It's not like you to give me excuses."

"That's not an excuse."

China looked away from him. The whiteness of his skull was giving her a headache. She needed to pray. That always settled her thoughts.

"We lost Saracen," he said.

She looked back at him. "What?"

"Saracen." His head tilted. "Saracen Rue."

"I know who he is!" she snapped. "What about him?"

"He's dead."

"Dead? But... No, the report you gave... you said the Shunter was dead."

"Yes, the Shunter died, and so did Saracen."

She flung herself out of her throne, almost teetering on the dais. The sea of energy crackled beneath her. "By the Faceless, Skulduggery! I sent you to kill Mevolent and you come skulking back with two of your own dead! What about Serpine? Why is he alive?"

Skulduggery was silent for a moment. "He proved useful."

"I don't care what he proved," China sneered. "I promised him freedom in exchange for his help. What am I going to do now? I can't let him roam our world, can I? He's Nefarian Serpine! I told you to kill him once the mission was done!"

"The mission wasn't done until two hours ago."

"But it *is* done, yes? It's done now?"

"Yes."

She raised her eyebrows.

"You want me to kill him," Skulduggery said.

"I want you to carry out your orders."

"Send someone else."

"I sent you."

"And that's not what I do."

China returned to her throne and laughed. "Oh, really? Tell that to Detective Somnolent."

He didn't respond, and she shook her head. "Go. Leave me. I must pray."

He left.

126

She lay beside Militsa in the dark.

"I'm not sure how to explain it," she said. "I might need a few days to, I don't know... organise it in my head."

"That's OK," Militsa said, as she softly stroked Valkyrie's hair. "You talk about it whenever you're ready to talk about it."

Valkyrie took a deep, deep breath, like it was the first breath she'd taken in a long time. "I hated being away from you."

"Me too."

"I'm never going to an alternate dimension again."

"Swear?"

"I swear."

The door opened a little and Xena came in, jumped up on the bed, and flopped down across Valkyrie's chest. Valkyrie laughed, and scratched behind the dog's ears.

"I've been calling in on your family," Militsa said, "doing my best to keep them optimistic. They're going to be so happy to see you."

"First thing in the morning, I'm there."

"You should crawl under the tree and when they walk in you should just shout *Merry Christmas!* That'd be cute."

"What?"

Militsa frowned at her. "Tomorrow," she said. "It's Christmas Day, tomorrow."

"It is?"

"You didn't know?"

"There weren't exactly a whole lot of decorations up where we were. I don't have anything for them, though."

"What, like presents? Sweetums, you are the present."

"Oh, yeah," Valkyrie said. "I suppose I *am* a gift."

Militsa laughed.

127

Christmas morning.

Valkyrie raised the key to the lock and kept it there, as if it was frozen in place. Her hand was steady, though. That was nice. As excited as she was, at least her nerves weren't showing.

But just walking in, after all this time, after 219 days away... No. Knocking would be better. Allow them to open the door, invite her in. Back into the house. Back into their lives. Valkyrie raised her fist, went to rap her knuckles.

Wait. Wait.

Why the formality? Why the stiffness? She was home. She'd always walked right in before – when she remembered her key, that was.

She shook her head at her inability to make a decision on this. Finally, she just slid the key in the lock and walked in.

128

Sebastian used to love Christmas, but that was back when he had a family, back when he had a normal life – if his life could ever be described as normal.

But he hadn't had anyone to buy presents for lately, so he couldn't allow this opportunity to pass him by.

He stepped into the room. Darquesse floated.

"Merry Christmas," he said, holding out the gift.

Darquesse didn't reach for it. Didn't even open her eyes. "Thank you," she said.

"It's, um, it's—"

"Baby shoes," Darquesse said. "I know."

"I just thought, seeing as how you don't have any family or, like, friends, I thought I'd... I thought you could use whatever support I can give."

She opened her eyes and looked at him. "Thank you. The shoes are lovely."

He smiled. "You haven't even—"

The box floated from his hand and disappeared, leaving the tiny yellow shoes to spin slowly through the air.

"Lovely," Darquesse repeated. "But I didn't get you a present."

He shrugged. "That's OK, you didn't have to."

"But it's tradition. What would you like?"

Sebastian laughed. "Really, you don't have to—"

"You'd like your family back."

His laugh faded. "No, I wouldn't."

"Of course you would. I know your thoughts."

He shook his head. "No. Thank you, but no."

"Their absence makes you unhappy."

"Yes. But I don't want you to fix it. Please."

"Very well. In that case, maybe a pony?"

He frowned. Darquesse was smiling.

"A joke," Sebastian said. "You told a joke."

"I did. Was it funny?"

"Yes."

"Oh, good. It's only my second one. I was worried."

"So how's the little one doing in there?" he asked, nodding towards her stomach. "Is she ready to come out?"

"Today?" Darquesse said. "No, it will not be today. The virgin birth of this world's next god shall not take place on Christmas Day."

"I just thought it'd be kinda cool..."

"No, Sebastian."

He sighed. "Fair enough."

"Although it would be kind of cool," Darquesse said, and laughed, and Sebastian laughed along with her.

129

Valkyrie opened the door and took in Skulduggery, standing there in a navy blue three-piece suit with a crisp white shirt and a navy blue tie. "Damn," she said, "you look good."

"Thank you," he replied. "I know. Is that dog of yours around?"

"She's barely left my side all week. What's the matter? Do you not want to get any dog hair on your trousers?"

"If I could at all avoid it."

"No problem." She motioned for him to come in, then shut the door and gave a low whistle. Xena came bounding in from the living room.

"Oh, dear," said Skulduggery, catching the dog when she jumped into his arms. Her slobbering knocked his hat off, but Valkyrie caught it before it hit the ground.

"I'm about to make myself some tea," she said, leading the way to the kitchen.

"Your dog is gnawing on my head."

"She's just happy to see you."

They got to the kitchen and Valkyrie filled the kettle with water, then flicked it on and turned, leaning against the worktop. "Are you going to this thing tomorrow?"

"I'll be there," he said, managing to put Xena down. She went to jump up again and he said, "Sit," very sternly, and Xena obeyed. He *did* have a commanding voice.

"I don't know if I will," said Valkyrie. "Militsa wants to go to a party tonight, but I hate New Year's Eve stuff and I'm really not in the mood to be around people right now. I think I'll skip China's speech tomorrow as well."

Skulduggery waved his hands, and a few of Xena's discarded hairs drifted from his jacket. "You might not be able to do that," he said. "We may have a problem."

Valkyrie groaned. "Another one? So soon? Let someone else take care of it, please. We've just got back from the last one."

"The last one isn't over," he said. "Not yet."

She frowned. "Explain."

"One of China's people was going over the footage taken of the battle. All those people coming through the portals."

"And?"

"They noticed something in all the chaos – three people carrying a body through, and then disappearing with it."

"A body? Like a corpse? There were loads of corpses. We were *fighting* corpses, for God's..." She faltered. "Whose corpse?"

"We couldn't make it out clearly, but earlier today I shunted back over to our friends in the Resistance. Meritorious has taken control of Tahil na Kurge. It's an uneasy situation, but he was responsible for sealing the gates once again, so the people are inclined to do what he says. For now. His first priority is dealing with the millions of walking dead outside the walls, but they pose far less of a threat now that the Necromancers have been taken out of the equation."

"Skulduggery," Valkyrie said. "Whose body was brought through the portal?"

He sighed. "I asked Meritorious if they had recovered Mevolent's remains. They had not."

She sagged. "Aw, no. Aw, no, no, no."

"China remembered what you said you'd seen on one of your first trips to the Leibniz Universe."

"The pool," Valkyrie muttered. "The Redhoods killed Mevolent and he was taken into this horrible-smelling pool of something black."

"And what did Baron Vengeous say?"

"He said that Mevolent died every day, in order to show death that he was its master, or some such rubbish."

"And then what happened?"

"Then he came back to life. So you think he's going to come back?"

"China came to me with the suggestion," Skulduggery said, "and I don't disagree that it's a distinct possibility. It all depends on who took his body."

"Aw, crap."

"What?"

"He'd been talking to Serafina. Professor Nye told me. They had some communications device that allowed them to chat. He probably arranged this as a contingency plan if something went wrong." Valkyrie brightened. "But all you have to do is bring Serafina in for questioning."

Skulduggery grunted.

"What?"

"Since we've been gone, China has given even greater power to the religious organisations in the city."

"You mean the Church of the Faceless."

"Yes... but also their rival church, of which Serafina is the head."

"So?"

"So they have quite a broad immunity from any investigation."

"Even ours? We're Arbiters, for God's sake. The Arbiter Corps was set up so that we could go after the people in power."

"We can," Skulduggery said. "We can go after Elders, whole Councils... even the Supreme Mage herself. But, according to the law, the religious leaders are out of our reach."

"Even though Serafina is probably resurrecting Mevolent as we speak?"

"Even though."

"Xena, here," Valkyrie said, crouching down when Xena came over. She cuddled her dog. "So what do we do?"

"We do what we always do," said Skulduggery. "We go in, and we make trouble."

130

Midnight came, and all around Corrival Academy, the students who'd stayed in Roarhaven for the Christmas break cheered and wished each other a Happy New Year.

"Happy birthday, Omen," said Auger.

"Happy birthday, Auger," said Omen.

One more year to go until they turned seventeen. After that, the prophecy would result in the death of either the King of the Darklands, or of the Chosen One. One more year.

"Prophecies suck," said Omen.

"Yes, they do," said Auger.

131

The Circle zone was filled with people. Only eight days earlier it had been the site of a full-on battle, but now it was covered in balloons and ribbons and New Year's Day cheer. Elder Praetor had just made a speech, and now it was Elder Vespers' turn. Valkyrie sat on a rooftop high above, legs kicking, not bothering to listen to what was being said.

Skulduggery drifted over, landed beside her.

"Any movement?" she asked.

He shook his head. "Serafina's mansion is as still as a corpse."

"That's unnecessarily morbid."

"And, like a corpse, its eyes are sewn up tight."

"And that's unnecessarily graphic."

"Every door to that place is sealed shut," he said, "every window covered... We have no idea what's going on inside."

"Saracen would be handy to have around, right about now."

"I swear, the one time he'd be useful..."

They laughed together, softly.

"OK," said Skulduggery, "the Supreme Mage is about to arrive, so let's mingle with the crowd. If you see anything strange, send out a bolt of lightning."

"Sure," said Valkyrie. "Hey... is China all right? It's just that she hasn't asked to see me since we got back, and she always asks to see me. I'm her favourite."

Skulduggery stepped off the roof and hovered there. "In all honesty, I don't know," he said. "We'll have to keep an eye on her. The Church of the Faceless, Creed... all of a sudden they have influence over her, and China isn't the kind to be influenced."

Valkyrie grunted. "Followers of the Faceless Ones are up to something sneaky," she said. "I am shocked, I tell you. Shocked and appalled."

Skulduggery drifted away and Valkyrie let herself drop off the edge, then swooped over the heads of the crowd. She even got a few cheers, which took her by surprise. Someone in this city, it seemed, might be close to forgiving her.

She touched down to one side of the crowd as China came out of the High Sanctuary and made her way to the podium. The crowd applauded, though more out of duty than love, it appeared.

Someone nudged past Valkyrie, and Valkyrie frowned, turning to look at her as she went. A little old lady, moving slowly, moving stiffly, head down and shawl up to cover her head and hide her face. Something about her, though.

Valkyrie walked after her. "Excuse me," she said, but the elderly woman didn't turn and didn't stop, and a buzzing grew behind Valkyrie's eyes and she was filled with a sudden need to shrug and go on about her day. Just like that time, years ago, when she'd approached the Book of Names in the Sanctuary, back in Dublin. The Will of the Elders, Skulduggery had explained. The closer you got to it, the less you wanted it.

Valkyrie frowned. That's what was happening here. This was an attack.

She focused inwards, concentrating on the buzzing, isolating it and examining it, tracing it back to its origin. The little old lady. Of course.

Valkyrie strode up, easily outpacing her, got in front and pulled away the shawl. Wrinkles, lines, bags under blue eyes. Good cheekbones and a strong jaw. Thin lips forming a grim, determined line. This old woman had once been outrageously pretty. Still was.

But Valkyrie knew the face. She'd seen it before, in that tower in Greymire Asylum.

"You can't move," Solace said, and Valkyrie's body turned heavy. Her mouth went slack. She swayed. A frantic part of her mind recoiled, thrashed, screamed. "You can't move and you can't speak." Valkyrie tried fighting it, tried reaching inside her own mind to free herself, but that voice – rich, melodious – thrummed within her skull and wouldn't leave her alone.

"You're a strong one," Solace murmured. "But not disciplined. You need practice. That's unfortunate." She stood up on tiptoes and whispered in Valkyrie's ear. "Kill yourself."

Then she walked on, disappearing into the crowd.

Valkyrie stayed where she was, hands by her sides. Her mouth was still hanging open. A thin sliver of drool was making its way down her chin. *Kill yourself.* Permission had finally been granted.

She was moving, her legs taking her towards the nearest City Guard. It wouldn't be too much trouble to knock him down and take his gun and use the gun to end her life. All those years of hating herself, all those years of guilt she'd been storing up, they could now come to an end. She wanted to turn and thank the old woman but, of course, her body kept going forward.

The City Guard nodded to her, waited for her to say something. She just gazed at him. He was frowning now – maybe at the way her mouth hung open, maybe at the strange look in her eye.

Valkyrie touched his arm and shocked him, just enough to knock him out. He crumpled and she took the gun from his holster. It was black and shiny. Its grip was textured. She could smell the sweet oil. Her thumb flicked off the safety. Her other hand took hold of the slide and racked it. A bullet was now in the chamber. All she had to do now was raise the gun and press it against her temple, or under her chin, and pull the trigger.

The gun stayed where it was. That was odd. That was funny.

Valkyrie frowned at it and it still didn't move.

A thought nagged at her. It was small and quiet, but it poked and prodded, somewhere at the back of her mind. She couldn't hear it, though. Couldn't quite make it...

No, wait. There it was. Becoming louder. More confident. It was no longer a thought, and it was now a certainty. Valkyrie may have wanted to die once, but not any more. The guilt was still there – of course it was, there was so much of it – but it no longer dragged at her. It no longer controlled her. She wasn't the dreadful things she had done – she was merely a woman who had done dreadful things. And, as such, she could get by them, and make up for them. As such, she could be redeemed. Even forgiven.

She didn't reach in with her magic and quash the voice that reverberated in her head. She didn't need to. She just wiped the drool off her chin and closed her damn mouth. Next, she slid the magazine from the pistol and stripped it down and let the pieces fall. Then she rolled her shoulders, and looked round as China screamed.

132

Walking fast.

"You're sure it was her?" Skulduggery asked.

"I'm sure," Valkyrie said. "I stole her music box, for God's sake. I tend to remember the faces of little old ladies I steal music boxes from. Wait – you don't think that's why she attacked China, do you?"

"Over a music box? I do not."

They burst into the Council Chamber, where Praetor and Vespers and some old guy who looked like he should have had a beard were fretting over stacks of reports.

"Detectives!" cried Vespers. "Finally! What have you learned?"

"The Supreme Mage's attacker is a woman named Solace."

"What does she want? What is she after?"

Skulduggery glanced at Valkyrie, and she sighed.

"I'm going to need you all to pay close attention to this next bit," she said. "Solace was one of Serafina Dey's handmaidens who ran away to marry Caisson, the son of Abyssinia and the Mevolent of *this* dimension. She was discovered and dragged back, and, when Caisson went after her, he ended up killing his father. In retaliation, Serafina had him tortured for nearly a century. We think Solace had some kind of breakdown over this, and China had her committed to Greymire Asylum. Caisson was freed back in February, and then he freed Solace, without any help, completely on his own. Then Caisson was killed, and his body was possessed by the spirit of his grandfather, the King of the Darklands. And I think that's it. Skulduggery?"

"Sounds about right."

"So that's who Solace is, and that's why she doesn't like China. Now – how *is* China?"

"I'm not sure I got all that," the new old guy admitted.

"Doesn't matter. How's China?"

"Physically, she's unharmed," he answered, fussing nervously with the clasp on his cloak, "so whatever is causing the Supreme Mage this degree of anguish is, according to our Sensitives, of psychic origin. Attempts have been made to sedate her, but nothing is having an effect, and so it has proven necessary to restrain the Supreme Mage for her own protection." He tried a sudden smile. "We haven't been introduced, Detective. I am Grand Mage Rubic, formerly headmaster of Corrival—"

"Don't care," Valkyrie said.

Rubic immediately started nodding. "Yes, of course, of course, more important matters, absolutely."

"We need to get into Serafina Dey's mansion," Skulduggery said. "We don't know why Solace chose now to incapacitate China, but if Serafina *is* working on resurrecting Mevolent and if they've been waiting for the perfect time to strike, this is it."

"Getting on to the High Superior's property is, uh, not as easy as it would first appear," said Vespers. "The new addenda to the Religious Freedom Act give any head of a religious order certain *immunities* from normal procedure, but I'm – I'm sure we can find a loophole. Grand Mage Praetor?"

"We drew up those addenda," Praetor said. "You know damn well there are no loopholes. Detective Pleasant, if you have good reason to believe that what you're saying is correct... you may have no other choice but to break the law that we put in place."

"Oh, dear," whimpered Rubic.

"I don't know about this," Vespers said, shaking his head. "You see, this is why our priority should be the selection of a temporary Supreme Mage. We can't be seen as rudderless in a time of crisis."

Valkyrie frowned. "Why do you need one? You three can make decisions, can't you? You're China's advisors."

"I have only recently been appointed," Rubic said, looking suddenly terrified. "Leading is not what I signed up for. I'm a headmaster, for goodness' sake."

"Do whatever you have to," Skulduggery said, "but, while you're doing that, put us in charge of the City Guard."

Vespers sat back. "Um," he said.

"You have reason to believe that Commander Hoc isn't up to the task?" Praetor asked, frowning.

"Hoc can still issue orders," Skulduggery said, "but his orders will be coming from the Arbiter Corps."

"And do you have a strategy?" Vespers asked.

"If I'm wrong, and Mevolent isn't about to return, then we still need to apprehend Solace before she goes after China again, so we'll need a grid search of the entire city. If I'm right, and Serafina *is* bringing Mevolent back to life, then we'll want him to be corralled when he shows up. We have to keep him in one spot so that Valkyrie can use the Sceptre against him."

Vespers took a breath. "That seems like a sound strategy to me."

"And me," said Praetor. "We simply can't allow Mevolent to gain any sort of foothold here. If he is alive, we have to do whatever it takes to—"

The door burst open and Cerise barged in. "Sorry," she said. "Sorry. But Mevolent."

"What?" Vespers said. "What about him? *What about him?*"

"What do you think?" Valkyrie asked, following Skulduggery out the door. "He's here."

133

The Cleavers and the Sanctuary sorcerers kept well back as Mevolent walked into the Circle zone.

He was clad in his battlesuit of leather and chainmail, and wore the metal helmet that turned his head into some kind of monstrous cathedral.

Serafina was by his side, resplendent in a dress of shimmer and silk and the bones of her enemies.

Her family came behind – the Unveiled. Her sisters – Runc, the tall one, the strong one, the one who'd fought in the war, and Kierre, smaller, lighter, the assassin who'd killed Caisson. Her brother – Strosivadian, the monstrous one, the one Valkyrie had only ever seen pictures of. He was quite a sight to behold, in the twisted flesh. Behind them came the worshippers, the Faceless Ones fanatics, the members of the Legion of Judgement.

"I'd tell you to go back home," Skulduggery said, "but they don't want you, either. So that makes you our problem."

Mevolent spoke softly, but his voice carried on the wind. "Your army cowers behind you."

"You think that's an army?" Skulduggery asked. "That's not an army. That's an audience. They're going to watch as we take you down."

"You," Mevolent said, "amuse me."

Skulduggery shrugged. "I *am* very funny. Tanith?"

Tanith, standing on a lamp post with the bow in her hands. Mevolent turned his helmeted head ever so slightly.

She fired off an arrow. One of the worshippers leaped in front of Mevolent, took the arrow in his chest. Dead before he hit the ground.

Valkyrie heard Tanith mutter the word, "Idiot," as she nocked another arrow. She let it fly and another worshipper leaped in, sacrificing herself to save her master.

"Well," Skulduggery said, "that's clearly not working." He looked at Valkyrie. "I don't like to ask..."

"You don't have to," Valkyrie said, her heart heavy in her chest. She stepped forward, Sceptre in hand. "You have one chance to surrender," she called.

Mevolent spread his arms wide. "If you think that weapon can end me, use it."

He wasn't going to surrender. He was just standing there, waiting. Waiting for her to kill him.

"Would it make it easier," he asked, "if I were to attack you?"

"It would, actually."

"Sadly, I cannot do that. If you wish to execute me, you will have to strike me down when I am unarmed, and pose no threat to you."

"You always pose a threat."

"Then you should have no trouble with the execution. It is what your Sanctuary masters demand, is it not? The murder of the messenger, the conduit between the faithful and the Faceless Ones?"

"I'm not getting into an argument with you. You're the bad guy. You have to be stopped."

"I have broken no law in your world. No law in your entire universe."

"Still a bad guy."

Tanith fired off a sneaky arrow when everyone was distracted, but a worshipper got in the way again. Valkyrie gave her an appreciative smile, and got a commiserative shrug in return.

Mevolent removed his helmet. Dropped it. "You see?" he said to his followers. "This is what they want – to silence me. To erase me. To stop me from reconnecting you with our gods."

His worshippers screamed and shouted and cursed, their faces red with outrage, wet with tears of righteousness. The fervour on display was terrifying.

Valkyrie raised the Sceptre, said, very loudly, "Mevolent, by the power vested in me by the Arbiter Corps, I sentence you to death," and black lightning streaked from the crystal and hit Mevolent in the chest, dead centre.

His body exploded into dust, and his followers shrieked in anguish.

Serafina stared at the space where Mevolent had been, her face blank, as if she couldn't believe what had happened. The dust had stained her beautiful dress.

Valkyrie lowered the Sceptre, the world suddenly very narrow around her.

"You did the only thing you could do," Skulduggery murmured in her ear, his hand on her shoulder.

She nodded dully. Cleavers were stepping past her now, approaching Serafina and the rest. Valkyrie turned, started walking against the grey-suited flow, filled with an overwhelming desire to be alone. A sorcerer congratulated her. Another slapped her on the back. Another tore the Sceptre from her grip.

"Hey," she said, as the sorcerer drew himself up to his full height, close to eight foot tall, with Mevolent's face and the veil over his eyes, and he held the Sceptre in both hands and then snapped it, and there were shouts and cries and Valkyrie stumbled away as Mevolent dropped the pieces to the ground. Skulduggery leaped in, God-Killer sword slashing downwards. Mevolent swayed to one side, and simply gestured, and Skulduggery hurtled backwards and the sword fell into Mevolent's hand.

The sword swung. Cleavers and sorcerers came apart.

It swung again. Valkyrie ducked, scrambled and fled.

134

The High Sanctuary was in lockdown. Roarhaven's streets were empty, its people huddled behind barricaded doors.

"I don't understand what happened," Valkyrie said. "I don't understand. I killed him. He was in front of me and I killed him. Skulduggery, what the *hell*?"

For a moment, the only sound was the crackle and hum of the sea of energy off the edge of the platform. China's throne stood empty on its dais. Valkyrie paced. Tanith sat on the floor with her back to the wall. Skulduggery stood very, very still.

"It must have been a reflection," he said.

Valkyrie spun. "A reflection? Seriously? We were fooled by a goddamn reflection? This isn't supposed to happen! We're supposed to be able to tell the difference!"

Tanith shook her head. "He kept the helmet on for most of it."

"So what do we do now? He destroyed the Sceptre. Destroyed it! And he has the God-Killer sword!"

"We still have God-Killers of our own," said Tanith. "The dagger and the bow and the spear. That's more than enough to put him down."

"Only if we know where he is," Valkyrie said. "And we have no idea."

The doors opened and the Grand Mages hurried in with Commander Hoc.

Hoc grimaced when he saw them. "Do they have to be here?"

Valkyrie was in no mood for this. "What the hell does that mean?"

"It means all this is *your* fault," Hoc responded sharply. "You met Mevolent out in the open, where you had him dead to rights, and you practically *handed* him the only weapon he couldn't defend himself against. To call this a *monumental* failure in judgement would be understating the sheer *incompetence* on display. And you wanted control over the City Guard? Seriously?"

Valkyrie struggled to keep her voice even. "We didn't meet him out in the open. That wasn't even *him.*"

Hoc loomed over her. "That is not the persuasive argument you seem to think it is, Detective."

Tanith was suddenly there, shoving Hoc away. "Get the hell away from her."

He snarled as he came back. "You touch me again—"

Energy crackled from Valkyrie's eyes and Hoc recoiled sharply, and then Vespers was pushing his way between them.

"Stop this! Stop this at once! If you wish to fight, may I remind you that a battle awaits us out there on the streets of our city! Not in here!"

Valkyrie forced herself to be calm, and Hoc smoothed down his jacket.

"Serafina's mansion," Skulduggery said. He hadn't moved from where he was standing.

"We sent the Cleavers in fifteen minutes ago," Praetor said. "Empty."

Skulduggery inclined his head. "You broke your own law?"

"We circumvented it," said Praetor, "with guidance from our new – *acting* – Supreme Mage."

"So which one of you got the job?"

"None of us were comfortable with the responsibility," Vespers admitted. "We thought we should choose someone with a... a *higher calling*, if you will."

Valkyrie frowned. "What do you...?"

Footsteps approached. The Grand Mages bowed their heads, as did Commander Hoc.

And Damocles Creed walked in.

"You're kidding," Valkyrie whispered.

"Let's skip the pleasantries, shall we?" Creed said. He was dressed in old jeans and a stained white T-shirt that showed off his heavily muscled arms. He looked like he'd been pulled out from under a car.

Then Valkyrie realised he was using a rag to wipe oil off his hands. He *had* been pulled out from under a car.

"The situation is this," he said. "Mevolent, my sisters and my brother are loose. They might be in the city; they might have teleported out. We don't know. We don't know much at all. What we do know is that the Sceptre of the Ancients has been damaged – beyond repair, according to the experts who've recovered the pieces. That leaves the bow as the only long-range weapon sure to kill him. Everything else, we'll need to get in close. As we all know, the closer we get, the more remote the prospect of success."

He approached China's throne, but turned instead of sitting. "Detectives, Miss Low – I understand that you may have some reservations about working with me. I urge you to put those reservations aside until this current crisis is over. Hopefully, Supreme Mage Sorrows will return to us very soon and we can all go back to hating each other. Until then, we must struggle onwards. Agreed?"

A moment of silence.

"Agreed," Skulduggery said.

Creed nodded, and sat. "Suggestions, Detective Pleasant?"

"We target the followers. The Legion of Judgement could be providing support. If we can get a list of their names, we can narrow the search."

Creed nodded. "Commander, can you get this information?"

Hoc bowed stiffly. "Of course, Supreme Mage."

"The Church of the Faceless will help in any way we can," Creed said. "My priests will ask our congregation if they know of anyone who might be willing to talk to us."

"There's a scientist working here," Skulduggery said. "His name is Destrier. I'd talk to him, if I were you. He might have some ideas."

"Grand Mage Vespers, will you send for this man?"

"As you wish," Vespers said, bowing and hurrying from the room.

"Any other suggestions?" Creed asked. "Any ideas for how to find Mevolent, should he still be in Roarhaven?"

"I'd like to try scanning for him," said Valkyrie.

Creed looked at her. "Our Sensitives are already searching, but finding someone like Mevolent through a psychic sweep is... unlikely."

"I know. But I work differently. I might be able to catch something they don't."

"Then by all means," Creed said.

Valkyrie hesitated. "I'll need to do it from outside the High Sanctuary, though. The shields interfere with my range."

Creed considered it. "I can't let you go out there alone, Detective Cain."

"I'll be with her," said Skulduggery.

"And me," said Tanith. "Dexter, too."

"Very well," Creed said with a sigh. "Do your very best not to get yourselves killed, would you? China will be ever so mad with me if she gets back to find I've broken her favourite toys."

135

It was eerie, walking around Roarhaven when it was like this. It reminded Valkyrie of the towns and villages they'd passed through on their hunt for Mevolent. And here they were, doing the exact same thing, looking for the exact same man.

It was a cold night in January. Dry, though, so at least there was that. Valkyrie, Skulduggery and Dexter walked the empty streets and Tanith walked the rooftops above them. She had the bow, Skulduggery the dagger, and Dexter held the spear. Valkyrie led the way, her mind open, searching through the anxious thoughts of a thousand frightened minds in her vicinity, discarding them as she went. Whether the people could feel her clumsy probing was immaterial – she was trawling for something bigger. Something a lot bigger.

Her attention snagged on something – a consciousness. She tried to examine it, but the consciousness retracted. She sent her mind after it, this consciousness, as it twisted, trying desperately to get away. She almost had it, but it wriggled. She found it again, closed in, pursuing it wherever it led her until she realised it was leading her into a trap.

Heavy walls *thunked* down around her thoughts and her body stopped walking. She was dimly aware of shouts, dimly aware of Rune leaping at Skulduggery, of Dexter stumbling away from Strosivadian, of Tanith struggling with Kierre.

Hello, Valkyrie.

Mevolent's voice in her head.

Apologies for tricking you. I do not possess your gifts, and so I had to lay a trap. Please do not feel bad. You are powerful and new – but I am old, and patient.

He stepped into her thoughts and she gasped as her mind opened around him.

Look at everything you can do. It is a marvel. Compared to you, I am nothing. I am a limited man.

Skulduggery slashed at Rune with the dagger. She swayed back. Dodged. She had hammers in her hands – light enough to move quickly, heavy enough to break bones.

You are a threat to me, Valkyrie – you, above all others. I'm afraid that's why you must be killed.

Strosivadian tore the spear from Dexter's grip.

This brings me no pleasure. There is much I could learn from you.

Tanith had dropped the bow and taken out her sword. Kierre had two swords of her own.

I assure you, your world is safe in my hands. Its people will need to be restructured, and change is often difficult. But they will soon grow to love their new station.

Mevolent, landing before her, in a dark suit with a cloak, the streetlamps reflecting off the screaming helmet. The God-Killer sword in his hands.

I can feel you trying to communicate. It is really most impressive, but I'm afraid I cannot allow...

What's this? What's this you're trying to...?

He paused, the sword raised and ready to swing.

The King of the Darklands lives?

Valkyrie roared and the lightning exploded from her eyes and sent Mevolent spinning backwards.

She gasped, her body once more back under her control, her mind once more free of those walls. Sound rushed in, the sound of fighting: metal clashing with metal, fists colliding with flesh, hammers cracking bones. She blasted Strosivadian, blasted Rune, didn't have time to blast Kierre because Mevolent was on his feet.

Valkyrie pulled her hood up, pulled her mask down, and flew at him as he reached for the fallen sword. He moved back at the last instant, punched her, and she hit the ground, went skidding. Then he was hauling her up, throwing her against the wall. She dropped and he kicked her and she crunched back into the bricks. Unable to breathe, she lay there and did her very best to curl up. He stomped on her hand. She screamed. He took hold of her hood and slammed her head into the floor. Dazed, she couldn't do anything to stop him as he peeled the mask from her face.

He picked her up, held her one-handed. She was a rag doll in his grip. His fist sank into her belly. She couldn't cry out. Couldn't make a sound. He turned her round, one arm choking her, the other hand gripping her chin.

He was going to pull her head off.

He'd done it once before, back when she'd allowed Darquesse to take over. He'd pulled her head off and thrown it away, and she'd had mere seconds to reattach it before brain death set in. Now he was back to finish the job. No preamble. No talking. He wasn't giving her the slightest chance to fight back.

Time slowed as Valkyrie's thoughts quickened. Her tendons stretched. Her vertebrae started to crack. The pain was unbearable.

He wasn't giving her a chance to fight back. Why? Because he knew something she didn't. Because he knew Valkyrie could win, perhaps, if only she could survive the next few seconds.

This idea filled her with the most peculiar sort of giddiness.

She called on her magic to reinforce her tendons, to strengthen her vertebrae. She felt the magic in her bones, in her blood, in her muscles. She felt her skin toughen. Her lips went dry.

She encircled his wrist with her fingers and pulled his hand away from her chin. She gave it a squeeze and felt the bones bend and then break.

Mevolent, to his credit, didn't so much as grunt.

Still holding his wrist, she turned, bringing the edge of her fist down into his ribs. He sagged sideways.

She hit him with her open palm, straight to his sternum, feeling it cave in, sending him backwards.

He staggered but didn't fall. She smiled at him.

He swept his hand up and Valkyrie was scooped off her feet. He flicked that hand and she hurtled into the wall. Her shoulder crunched. Her clavicle snapped. Her knee fractured.

She fell in a heap, eyes wide, trying to remember how to shut off the pain, but it was too late, and the pain came crashing down on her like a wave and all the strength left her body as an agonised moan slowly rose from somewhere deep inside.

But Mevolent wasn't finishing her off. He wasn't killing her. He was looking to where the King of the Darklands stood, in the body of Caisson, son of Abyssinia. The Unnamed.

136

They flew at each other, Mevolent and his old master.

They collided in the street, the King of the Darklands and his one-time protégé.

They were a blur of fists and magic that lifted off the ground and hurtled into the night sky.

Tanith dropped to the ground. She grunted and rolled, leaving streaks of blood on the road. Her arms, legs, torso – they were crisscrossed with slashes, both shallow and deep. Kierre followed her down. Blood trickled from a single cut along her left shoulder.

Dexter drove Strosivadian back with a sustained stream of energy from both hands. Strosivadian crossed his wrists before him, taking the streams on his armoured forearms. Grimacing. Snarling. The streams faltered as Dexter began to weaken, and now Strosivadian was powering forward.

Skulduggery had lost his hat somewhere along the way. He lunged at Rune with the dagger, close enough so that it would be virtually impossible to miss. But she dodged and struck at his arm with a hammer. The dagger fell. He tried to push at the air and she moved around him, tripped him, hit him with the other hammer as he tumbled, cracking his skull.

Valkyrie was in too much pain to even try to get up.

137

There was a popular bar on Memory Lane – closed now because of the curfew – that pretty much exploded when Mevolent and the Unnamed crashed into it.

Temper followed the battle through the multiple rows of monitors in the Surveillance Room. He and four other City Guard officers stayed on their feet, moving from a monitor on one side of the room to a monitor on the other. A punch from Mevolent would send the King of the Darklands halfway across the city, and a kick would send Mevolent right back again.

They burst through the wall of the bar and took to the skies once again, grappling with each other, twisting into the night.

Temper's attention returned to the monitor showing Kierre kicking Tanith's ass. Skulduggery and Dexter weren't faring any better against their opponents – and it looked like Valkyrie was down.

"Dammit," he muttered, and ran for the door.

138

Omen watched the battle from the top floor of the school. He wasn't supposed to be there. He was supposed to be with the others, the students and staff, huddled in the Safe Area. Like there was any Safe Area when it came to this stuff.

He ran from window to window. It was hard to make out, but he could tell it was Mevolent by that terrifying helmet. The other person... they were moving too fast, but it had to be Valkyrie. No one else could take on Mevolent like that.

They disappeared from view, but Omen heard the crash all the way across the city as they collided with something. A building or a street, most likely. He could only imagine the damage they were doing. A lamp post spun through the air in the distance, tossed as easily as a toothpick.

There was a speck, getting closer, and suddenly Mevolent was hurtling towards the school.

He hit the East Tower and bounced off, fell to the courtyard. Omen ran over, pressed his face against the glass. He was down. Mevolent was down. He was trying to get to his hands and knees, but he kept collapsing.

She'd done it. Valkyrie had done it. She'd beaten him. She'd—

Mevolent's opponent dropped gently from the sky and Omen went cold. It wasn't Valkyrie. It was a man wearing the body of Abyssinia's son, Caisson. It was the King of the Darklands.

The King pulled the helmet from Mevolent's head and threw it to one side. Mevolent got to his knees, but the King grabbed his face with one hand before he could stand. Mevolent stiffened. The King was draining his life force.

Then the King stopped, like he'd heard something. He turned, looking towards the school.

Auger.

The King left Mevolent to crumple, and walked over to the main building, disappearing from Omen's line of sight.

Omen bolted.

The corridors echoed with his footsteps.

There was a crash somewhere below him. The crash of a wall being smashed through.

Ran to the staircase. Leaped. Used the air to cushion his fall. Down he went. Down and down.

Screams. Shouts.

More stairs. Leaping down.

Landed badly, hurt his feet, kept going. Using the air to throw open doors. Sprinting through.

Got to the dorms. Long, long corridors. Gasping for breath, not slowing down.

Auger's room. Door opens. The box under the bed shooting into his hand. Grabbing the knife in its sheath, dropping the box, running again. More running.

Students, coming the other way. Panicking. Yelling and crying and being scared and being brave. Running through them, screaming at them to get out of his way.

The Safe Area. Cafeteria. More students, huddled.

Kase and Mahala. Never and Axelia. Running past them all.

The King of the Darklands throwing back Peccant and Miss Wicked and Miss Gnosis and Hunnan and a dozen other teachers. And Auger.

Omen skidded to a stop beside his brother, trying to get his breath back, pressing the Obsidian Blade into his hand.

"Not the time," Omen gasped. "We have... another year."

"Prophecies," Auger murmured, sticking the knife into his belt. "When have they ever got it right?"

The King of the Darklands turned to them. He'd found the one he'd sensed.

"My name is Auger Darkly," said Auger, his voice shaking only a little as he stepped forward. "A thousand years before I was born, a Sensitive foretold of the day when you and I would battle. She said one of us would walk away. The other would fall."

"It was longer ago than that," said the King of the Darklands, "and the witch told me of the vision herself. She said if ever I were to die it would be by your hand, Auger Darkly. If you fail to kill me here tonight, if I instead take your life, then I will live forever."

"I'm here now," Auger said.

"As am I," said the King. "You're strong. I can sense that. I can see that you're fast. Intelligent. All these things I can sense in you. I look in your eyes and I also see courage, and decency."

"I look in your eyes and I see a murderer," Auger said.

The King smiled. "Then who are we to keep destiny waiting?"

Auger ran at him.

Omen watched as his brother attacked. As he spun and jumped, kicked and punched. As he realised how useless any of this was against his enemy.

Auger reached for the knife in his belt – but the King caught him with a slap and Auger flew backwards into the wall.

The Blade went spinning away.

"I expected more," the King said, and placed his hand on Auger's throat.

Omen screamed and charged. The King watched him come and swiped at him, but Omen dropped, sliding with all his weight into the King's legs.

And the King fell, tumbling over him, and Auger kicked him in the face as Omen scrambled up.

"Enough!" the King roared. "Enough of this!"

He grabbed Auger's wrist and Auger gasped, stiffening just like Mevolent had.

And then a small fireball dropped on to the King's back and went out.

The King turned.

Omen didn't know the girl who had thrown it. Looked like a typically terrified First Year. She snapped her fingers repeatedly, but couldn't get a second fireball going.

Then Never snapped his fingers. And Kase and Mahala and Axelia.

The cafeteria was suddenly full of snapping, clicking fingers, and now fireballs were exploding all over the King of the Darklands as he let go of Auger and stepped back to shake off the flames.

Omen dropped to his hands and knees, saw the Blade on the floor beneath a table.

Three dozen individual blasts of wind filled the cafeteria, driving the King back a few more steps, throwing the tables and chairs against each other. Omen dived, grabbing the Blade before it disappeared under all that furniture.

Then Never was beside him, pulling him up, teleporting them both to the space right behind the King.

Omen tore the Obsidian Blade from its sheath and lunged, but the King twisted, the edge of his hand knocking into Omen's forearm, shattering the bones.

Omen hollered in pain and the Blade flipped through the air. Auger caught it.

The King recognised the weapon. Went to seize Auger's wrist.

Auger tossed the Blade up. As it spun, he knocked the King's hand to one side, flicked his fingers into the King's eyes, struck the Blade's handle, and sent it spinning again. His hands blurred, catching and tossing the knife while the King tried grabbing it, moving too fast to stop.

Then Auger snatched the Blade from the air and buried it in the King's neck.

The King of the Darklands stiffened and everything went very still and very quiet.

Blood pumped from the wound. Auger tried pulling the dagger out, but the blade snapped off. He stepped away, wincing, blinking madly, with only the handle in his grip.

The King's hands went to his throat. They tapped against the bit of blade still sticking out. His mouth opened and closed.

He let out a breath and then it was as if he was being erased. It happened quickly, yet seemed to go on forever. Emptiness spread from his wound and took his neck. Where once there was flesh and blood, now there was nothing.

It didn't stop there. The emptiness spread from his chin up to his crown and also started downwards from his shoulder. His head was gone and so was an arm, and his stomach was next and the other arm. He took a step to keep his balance and Omen could see his insides briefly before they, too, were scrubbed from existence. His legs went, and his knees and his shins and his ankles and his feet and then it was done and he was gone.

139

Valkyrie howled as she propped herself up into a sitting position, her back against the wall. Broken leg. Broken shoulder. Broken whatever. She gritted her teeth as she raised her right arm. Screw it, she'd had worse.

Energy crackled around her finger, and a streak of lightning missed Strosivadian by about three metres. She hissed, aimed again. Dexter was getting pummelled, the spear lying somewhere in the dark. He didn't have long.

She took a breath and let it out as she turned her head slightly, aimed right down her finger... and the lightning caught Strosivadian in the neck. He jerked sideways, went tumbling, leaving Dexter to gasp and spit blood and roll over.

Skulduggery staggered. Fell to one knee. Got up and fell again. Rune walked after him, hammers in her hands.

Valkyrie aimed, her hand trembling. She missed. Missed again. Rune looked up, scowled at her.

Skulduggery took advantage of the distraction and the air rippled and he launched the God-Killer dagger straight for Rune's chest – but she smacked it with a hammer and sent it whirling across the street where it clattered into the wall beside Valkyrie's face, barely missing her.

"Bloody hell," Valkyrie muttered.

While Rune started kicking Skulduggery, Valkyrie readjusted

her position, waited for her head to stop spinning, and went to aim again – but Rune was walking towards her.

Valkyrie's eyes lit up and Rune immediately hurled a hammer and Valkyrie cursed, crossing her right arm over her face – but the hammer never hit. She peeked out, saw the hammer being yanked through the air by a black tentacle that retracted into Temper Fray's hand.

Temper put the hammer on the ground for Rune to pick up, and backed away. "Kierre," he said. Then, louder, "Kierre."

Kierre stopped strangling Tanith long enough to look round. She released Tanith entirely and straightened. "You shouldn't be here," she said.

"I'm asking you not to do this," said Temper. "All of you. Please."

"They attacked our Deliverer," said Rune.

"Of course they did," Temper responded. "You know what the old Mevolent did. You know the new one will be even worse."

"We supported the old Mevolent," said Strosivadian, getting to his feet and rubbing his neck. "We support this one."

Temper nodded. "And I'm asking you not to."

Kierre frowned. "You must know we can't just walk away, Temper. This is the right thing to do."

"Millions – *billions* – of people will die."

Rune sneered. "Barely people."

Temper ignored her. "Kierre, if you love me, you'll stop this. You'll spare my friends and walk away."

"And if you love me," said Kierre, "you'll join us. Come on, Temper. This is what you were born into. You're a believer. You believe the Faceless Ones belong here. You believe in the natural order."

"Not any more, I don't."

"Then come away with just me."

Temper hesitated. "If I do, will you spare my friends?"

"You'd... you'd do that?"

"I love you, Kierre. I'd do that."

Kierre looked at her brother and sister, eyes wide and pleading. Strosivadian grunted. "Very well."

Rune picked up the hammer. "Serafina won't be happy."

"Serafina is never happy," said Kierre. "That's her job, as eldest sister." She ran over to Temper. "We won't hurt your friends any more. You'll come away with me now?"

"Well," he said, "I've got some things to clear up—"

"But you said," Kierre interrupted. "So come away with me now, before anything else happens. Please."

Temper looked around, looked at Valkyrie, then looked back at Kierre. "Yeah," he said, "OK."

Valkyrie tried to shake her head, but that was way too painful, and, by the time she'd gathered the strength to call out, Temper and Kierre had already disappeared into darkness.

Rune picked up Skulduggery's hat and brought it over to where he lay in the middle of the street. She placed it on his chest.

"Thanks," Valkyrie heard him murmur.

Strosivadian hunkered over Dexter. "I think I may have killed this one," he said.

"No," Dexter said, waving a hand weakly. "I'm alive."

"Oh," Strosivadian said, "my apologies. You look dead."

"Probably because you've beaten me to a pulp."

Strosivadian straightened. "Undoubtedly." He looked at his sister. "Where is Serafina? She should have been here by now."

"Where Serafina is depends on where Mevolent is," Rune said, and then, as if the mere mention of his name was enough to summon him, Mevolent floated down from above.

He was pale, unsteady – but he was here, and the King of the Darklands wasn't. Valkyrie tried pushing herself up.

"Stop," Mevolent said. "You've lost."

"No."

He walked over, and sat down beside her. "Yes," he said. "It's OK to lose. It's OK to be beaten."

She sagged back against the wall, the pain threatening to overwhelm her.

"You fought well," Mevolent continued. "You have been a worthy opponent, but you have failed. It's OK to fail. It's OK to die."

Her broken shoulder made turning her head impossible, so she looked at him out of the corner of her eye instead. "You're not as bad as I thought you'd be, you know that?"

"That's very nice of you."

"You think... you think we could have been friends under different circumstances?"

"I do not know. I have never been one for... friends."

"I think we could have been," Valkyrie said. "I think we'd have been best friends. Give me a hug, best friend. One last hug before you kill me."

"So you can stab me with that dagger in your hand?" Mevolent asked.

She paused. "You can see that, huh?"

"It is quite obvious."

"So you gonna give me that hug, or not?"

Mevolent actually smiled. "I think not."

"Ah," she said, "go on."

He laughed then, and so did she. It hurt like hell, but she laughed, and she didn't even complain when he gently took the God-Killer dagger from her hand and placed it well away from her.

"Would you like to die sitting, or on your feet?" he asked.

"May as well stand," said Valkyrie. "At least they'll say that about me."

He helped her up and let her lean against the wall, cradling her left arm.

"Don't," Skulduggery said, trying to get up. She heard the sound of broken bones falling on asphalt, and she winced.

"Skulduggery," she said, "it's OK."

534

"You're not going to die tonight," Skulduggery said, managing to stand. His right leg gave way with a snap, and Mevolent watched him crumple.

When Mevolent turned back, Valkyrie stood as tall as she could. "Not the face," she said. "I want my family to be able to see me one last time."

He nodded. She closed her eyes.

140

"Mevolent."

She opened her eyes again.

Everyone was looking to Valkyrie's right, to whomever had spoken. Grimacing, she repositioned herself so that she wasn't missing out.

Creed, wearing a heavy coat lined with fur, his bald head gleaming and his hands in his pockets, stepped from the shadows.

"You've done quite enough damage, I think," Creed said. He didn't look even slightly worried. "You are to stand down immediately and allow the City Guard to take you into custody."

Officers of the City Guard appeared beside him – maybe a dozen of them. Some Cleavers, too.

"Is this it?" asked Mevolent. "Is this the army you've gathered?"

"You and armies," Creed responded, sounding puzzled. "I don't get the obsession, I really don't. Why would I need an army to fight you?"

Mevolent walked into the middle of the street. "Do you intend to face me alone?"

"I don't intend to face you *at all.* This whole thing, the fighting in the streets, throwing each other through buildings... I've always found it a tad *redundant.*"

"So you expect me to surrender, is that right? And then you will incarcerate me?"

"Yes."

Rune laughed. Creed looked at her, and then at Strosivadian. "My second-favourite sister and my least-favourite brother... After all this time, I had hoped you would have seen the error of your ways and come over to join the Church of the Faceless. It's been so sad watching you waste your time with the Legion. The Faceless Ones do not hear your prayers, my siblings."

Strosivadian folded his massive arms. "And they listen to yours, do they?"

Creed smiled. "They will."

"I am curious," Mevolent said, and Creed looked back at him. "How do you intend to keep me incarcerated when you know that there is no prison that could hold me?"

Creed stepped to one side. "I'm going to put you in this," he said, as a platform was wheeled forward. Upon that platform were four metal columns at least three metres high. "It's called an Eternity Gate. I don't think you have anything quite like it in your reality. It will freeze you in time, and stretch a moment into a millennium."

A small, slight, nervous man came into view, hands tapping off each other. "Longer," Destrier said.

Creed looked at him. "Longer, you say?"

Destrier nodded, then frowned. "Obviously, it depends on how long you judge a moment to be, but, um... the Eternity Gate, such as it is, came about as an offshoot of my primary focus, which—"

Creed smiled, and patted Destrier on the shoulder. "That's OK, my friend. Mevolent doesn't need to know the finer details. All he needs to know is that this will be his prison cell for the next few thousand years."

Mevolent was no longer finding this amusing. "And how will you get me inside?"

"I'll ask you," said Creed. "Politely, of course. But if you feel you'll need an incentive..." He disappeared for a moment, back into the gloom – and re-emerged with the tip of a knife resting on the top of the binding collar that encircled the neck of Serafina Dey.

Rune snarled and Strosivadian roared, but a raised hand from Mevolent stopped them before they rushed forward.

"If you co-operate," Creed said, "Serafina remains alive. If you do not, I will cut her throat right here, in front of you."

"You would kill your own sister?" Mevolent asked, teeth bared.

"I would. Quite happily."

Serafina sneered. "You've always been a coward."

"Your insults were more creative when we were younger," said Creed.

"That's because you were more interesting as a child. As an adult, you have done nothing but disappoint me. Mevolent, the moment he cuts my throat, please kill him."

Creed pressed the knife deeper, drawing blood. "You think he'll let any serious harm come to you? He's already lost the Serafina in his reality. I daresay he couldn't bear to lose you again."

"If I do this," Mevolent said, "you will release her?"

Serafina glared. "Do *not* give in to him."

"I'll keep my word," said Creed. "Serafina will be free to leave the country, so long as she agrees never to return. If we find that she has returned, or that any of my other siblings have returned, a death notice will be circulated and I, personally, will not rest until the love of your life is dead."

Mevolent walked to the Eternity Gate. Destrier fussed around, attaching a metal step to the platform. Mevolent looked at it. Looked at Destrier. "Thank you," he said.

Destrier nodded, terrified, and backed off as Mevolent stepped up halfway.

"Mevolent, stop," said Serafina. "Don't do this. I beg you. I lost you once. Don't make me go through it again."

"I'm afraid I'll have to hurry this along," said Creed. "Step all the way in there, there's a good boy. Go on. Just one more—"

"No," Serafina whispered.

She reached up, her hands closing around her brother's, and she plunged the knife into her throat.

Mevolent roared and leaped down, shoving Creed away and catching Serafina before she fell. Blood washed over him.

"I'm sorry," Serafina said, touching her hand to his face, leaving a bloody handprint on his skin. "You deserve life. You deserve this world. I... I wanted to give it to you. I only hope, in some small way, I measured up to the woman you loved."

"You are the woman I loved," Mevolent said softly. "You are pure, you are perfect, no matter what reality you are in. Fate tried to keep us apart, but we found each other despite it all."

"I don't... want to leave you."

"You don't have to," Mevolent said.

He kissed her, and she kissed him back, and he gathered her into his arms and stepped up into the Eternity Gate. Destrier hurried forward and flipped the switch. A blue energy field rose between the columns, sealing Mevolent and Serafina within her last moments, forever.

141

Omen's parents were on their way. They'd been holidaying somewhere remote, somewhere with skis. When news reached them of what had happened, they'd demanded a Teleporter be sent to bring them back. Supreme Mage Creed didn't seem interested in playing their games, however – not now that the Chosen One had fulfilled his purpose.

Omen dreaded to think what mood they'd be in when they got back. They had expected another year of people fawning over them – a year of increased visibility and opportunities. A year of increased importance. They'd gone away as rock stars – or as the parents of a rock star, anyway – and they were set to return as nobodies.

He was curious to see how they'd handle it.

It was almost time for lights out, and Omen went to call in on his brother.

"Crazy times," said a voice from the darkness and Omen jumped sideways with a yell that turned into a laugh.

"Please stop doing that," he said as Crepuscular stepped out.

"Naw," Crepuscular said, "it's way too much fun. You look relatively uninjured after your scrape with destiny."

"And so do you, after your scrape with Reznor Rake. What happened with him?"

Crepuscular pushed his hat back a little. "He got away,

unfortunately. But I heard your brother broke the Obsidian Blade, so the good news is that Rake's got no reason to come after you again. Apart from revenge."

Omen's smile dropped. "You think he will?"

"Probably not. Hopefully not. I don't know, to be honest. Best be vigilant, just in case. Sorry I was late that night, by the way. I had a thing."

"You turned up when I needed you," Omen said, "and that's what matters. Thank you."

"Just doing my job as a card-carrying good guy."

A thought occurred, and Omen frowned. "How'd you get in?"

"Here? I'm a sneaky one, Mr Darkly. I can get anywhere if I put my mind to it. I'm on my way to something, but I thought I'd stop by and wish you a belated Merry Christmas, and a Happy New Year, and the happiest of birthdays. I don't have any presents for you. Sorry."

"You probably saved my life," Omen said, "so that's enough."

"I suppose it is. Call me if you need me again, but, in the meantime, remember the golden rule."

"Don't tell anyone about you," said Omen. "I won't, I promise."

"Good man," Crepuscular said. "See you soon."

He stepped back into darkness. Omen stood there.

"I'm waiting for you to go," said Crepuscular from the shadows.

"Right, sorry!" said Omen, and hurried on. He got to the next block of dorm rooms, and knocked on Auger's door. A moment later, Never opened it.

"Hey," she said.

"Hey," said Omen. They kept their voices down. "How's he doing?"

"Resting. You want to talk to him?"

Omen shook his head. "It can wait until tomorrow. How is he, um... psychologically?"

Never smiled a little. "I don't actually know. He said he'd been waiting for this for his entire life, but it still managed to take him by surprise."

Omen offered a shrug. "The prophecy said that the battle would take place when he was seventeen. It was a whole year wrong."

"Prophecies suck."

"Yes, they do."

"You sure you don't want to say hi? I've got to head back to my room anyway, and he'll talk to you. You'll understand what he's going through."

"If he's sleeping," Omen said, "let him sleep." He smiled. "We've got our whole lives to talk."

142

Militsa left for work and Valkyrie had a long, long shower. Reverie Synecdoche had mended her broken bones and Valkyrie had let her do it without latching on to her power, but, while she had not even one bruise remaining, she still ached. Not a physical ache, not an ache of pain, but the ache of an exhausted mind.

She stepped from the shower, dried off, rifled through the drawer Militsa had given her for clothes, found a little square of paper in there, a square with a familiar sigil.

She held it, looked at it, remembering how it tasted when it dissolved on her tongue. Remembering the flush of magic that came next. Enough to make her feel invincible. Enough to make her forget the awfulness.

Xena nudged her.

"Yeah, yeah, hold on," she said, tearing the paper into little bits. She dressed in jeans and a rollneck sweater, then pulled on a heavy coat and found the lead. She stepped out of the front door.

"How long have you been waiting here?" she asked.

Skulduggery turned. "Not long," he said, scratching Xena behind the ears. They started walking.

"China has been put into an induced coma," he said, "for her own safety. The doctors say there's no telling when she might recover."

"Have you been able to see her?"

"Not as yet. Security has been heightened because of recent events and, of course, Solace is still out there."

"You let a little thing like heightened security stop you?"

"When it's this heightened, yes. Cleavers everywhere. All manner of sigils on the walls, some of which I don't even recognise..."

"One might think that Creed just doesn't want anyone getting too close to China."

"One might, yes."

Valkyrie looked around, made sure they were alone. "And we're stuck with him, are we? As Supreme Mage?"

"For the moment."

"Isn't that a conflict of interest? Being Arch-Canon *and* Supreme Mage at the same time?"

"Not according to either the Church of the Faceless or the High Sanctuary," said Skulduggery.

Valkyrie raised an eyebrow. "Well, so long as everything's above board."

Xena found a particularly interesting scent beneath a bush and they waited for her to finish investigating.

"We're going to have to tread lightly," Skulduggery said. "As Arbiters, Creed has no jurisdiction over us – but there are many options open to him if we prove to be too much of a nuisance."

"And will we prove to be too much of a nuisance?"

"Oh," Skulduggery said, "I fully intend to be."

Xena caught another scent and started tracking it. They followed along behind.

"Have the Unveiled headed home yet?" she asked.

"They left yesterday. They're demanding that Serafina be released from the Eternity Gate, and I'd say they'll keep demanding that for the next few hundred years, but they don't have much hope of that ever happening."

"Did you see the crowd that gathered outside the High Sanctuary yesterday?"

"I did. Creed might have to move the Eternity Gate to a secret location if this keeps up. He can't let that level of disruption continue."

"I'll say one thing about Mevolent supporters, they do have some catchy chants. The one about killing all mortals? That's an *earworm*, you know? I was humming it all day."

"And how are you, Valkyrie?"

"All healed. What about you? Did Reverie patch you up or did you have to dip into your stash of replacement bones?"

"She patched me up."

"Rune looked like a handful."

"Yes. Fighting her is never fun. I'm glad I don't have to do it too often. But I wasn't enquiring as to your physical state."

"Ah," she said. "You want to know how I'm doing inside my *brain*. I'm doing fine. I'm doing much better. I might start seeing a therapist, actually. I've said this before, but now I think I will. It's good to talk to someone about this stuff. Sometimes I can only figure out how I feel about a thing if I *tell* someone how I feel about a thing. Does that make sense?"

"As much as anything can."

"And I'm taking a break. Just a few weeks, but I'm going to spend that time with my family, with Militsa, with my dog, and I'm going to chill, and work out, and go for runs, and I'm going to catch up on everything that's happened in the world since we've been gone, and watch loads of movies and TV shows and read about fifty-seven books. And all that starts now."

"Good," Skulduggery said. "That's healthy."

"I thought so."

"And then you'll be back, will you?"

She smiled at him. "Of course I will. I can't stay away from you, you know that."

The way his head tilted, Valkyrie knew that pleased him.

*

545

She got back and had something to eat, then loaded Xena into the car. She stopped outside Reverie's clinic on the way out of the city. Reverie was waiting for her inside.

"Are you sure you're OK with this?" Valkyrie asked.

Reverie smiled. "I'm fine with it," nodding to the room ahead of them – the one guarded by two Cleavers. "He's in there."

Valkyrie walked in. Serpine sat on the bed. His coat was off and his sleeve was rolled up.

He frowned. "What are you doing here?"

"I'm the one who asked Doctor Synecdoche to invite you to come here," she said. "How are you doing, Nefarian?"

"I'm doing wonderfully, thank you."

"Enjoying Roarhaven?"

"Not really," he said. "My immunity has been slow to materialise, so I'm escorted everywhere by two very serious, very dull Cleavers. And yesterday I was told that, since my original deal was with China Sorrows, it will have to be reviewed by Supreme Mage Creed to establish if it's still viable."

"I'm sorry about that."

"I'm the one who closed those portals, remember. I'm the one who saved this world."

"I remember."

He sighed. "So you persuaded the doctor to fit me with a prosthetic hand? How nice of you. It almost makes up for the skeleton allowing them to take my real one."

"You're not here to get a prosthetic, Nefarian. I'm going to try something."

Reverie came in, sat on the chair by the door. Valkyrie went over and put her hand on her shoulder.

"Absolutely positive?" she asked.

Reverie smiled. "I'm always open to new experiences."

As gently as Valkyrie could, she slipped into Reverie's mind and went straight for the knowledge. Corridors formed between them and doors in her own head swung open, and once more she understood the human body, once more she understood how it worked.

She took her hand away and watched Reverie slump in her chair, eyes fluttering. Satisfied that she was all right, Valkyrie crossed the room to Serpine. She took his wrist with her left hand, covered the stump with her right.

Serpine frowned. "What are you doing?"

"Hush," she told him.

"It's warm. What are you...? Ow."

"Hush, I said."

"Tell me what you're doing to me."

"I'm growing you a new hand," Valkyrie said, closing her eyes. "I'm giving you the chance you didn't give that guy you stabbed in his sleep. I'm giving you the chance to heal – maybe even grow to be a better person. Maybe you'll take it. Maybe you won't. But what else can I do, right?"

"How can you—" he began.

But her mind was in his nerves, in his muscles, in his bones. "Shut up," she said. "And let me work."

143

Temper Fray and Kierre of the Unveiled watched from the rooftop.

When they were satisfied he was alone, they moved. Temper climbed down, jumped when he had to. Kierre just walked, and disappeared into the shadows.

Adam Brate saw Temper, waved to him, hurried over.

"I don't like this, man," he said. "Too exposed. Anyone could be watching."

"Don't worry," said Temper, "this won't take long. I just wanted to tell you that I'm leaving."

"Leaving Roarhaven?"

"Yeah. Can't tell you where I'm going – you understand – but I just wanted to say thank you for all your help, and please, if you have any tips in future, if you find out that Creed is up to something weird, if you find out anything more about the Kith, get in touch with Skulduggery and Valkyrie. They can help you."

"I will, man. I will. Wow – I can't believe you're going."

"Yeah," Temper said, smiling. "Me neither."

"You take care of yourself."

"You too, buddy."

Brate gave him a salute that was all wrong, and turned and started hurrying away.

"Hey, Adam?"

Brate turned, and froze when he saw the gun in Temper's hand. "What? What the hell, man?"

"I know you're working for Creed, Adam."

"No. No way. Come on, man!"

"How many times have I told you? You've got to be more subtle. I told you I suspected Creed's involvement in Drang's murder and, the next thing I know, I'm off the case."

Brate's hands were up. "That doesn't prove anything, Temper! I was asking around! People talk!"

"Oh, don't worry, that's not everything. I gave you a test, too. I told you I'd found out that Drang was investigating a link between Creed and Praetor and Vespers. And what happens next? Mr Glee comes to kill me."

Brate licked his lips. "I don't... I don't even know who that is."

"But the thing I don't understand is, as you're working for Creed, why did you lead us to the Kith last year?"

"Maybe he's not only working for my brother," Kierre said, emerging from the darkness, and Brate yelped and jumped away. "Maybe he's got more than one master."

"Is that right, Adam? You got more than one master?"

"Temper... please... you've got this wrong. You've got it all... You've..." And then he burst out laughing. "Dammit! I just could *not* keep a straight face!"

He dropped his hands by his sides and Kierre took her spear in her hand. It lengthened and she held it ready.

"I admit it," said Brate, "you're smarter than I gave you credit for. You got me, my friend. You got me good. Bravo, sir. Bravo."

Temper chambered a round into the gun. "Who are you working for, Adam?"

"I don't think I'm going to divulge, to be honest. The game's still being played, and a lot of pieces are still on the board. But well done, you, for taking me off. I didn't see that coming, I really didn't."

"You're under arrest, Adam."

Brate squinted at him. "Are you even a cop? Didn't you quit?"

"This'll be my last act as a City Guard."

A chuckle. "I wish I could accommodate you but, like, there are people who play the game that you see, and then there are people who play the game that you don't see. The long game." Another smile. "That's us, buddy. I'll see you around."

And then he teleported.

144

February was a beast of a month.

It brought snow – proper snow, the kind that fouled up roads and cut off power and generally made life a very pretty misery – and freezing temperatures.

It also brought Darquesse's baby.

Sebastian stood against the wall as the other Darquesses did what they did. The pregnant Darquesse was allowing herself to feel every last bit of pain – and, by the hollers and the curses, that pain was significant.

"It's coming," said a Darquesse.

Suddenly Sebastian was being pulled forward by one of them.

"What?" he said. "What are you doing? What's happening? I don't want to do anything. I don't want to – oh, God. Oh, God. That's a baby's head. Oh, God."

"You're going to deliver this baby," said one of the Darquesses.

"No, I am not."

"Yes, you are," said another, as she melted into the pregnant Darquesse.

"You're going to raise this child," a Darquesse at his shoulder said. "She will grow up quickly, and she will be me, but she'll also be her, and she'll need a parent."

"What?" Sebastian said dully as his hands were guided down.

"Take hold of the baby's head."

"Ohhhh, Jesus."

The Darquesse melted into the pregnant one.

That left three Darquesses who weren't giving birth.

"I don't know what to do," Sebastian said. "Please come over here and help me."

"You'll do fine," the three of them said, melting into each other. "Raise the girl like you would raise your own child."

"I can't do that. I don't know the first thing about babies or children."

"A child is just a small adult," the Darquesse said. "And a baby is just a small child."

She melted into the Darquesse giving birth, the one sweating, her hair matted to her head, the one who was now locking eyes with Sebastian.

"I need to understand why this world is worth saving," she said, breathing heavily. "I've done my research. I've collected my information. Now I need a reason to save you all. I'm going to push again, and this time the baby will come out."

"That's not a good idea."

"It will be yours to raise."

"But what about you? You'll raise her with me, right?"

"Don't be silly. How could I raise myself?"

And she pushed, and as she pushed she melted into the child, and Sebastian roared in fear as the baby slipped into his waiting hands.

And then they were alone, just him and the screaming, crying baby. He stared at her, all slimy and gross.

At least he knew what to call her.